Praise for
All That Is Mine I Carry With Me

"Gripping . . . a masterly piece of writing."
—*The New York Times Book Review*

"Part crime drama, part psychological suspense, Landay's new novel . . . is absolutely unputdownable, with an ingenious plot and a cast of comprehensive, accurately depicted characters."
—*Library Journal* (starred review)

"An all-encompassing look at family dynamics through several decades, at the legacy of violence that looms over this family and how this determines each child's future . . . a master class in juggling genres into a cohesive story. . . . Landay shapes each character as realistic, flawed and all too human."
—*South Florida Sun Sentinel*

"[A] gripping, slow-burning, yet tension-packed family drama . . . a haunting story of family trauma, family secrets and fraying sibling bonds."
—*The Patriot Ledger*

"Thought provoking . . . captivating . . . You will be thinking about this book after you finish it."
—*The Times Leader*

"An intriguing mystery with several possible solutions . . . a page-turner . . . The story is compelling and satisfying."
—*The Portager*

"Told from different points of views of the various characters, this is a master class in how to write a compelling novel. Author Landay is known for *Defending Jacob*, which became an Emmy-nominated series, [and he] brings the same kind of thought-provoking, character-driven story to this one. Readers will not be able to put it down."

—Red Carpet Crash

"While the novel whipsaws back and forth between 'did he or didn't he?' it also presents a sensitive portrayal of perhaps the most complicated kind of family life. . . . [An] emotionally charged, layered novel . . . a nuanced look at the devastating toll an unsolved disappearance can have on a family, and the crushing effect that years of doubt can have on the psyches of those left behind."

—Criminal Element

"A wonderful, well-written novel that crackles with suspense."

—STEPHEN KING

"This novel is an enthralling mystery and a haunting family tragedy about the lifelong effects of trauma and suspicion on a family following a mother's disappearance: heartbreaking in places, with deeply drawn characters and all the thrills of a classic whodunnit. I couldn't put this down. You won't be able to either."

—ALEX MICHAELIDES, *New York Times* bestselling author of *The Silent Patient* and *The Maidens*

"*All That Is Mine I Carry With Me* is astonishing, powerful, and provocative. It explores the dynamics of family and the ways in which vengeance can control and destroy the ones we love. This book is worth the excruciating wait for another William Landay."

—LOUISE PENNY, #1 *New York Times* bestselling author of *A World of Curiosities*

"*All That Is Mine I Carry With Me* is masterful, original, and riveting, and the best book I've read in quite a while. With its subtle mystery and compelling portraits of how lives are transformed in the aftermath of violent crime, it possessed me from the very first line to the last page."

—SCOTT TUROW, *New York Times* bestselling author of *Presumed Innocent* and *Suspect*

"The last time I went numb reaching a pivotal moment in a book was more than a decade ago. That book was *Defending Jacob*. It just happened again with *All That Is Mine I Carry With Me*. When I finished, I was overwhelmed. It's the best novel I have read in years."

—LINWOOD BARCLAY, *New York Times* bestselling author

"Riveting, intense, and breathtakingly compelling . . . William Landay has brilliantly broken every rule of storytelling in this haunting masterpiece of a novel—part legal thriller, part family drama, and part literary tour de force."

—HANK PHILLIPPI RYAN, *USA Today* bestselling author of *The House Guest*

"With *All That Is Mine I Carry With Me*, the masterful author of *Defending Jacob* has created something riveting, unforgettable, and original—unlike any other crime novel I've read."

—JOSEPH FINDER, *New York Times* bestselling author of *House on Fire*

"An absolutely compelling read, it perfectly blends nuanced and affecting writing with being a real page-turner."

—CLAIRE FULLER

By William Landay

All That Is Mine I Carry With Me

All That Is Mine
I Carry With Me

A Novel

William Landay

BANTAM
NEW YORK

Omnia mea mecum porto

2024 Bantam Books Trade Paperback Edition

Copyright © 2023 by William Landay
Book club guide copyright © 2024 by Penguin Random House LLC

Published in the United States by Bantam Books, an imprint of
Random House, a division of Penguin Random House LLC, New York.

BANTAM & B colophon is a registered trademark of Penguin Random House LLC.
RANDOM HOUSE BOOK CLUB and colophon are trademarks of Penguin Random House LLC.

Originally published in hardcover in the United States by Bantam Books,
an imprint of Random House, a division of Penguin Random House LLC, in 2023.

Grateful acknowledgment is made to writersinkpodcast.com for permission to
reprint an interview between William Landay and Christine Daigle (writersinkpodcast
.com, Episode 178). Interview has been edited for clarity and length. Used by
permission.

ISBN 978-0-345-53186-5
Ebook ISBN 978-0-345-53185-8

Printed in the United States of America on acid-free paper

randomhousebooks.com
randomhousebookclub.com

9 8 7 6 5 4 3 2 1

Book design by Diane Hobbing

BOOK 1

AFTER I FINISHED writing my last novel, I fell into a long silence. You might call it writer's block, but most writers don't use that term or even understand it. When a writer goes quiet, nothing is blocking and nothing is being blocked. He is just empty. I don't know why this silence settled over me. Now that it's over, I don't like to think about it. I only know that for months, then a year, then two years, I could not write. It did no good to struggle; the more I struggled, the tighter the noose became. I could not write, then I could not sleep, then I could not bear my own presence and I began to think dark thoughts. I won't dwell on the details; in my profession, there is a saying that a writer's troubles are of interest only to other writers. I mention my silent period here only because it is the reason I wrote this book, for it was during this time, when I would have grabbed at any plausible idea for a story, that I got an email from an old friend named Jeff Larkin.

I have known Jeff since we were twelve years old. We met in September 1975 when we entered the seventh grade together at a very august and (to me) terrifying private school for boys, and we became pals almost immediately.

Let me say, I am uneasy about starting a book this way, with friends and confessions about my childhood. I am not nostalgic for that time in my life. I'm not even sure an honest account is possible. I do not trust my own memories. I tell myself so many stories about my past, as we all do. Worse—much worse—I don't think a writer ought to insert himself into his stories this way. It generally distracts more than it deepens. A writer's place is off-stage. But what choice do I have? If I am going to tell this story, there is no way around a little autobiography. So:

When I was in sixth grade, my teacher called my parents, out of the blue, to suggest I was bored at school, which was certainly true. Had they considered sending me to a private school? Some-place rigorous and rules-y, where I would not continue to be (I will paraphrase here) a daydreamer and a smart-ass. My folks had never thought of it. They had both gone to public schools, and they presumed that fancy private schools were for Yankees. But Mom and Dad grasped the teacher's essential meaning: what I needed was a swift kick in the pants.

So the next fall I found myself at a school that probably had not looked much different twenty or even fifty years earlier. There were no girls. There was a school necktie. Spanish was not taught, but ancient Latin was required. The gym was called a "palestra"; the cafeteria, the "refectory." Portraits of mustachioed old "masters" hung in the hallways. There was a half-length painting of King Charles I gazing down at us with his needle nose and Van-dyke beard, which alone might have cured me of daydreaming and smart-assery. Even my parents were dazzled and intimidated by the place. My mother warned me, "They smile at you, these WASPs, but I promise you, behind closed doors they call us kikes."

Jeff Larkin felt no such anxiety when he arrived at school. He was a prince. His older brother, Alex, was a senior and a three-sport star, with the heroic aura that surrounds high school ath-letes. Jeff's dad was well known too. He was a criminal defense lawyer, the kind that showed up in the newspaper or on TV stand-ing beside a gangster, swaggering on about the incompetence of the police and the innocence of his wrongly accused client. There was a dark glamour to Mr. Larkin's work, at least before the ca-tastrophe, when his association with violent crime stopped being a thing to admire. But that came later.

Forbidding as the school was, at least I had a new friend. Jeff and I hit it off right away. We were inseparable. It was one of those childhood friendships that was so natural and uncomplicated, we seemed to discover it more than we created it. I have no adult friendships like the one I had with Jeff. I am sure I never will. Once we slip on the armor of adulthood, we lose the ability to form that kind of naive, unqualified connection.

But forty years later, when I got Jeff's email in 2015, we had been out of touch for a very long time. He reached me by sending a fan email from my author website, just as any stranger would do.

"Hey," his email read in its entirety. "Loved the book. Mr. K_____ would be proud." (Mr. K_____ was a beloved English teacher.) "You up for a beer sometime?"

"I'm up for three," I emailed back. "Or forty-three. Just name the place."

THE place he named was Doyle's, an ancient pub in Jamaica Plain, now gone. It was a nostalgic choice. In our twenties, Jeff and I hung out there night after night, shooting the shit. The place had changed over the years. It was bigger and brighter now, more of a family restaurant than the grungy, patinaed old pub I remembered. But the long bar was still the same, and the ornate Victorian mirror behind the bartender.

When I arrived, Jeff was waiting at the bar. His hair was gray, and his face was fuller and more deeply lined than I had expected, but when he saw me and stood up, grinning, he became my old friend again.

"It's the famous author, Philip Solomon," he teased. "What an honor." And we hugged in the clumsy, equivocal way men do.

For the next couple of hours, we drank and bantered as we always had. We picked up our conversation after twenty-odd years as if we had just seen each other the day before. I am a shy man, and I was particularly quiet during that hard time, but this night I yammered like a fool and I laughed harder than I had in a long time.

It was late, around midnight, when Jeff finally mentioned his mother's case and the forty years of misery that followed. We had moved from the bar to a booth by then. His voice was low and confidential.

"You heard about my dad?"

"No."

"He has Alzheimer's."

"Whoa. I'm sorry."

"Convenient, isn't it?"

"That's not how most people think of it."

"He gets to forget. Or pretend to."

"You think he's pretending?"

"I don't know. Haven't seen him. I get my information from Miranda."

Miranda is Jeff's little sister, younger by a year and a half.

"Miranda talks to him?"

"She's taking care of him."

I made a face: *Really?*

"She wants me to go see him. Before it's too late."

"So go. What's the difference?"

"I wouldn't give him the satisfaction."

"He has Alzheimer's. He won't remember anyway."

"That's what Mimi says. She says it's gone on long enough."

He put on a mocking tone: "I'm *lost in the maze of hate.*"

"The maze of hate? That's a thing?"

"Don't even—I can't." He shook his head. "Miranda."

"It's a good name for a band, Maze of Hate."

"She says when I hate him, I'm only hurting myself."

"That could actually be true."

"Maybe. Doesn't mean I'm gonna stop."

"Attaboy. You stay in that maze of hate. Great decision."

"You should call her, Phil. She'd love to hear from you."

"Miranda? Nah. Well, maybe. I dunno."

"Don't worry, I won't tell your wife."

"That's very considerate, thank you."

He gave me a dopey drunk grin. "Maybe it'll give you something to write about."

Some background:

Jeff's mom, Jane Larkin, disappeared on November 12, 1975. It was only a couple of months after Jeff and I started school, but I did meet Mrs. Larkin a few times. Looking back now, she does not seem to have left much of an impression on me. I don't have compelling memories or revealing personal anecdotes about her that I can share with you. Probably, to my twelve-year-old self, she was like any other mom. Certainly there was nothing about her to suggest she was about to become a sort of celebrity, the Woman Who Vanished.

But after her disappearance, a celebrity she was. In the fall of '75, believe me, if you lived in Boston, you knew who Jane Larkin was. The local media feasted on the story, particularly in the first few weeks after her disappearance. It is that shower of news updates, not Mrs. Larkin herself, that I remember best.

One photograph in particular sticks in my memory. It was a staple of the news stories. I presume the picture was provided by her husband when Mrs. Larkin first went missing. It was a formal portrait. Her body was angled, left shoulder forward, and she looked directly into the camera, as if she had just heard you come into the room and turned to look at you. The corners of her mouth were teased upward, her lips slightly parted, an expression that was not quite a smile. I see now, forty years later, that there was a sexy quality to this pose. That is why the newspapers liked it: that little smile was a come-on. Jane Larkin was only thirty-nine when she disappeared, and her attractiveness was an essential part of the story's allure. It was a hammer that people could use to bash her husband when he became a suspect: How could a man with such a beautiful wife dare to want more? How could he presume to feel unsatisfied? Who did he think he was?

A few days after my dinner with Jeff, I did go visit his sister, Miranda. And, yes, I did tell my wife, though I described Miranda only as an "old friend," a bit of husbandly understatement.

The truth is, when we were kids I had a devastating crush on Miranda Larkin. She was absurdly pretty. And somehow catastrophe only made her lovelier, left her with an irresistible brooding, damaged quality. She was two grades behind us in school but years ahead, one of those weirdly mature kids—a grown-up trapped in a teenage body. Brainy, a little actressy, unfathomably well-read. I remember once, when she discovered I was a reader, she asked me, "Have you read the Russians?" I was probably fourteen. I was not sure who the Russians were. It seemed to me there were a lot of Russians. My taste ran more to Alistair MacLean, Irwin Shaw, Robert Ludlum, Leon Uris—airport stuff. Suffice it to say, I have always been a little in awe of Miranda's intellect. (And I have secretly dreaded her opinion of my novels.)

Miranda was also an artist, though it was never clear what kind. It seemed she could do anything. She played guitar. She wrote—stories, poems, even a novel while still in high school. She painted—landscapes, still lifes, abstracts, rarely people. She never worked at any of these things for long. She fluttered from one to the next like a bird in a tree, testing one branch after another. But she always struck me as the real thing, a truly creative temperament. I am not an especially creative person myself—more of a plodder, a grinder, a mechanic—so I have always envied Miranda's instinctive, effortless creativity.

I lost touch with her around the time Jeff left for San Francisco, where he spent most of his twenties; he was the necessary link between us. So after a lapse of twenty-five years or so, I had to google "Miranda Larkin" to find out what she was actually doing. It turned out she was working as a photographer and a painter.

Her studio was located in a converted factory in Waltham.

Outside, the building looked desolate, the sort of abandoned red-brick mill that you find all over New England. But inside, the place was teeming with activity. The lobby directory listed several painters and photographers, a sculptor, a metalworking shop.

Miranda's studio was a single high-ceilinged room on the top floor, bright with sunlight from enormous multipaned windows. Don't imagine anything romantic or picturesque, though. The studio was more like a hoarder's attic. There was not much furniture: a battered oak desk with an enormous computer, a large worktable, one stool. And everywhere stacks of paper, mostly magazines and catalogues, a few books.

Standing amid all this mess was Miranda. She wore jeans and a baggy sweater. Her hair was gathered loosely in a topknot.

"Oh my," she said. "Phil, you look exactly the same."

"You do too."

It was not true. She was still lovely, but there was an austerity about her appearance now. She had gotten very thin—too thin, I thought, for the girl I remembered. No makeup, no jewelry. You could still see the beautiful woman under all that Pilgrim plain-ness, you couldn't help seeing her—high cheekbones, clear eyes, white teeth—but she seemed dulled, reduced, drawn. As a kid, she was radiant; not anymore.

I shouldn't have been surprised, of course; she had simply gotten older, and the work of caring for her father must have been exhausting. It was just that, during the long lapse between visits, Miranda Larkin had never aged a single day in my memory. In my mind's eye, she had always been sixteen years old (though she was actually older the last time I saw her). For a moment, but only for a moment, I even regretted seeing her and spoiling that vivid, precious memory.

She came over to give me a warm hug, just as her brother had. "My goodness, I'm happy to see you. I've missed you."

I nodded. Like a lot of writers, I think, I am more reticent in person than I am in my writing. So I could not quite bring myself to say, as any normal person would, *I've missed you too*. What I said instead, keeping the conversation comfortably on the surface of things, was "I love your pictures. Is it okay if I look?"

I browsed the artwork that was around. There were maybe a dozen photographs—mostly black-and-white street scenes—but the more interesting ones were unframed canvases, which were propped against the wall. These I loved.

"Miranda, these are just—wow."

The pictures mixed Miranda's own photographs and painting with clippings she had found—magazine ads, news photos, headlines—in mixed-media compositions. I don't want to claim too much for Miranda's art; this sort of Rauschenberg-style collage is pretty familiar by now, and of course it is hard to be objective about the work of a friend. But to me there was something fresh and alive about it. The arrangements were built around one or two of her own photos at the center, usually black-and-white, usually of people standing on the street. The subjects seemed to have been photographed without their knowledge. Their faces were hidden by slashes of paint or other clippings: swatches of fabric or newsprint, or little pastiches of old master paintings. They were not just decorative collages; they were portraits.

"Miranda, I'm speechless. They're stunning. Really, really beautiful."

"Thank you."

"I want one. How much are they?"

She shrugged.

"More than a car?"

"What kind of car?"

"Ouch, never mind."

"Well, they last longer than a car, so . . ."

"How do you get these pictures of people? Don't they mind?"

"I don't know. I've never asked."

"They don't know you're there?"

"No."

"How is that possible? Do you hide in mailboxes? Or behind a tree?"

"I don't hide. I have a little trick." She got a strange bulky box-shaped camera from her desk. "This is my secret. It's a Hasselblad. Do you know these cameras?"

"No."

"Come look." She stood close and flipped open a little frame at the top. "This is the viewer. You hold the camera at your waist or your chest, like this, and you look down into it. So all you do is, you don't face in the direction you're photographing. I look down into the camera but I point it sideways, so the person I'm taking a picture of doesn't know what I'm up to."

"That's it?"

"That's it."

"It's not fair, tricking people like that."

"Who said life is fair? Here, can I take your picture? For old times' sake?"

"Absolutely not. You'll put me in one of your paintings and I'll wind up hanging in some dentist's office."

"I promise, I won't."

"Forget it. And I'm not falling for your little camera trick, either."

"Fine." She folded up the viewer on her Hasselblad and returned it to the desk. "Here, sit. You want anything? Coffee?"

"No, thanks."

"Good. I don't have any."

She patted the stool, gesturing me over.

On the belly of her right arm, I glimpsed her old tattoo, which I had forgotten. In small letters, now a little blurry, it read *Omnia mea mecum porto,* Latin for "All that is mine I carry with me." She got this tattoo when we were just out of college, in the mid-1980s, when she was feeling quite lost. This was before the current fad for tattoos had got going, and I hated it at the time, not because I disagreed with the sentiment (I do not) but because I hated to see Miranda deface such a lovely arm. It was like scribbling with a Sharpie on Michelangelo's *David*. Now the tattoo struck me as quite modest. It was placed in such a way that only Miranda herself could read it comfortably: on the underside of her arm, in a single line of letters running from the middle of the forearm up to her elbow. It was like a little note that Miranda had written there just for herself.

She sat on her desk facing me.

"I was sorry to hear about your father."

"Were you really?"

"Well, no. I was sorry for you. Jeff said you're taking care of him."

"I am. It's complicated."

"I bet."

"Are you still writing, Phil? Where's the new book?"

"It's complicated."

"Why? Tell me."

"Nothing to write about."

"There's a whole world to write about."

"*Meh*. The world is such a mess right now. The whole novel thing—it feels trivial, telling little stories when everything is falling apart."

"Everything is always falling apart. We still need art."

"I know. It's just, I want to write something real, something complicated."

"So do it. Write something real. Write something complicated." She gave me a weary, mischievous smile. "Maybe I can help."

It was Miranda who first discovered her mother's absence, on Wednesday, November 12, 1975. She was about to turn eleven years old, a fifth grader. No shadow had fallen over her then. She was a curly-blond pixie, the sort of bright-faced child adults are drawn to.

She walked home from school that day carrying in her arms a

bulging three-ring binder, a bulky math textbook, and a paper-back novel, *Sounder*. She wore her favorite teal miniskirt and the bone-white ribbed turtleneck that went with it, her "school clothes."

She went to the back door of her house and, clutching her books against her chest, she twisted to press the doorbell. No answer. Someone was always home to meet Miranda, usually her mother, but that day the house was dark.

She put her books neatly on the stoop, then tested the doorknob. Locked.

She fetched the spare key from the garage, where it was hidden in an empty flowerpot, unlocked the door, and immediately returned the key to its hiding place, as she had been taught to do.

Inside, she called, "I'm home!" When there was no answer, she went to the foot of the staircase and aimed her voice up toward the second floor: "I'm *hooome*!" Still no answer.

She wandered through the first floor, up the stairs, checked every room. She called out, "Mom! Mom!" for a while, but the house was empty.

It did not occur to her to be frightened. Mom's pocketbook was in the front hall. She had probably just run out for a moment. Far from panicking, Miranda felt a little thrill of independence at having the house all to herself. She could not remember ever being left completely alone like this.

She took three Oreos from the kitchen, turned on the little black-and-white TV in the first-floor den, and settled in contentedly to watch *The Mike Douglas Show*. The Jackson 5 was on the show that day (Miranda would always remember this detail) and she luxuriated in the fact that Alex and Jeff were not there to change the channel to *The Three Stooges* or some stupid cartoon.

At four, when *Mike Douglas* ended, she turned off the TV and drifted around the house. In the quiet, it was easier to notice the house itself. Empty, it was not Miranda's home; it was just a building that, for now, her family happened to occupy. The house was eighty years old, very boxy and plain, with four flat, featureless sides, unlike the many grander wedding-cake Victorians in the neighborhood. Every surface had the patina of years, of human touch—the dark wood, the tarnished brass hinges and knobs, the wavy horsehair-plaster walls. The very age of the house prompted a troubling idea: Other families had lived here, had passed through the house. Other children had stood on these same chipped, creaking bird's-eye maple floors. And other families would occupy it after the Larkins were gone too.

The empty house made little breathing noises. The radiators knocked as they filled with steam, the pipes creaked inside the walls as they expanded and contracted, the boiler thunked on and off in the basement.

She shuffled into her parents' bedroom, crossing the usual borders. On Dad's night table there were only three objects, a Sony digital clock with little hinged cards that flipped to show the time, a copy of *Newsweek,* and a Horatio Hornblower novel with a sailing ship on the cover. Miranda opened the night table drawer, peered at the few neatly arranged things inside: a small box of Kleenex, a tube of cream, a few magazines turned facedown. Miranda turned the top magazine over. It was *Penthouse.* The glossy cover showed a woman in soft focus with her naked back to the camera. The model looked over her shoulder with a blank expression. Miranda studied the magazine cover, wishing she hadn't seen it, then replaced it precisely and closed the drawer.

In a high chest where Dad kept his clothes, there were stacks of dry-cleaned shirts, all folded and wrapped in plastic bags. She opened his closet, where business suits were arrayed neatly on matching wood hangers, grouped into blue suits and gray suits. His wingtip shoes were lined up on the floor, cedar shoe trees in all of them, black shoes and brown shoes and oxblood shoes.

On her mother's dresser was a wedding photo from seventeen years before, Dad in a short haircut, Mom in her white gown, hair piled high on her head like a top hat, both of them smiling. Miranda opened her mother's jewelry box, looked inside it. On a silver tray were coins, mascara, lipstick, a small tub of blush, and an irresistibly soft makeup brush. A Mason Pearson hairbrush with Mom's hair snarled in the bristles. An open pack of Larks (red with silver foil) and a ceramic ashtray filled with cigarette butts marked by her lipstick. Miranda swirled the makeup brush on her cheeks, nose, and forehead to feel its sensuous bloom of soft bristles.

By 4:30 daylight was faltering, the house became gloomy, and Miranda got very worried very quickly.

She considered calling her father at work. His office number was in the kitchen, in the address book. But Miranda had never called his office before and she was too shy to try it now. Who would answer the phone? How would she ask for her dad, what would she call him? "Mr. Larkin"? "Dan"? Anyway, he was at work, and Miranda understood, without ever having been told, that she was not to disturb him during the workday. Mom and the three children regarded Dan Larkin's work with reverence. The Law—that was what her mother called it—was demanding, abstruse, noble. No one in the family ever spoke cynically about it, except Dan himself.

There was no trusted neighbor or friend Miranda felt comfortable calling, either. Her parents had few friends, and none of those adults penetrated the Larkins' circle.

There was Grandma Lil, but she would surely overreact and rush right over in a flutter, when the truth was Miranda did not even know whether there was a problem.

There was Grandma Mildred, too, but that was much too scary an option.

So she waited. What else could she do? In the deepening gloom, Miranda turned on a single lamp in the little den on the first floor, and in the shelter of that warm light, she read *Sounder*, determined not to look up from her book until her mother got home. She was a good reader, but that day it was difficult. In the back of her mind, an idea tugged at her attention—as sometimes a stray thought will distract you from a book—that it was possible her mother would never come home again.

FORTY years or so later, when Miranda described this part of the story, in her cluttered studio, she paused here.

"Isn't that weird? Why would I think my mother was gone forever? It's like I already knew."

"I don't know. Maybe it's natural for a kid to think the worst."

Miranda accepted this and went on with the story: Jeff's return home from school, carrying his crimson football jersey with the shoulder pads inside so that it resembled a torso. Then Alex, towering over the two younger kids, reassuring them it was probably nothing. Dan's return home from work to discover his wife missing, the kids alone, no dinner on the table. The increasingly frantic phone calls to friends and, later, to the police, who refused to investigate that night because Jane could not be considered missing until she had been gone for forty-eight hours. Miranda lying in bed in a low panic, listening to her father's voice on the phone downstairs, frightened by his tone even when she could not make out the words, yearning for her mother to come lie beside her.

She told me, "I thought it was my fault. I thought I did something to make her go. That's how I knew she wasn't coming back."

"What could you have done?"

"I don't know. It makes no sense. But I still think it sometimes."

THE next morning, Miranda woke up early. The light in the house was dim, foggy. It was Thursday, a school day, but everything was wrong. It did not feel like a Thursday. It did not feel like any day at all. The day had come unmoored from the calendar.

There were voices speaking in the kitchen but they were all men's voices.

Miranda sensed right away that her mother had not come back. If she had, Mom would have come straight to her, to her room, to her bedside. Miranda was *almost* sure of it.

She had to pee but could not take the time. Barefoot, wearing her pink-striped Lanz flannel nightgown, she made her way down the stairs.

Three people were in the kitchen, framed in the doorway: Dad, wearing the previous day's starched blue dress shirt, uncharacteristically wrinkled and untucked; Alex; and a third man whom she had never seen before.

This third man might have been very handsome—he had square features and an appealing, level way of looking at you—but his face was marred by a large port-wine stain on the right side of his forehead. Miranda had never seen a face marked this way, and the surprise of the man's appearance, compounded with the off-kilter atmosphere in the house, left the little girl gaping.

Her father stepped forward to say, "Mom hasn't come home yet. We don't know anything. We're still waiting."

"But where is she?"

"I'm sorry, sweetie, we just don't know. That's all I can tell you."

Miranda absorbed the news and, with a quivery feeling, she stood frozen.

"This is Detective Glover. He's a policeman. He's going to help us."

The man gave her a half-hearted smile.

Her dad made no move toward her, to hug her as she yearned for him to do, so she turned and floated back up the stairs.

In her parents' bedroom, the Big Bed was rumpled but the sheets were still tucked in. Dad must have spent the night on top of the covers. On her mother's side of the bed, Miranda tugged the sheet open and climbed in. She snuggled down in the little hollow that Mom's body had impressed into the mattress, laid her head on the flat pillow Mom used, felt Mom's presence still on the sheets, her smell. She did not cry; it was not clear yet that a tragedy had occurred. She just lay there, luxuriating in her mother's lingering, ghostly companionship in the bed.

After a while, Jeff came upstairs to check on her. He was already dressed, in jeans and a T-shirt. Jeff was twelve and a half, and something had happened to him recently, a quickening in his body. Miranda thought he seemed suddenly much older than she was. The eighteen-month gap between them seemed to have widened. He was becoming a junior adult like Alex, leaving Miranda alone in little-kidhood.

"Hey, Mimi."

"You need to brush your hair."

"Yeah?"

"You look like the wild man of Borneo."

This was her mother's phrase. The kids had no idea where Borneo was or who was its wild man, but apparently he had messy hair.

"You okay, Mimi?"

"No."

He sat down on the floor beside the bed, knees up, back against the wall. "It's gonna be okay."

"Who's that guy downstairs?"

"He's a cop."

"Duh. I mean, what's he doing here?"

"Dad made the cops send someone."

"Why?"

"Cuz he's worried about Mom. *Duh*."

"You shouldn't call them cops. I don't think they like it."

"They don't care. They call each other cops, I think."

"What's that thing on his face?"

"It's just a birthmark. He can't help it."

"It looks weird."

"You look weird."

She smiled. "Where's Mom?"

"They don't know."

"Where do *you* think she is?"

"How should I know?"

"They must think something bad happened. That's why there's a cop here."

"No, Mimi. You shouldn't think like that. You'll make yourself sad. We need to stay cool."

"Stay cool."

"That's right. Stay cool."

"What if she had a car accident and she's out there somewhere waiting for us to come get her?"

"She's not. They checked all the hospitals and all the police departments. There weren't any accidents."

"Maybe she's hurt."

"Maybe. We just have to wait, Mimi."

"Maybe she's dead." Miranda grinned then covered her mouth, surprised at the weirdness of her own reaction, and buried her face in the pillow.

But Jeff laughed too. "She's not *dead,* you idiot. Why would she be dead?"

They waited a moment, listening for a sign that the adults in the kitchen, Dad and this weird-looking cop, had heard their inappropriate laughter.

"Maybe she just went away."

"Went away where?"

"I don't know."

"Why would she go away, Mimi?"

"I don't know. Maybe she was sad."

"Sad?" His tone became quite certain: "Mom wasn't sad."

"Maybe she had a boyfriend and they ran away."

"A boyfriend! What?"

"Yeah. Only, if she had a boyfriend and she ran away with him, she'd take us with her, wouldn't she?"

"No! Miranda, if you have a boyfriend, you don't want your kids around. You go off to, like, a hotel or something."

Miranda knew he was talking about sex and she could not bear to look at him. She knew what sex was, in a general way, but she did not like to talk about it, certainly not with her brother, and she *certainly* did not like to think of her mother doing it.

"Are they going to get a divorce?"

"I don't think so."

"How do you know?"

"Cuz they never fight."

"Oh." A pause. "What if she doesn't come back?"

"She's coming back."

"But if she doesn't. Will they still be married?"

"She's coming back, Miranda."

"Okay, but what if she doesn't?"

"Why wouldn't she come back?"

"Cuz maybe she doesn't want to."

"Of course she wants to!"

"You don't know. Maybe she doesn't want to be with Dad anymore."

"Well, she'd still come back to be with *us*."

"Maybe not. If she wanted to be with us, she wouldn't have run away."

"If she doesn't *want* to come back? I don't know. I guess they'll get divorced. It's okay, though. Lots of people get divorced."

"What would happen to us?"

"We'd go live with Mom, I guess."

"Why not Dad?"

"It's just not the way it works."

"Where would we live?"

"I don't know where! None of this is going to happen, Mimi. She's coming back, they're not getting divorced, there's nothing wrong. You just have to wait. Be cool. Be. Cool."

"What if she doesn't want to be our mom anymore?"

Jeff growled at her.

Miranda nuzzled her face into the pillow, thought about it. "Do we still have to go to school?"

"I'm going. I don't know about you."

"Do I have to?"

"Yeah. You're not sick."

"Maybe Dad will let me stay home."

"He won't. You have to go. You're not sick."

"If I go, what do I tell people about Mom?"

"Nothing. It's none of their business."

"None of their beeswax."

"That's right. I don't think we should tell anyone. It's none of their beeswax. Okay?"

"Okay."

"Really, Miranda. You have to promise, okay? It's embarrassing."

"Okay, I promise."

Jeff squinted at her, then decided to trust her. "Okay, good. I promise too."

Jeff did go to school that day, and the next day, Friday, as well. His behavior was normal in every way. He even played in his football game after school on Friday afternoon. I saw Jeff in school both days, and I did not have any idea his mom had gone missing until Saturday morning, when there was a story about it in the *Herald American,* which my own mother noticed. When I came down to breakfast Saturday, she held up the paper, showed me the story. "Isn't this your friend's mother?"

A few days after my conversation with Miranda at her studio, I called Tom Glover, the lead detective on the case back in 1975— the man with the port-wine stain above his right eye. I was having a hard time shaking the idea of this book. I doubted the story was rich enough to hold my interest (and yours), but the idea was worth a little digging, certainly.

I did not know Detective Glover. Before I became a novelist, I worked for a few years as an assistant DA in Middlesex County, which includes the city of Newton, but I had never handled a case of his or even met him. I knew he had retired from the force several years earlier, with the rank of lieutenant. Some of my old friends who had known Glover remembered him as smart, prickly, reserved. Not a bad guy, exactly, but then no one had his phone number, either. Still, I expected he would be happy to talk with me about the Larkin case.

He was not. When I called, he turned me down flat. "That's still an open investigation," he said. He made an insincere apology and, while he did not hang up on me, he made it clear he had no interest in prolonging our phone call. The whole conversation lasted only a minute or two.

Now, I am not so presumptuous as to think everyone should be eager to talk to me when I call for my novel research, but in fact most people are. It is flattering to be told that your life is the stuff of novels. Cops in particular have always been happy to talk. Maybe it helps that I used to be a prosecutor and that I am generally referred to them by another prosecutor or a cop. I am on the right team, at least I used to be. Whatever the reason, cops have always been receptive to my questions.

Glover's excuse was also ridiculous. The Jane Larkin case was ice cold. Talking to me could not possibly endanger the investigation. There was no investigation, just a bunch of forgotten old file folders in a storage unit somewhere.

I called Miranda to report all this. Evidently there was some frustration in my voice because she said, "Don't be mad at him. He doesn't mean to piss people off. Let me talk to him."

"You think he's going to talk just because you tell him to?"

"I know he will."

And Miranda was right. After she called Detective Glover, he did agree to meet. He was not especially enthusiastic about it, but he allowed me to come to his home, a little Cape-style house in Burlington, north of Boston.

We spoke in the living room. There was a small brick fireplace. On the mantel was an old picture of Glover's father in a Cambridge Police uniform. He looked like a thicker, coarser version of the man standing beside me, the raw material that had been refined in the next generation.

Glover himself was handsome, just as Miranda had described him, though he was now seventy-one years old. I could see how as an eleven-year-old girl she might have been awed by him. He had a guarded, diffident, watchful sort of manner, like a very smart, shy child.

About the port-wine stain, which Miranda had described several times and which I had prepared myself to ignore: In the actual event, I could not help being distracted by it at first. It lay on his forehead like a thought, and, watching him, I had the uncomfortable sense of his nakedness, as if what lay exposed was a private part of himself that ought to be hidden. Its color was not as lurid as Miranda had described. The stain was not the strawberry red that she remembered, but a darker nut-brown, not all that different from the surrounding skin. It is possible the stain had a brighter appearance when Miranda met the detective in November of '75, when Glover was thirty-one years old. Or maybe she simply saw it with a child's eye and could not help being fascinated by it. Because of the way it was placed on the right side of his forehead, as he turned his head, it created a two-faced, Januslike impression. His left side in profile was unmarked and strikingly handsome; his right side in profile was an entirely different face, dominated by the stain. I will say no more about it. Now that I know Tom Glover—I would even call him a friend—I understand that he would hate to be defined by it.

I want to get off the subject, as well, because as a writer I hate that port-wine stain. It is a clumsy, ridiculous device and, believe me, I'm embarrassed by it. I would no sooner give one of my fictional characters a port-wine stain to suggest some mysterious inner torment than I would give him enormous ears to show that he is a good listener. But the truth is Tom Glover did (and still does) have that port-wine stain, and I am determined to report this story exactly as I found it, so let's leave the damn thing on his forehead and move on.

THAT afternoon—Thursday, November 13, 1975, the day after Jane Larkin vanished—Glover was waiting in an unmarked car a half block from the Larkins' house when Miranda walked by, on her way home from school. In the rearview mirror on the driver's door, he watched the little girl shuffle toward him on the opposite side of the street. She moved slowly, head down, scuffing her feet, cradling her books and lunchbox.

Detective Glover had not been waiting for Miranda. He had been watching the house, or rather watching Dan Larkin, for nearly six hours now. He mistrusted Dan from the start. That morning Larkin had behaved in every way as a distressed husband might. He was worried sick about his wife; he said so several times. He would stay home from work all day in case she called. He asked Glover if it would help to call in the state police or even the feds; he had the connections, Glover only had to say the word. But there was something about Larkin's performance—wooden, self-conscious, calculating, meticulous—that ignited Glover's suspicion. It was possible, of course, that the guy just had a stiff manner, but Glover could not help doubting him. All that playacting.

What Larkin wanted, perhaps, was to establish for the record that he had reacted appropriately, and that was why he had demanded the police send someone so quickly: he wanted an audience to witness his distress. Later, if the case came to trial, Detective Glover could be called to testify to the whole show: the panic, the pacing, the fruitless phone calls to friends. It was a pitiless, cynical impression, even for a cop, and Glover did not entirely trust it. So all morning and afternoon he watched. He watched to see if Larkin really meant to stay home and wait for his wife's call, or if in fact he knew the call was not coming. He watched simply to see what Larkin would do next. He watched, in the end, because he did not know what else to do. There was no clear evidence that a crime had been committed and no leads to follow if one had been. Without more, until forty-eight hours passed, Jane Larkin's disappearance would not be a police matter at all, even as a (noncriminal) missing-person case.

The truth was Glover enjoyed surveillance. At least if he could be alone like this. There was something peaceful in watching, motionless and silent, hidden, like an owl in a tree. A lot of detective work, it turned out, amounted to no more than being watchful, and his whole life had prepared him for it. To be acutely self-conscious is, equally, to be acutely other-conscious—to observe people and note their reactions, to watch them watching you.

That morning Miranda had been too shy to speak with him, and Glover considered letting her walk past now, but the little girl recognized him and stopped. There was no more than ten feet between them as he looked through the open car window. She was looking at the unmarked side of his face, but Glover could see her thinking, remembering the stain, painting it onto him.

He allowed her a moment to work through her thoughts.

"She didn't come home, did she?"

"No. I'm sorry."

The girl's eyes dropped and she stood there, frozen.

"We'll find her," he said. He did not believe this, at least he was not sure of it, but it seemed like the kind of thing one ought to say to a child. "You want to talk about it?"

The girl managed to shake her head, eyes fixed on her own toes.

"Are you okay?"

No response.

"You want a ride home?"

"I'm not allowed to take rides from strangers."

"I'm not a stranger, I'm a policeman."

"It's the same thing."

"True."

A beat.

"I don't want to go home anyway."

"Why not? Your dad's there."

"I don't *want* my dad!"

And with that, after nearly twenty-four hours of waiting, it was all finally too much for Miranda. She fought to contain her emotions for a moment, and there were a few sniffles. Then she surrendered. Her books slipped out of her arms and cluttered around her feet, and all at once the little girl was sobbing so extravagantly, so unapologetically—her shoulders bouncing and shrugging, her breath coming in wet gasps—that Glover was awed by her lack of inhibition.

Glover, poor childless Tom Glover, had no idea how to respond. He stared at her a moment, wondering at her capacity for release. He wished she were a boy; then he would have some idea how to talk to her and shut this whole thing down. He looked around to see if anyone else was nearby, but there was no one. Finally, diligently—what choice did he have?—he forced himself out of the car and quick-marched across to her. He said, "Shh, shh," and put his hand on her head, testing it first with his palm as you would tap on a stove to see if it was hot. When that did not work, he knelt beside her, and Miranda abruptly threw herself against his shoulder and tossed her arms around his neck and went right on sobbing, so that he hardly had any choice but to wrap his arms loosely around her, and when she tightened her grip, he returned a cautious squeeze, and for the first time the gravity of what was happening to these kids sunk into Glover, and it became more than an idea, a case to be solved. They stayed like that for a few seconds. Glover was startled by his own emotion as much as Miranda's. He was pierced. He resolved not to move until the little girl released him.

When she finally unclinched her arms, his shoulder was wet with tears and snot, and he understood that he—his shoulder, his awkward, inexpert touch—had somehow comforted this child. The strange emotion was sinking away, and he struggled to name it before it vanished. Not pity, not protectiveness, not love. It was a kind of covenant between them.

"Here," he said, "let's pick up your books."

"I don't care about my books."

"Well, I can pick them up for you."

He collected them, arranged them, and offered them to her.

"I don't want them."

"No? Okay. So, um, why don't—I can carry them home for you."

"I don't *want* to go home. I want my mother."

"We can go see if she came home."

"You know she didn't. You already said so."

"Well, maybe she called, maybe there's news. Your father will know."

"You're just trying to get rid of me."

"I am *not* trying to get rid of you. Why would I want to get rid of you?"

"I'm not a little kid. You don't have to talk to me like that." She refused to look at him.

"Okay. We could go sit by the lake. You want to go sit by the lake? We can just hang out until you're ready to go home." This was Crystal Lake, a block away.

"I'll never be ready."

"Well, then I guess we'll just sit there all winter."

He had not meant it as a joke and he did not see anything funny in it, but the little girl laughed, so Glover did too.

He left the books in his unmarked Ford, and together they walked to a shady slope beside the lake. They sat down on a wood-slatted bench there, Miranda to the detective's right, the same side she had chosen to walk beside him. He thought she must be choosing this side because she was curious about the port-wine stain, but she was not stealing any glances at it. It occurred to him that she took this side to put *him* at ease, to show him that she was not fazed by it, that he needn't be self-conscious. He liked her so much for this gesture that he immediately convinced himself that it was impossible, she had not done it at all. It was just a coincidence that she had chosen to sit on his right side, because children are not so kind and neither, generally, are adults.

"Do you want to talk about it?" he said.

"No."

"Do you want to talk about anything?"

"No."

They sat there in silence for a long time, or what felt to Detective Glover like a long time.

"What's your name?"

"Detective Glover."

"No, your real name."

"It's Tom."

"Tom. Do you like being a detective, *Tom*?"

"Not really."

"Why not?"

"I don't know. I suppose it's because I meet a lot of unhappy people."

"Like me?"

"Like you."

"You meet happy people, too, don't you?"

"Not many. Happy people don't call the police a whole lot."

"How do you get that job?"

"Well, you start by being a police officer, the kind that wears a blue uniform."

"Did you wear a blue uniform?"

"Yes. I used to."

"Why blue? Why not green?"

"I don't really know. I guess people just like policemen to wear blue. I used to wear a green uniform, in the army. I've worn lots of uniforms."

"But now you don't."

"Now I don't. Not anymore. I wish I did. It's easier. You don't have to think about what to wear."

"Can you find my mom?"

He looked down at her. "Yes."

"Do you know why she ran away?"

"What makes you think she ran away?"

"Because she left."

Glover nodded. He looked out at the lake, not at the girl. He waited for her to speak.

"Do people ever just leave like that?"

"Sometimes."

"And then they come back?"

"Sometimes."

They watched a duck capsize itself to snap at something under the surface.

"Why do they leave?"

"I don't know. Lots of reasons, I guess. What makes you think your mother would run away?"

"I don't know."

"Did she fight with your dad?"

"Sometimes, I guess. Everybody fights."

"What did they fight about?"

"They didn't, like, *fight* fight. Just regular fighting."

"Well, like what would be an example of them fighting?"

"I don't know. Don't you ever fight with people?"

"Sure. Did they have a fight recently?"

"No."

"Maybe about money?"

"No."

"About something else?"

"No."

"Maybe about something your father did?"

"No. There was no fight. I told you."

"Did you ever see them do worse than arguing?"

"Worse like what? I don't get it."

"Did your mom ever get hurt? Bruises, black eyes, anything like that?"

"You mean, by my dad?"

"Yeah."

"No!"

"Your dad never hit your mom? Or pushed her?"

"No! Never."

"Threatened her?"

"No."

"You'd tell me if he did?"

"Yes."

He leaned back, folded his arms, stretched out his legs, and crossed them at the ankles. "Did you see your dad yesterday morning before you left for school?"

"I see him every morning."

"Was there anything unusual about him? How he looked, how he acted?"

"No. He was happy."

"He wasn't angry or nervous or anything?"

"He was just normal."

"What was he wearing?"

"A suit."

"What color, do you remember?"

"Gray."

"You remember his shirt?"

"Yeah."

"What color was it?"

"Blue. Light blue. With a white collar."

"That's pretty good. How do you remember that?"

"When he comes down for breakfast, he always does the same thing. He hangs his coat over the top of the kitchen door, and when he sits down, he flips his necktie over his shoulder like a scarf so it won't get dirty."

"He must have been eating something messy."

"No, just a muffin."

"That can be messy, can't it?"

"No. He used a fork and knife."

"Why would he eat a muffin with a fork and knife?"

"He always does. He says it's greasy. He doesn't like to get grease on his fingers."

"Hm. Okay. But you remember him wearing that shirt specifically?"

"Yes. It's my favorite. It has little holes in the collar for a clip that he wears."

"You have a good memory. How about the tie, do you remember that too?"

"Yeah. It was red with, like, decorations."

"Decorations?"

"You know, a pattern." She pronounced it *patterin*. "Like little flowers, kind of."

"Have you seen that tie before?"

"All the time."

"But he has other red ties too?"

"Yeah."

"But you know the specific red tie you mean?"

"Yeah."

"Would you recognize it again if you saw it?"

"Yeah."

"Did he have any marks on him yesterday morning, scratches or bruises or cuts, anything like that?"

"No, I don't think so."

"But you're not sure?"

"I don't remember any."

"On his neck?"

"I don't remember."

"How about your mom? Did she seem scared, upset, agitated?"

"Agitated?"

"You know, weird."

"No, she was normal too."

"Does your dad like to garden or work outside?"

"No. Why are you asking me that?"

He smiled down at her gently, like a kind uncle. "No reason. Just making sure you're still listening."

"My mom likes to garden sometimes. She plants flowers. But only sometimes. Daddy doesn't."

"Okay, this is going to be a weird one. You ready?"

"'Kay."

"Does your dad keep his car very clean?"

"Pretty clean, I guess. Just regular."

"Does he take it to the car wash?"

"I don't think so."

"Does he wash it himself, in the driveway?"

"No, never."

"Does he ever have anyone else clean it for him?"

She looked at him. "You think my dad did something to her, don't you?"

"Why would you say that?"

"All these questions about him."

"I don't think anything. I just notice things sometimes. I'm a good noticer. I get the feeling you're a good noticer too. Is that true?"

"I don't know. I guess."

He thought about what the girl might say when she got home. "I don't think your dad did anything at all, Miranda. I just want to find your mom, that's all. Okay?"

"Okay."

"You believe me?"

"Yes."

Glover paused. He'd gone too far, trusted a child more than he should have. "Is there anything you want to ask *me*?"

"About what?"

"About anything."

She made a concentrated face—lips pursed, brow furrowed. "I don't know if I can ask this."

"You can ask me anything."

"It's not about my mother."

"Okay."

"Did you always have that mark on your face?"

"Yes."

"How did you get it?"

"I was born with it."

"So you had it when you were a kid?"

"Yes."

"Were other kids mean to you?"

"Sometimes."

"Did you wish you didn't have it?"

"I did back then, yes."

"But not now."

"I don't think about it anymore. It's just a part of me. It wouldn't do any good to wish I didn't have it, so I don't waste time thinking about it."

"It's not so bad, you know."

"I know."

"Is it okay that I talked about it?"

"Sure."

"Does it feel any different? I mean, like, if I touch it?"

"No. It's just skin. Same as yours."

"Can I touch it?"

He hesitated. "I guess."

That momentary hesitation had nothing to do with a social taboo about physical contact with children. Times have changed. Today, a man in Tom Glover's situation might say no for that reason, however innocent the touching. But that day in 1975, Glover's hesitation was entirely personal. He simply did not like to be touched.

Miranda stood in front of him. The bench was on a downslope; standing, she faced him eye to eye. With great concentration, she laid her left hand on his forehead, with her palm on his temple and her fingers stretched across his brow. The stain was bigger than her hand, so she had to reposition it to cover as much as possible. Glover felt her warm hand come off his forehead and resettle itself each time, like a dog carefully positioning itself on its bed.

"There. It's gone."

He gave her a suffering smile. "Thank you."

When he finished describing this scene to me, forty years later, in the cramped living room of his house, Glover smiled at the memory of little Miranda.

He said, "There's one other thing that happened that day. It has nothing to do with the Jane Larkin case. It just kind of sticks in my mind."

"You must think it's part of the story if you're remembering it now."

"It's part of the story *for me*." He massaged his jaw, frowned, shrugged. "I don't know. I'll tell it, you can decide. Put it in your book, don't put it in your book, whatever."

"Okay."

"So I'm sitting on the Larkin house. I've been there all day, except for the time I was with Miranda. This is about six, seven o'clock at night, maybe, something like that. And nothing happened, of course. Mrs. Larkin didn't come home. Mr. Larkin never left the house, never called the station, never did anything. He's just lying low. He knows I'm watching—he's not going to give anything away. So I finally give up, I leave.

"And I'm driving—you know the woods where Hammond Pond Parkway meets Beacon Street?"

"Yeah, I know where you mean."

"So I'm on Hammond Pond Parkway there, and I see this thing on the road, so I stop to clear it away before there's an accident. It's a—whattaya call it?—a headlight assembly. It's smashed. There's broken glass everywhere. There's blood on the grass, and the grass is all matted down. And I can see where the blood goes off into the woods.

"So I follow the trail. It's twilight, but it's a little darker in the trees, gloomy. I follow the blood.

"I come to a little clearing, and there's a deer lying there. On her side. Not a big one. She's struggling. Breathing real heavy, panting. She picks up her head and looks at me, but that's all she can do, she can't really move. There's foam in her mouth. Her back, her haunch—her whole back leg and hip are just blood. It's all torn open, the skin is ripped off, and I can see the . . . you know, the meat. I don't know how long she's been lying there, but there's a lot of blood on the ground underneath her. It's obvious she isn't going to make it.

"So I call it in on the radio. What should I do? The desk sergeant says, 'Nothing. Just leave it.' Because it's not a police matter. No crime's been committed, no people are hurt, no public-safety issue. It's just an accident. It's a wild animal; they die all the time.

"So I wait there, I stay with this deer. Something about it—I just can't leave her there to die alone.

"Only it takes a long time. She doesn't want to die. Every now and then she picks up her head, or she tries to use her front legs to get up. At one point, I go back to my car and wait, hoping she'll die in the meantime. But when I get back, she's still awake, obviously suffering. Something has to be done. And now the light is starting to fade.

"I was just a young guy at this point. And I'm not a hunter, I've never killed anything. So I radio in and I tell them I want to put this thing out of its misery. Can they send over animal control or someone? They tell me animal control won't come for a deer in the woods; deer are *supposed* to be in the woods. So you'll have to do it. Only I don't know how, and I don't want to make things worse by doing it wrong. So the dispatcher finds a cop who's a hunter, and the guy tells me, 'Get as close as you can but not too close, because you could get a hoof in the face. Aim for the spot right where the neck meets the skull, just below the skull, so you can put the bullet right in her brain. She'll never feel a thing,' he says.

"So that's what I did. I got up as close as I could and I shot her."

Me: "And?"

"It just feels like part of that day somehow."

"It bothered you, obviously."

"No. That's the thing. It bothered me right up until I pulled the trigger. I didn't think I'd be able to do it, but once it was over, it was like nothing. Didn't matter at all. It's just that it was my first time." He batted away the memory with the back of his hand.

"It's just something that happened. Forget about it. Just a strange day."

THAT same evening—day two, soon after Glover shot the deer—Jane's older sister, Kate, appeared at the house. Neither Miranda nor Jeff is sure now how Kate got word of the disappearance; presumably Dan called and told her.

For Miranda, it was an enormous relief to see Aunt Kate. It meant the Larkins were not so alone, and Miranda was not the only girl, and her dad was not the only adult. Even Aunt Kate's physical appearance was reassuring; she looked enough like Miranda's missing mother that seeing Aunt Kate in the house felt vaguely like having her mom back home. Aunt Kate might even be a *better* version of Mom for this crisis: she was leaner, harder than her younger sister, with none of Jane's kittenish warmth. She was tough.

(A side note: Today, you can hardly miss how the adult Miranda is so much more like her Aunt Kate than her warmer, "softer" mother, Jane. I have met Aunt Kate, now in her eighties, and she has some of Miranda's chilly beauty and self-possession. There is even something in their voices that sounds alike.)

At the sight of her aunt, Miranda began to lose her composure.

Aunt Kate stepped around Dan and dropped down on her knees to entangle Miranda in a hug.

Miranda allowed herself to be gathered in close, though the cold still clung to Kate's puffy down coat and to her cheeks and ears. "Oh, sweetheart. You must have been so worried. Don't you worry. We're going to figure this out."

The boys were there, and Kate greeted each in a carefully modulated way—a more restrained hug for Jeff, who needed more nurturing than he let on, and a formal kiss for Alex who bent down, stiff as a jackknife, to accept it.

They settled in the little den on the first floor where the family always gathered, where Kate said in a peremptory way, "What's going on? Tell me everything."

Dan told her what little they knew, which was not much more than the bare fact that Jane had not been home the evening before to meet any of them. "We haven't heard a thing, Kate. There's nothing to do. We're all just waiting. We're trapped here."

"Something happened. This is so unlike her. To just leave like this? No way. I can't imagine it. She wouldn't do this. Something must have happened."

"Do you know anything, Kate?"

"Of course not."

"Was she unhappy?"

"Jane? *Jane?* No. If she was unhappy, she never said anything to me."

"I mean, was she unhappy with *me,* Kate? Be honest."

"No, she never said anything like that, never."

"Then why would she leave?"

"Oh, Dan, stop. Obviously there's been some kind of accident. Or something."

"They've checked, they've checked." He fell back in his chair, hand-mopped his face.

"She wouldn't just *leave.* She wouldn't do that to the kids. Or you. Is it possible that one of your clients . . . ?"

"My clients? No. No one would do this."

"Well, *something* happened to her, because she would not just leave, I'm telling you."

Dan said, "Kids, can you leave Aunt Kate and me alone for a minute so we can talk?" When they had shuffled out, he slid forward on his seat cushion and murmured, "Kate, did she ever talk to you about anyone?"

"Anyone like who?"

"You know what I mean. Was there someone else?"

"Oh God, no. Jane? Are you crazy?"

"There has to be a reason why a woman leaves her husband."

"Dan, let me tell you something about Jane: she is a horrible liar. If she was unhappy or if she was seeing someone, you would have known it. You especially. No way she could have pulled that off. It's not her. She's too *good* for that."

"Women have secrets."

"*People* have secrets, Dan. But not Jane, not like that."

"And if she was unhappy, you would tell me?"

"Yes, I would. Of course I would. She's been unhappy in the past. We both know that. But not now. My impression was things were getting better, no?"

He drooped back into the chair. "I still think she was unhappy."

"Why would you say that? Were *you* unhappy, Dan?"

"No more than anyone else."

"That sounds like yes."

"No. I wasn't unhappy. Maybe not completely satisfied anymore, but not unhappy."

"What does that mean?"

"You know what it means, Kate. Jane and I have been married twenty years now." (It was actually seventeen.) "Things change. It's natural, it's the same for everyone. Be honest. We're not kids anymore."

"Dan, I'm not a kid but I'm not unhappy."

"I didn't say I was unhappy. I said unsatisfied."

"Did Jane know you were . . . unsatisfied?"

"Maybe. I don't know. I'm sure she probably did. How could she not?"

She searched his face for a moment. "Have you told my parents?"

"No. I couldn't deal with it, frankly. It's not a phone call I'm looking forward to."

"Do you want me to tell them?"

"Yes, believe me. But I can't let you. I have to do it. I'll call them."

"You want to call them now, together?"

He thought it over. "No. Let me give it one more day. Maybe

she shows up and it's all just a big misunderstanding. No need to flip them out for no reason."

Kate accepted this without comment. She seemed resolved to give Dan whatever sort of help he needed and to avoid arguing with him, as she often did.

"The police seem to think she might come back."

"Okay then. We'll wait if that's what you want."

"That's what they're telling me."

"Okay. I believe you."

"Do you?"

"Yes."

"I'm not sure what to believe myself."

Kate had never quite connected with her brother-in-law, never quite "got" him. She liked Dan well enough, she told me years later. He was smart and pleasant. Certainly she understood what Jane saw in him: he was her type, successful and blandly handsome, with the sort of me-first attitude Jane always went for in men. Back when they were kids, Jane used to make a fool of herself over boys in a way Kate never did. But between Kate and Dan? The connection had never been more than a formality, a thin line linking them on the family tree. Kate had said to her sister once, cautiously, that there was something about Dan, an elusive quality, that made her think of Gertrude Stein's famous put-down of Oakland, that "there's no *there* there." Jane laughed it off. She said she did not even know what that meant, "no there there," it was just one of those clever-sounding phrases people like to say. So Kate had never raised the subject again. But at this moment, when she was trying her hardest to love Dan, to be there for him, she got the feeling again that there was nothing inside Dan to connect with. Whatever that essential thing is—the little pilot that sits inside our heads, the self, the soul, call it whatever you want—Kate could not seem to sense it in Dan. He was hollow.

Why, exactly, did Dan make her feel this way? What was it about him? The reasons seemed to dematerialize the moment she tried to name them.

He had a guarded personality. So what? Did everybody have to be an open book?

He could be remote, aloof, or lost in thought. So what? Probably he had more important things on his mind than the latest family gossip.

The flaw might have been Kate's, too, remember. If she found Dan hollow, maybe her imagination was just too weak to conceive a person so different from herself. Her empathy could not extend that far. We are all sealed up alone. We all carry the center of the universe inside our own heads. It is, for each of us, a point a few inches behind our eyes where the binocular lines of vision converge. Only a narcissist or a child is fool enough to believe it. Of course Dan was not hollow, no more than Kate herself. She knew all this.

So Kate made a conscious effort to connect with her brother-in-law that night, to accept him unconditionally, be a sister to him. And yet, and yet.

JEFF. Somehow I have let Jeff slip offstage. It's what he would have liked to do back then, as all this was unfolding. Jeff kept his secrets. It never bothered me. He went through a lot, obviously. It was his right to talk about it or not, as he chose. Anyway, I have always understood isolatoes like him. Honestly, it is you extroverts that mystify me, always bounding up with your tails wagging, wanting more and more and more. To me, Jeff's reticence seemed perfectly natural.

For us new boys at school, this was an intense period even before Mrs. Larkin went missing. In those first few weeks and months of classes, all of us were reeling. Private school was much more demanding than public school had been. We were overwhelmed. We were *meant* to be overwhelmed. Our new school was famous for its rigor—the struggle maketh the man—so terrorizing the incoming seventh graders was terrifically on-brand.

One aspect of school life did feel easier, at least: the daily schedule, which gave us our first taste of independence. The days included free periods when we could do whatever we liked, so long as we did not leave campus. Jeff and I, and all of our friends, spent most of our free periods playing basketball in the gym. Jeff was never that into it. He would play but it was just to kill time, and he was not very good. When he first arrived at school, the older boys used to eyeball him for signs of his older brother's talent, but he did not have Alex's skill or ruthlessness. The truth is he never cared about basketball. Jeff just wanted to hang out, and back then the gym was the place to do it.

It was in that lovely old gym, between classes, that Jeff and I first talked about his mother's vanishing. This was the Monday after Disappearance Day. As I mentioned, my own mother had seen a story about the disappearance in the paper on Saturday, and I came to school burning to ask Jeff about it. I did not have the chance until I found him in the gym midmorning.

The gym was silent. When I came in, I thought the place was empty and I picked up a ball before I noticed him, alone, slouched in the top row of the wooden stands. There was a vacant look on his face. I remember that lost expression of Jeff's very clearly, even now. I think I knew, before I even spoke with him, that a terrible thing was happening. I knew that Jeff's mom had not just slipped away for a few days, it was not just a misunderstanding, as my own parents had been speculating. I felt the change in Jeff immediately. At that age, I had never seen terrible things, not up close. It scared the shit out of me.

This is the story Jeff told me that day:

"A few months ago, my dad took Miranda and me out for pizza. It was a Friday night. It was *really* warm, so I think it was, like, July, maybe? Something like that.

"My mom didn't come. She said she was too tired, she wanted to sleep. 'I'm gonna take a pill.' So we're like, 'Okay.' That sounds like a big deal, I guess, but it wasn't. She always has trouble sleeping, so she takes sleeping pills. But she was acting weird. And it was weird that Dad took us alone. That never happens. He was acting all pissy too. They must have had some kind of fight.

"So we go out for pizza, the three of us. We went to Pino's. We were out for like an hour, maybe more.

"When we get home, the house is all quiet and sweaty from the heat. My mom is sleeping upstairs, so we all stay downstairs so we don't bother her. We're being all quiet and stuff. We put on a Red Sox game, real low. They were playing the Royals, I think, and we watched for a while, and Miranda got bored and she went off somewhere.

"And this whole time there was a sound, like a humming sound. Real low. Just, like, in the background. Like a machine running somewhere in the distance, like maybe a dishwasher or an air conditioner or something.

"Then Miranda calls down from the second floor: 'Where's Mom?'

"And my dad's like, 'I thought she was sleeping.'

"So we start calling for her and looking around the house for her, and she's not answering. She's gone. She left.

"So we keep looking and looking.

"And suddenly I figure out what that noise is.

"I run out to the garage. The doors are all closed.

"I open the side door to the garage. It's kind of dark inside, but I can just make her out. She's sitting in her car with the engine running. Her head is tipped back like she's dead.

"So I'm standing by the little side door to the garage, and the button is right there to open the big garage door, so I just push it. The garage door opens, a little daylight comes in.

"So she wakes up and she looks up at me like *Ooh!*—like she's surprised to see me. 'I must have fallen asleep! I must have fallen asleep!' "

He mimicked her flustered voice with obvious scorn.

"So I was just like, *Okay, right, whatever.* It was bullshit, you know? It was pathetic. I was so mad. I wasn't sad, I didn't feel sorry for her or anything. I just *hated* her for it, you know? I just kind of walked away and left her there."

I said, "Why were you mad?"

"It was just so stupid. And selfish. She wanted to kill herself? Why? And what about us? We don't matter, we don't get a vote?"

"But it was an accident, wasn't it? Why would she want to kill herself?"

Jeff shrugged. "It's just how she is. She goes up and down. Anyway, she never said anything about it. We never talked about it. We just kind of pretended the whole thing never happened. It was like we agreed, without ever saying anything, that we were going to act like I never saw what I saw. Like I didn't know what she was doing.

"So that's just what we did. She told Miranda and my dad that she just fell asleep in the car, like it was just a funny story. She left out the part about the engine running and the garage door being closed. My dad and Miranda still don't know. I'm the only one. And now you."

By the way, I still wonder why exactly Jane Larkin would want to kill herself. Was that really what she was trying to do? The whole incident is still puzzling. Recently I asked a friend of mine who is an ER doctor whether Jeff's story rang true to him. He thought Jane's excuse was plausible but unlikely. People do make mistakes with prescription drugs. If it was a prescription, in 1975 the drug might have been Valium, which could have made Jane drowsy enough to fall asleep accidentally after starting the car. But he thought it was unlikely, and I do too. I am still not sure what to make of it. The only detail about the incident that I have been able to pin down firmly is the date: July 18, 1975. That was the only Friday that month when the Red Sox played Kansas City. (They won 9 to 3, getting a complete game from the crafty left-hander Bill Lee.)

Jeff, the only witness, did not have an answer in the gym that day, either. Why would his mother want to kill herself? He just gave a disdainful snort, the sort of sound that naive teenagers use to express their contempt for adults and their sloppy, botched lives. He said, "They weren't getting along. It was a mess."

I did not push him any further. It would have been unkind. Better to be loyal than logical.

Jeff said, "She's not coming back."

Only four days in, Jeff had already lost hope, just as Miranda had the day she came home to discover her mother missing. But Jeff never lost his composure. Not that day, not ever, at least in front of me. You could *feel* how devastated he was. A sense of tragedy hung around him like a cloud—not sadness, tragedy—but he never broke down.

THE same day Jeff related that story to me at school—Monday, November 17, 1975, according to my reconstruction—Jane's car was found at the Route 128 train station. It was a '75 Ford Thunderbird coupe, white with a brown landau roof and tan leatherette interior. The car was unlocked and undamaged. There was no sign of struggle. The key, removed from any key ring, was stashed under the visor on the driver's side. The car started easily; there was no sign of mechanical difficulty. When the state trooper turned on the ignition, the eight-track tape player started. Apparently when she turned off the car Jane (or someone) had been listening to "Cecilia," from the Simon & Garfunkel album *Bridge Over Troubled Water*. The trunk and passenger compartment were empty except for some small loose items: coins, pens, a ponytail holder, a sloppily folded road map in the glove compartment.

The car had not been hidden in any way. It had taken four days to discover only because the police had not started looking for Jane until Saturday, and even then they had not taken the case seriously, presuming that if Jane truly was missing, it was probably a personal matter between man and wife (an attitude more prevalent in 1975 than now, no doubt). Also, no one had thought to look at the train station because Jane had never been known to take the train. In fact, Tom Glover actually had prowled through the long-term parking lot at Logan Airport, guessing it might be more Jane's style.

The car was photographed from every angle, inside and out, before it was towed away to the Newton Police lot, where it was examined for fingerprints. Several prints were found, but all belonged to the Larkin family. The key, steering wheel, and driver's door handle—the parts necessarily touched by whoever abandoned the car there—all showed no prints.

Over the next few days, the detectives working the case—besides Glover, a state police detective was now investigating, plus others temporarily assigned to help with the legwork—tried to confirm the theory that Jane had boarded a train. They were unable to do so. They canvassed witnesses and conductors at the station and on various train routes. None remembered her specifically. In 1975, IDs were not checked and passenger manifests were not kept. Passengers commonly bought their tickets with cash, leaving no identifying record of the transaction. In the end, the detectives could neither prove nor disprove that Jane had actually gotten on a train.

THAT night, Glover confronted Dan Larkin with his suspicions for the first time. In hindsight, he says now, he regrets doing so. There was no upside in it, no tactical advantage. The detective just lost control of his emotions. He tipped his hand because he was tired and he wanted Larkin to know he wasn't fooling anyone. Today, Glover confesses that "I wanted him to know I was just as smart as he was." A more experienced—and more self-assured—man would not have made the same mistake, or so Tom Glover seems to feel.

For what it's worth, I don't see it that way. The mistake, if it was one, probably did not make any difference. Dan Larkin was an experienced criminal lawyer. He must have been on guard. He must have known he was a suspect, as any husband would be in the disappearance of a married woman. Glover was not giving anything away.

But every cop knows the self-lacerating guilt that comes with an unsolved or mis-solved case. The gnawing questions of "what if?" The shame of *personal* failure. Glover has taken this case hard. It is one thing to fail, as we all do, and another thing to live with that failure year after year, to carry it around in your pocket and worry it with your fingers.

The conversation took place in the Larkins' kitchen, after Glover told Dan they found Jane's car. The new evidence obviously created a dilemma for the detective: Should he continue to treat Dan as a victim whose wife was missing, and thus entitled to complete information? Or as a suspect, entitled to no information—or even false information if that served the cops' purposes? In the end, Glover held back a few facts, particularly the lack of fingerprints, which by the evening was already known to the investigators. But he gave Dan enough detail to keep up the pretense that they were still on the same side.

When the conversation seemed at an end, Glover added, "You mind if I ask you something? Didn't you represent Vincent Tancredo?"

Dan bowed his head and gazed at Glover from beneath his brows, taking a moment to recalibrate. "Why do you ask?"

"It's a famous case. I'm curious. What was he like?"

"I have no idea. Vincent was a client, not a friend."

"You spent a lot of time with him. You must have some impressions."

"Not really."

"Was he smart?"

"Not especially."

"Did you like him?"

"There was nothing remarkable about him. He was just a guy. Same as anyone. Same as you."

Some background: Vincent Tancredo's wife, Janice, had been murdered in April 1972. The body was found in her car, folded in the footwell behind the driver's seat, covered with a blanket. The car, a forest green '69 Buick Wildcat convertible, was parked in the lot at the Faulkner Hospital in Boston, where Janice was a nurse in the ICU. She had worked a regular shift one day but never returned home. When Janice's husband reported her missing the next afternoon, the car was quickly found. No one had thought anything of the parked car until then; the staff was used to seeing her car parked in that area for long periods.

Glover said, "It's the car that makes me think of it, is all. I spent the day with your wife's car in that lot today. It just made me think of Tancredo, how that case got started."

"Mm-hmm."

"They said he was a mastermind. Was he?"

"Vincent? *Pf,* no."

"He was a doctor."

"So?"

"He must have had something on the ball."

"You think? You ever heard the old joke: What do they call the dumbest guy in his med school class?"

"I don't know. What?"

"'Doctor.'"

"Well then, there's a thought: you don't even have to be that smart to get away with murder."

"Who says he got away with murder?"

"Everyone."

"Not me."

"Of course. You're his lawyer."

"That's not it. If Vincent got away with murder, I'd have to agree with you: it doesn't take a genius. Since he did not do anything at all, I'm not sure how you can draw any conclusions from the case. There was no evidence, that's all we can say for sure."

In fact, there was substantial evidence that Vincent Tancredo strangled his wife to death. It was simply a circumstantial case—lots of evidence establishing motive, means, and opportunity, but no direct proof of the act itself. The particulars were banal: a bored husband with a growing appetite for the high life and for women not his wife, and without the means to pay the tab. There was a girlfriend, there was a life insurance policy on Janice Tancredo. It was a string of clichés, as domestic murders often are. What made it interesting—really the *only* thing that made it interesting—was that he got away with it. The district attorney held off indicting the case for nearly two years, hoping for more evidence. It never came, and the DA decided, unwisely, to play the cards in his hand rather than wait to be dealt an ace. At trial, day after day Dan Larkin harped on the insufficiency of the evidence; Vincent Tancredo never left his seat to testify, and the jury came back not guilty after just a few hours of deliberation. Game over.

"Maybe I'm just naive—"

"Oh, I doubt that, detective."

"But I look at that case and I think, *Y'know, maybe it's not so hard to get away with it*. Hasn't that ever crossed your mind? It must have, right? You watch case after case, you see the mistakes these guys make, you see patterns, you learn."

"I see people, not patterns."

"Yeah, I know, you have to say that. But that's the dirty little secret, isn't it? It's not so hard to get away with it, you just have to know what you're doing and not make stupid mistakes. Most people are amateurs at murder. They make mistakes. Not you."

"Yes, detective, I'm a real expert at wife-murdering."

"I didn't say—"

"Yes, you did."

Dan had a way of staring, of locking eyes without blinking. In court, he used it to make witnesses uncomfortable, make them fidget, which juries misread as a sign of dishonesty. Now he fixed his eyes on Tom Glover.

A long moment passed.

"Detective—Tom—let me help you. Don't play little games like that. This isn't the movies."

Dan softened his tone, allowed the witness to relax. He liked to say, *You cannot endlessly flog a witness; you have to show him a* little tenderness, too. Take his side now and then, give him hope, or you will lose him, he will simply go silent.

"Listen. Forget Vincent Tancredo. It's not necessary. You don't have to play games with me. I understand what you're thinking. It's natural for you to have these questions. You have suspicions, of course you do. You're doing your job. In your shoes, I would suspect me too. From now on, just ask me straight out, all right? Ask me anything at all. I'll answer every question you have."

Glover said nothing. His head was empty, he had no idea what to ask next.

"How old are you, Tom?"

"Almost thirty-two."

"Almost thirty-two. Never had a case like this, have you?"

"No."

"Look, I think you want to hear this from me, Tom. I want to be crystal clear. I don't want anyone saying, down the road, *Why didn't that rat-bastard Larkin ever deny it?* Okay? So listen: I did not harm Jane. Not in any way, ever. I have no idea where she is or what happened to her. My wife is missing and I don't know why. I am devastated—devastated, Tom, do you understand that?"

"Yes."

"Now, do you have any other questions for me?"

"No."

"Good. Because I want to answer all your questions, Tom. I want you to know you can ask me anything. I'm not asking you to trust me; that wouldn't be reasonable. Just be up-front with me."

"Okay."

"Because I trust *you,* Tom. I do. I've never refused to answer any of your questions. I've never hid behind the Fifth Amendment. Never asked you to get a warrant to search anywhere you liked. I've barely slept or eaten in days, but I've still been ready to help in any way you asked, haven't I?"

"Yes."

"Now, does that sound like a guilty man, Tom? Does that sound like a murderer?"

"No."

"Good. Then go find my wife. Please. Find my wife. Can you do that?"

Glover did not answer. He stood there feeling like Dan had picked his pocket.

"Okay then. I think it's time for you to go, detective."

Glover turned to leave, anxious to be out of that house, and only then saw Alex looming in the kitchen doorway. Alex's arms were folded. Glover approached Alex, who was a good six inches taller, but the young man did not immediately move aside. "Excuse me," Glover had to say, whereupon Alex turned his body, leaving a narrow gap for Glover to squeeze through. "Excuse me," Glover repeated, a little more firmly, and the young man stepped back out of the doorway to let him pass.

In the front hall, he saw Miranda sitting on the landing halfway up the staircase, in her nightgown. Miranda's eyes were wet with tears. The little girl waved to him weakly. Miranda was only a few feet away—eight steps up—and Glover wanted to say something, to help the kid somehow, to be kind to Miranda as she had been kind to him. But, caught between Miranda's despair and Alex's contempt and Dan's manipulations, he fumbled for the right words, then could not find any words at all. He stood there a moment, absorbing his failure, then let himself out.

WHEN Glover related this incident to me, I thought I might look up Vincent Tancredo to see if he would speak with me. It would make a nice sidebar. Did he have any memories of Dan Larkin? Did he recall any of their conversations? What was Dan like in court? But Vincent Tancredo died in May 2005, of "natural causes," according to his obituary in the *Globe*. He was eighty-two years old, which—in one of those nice symmetries that are quite common in life but that novelists ought to avoid—was precisely twice his wife's age when she was killed.

The two cases were not especially alike, but it is understandable that Tom Glover connected them. There was the bit about the women's cars, both abandoned in public parking lots, and the similarity of their names, Janice and Jane. And of course they had Dan Larkin in common. Glover drew a perfectly logical inference, or at least an inference that might have seemed obvious to a cop: after a smart lawyer like Dan Larkin had watched enough of his own clients go free despite committing all sorts of crimes including murder, it must have been natural for Dan to think, *You can get away with anything if you're smart enough.*

But from the cops' point of view, the Jane Larkin case had two enormous problems that the Janice Tancredo murder did not. First, there was no body. Understand, the prosecution is not required to produce a corpse in order to prove that a killing has occurred. The corpse is simply the best and commonest evidence. So if, in the early days of the investigation, you were inclined to suspect Dan Larkin of murder, you had to assume—had to guess, really—that Jane was in fact dead. Most people had no problem making this leap. With each passing day, it seemed less and less likely that Jane was lost, injured, unable to get to a phone, unaware of the panic her disappearance had caused, etc. Jane was dead—everybody knew it. If nothing else, the thinking went, a mother would not just up and leave her children. Within a week or so of the disappearance, a tentative consensus was reached that Dan was probably guilty of *something.* The only remaining drama was what that *something* might be. The lack of real proof did not help Dan in the "court of public opinion" or with the professional investigators. You see, suspicion does not need proof; it feeds just as well on the absence of it.

The second problem with the case against Dan was that he had no obvious motive to kill his wife. That was about to change.

Now I must tell you something out of chronological order again, because it was not until late in the process of writing this book that Alex consented to an interview, and it was Alex whose view I most wanted on this question of motive, for reasons that will become clear in a moment. By the time we spoke, I had a nearly completed draft, so I was able to squeeze him with the usual reporter's blackmail: *The book is going to be written with or without your cooperation, so if you want your side to be heard . . .*

The interview took place at the law firm in downtown Boston where Alex is now a partner. The firm is a very old and prestigious one. I will not name it; suffice it to say the name would be familiar to any Boston lawyer. Coincidentally, I worked at this same firm briefly, as a wildly overpaid and underworked summer associate during law school. In those days—it was the summer of 1989— the firm was transforming from a gentlemanly old Yankee firm into the national "Big Law" colossus that it is now. But the future of the firm was clear, and I knew damn well I would never make it there. As a lawyer, I was headed in a different direction.

But as ill-suited as I was to life in a big law firm, Alex Larkin was fairly made for it. I remember him sauntering in the hallways that summer, in his tailored suits and silk suspenders, tall and handsome with his athlete's strut. He was in his early thirties then. His hairline had begun to recede, so the gulf in years between us felt wider than ever. He had a young man's arrogance— there is no kind word for it—a quality I detest, but I could not dislike Alex or even blame him for being full of himself. He had been a star for so long. I still thought of him as a star too. The idols we choose in childhood, we keep.

One other memory sticks out from that summer of 1989: no one at the firm ever mentioned the business about Alex Larkin's mother. It was as if they had all agreed it would be impolite to gossip about it. Or maybe they just never connected Alex to the case, which by then had been out of the news for many years. Alex acted as if he had forgotten it too. In fact, he never showed any sign that he was troubled by anything at all.

When we finally met to discuss this book, almost thirty years later, in early spring 2017, it was this young, princely version of Alex that I was expecting to find. And indeed, though he was fifty-seven now, that is exactly the Alex I found. Unlike Jeff, who had struck me as so worn and weary in middle age, Alex wore his years beautifully, like his tailored suit and his Rolex watch and his delicate reading glasses. This was the final, consummated version of Alex Larkin, the fulfillment of all his earlier promise.

We met in Alex's corner office, which had a sweeping view of the Seaport District and Boston Harbor. After a grave handshake, he went behind his desk, a monolith of dark wood, the sort of power desk that makes you wonder how such an enormous object could be moved to an upper floor like this. My manuscript pages stood in a shaggy pile in front of him. (Alex had insisted on a printed manuscript, not a digital file.) He leaned in his chair, as big and supple as a leopard.

"Well," he said, "honestly I'm not much of a reader, Phil, but for what it's worth I thought it was good. I can't say I enjoyed reading it, of course, but it's well done."

"Thank you. I know it's an uncomfortable subject for you."

"But not for you."

"Of course for me too. It's not the kind of thing I'm comfortable writing about. I've said as much to Jeff and Miranda. Hell, I say it in the book. I don't like writing about friends."

"Is that what we are, friends?"

"Yes."

"But you're going to publish it anyway."

"I hope so, yes. I mean, I have qualms. I don't feel great about it."

"So why publish it? Why not listen to your conscience?"

"Because that's what I do."

"Pick at people's bones?"

"No."

"What about me? Don't I get a vote?"

"Afraid not."

"So if I ask you not to publish it? What then?"

"It would depend on the reason, I guess."

"How about decency? Friendship? My father is a very sick man.

You know that, don't you? He's dying. Do you think it's right to go after him now, when he can't fight back?"

"I'm not going after anyone. I'm just trying to tell the truth. My job is to be honest."

"Oh, don't make it sound so virtuous. Sometimes honesty is cruel. You don't *have to* come out and say these things."

"It's what writers do."

"It's not what novelists do."

"It's precisely what novelists do."

"Novelists tell *stories,* Phil. They write fiction."

"That's what I've done."

"Barely."

"It's a novel, Alex. That's what I'm calling it."

"I thought you were honest. That's what you just said."

"I'm honest in my way. As honest as I can be."

"Do you dislike my father, Phil?"

"I don't have strong feelings about him either way."

"What *is* your opinion of him?"

"I don't know him."

"Come on, you must have some opinion. You knew him. Did you like him? Did you think he was a likable man?"

"Those are two different questions. I don't think he's especially likable, no. That doesn't mean I dislike him."

"But Jeff does. You know that, don't you? Jeff dislikes him intensely."

"You'd have to ask Jeff about that."

"Jeff's not here. I'm asking you."

"I think Jeff's feelings about his dad are pretty tangled at this point."

"But in these pages you parrot what Jeff tells you uncritically."

"Not sure I'd use the word *parrot.* I report. And not uncritically."

"Use whatever word you want. It's very one-sided."

"Well, I might parrot the other side, too, if you'd tell me anything. You've refused to talk to me. What can I do?"

"It's too late now, isn't it? The book's already written."

"There's time. Anything you give me, I'll use."

He smiled but let the invitation pass. "And Glover. He's obviously a major source. Obviously you consider him reliable."

"I do. I think he's honest."

"He can be honest and unreliable, honest and wrong. The world is full of honest fools."

"Glover's no fool."

"No. I take that back." He frowned at the manuscript in front of him. "I assume you've cleared this with your publisher's legal department."

"Not yet."

"Well, libel's not my area of expertise, but it seems to me my father will have a terrific cause of action. I certainly know a few good attorneys who would leap to take the case."

"Alex, if you think I've got anything wrong on the facts—"

"The facts? I wouldn't even know where to begin."

"Tell me. Tell me what mistakes you saw. I'm happy to make corrections."

"No. Because what I tell you are not *facts,* it's just testimony. You're a lawyer, you know that. You can't trust every witness, including me. Witnesses make mistakes even when they're not lying. They misperceive, misremember, misstate. Come on, this is first-year law-school stuff. You seem to think that just repeating what people tell you, even Miranda or Jeff, is all you're obligated to do. As if all the things they tell you are the gospel truth, as if a thing becomes a fact just because someone says it."

"Look, I know you're angry, Alex, but again if there's anything you'd like me to correct, I'd be happy to do it."

"But the onus is on me, isn't that right? What if I don't want to *correct* anything? What if I don't want any part of this? What if I just want to be left alone?"

"You have that right. But Miranda and Jeff want something different. Are you going to sue your own brother and sister?"

"Of course not. I'll sue you. And your publisher."

"For reporting what Jeff tells me? A firsthand witness? No, you won't."

"Jeff. Jeff." He closed his eyes and soothed his forehead with his fingers like a weary father.

Jeff would have winced. He had always described his ambivalent relationship with his older brother using words like *arrogant, oblivious, narcissistic*. He thought Alex escaped the worst of it. When their mother disappeared, Alex was already a young man. In less than a year, he would leave home for college. Alex was old enough to handle the blow—better than Jeff and Miranda, at any rate, who were still kids. Jeff was right to be angry with Alex, I think, but I "get" Alex a little better now. He was not oblivious or narcissistic, no more than a lot of young people anyway. He just did not grok how *deeply* his younger sibs had suffered. Why had Jeff and Miranda allowed themselves to be so wounded? Why stew over things you could not change, year after year? What was the point? And what could Alex do for them anyway? Babying Miranda and Jeff had always been their mother's job; Alex was not equipped to stand in for her (which is forgivable) and he did not have any interest in trying (which probably is not).

"Alex, I think Jeff is just trying to make sense of what happened. To me, that seems perfectly natural. Don't you feel any of that yourself?"

"No. It's over."

"How is that possible? How can you be so . . . serene?"

"I am not serene. You have no right to say that. You can't possibly understand."

"Sorry. Maybe that's the wrong word. It's just that you seem to have the whole thing settled in your mind. How do you explain it to yourself? What's the story you tell yourself about it, about what really happened?"

"You mean, do I think my father is a murderer?"

"I didn't say that."

"It's what you meant. The answer is no, I do not."

"You've never had any doubt? Even for a moment?"

"No. I trust him. That's never changed."

"But there were things about him you didn't know."

"Of course."

"Like Sarah."

"Yes. Like Sarah."

"Tell me about her."

"What is it you want to know?"

"When did you find out about her? What was she like? Did you like her? Tell me anything at all. What was your first impression?"

He eyed me. "Are we on the record?"

"Yes. Always. I'm not a journalist, I don't know how to go off the record."

His hand hovered over the manuscript a moment, like a spider descending, then touched down on five fingertips.

"She came to the house." He stopped there.

"When? When did she first appear?"

He sat a moment in silence, considering whether to speak to me about the case. Then:

"About a week after my mother went missing. Maybe two weeks, I'm not sure now."

"How did you feel? What did you think when you saw her?"

Another pause. Alex still hesitant to share information.

I waited. Hoped.

"I thought she was beautiful. When she stepped in the door, it took my breath away. I'd never seen a woman that striking. She was luminous."

I smiled. "Oh my."

"She'd been a model when she was younger, did you know that? She was a Breck girl. When I met her, she was forty or forty-one—a couple years *older* than my mother, by the way. Make sure you include that, Phil."

"All right."

"It was late at night. There was a knock on the back door, very quiet. My dad was obviously nervous when he heard the knock. We'd been cooped up in the house a long time and we were jumpy.

It might have been the cops or some crazy person who read about us in the newspaper. Whoever it was, they hadn't rung the doorbell in front. They sneaked around to the back where it was dark. It was just odd. It even occurred to me that it might be my mother finally coming home because nobody outside our family used the back door at night.

"My dad opened the door, and Sarah stepped in and they kissed."

"And then?"

"No, not 'and then.' This was—this was a real kiss. If you saw it, you *knew*. They kissed like lovers, like a young couple that had been separated a long time. My father was not a passionate man, but the way he kissed her—he put one hand behind her head, his left hand, with his wedding ring, and one hand around the small of her back, and he held her that way for a long time. I think he completely forgot I was there. Then again, just imagine the strain he was under, the pressure. Try to be a little compassionate here, Phil. Imagine how he felt. Alone, under siege. And then here she was, suddenly, the woman he loved. Imagine how he must have felt."

"I'm trying to imagine how *you* must have felt. It must have been a shock."

"A shock? I was blown away. Blown away."

"You'd never seen her before?"

"Never."

"Never heard of her?"

"Never."

"Never had any idea your father was . . . ?"

"God, no. We had no clue. My father is a very careful man, very meticulous. I had no idea who this woman was, no idea she even existed."

"And your mother? Did she know?"

"I don't know. I doubt it."

"So, what were you thinking as you watched them kiss?"

"Honestly, I thought my dad suddenly looked twenty years

younger. He was a different man. He wasn't my father anymore, just some guy named Dan Larkin who I'd never met. He was *alive,* you know? That's the only way I can think to describe it."

"You sound jealous, if you don't mind my saying."

"Aren't *you* a little? Imagine how it would feel to be suddenly fully awake."

"In love, you mean. You're saying he was in love."

"In love—I don't know. I can't say exactly what he was feeling. That would be speculation. All I can say is I watched him kiss this woman with such *desire.* That was the surprise. This was my *father.* Young people always think their generation invented sex. They can't imagine that their parents ever felt such passion."

"And then?"

"Sarah said, 'I had to see you. I've been so worried. I knew you couldn't call and I shouldn't come, but I *had* to.' My dad told her, 'It's all right. It's done. I'm glad you're here.'

"He introduced me to Sarah. He did not make a big deal of it, he did not seem the least bit embarrassed or apologetic. He just said, 'Alex, this is my friend Sarah,' like he was introducing a golf buddy or a work friend or something, like that kiss hadn't just happened. She, at least, seemed a little embarrassed. She shook my hand, then they went into his study."

"Describe her. What was she wearing? Do you remember?"

"Of course I remember. Slacks and a cream-colored blouse. Her shoes were like little slippers—expensive looking. Her hair was in kind of a loose ponytail, some complicated thing, I don't know what it's called exactly."

Alex gazed past me, wistful at the memory of Sarah. I imagine he was reexperiencing the intoxication he felt upon seeing her, the awe, in her vanilla blouse, the little cleavage of her toes winking out from her open-top shoes.

"Where were Jeff and Miranda?"

"Upstairs, I guess. I don't remember. Miranda must have been asleep. She was little."

"They didn't see it? Didn't hear it?"

"No."

"And you didn't tell them?"

"I told Jeff. Miranda, no."

"Why not?"

"Because she wouldn't understand. She was too young."

"What wouldn't she understand, exactly?"

"Just the way my dad looked at Sarah. What he *saw* when he looked at her."

"And that was . . . ?"

He tipped his head and shrugged. *You know.*

"Your mother was attractive, too, wasn't she?"

"Of course, of course. I'm not being disrespectful. But this was different. Let me be clear: I'm not saying my father was right to fall for her; only that as a man, I can understand how it happened."

"Why did you think Jeff would understand that but Miranda wouldn't?"

"He was a little older."

"He was just a kid."

"He was thirteen, Phil. That's not a kid, it's a young man. Remember what you were like when you were thirteen."

"I'd rather not."

"Imagine your friend Jeff, then. He was no kid."

"I remember Jeff at thirteen. So did he understand?"

"I think he understood up here"—he pointed at his temple—"not here"—he indicated his heart.

"But you understood."

"I understood that people fall in love."

"Even married people?"

"I'm not sure that's a serious question. These are human beings. Flesh is weak."

"And you understand now. You forgive him."

"I forgive him for being human, yes."

"That's a lawyerly way to phrase it. I don't think the charge against your dad has ever been 'being human.' I think Jeff would say—at a minimum—that he betrayed his wife, he cheated."

"I'm not condoning it, Phil. I said I could forgive him. You can't forgive someone who's done nothing wrong. My point is: the thing he's been accused of—the thing *you're* accusing him of in this book—is a hell of a lot worse than adultery."

ALEX's discovery of his father's affair put him well ahead of the detectives. It would be weeks before they discovered Sarah Bennett's relationship with Dan. First they had to rig the Larkins' home phone with a pen register and a phone trap, which were the pre-digital devices used to capture outgoing and incoming calls, respectively. In those years, there was no way to review local telephone traffic on that line in the weeks leading up to Jane's disappearance; no such records were kept. On the other hand, pen registers and phone traps did have the advantage of not requiring a warrant, because they captured only the time and number dialed rather than recording the actual conversation, as a phone "tap" does. So, once the trap was in place, the investigators were able to monitor Dan Larkin's phone traffic despite the near-complete lack of evidence against him. Those phone logs led the police to Sarah. From the pattern of calls, the investigators might have guessed that Dan and Sarah had initially tried to hide their affair. There were no phone calls at first, then a few, often late at night, and finally the calls became quite frequent as, apparently, Sarah's discipline broke down. Of course Dan must have presumed the affair would be discovered eventually. So he made no serious attempt to hide it beyond telling Sarah to keep her distance until things cooled off, and when she was not able to do that and the affair was discovered, he readily admitted it to the detectives.

In terms of actual evidence, it hardly mattered. The discovery did not move the case ahead all that much. The question remained: if Dan Larkin wanted to be rid of his wife, why not just divorce her? That puzzle, more than anything else, stymied the investigators. After all, husbands leave their wives all the time but almost never kill them. The answer was not money, either. Dan could have afforded a divorce, even an expensive divorce, and there was no insurance policy or other financial reason to kill Jane.

Only Tom Glover was not dissuaded by this problem. To him, the affair was a smoking gun. It completely answered the question of motive: Dan did not want Jane anymore; the rest was just details. Almost forty years later, Glover still had no doubts. In one of our 2015 interviews, he said, "[Dan] didn't want to just be separated from her. He wanted Jane not to exist, he wanted to erase her. There was no room for an ex-wife in Dan's new life with his new woman."

It sounded a little fanciful to me. It just wasn't enough to establish motive. Certainly it would not be enough to a jury. I suspect that Glover's frustration led him to overvalue the affair. Emptyhanded, the investigators were desperate for a break in the case. Also, Glover may have been a little prudish about Dan's adultery. As a monkish younger man, he might have attached too much significance to it. Marriage was sacred to him, perhaps because he was so profoundly alone then. (Glover would marry much later, about a dozen years after Jane went missing.)

In any case, Alex never shared his discovery of Sarah with anyone but his little brother. It never occurred to him to report The Kiss to the police, apparently. Make of that what you will. It must have been an agonizing position for a young man. He could betray his father by telling or betray his mother by not telling. Personally, I can't criticize him for keeping his father's secret. I probably would have done the same thing.

An aside:

In the same 2015 conversation in which Tom Glover discussed Dan's affair, I made an interesting discovery: to this day, he keeps a picture of Jane Larkin in his wallet. He produced the photo without my asking. I simply mentioned that this case seemed to have affected him in an unusually deep way, and he took out his wallet, tweezed the photo out with his fingertips, and held it up like a passport, the proof of his devotion to Jane.

I asked, "Does your wife know you carry that around?"

"It's okay. You can't cheat with a picture."

That was not true, of course. You can cheat with a picture. You can fall in love with an image of someone, with a memory or an idea of her. For that matter, the image is generally easier to love than the actual person, since the image will never change, never grow old, never argue or disappoint you.

I suspect that Glover is not the only old cop who carries a victim's photo in his wallet. Many more, I am sure, carry a mental image, a face they cannot forget. Detectives, even the hard ones, often develop tender feelings for some special victim. Even homicide victims inspire this sort of devotion, despite—or because of—the fact that they can never be known.

Obviously Jane was important to Tom Glover somehow. At least, his *conception* of Jane was important, what she represented, since he never actually met her. Maybe Alex was right: People fall in love in their different ways. Flesh is weak.

GLOVER arrived at the head of a search-warrant team on December 2, at around five o'clock P.M. There were a dozen or so cops, state and local police, all in plain clothes. Glover wore a tie and sport coat.

Marked cruisers idled at either end of the street, sealing off traffic, discouraging gawkers.

Miranda stood behind her father as he opened the door to the phalanx of policemen. Seeing them arrayed on the little porch, she thought that even Glover's fellow cops hung back from him a little, or he from them.

To her, Glover seemed different that day than he had earlier, when they sat together by the lake. Harder, resolved. Gone was the deferential, tentative man she had met. Glover had apparently reached a conclusion about Miranda's dad. His investigation was over; he was only interested in gathering evidence now, building the case against him. Even so, Miranda liked him and felt hurt when her new friend did not acknowledge her somehow as he stood on the front porch.

Dan Larkin eyed him—with contempt, Miranda later recalled. (Miranda told me, "Do you know what Tom Glover was to my dad? He was the little piece of gristle that you chew and chew but you can't swallow and you can't spit out. Dad just wanted to spit him out, but he never could.")

"We have a search warrant," Glover announced. He handed over a paper.

"You didn't need to do all that, Tom. You know that. I've told you, you can search here anytime you like."

"Are you consenting to the search, then?"

A beat.

"No. I do not consent. Give me a minute to read the warrant."

Larkin stood in the doorway, reviewing the document with a theatrical frown of disapproval. He lingered over the affidavit, Glover's sworn statement of the facts justifying the search. He extended this moment longer than necessary, until the cops began shifting their feet like horses in a starting gate.

"This won't stand up."

"We'll see."

Larkin turned to his little daughter. "Come on, Miranda. Let's go sit in the living room while the policemen do their work."

"What are they doing?"

"They're looking for Mom."

"Here?"

"Mom's not here, sweetheart. I don't think these men know what they're looking for. But we'll let them have a look so everyone is satisfied, and when Alex and Jeff get home, we'll have our dinner, okay?"

So they sat on the couch and waited. Miranda slumped against her father's hip, an encroachment he might not have tolerated had they been alone.

At length, Glover came down from the second floor with a pile of clothes.

"We're taking these suits."

"Which suits?"

"All the gray ones. Are there any missing? At the cleaner?"

"No, that's all of them. Those are good suits. I expect them all back."

Glover ignored him. "The shoes too."

"Just take the black." Larkin's eyes flicked down and up, registering Glover's outfit, a wide-lapeled plaid blazer and a wide tie of a different plaid. "You don't wear brown shoes with a gray suit. But you knew that."

Glover ignored him.

"Tom, would you at least explain why you are taking my suits? Do you really think, if I were going to kill my wife, I would put on a suit to do it? Is that your theory?"

"We need to get into the garage, Mr. Larkin."

"Is that your theory, detective? I wore a suit to a murder?"

"The garage, please. Is it electric? I need you to open the door. And I need your car keys."

"Tom, how many murder trials have you seen? Do you even know—"

"The garage, please."

A sigh. "Of course. Let me get it for you."

Larkin went into the kitchen, followed by Glover, and fished a remote control out of a cluttered drawer. He pointed the remote control, a bulky plastic block, out the kitchen window toward the detached garage.

Watching Larkin with the remote, Glover frowned. "Is there something on your fingernails?"

"No," Dan said.

"Yes, there is. What *is* that?"

"Oh. It's polish."

"You wear nail polish?"

"Clear nail polish, yes. It makes your nails stronger, it looks neater. Makes you look finished. You should give it a try, Tom. Take a little pride in your appearance."

Glover winced, as if Larkin had suggested he take up cannibalism or bestiality. "Car keys."

(Miranda would remember Glover's reaction, one of the first cues she had that her father's fastidiousness might be odd. It surprised her. She had always adored the way her father dressed, especially his work suits—the contrasting white collars, French cuffs, vests, gold collar pins. Miranda's mom used to tease Dan about all this, especially the way he kept his hair carefully blown out and sprayed, even on weekends. But Miranda had no way to judge which parent was right. It is hard for a kid to gauge a parent's quirks. Every family is odd, but every family seems normal to a young child born into it, for a while at least.)

They spent another hour searching the car and the garage. They swept the garage floor and sifted through the dust pile. They took the Larkins' heavy digging shovel away with them, but left the snow shovels.

They pulled the car out of the garage and swarmed over it. It was a 1973 Mercedes 450 SEL sedan, white with a black interior, for which Dan had paid an appalling $26,000, precipitating a fight with Jane. Miranda stood on the back patio and watched the detectives. They removed the floor mats from the car. They removed the jack and the L-shaped lug wrench from the trunk and put both in evidence bags. At one point, she remembers, Glover leaned so far into the trunk that his feet came off the ground. When he emerged, he was pulling the fabric liner off the trunk floor, tugging and tearing it away, torquing his body for leverage. She thought: *Dad will be mad at Tom for doing that. He loves that car.*

Before the cops left, Glover asked Dan if he could speak with Miranda alone.

"No, you may not."

"She can talk to me or the DA can subpoena her to the grand jury. Don't make us do that. She's just a kid."

Dan hesitated. "You're not taking her anywhere. I have to be present."

They went up to the master bedroom, accompanied by a state trooper to ensure there were two witnesses to whatever exchange was to take place. The room was messy—drawers left open, clothes strewn about—but no real damage. They were still treating Larkin with a little reserve, Glover thought, because they were uncertain and because they were intimidated by him.

On the bed was a pile of silk neckties, reds and yellows and blues, with splashes of green and pink, repp stripes and foulards and polka dots.

Glover got down on one knee and said to Miranda, "Do you remember you told me your dad wore a red necktie the day your mom went away?"

The girl nodded.

"I want you to look through these neckties—be very careful, take your time—and tell me if that red necktie is here."

Miranda stood at the foot of the bed and looked. She spread them out on the bed, felt their cool, slick surfaces, folded and arranged them in groups by color as her dad would have wanted, to appease him for her disloyalty in cooperating with the policemen. When she was satisfied, she looked at Glover—but not her father—and shook her head. "No."

THE district attorney for Middlesex County at the time—thus the man who would decide whether Dan Larkin would be charged with any crime related to his wife's vanishing—was John Kearney. He had been in office since 1959, long enough that most voters could not remember the DA's office without him. He was sixty-four but looked older. His hair was white and he was mostly bald, with just a few wisps remaining on top. His face was jowly. To voters, inside the county and out, he was the picture of an old-school, sharp-elbowed Irish pol. He had a reputation as an aggressive prosecutor too—a strict law-and-order man, blunt, fearless, the kind of DA "who would indict his own mother." It was a persona he had carefully crafted and clearly enjoyed. Over his fifteen years in office, he had been involved in a number of high-profile prosecutions, including the Boston Strangler case.

But beneath the surface, in 1975 Kearney was becoming vulnerable. His health had begun to fail in small but noticeable ways. In conversation, he sometimes paused to swallow with great effort. His voice could be slurred and soft, especially when he was tired. Walking, he was unsteady, off-balance, stiff-legged. These were early symptoms of Lou Gehrig's disease, though Kearney's illness was a closely guarded secret. Reporters were told that he had a "viral infection." To squelch rumors about his health, Kearney's inner circle constantly talked up his strength and sharp mind. The secret was easier to maintain in 1975 than it would be now, perhaps; most voters never heard him speak or saw him walk.

Even if he had been healthy, Kearney's political future would have been cloudy. He had never been able to jump from the DA's office to a higher job. He was drubbed in 1964 when he ran for governor and drubbed again in '72 when he ran for U.S. Senate against Ed Brooke. That last failure damaged his image badly. Kearney was comfortably reelected to a fourth term as district attorney in 1974, but a new narrative emerged: Kearney was yesterday's man. Too old, too long in office, the public had tired of him. Kearney had been in politics, one way or another, for nearly three decades. Before taking office, he had been a longtime campaign organizer for John Kennedy, an insider and confidant beginning with Kennedy's first run for the U.S. House in 1946, when both men had just returned from Navy service in the Pacific. But in 1975, that all felt like ancient history. Kearney could no longer play up his link to President Kennedy; it only called attention to his age.

Sharks were circling. Younger, TV-friendly candidates had

begun to plan for the 1978 election. Momentum was growing to dump the old man for a more polished, more modern sort of politician.

This was the man who would decide Dan Larkin's fate at this crucial stage of the process. The charging decision is one of the prosecutor's great "soft" powers; he has the sole discretion to decide whether a suspect will be charged and with what crime. Did Kearney's circumstances—his age, illness, precarious political position—have any effect on his decision in the Larkin case? There is no way to know for sure, but I suspect they played to Larkin's advantage. A man in Kearney's position, late in his political life, is free to follow his conscience. He is less likely to be stampeded into an indictment when the evidence is not there.

There was something else, too, another reason Dan Larkin was fortunate to have Kearney in office just then, as he was fortunate in so much else. Kearney's unique experience made it quite easy for him to believe in Larkin's innocence. But then, maybe Dan knew that too.

THE charging conference took place in Kearney's corner office on the second floor of the then-new courthouse in East Cambridge. It was shortly before Christmas. The room was paneled in walnut and adorned with plaques and photos of the district attorney with various politicos, including JFK and RFK, but the building's grim design and shoddy construction—thin carpet over hard concrete-slab floors, molded-concrete facades, drafty windows—made the room feel shabby and cold.

As Glover recalls now (he did not preserve any notes from the meeting), six men sat at a round table, representing the DA's office and state and local police. On the table in front of them were a few thick file folders. The first assistant DA—Kearney's top aide—had a three-ring binder, the so-called murder book, the repository of all the most important original documents and notes in the case.

The day before, Dan Larkin had broken his silence in the media, telling a *Globe* reporter this: "I am entitled to a decision. I am an innocent man. There is no evidence that I have done anything at all. The district attorney ought to do the right thing and clear my name of these rumors once and for all, rather than let an innocent man be dragged through the mud."

(From this detail, we can date the meeting precisely. It was Thursday, December 18, 1975. The article Glover remembers was a page-one story in the *Globe* titled "Vexed Larkin Decries Rumors.")

To some extent, Dan was right: he *was* being dragged through the mud. The public's perception of him was changing. The same newspapers that for weeks had treated Larkin as a victim—referring to him as *bereaved, grieving, stricken, distraught*—were now openly suggesting he was a suspect. The latest police search of Larkin's home had been written up in all the local papers. The *Globe* and *Herald American* both included photos of plain-clothesmen around the house. If Dan was indeed innocent, then it was all grossly unfair.

On the other hand, Dan could not force the district attorney to do anything, let alone clear his name. The DA was perfectly within his rights to keep the investigation open indefinitely, in the hope that new evidence would turn up. Suspects in this position usually keep quiet, at least the smart ones do. Tactically, there is nothing to gain and much to lose by talking. So why did Dan Larkin break his silence?

The men at the conference table discussed this awhile. Maybe Larkin was guilty—and he was protesting too much. Or trying to rush the state into a hasty indictment, before the evidence was fully developed. Or maybe he was speaking to potential jurors, already arguing his "story of the case," that he was the victim of a rush to judgment. Whatever his true motive, they were all certain he was up to something. He was a defense attorney, after all, and a particularly slippery one. To a man, they were sure that Dan Larkin had never said anything impulsive or stupid in his life; he was not going to start now.

Kearney had been leaning back in his chair, listening to all this. He said, finally, "Maybe Larkin said it because it's true. Maybe he really didn't do anything. Maybe there's a reason we're not finding any evidence."

The first assistant said, "We're going to have to make a decision soon anyway. We're about to dismiss the grand jury. The session ends first of the year. I can hold them over, if we're close. Are we close?"

The DA turned to Glover with raised eyebrows. "What do you say, detective?"

Glover did not feel confident among these men, who were more experienced and seemed to know one another. "Well, I think if we had a little more time—I think we've got the right guy, I really do."

"It doesn't matter if he's the right guy if we don't have a case, now, does it? We need evidence."

"We're still working on it."

"Could you be wrong?"

"No. I don't think so. He's the only one that makes sense."

"Does he, though? I have to tell you, detective, I'm uneasy with the whole direction of this case. I'm not entirely sure we've heard the last of Mrs. Larkin. It seems to me that the likeliest explanation for a woman disappearing into thin air is that she left of her own accord. Isn't that possible?"

"We've considered that. I just don't believe it. A mother leaving her children with no warning?"

"Stranger things have happened."

"Everything I've heard, it doesn't sound like this woman would do that."

"Tom, have you ever heard of Joan Risch?"

"I don't think so."

"Well, I'll tell you a story, then. Joan Risch disappeared in October 1961. It was my third year as district attorney. When I first saw the case, I felt exactly as you do now. Mrs. Risch lived in Lincoln. She was thirty-one or thirty-two. She had two young children whom she adored, by all accounts. Everyone said she would never leave them, either.

"There was nothing unusual about her behavior. The day she disappeared, she took her daughter to the dentist in the morning, then went grocery shopping.

"Around four in the afternoon, her daughter came home from playing at a friend's house. The little girl saw blood on the kitchen wall. There were signs of a struggle: the phone book in the kitchen was open to the emergency numbers; a chair was overturned; the phone had been ripped off the wall and thrown in the trash can. There was a trail of blood leading from the kitchen out to the driveway.

"That afternoon, she was seen wandering near Route 128, which was just being built at the time. Witnesses said she was bloody and seemed dazed, but nobody stopped to help her.

"She's never been seen again.

"Now, in the Joan Risch case, there was some real evidence— more than we have here. Witnesses saw a gray sedan parked in the Risches' driveway that afternoon. There was a bloody palm print on the kitchen wall and a few fingerprints, none of which we've ever been able to identify, so *someone* was in that kitchen with her. It wasn't her husband or anyone else in the family. Anyway, the husband was out of town on business that day. His alibi was rock-solid. We ruled him out immediately.

"So clearly Mrs. Risch had been murdered by a mysterious intruder of some kind. There was no doubt. I sat at many meetings just like this one, and *everyone* was sure of it.

"But then strange details started to emerge. Mrs. Risch had worked in publishing in New York before she ended her career and got married and settled for the quiet life of a suburban wife and mother. A few of her friends began to tell us that Mrs. Risch was not happy with the choices she'd made. She was bored. She missed the glamour of being a publishing girl in New York City.

"Mrs. Risch still loved books, though. She was an avid mystery reader. That summer, she'd borrowed over thirty books from the public library, all on the subject of murder and disappearances. She'd been studying how women disappear.

"Then the blood, it turned out, was less than first thought. The experts thought it likely came from a superficial wound.

"And there were stories about Mrs. Risch too: that she'd been abused as a child, that her own parents had perished in a mysterious fire when Mrs. Risch was nine years old. Perhaps she was a disturbed woman.

"So," the DA said, "what happened? Did Joan Risch run away? Or was she murdered? To this day, nobody knows. It is an open case. Now, Mr. Glover, does that story alter your opinion in this case?"

"No."

"Why? What makes you so sure?"

"Look, I admit it is possible Mrs. Larkin ran off. Anything is possible. But I just don't believe it. We haven't heard one thing about Jane Larkin to suggest she wanted out. Everyone says she was devoted to those children, she would never leave them."

"What is your theory, then? Make your case."

"I think her husband wanted her gone. He wanted to be with his girlfriend. We have a solid motive.

"I think he left that morning and he signed in at the Social Law Library in town just to establish an alibi. But he did not stay there. He drove back home and he killed her. I don't know how; we'll know when we find the body. Then he took the body somewhere to dump it. He was very careful. The cars were both scrubbed clean, no prints, no blood, no hair, no damage or sign of struggle. Mrs. Larkin's car in particular looked freshly scrubbed. The shovel in the garage also looked freshly cleaned and wiped down, so I suspect he buried her or sunk the body in a lake somewhere. I have no idea where.

"Also, Dan's appearance was different that night than when he'd left in the morning. His red tie was gone, and there was dirt under his fingernails the next morning. You don't get dirt under your fingernails if you're reading law books.

"The car at the train station is a red herring. Dan left it there for us to find. There were no prints on it; if Jane was the one who dumped it there, she wouldn't have wiped it down.

"And if she ran off, what is she living on? She did not take any cash or checks or credit cards."

The DA shrugged. "Maybe she's getting help. Maybe she's got a boyfriend. Either way, it's all just guesswork, isn't it?"

"Every case starts with a theory."

"Yes, but the theory, if it's right, is confirmed by real proof eventually. And we don't have that. We don't have the body, we don't have a weapon, we don't have witnesses, we don't have a history of abuse or violence. The reality is we have nothing."

"Dan Larkin is a very smart, careful man."

"Is he? Is anyone *that* smart? Could he have killed his wife and not left *any* evidence for you to find? Really? Not one mistake?"

Glover said nothing.

Kearney turned to his first assistant. "George, what do you think?"

"It's an easy call. There's no case here, we have zero evidence. Dismiss the grand jury and keep digging. That's all we can do."

Kearney: "Anyone disagree with that?"

The others shook their heads.

Kearney: "Tom, I can see you're disappointed. But I'm not going to indict a man for murder only to have the victim stroll into court, alive and well, after hiding out in Canada or Florida or Timbuktu. You don't want me to look like a fool, now, do you?"

"No, sir."

"Good. The case is still open. Keep digging."

"Yes, sir."

"Change my mind."

"Yes, sir."

"Good." The district attorney turned to his first assistant: "I want you to release a statement. Bring this thing to a close somehow. Turn down the temperature before Dan Larkin gets tarred and feathered. Keep it simple: no charges are imminent, the case remains open, we'll continue to investigate, anyone with information is encouraged to come forward, et cetera."

"You want to mention Larkin by name, clear him like he asked?"

"No. He *hasn't* been cleared."

"It's a hell of a thing if he didn't do it. All those rumors."

"Well," the district attorney said, "it's also a hell of a thing if he did."

The following year, on the anniversary of Jane's disappearance, the press would inquire about the case, and the DA's office would issue a similar statement: no charges forthcoming, no active leads, case remains open. A year later, on the second anniversary, a similar statement. After that, the press stopped inquiring.

THE case might have ended there—in a way, I suppose it did. The district attorney's statement had precisely its intended effect: the fever broke, people began to lose interest in the case. It gave the drama a kind of provisional if unsatisfying closure. The story did not end; it just stopped. The investigators—and we, the leering public—resigned ourselves to waiting.

For Dan, the DA's decision not to clear him explicitly was devastating. It sealed his reputation. For the foreseeable future, most people would assume that Dan had something to do with his wife's disappearance, though precisely what it was, nobody knew. This was the shadow my friends Jeff and Miranda would live under for a very long time.

Inside the Larkins' home, life did not return to normal, of course, but it did go on. The days and weeks continued to pass. The kids' lunches had to be made every day, laundry washed and folded, groceries bought, meals cooked. Miranda, still only eleven years old, was more needy than the boys. Someone had to meet her after school and get her to ballet class on Tuesday and Thursday afternoons. Dan returned to work. He had zero interest in the mundane details of running the house. Nor, in those early weeks and months, did he dare bring his girlfriend Sarah into the house to help. So for the most part it fell to Jane's sister to fill the void. Kate did the grocery shopping and the laundry. Kate was at the house in the afternoons to meet Miranda after school every day.

Ever present, amid all this pretend normalcy, lurked the ghost of Jane. Miranda says now, "It was like living in this in-between state. We kept imagining she would walk in at any moment. My father was telling us that Mom was alive somewhere and we should not give up. Jeff and I both figured he did not want to tell us Mom was dead because then he'd have to deal with two hysterical little kids."

One's heart goes out to these children, of course, but I can't help thinking of Kate too. Every day, she came to her sister's home and stood in her sister's place. Every day, she tried to give her niece and nephews some of the things that Jane would have. Her own kids were old enough that Kate could spend the afternoons with Miranda, driving her to ballet or watching TV, or just ensuring that Miranda would not come home to an empty house. So every day she came, and every day she seethed.

One afternoon—Miranda thinks it was just a few weeks after the district attorney's disappointing decision, when the wound was still raw—the two sat side by side on the couch watching a game show on TV. Miranda cuddled against her aunt. She craved contact, and Aunt Kate pulled her close, though Kate's body was leaner and harder than Miranda's mother, less good for snuggling.

"Miranda, can I ask you something just between you and me?"

"Okay."

"This is something you won't tell your father, it will be just our secret."

"Okay."

"You're sure you can keep a secret, just you and me?"

"Yeah."

"Are you afraid here?"

"Afraid of what?"

"Him."

"No."

"You would tell me if you were?"

"Yes."

"Do you feel safe here, in this house?"

"Yes."

"Has he ever done anything or said anything that made you feel frightened or worried?"

"No. I don't think so."

"Because you know, if you want to come live with me and Uncle Stephen, you can do that. You would be safe. Nobody would be able to get to you."

"What do you mean, get to me?"

"Nothing. We're just talking. I just want to be sure you know: if you're ever afraid, of *anybody*, you can come to me. You know that, right?"

"I guess."

"Okay then." She kissed the little girl's forehead.

Miranda understood what her aunt was implying, but the thought of being turned out of her home, of being orphaned by a wicked father, seemed ludicrous, a Gothicism right out of Dickens. Besides, Miranda was genuinely not afraid, even though she understood the possibility that her father might have done something horrible. He was her father, after all. She could not have stopped loving him even if the worst was true.

Kate was not through with the subject, however. She brooded over it the rest of the afternoon, saying less and less to Miranda as the house darkened.

By the time Dan got home that evening, around 5:30, before either of the boys, his sister-in-law was boiling, and she was not very good at—or interested in—hiding her emotion.

Kate lingered in the kitchen, gathering up her purse, slowly buttoning her coat. She planted a decorous kiss on the top of Miranda's head, then stood by Miranda a moment too long, as if reluctant to leave, and it occurred to the little girl that her aunt wanted to take her away right then and there, whether Miranda wanted to go or not.

Kate glared at Dan until he could not ignore it any longer.

"Is something wrong?" he said.

"You know what's wrong."

"It's a tough time. I know. We're all . . ."

"That's not it." She would not take her eyes off him.

"What, then? Tell me."

She moved closer, as if she intended to keep Miranda from hearing. But when she spoke, she did not lower her voice. "I know what you did." She pointed her finger at him. "I know what you did."

BOOK 2

HE KILLED ME. You know that, don't you? He killed me because he was bored, he was disappointed. That's what it comes down to. He was disappointed in his life. He was disappointed in his marriage. Mostly he was disappointed in me. I didn't make him happy anymore, I didn't excite him.

I was unhappy too. That's over, at least.

To my kids, Alex, Jeff, and Miranda:

There are a few things I want you to know, things I did not have the chance to say before I left.

First, I do not hate your father. I am angry, yes. I do not forgive him, and I do not love him anymore. I should have got rid of him. But I could never bring myself to hate him. It would be like hating myself; there is no me without him. We grew up together. We were kids together. We made each other.

And of course we made *you*. Without your dad, you three precious, beautiful kids don't exist. So how could I ever regret my life with him? The end does not erase everything that came before. It does not erase *you*.

So here's the thing: I do not want you kids to hate him, either. Certainly I don't want you to hate him *for me,* out of loyalty. I want you to be happy. That is every mother's wish for her children: just be happy. Simple as that. Let it go. After all these years, I want it to stop—all the smoldering and contempt, the grievance, the sadness. Especially you little ones, Jeff and Miranda: let it go, do you hear me? Let *me* go, for your own sake. I do not want to be the source of your unhappiness, not for one day more. If you need to forget me, if that is the price of your happiness, then do it. Do it today, do it right now. We all have to say goodbye eventually. Let that be the last thing I teach you: how to say goodbye.

WHEN I died, they made me a saint. The newspapers all said I was docile and simple and pretty and sweet—a lamb to slaughter. None of it was true, at least no more or less than it is true of you.

A few were not as kind. They said: Why would she ever have married this monster? How could she not have seen the murderer inside him? Isn't this whole thing partly her own fault, really, for putting herself in harm's way? For being naive or stupid, for misjudging this evil man. For staying with him despite the signs that *must* have been there.

Listen, there were no signs. When I met Danny Larkin at Brookline High School in 1952, he was a sweet, smart, nerdy sixteen-year-old boy. He wore sweater-vests and khakis pressed by his mother's housekeeper. He sometimes wore a blue-and-red band on his upper arm to show he was a class marshal—one of the kids who told us not to run in the hallways. He was skinny; his watch flopped around on his wrist, the seat of his pants bagged where his flat butt did not fill it out. His hairline was too high, which made his forehead too prominent for a teenage boy. He was also smart and the most self-assured person I had ever met. He was *different,* not like the other boys. But believe me, he was just a kid—about as far from being a monster as any of us.

I understand why people want to blame me. You want to reassure yourself about the man beside you, staring at the TV or snoring in bed. But I was not stupid or naive about Dan.

I suppose I must have known who Danny Larkin was during our freshman and sophomore years at Brookline High. Our class was not that big, everybody knew everybody. But I did not really meet him until we were juniors.

That fall there was a little controversy. To celebrate Armistice Day, the school showed a short movie called *A Time for Greatness*. It was about the evil of war, and it suggested that America take a more pacifist, diplomatic approach to settling our quarrels with other countries. The film was produced by the Quakers, which did not help. Well, it seems quaint now, but you can imagine the reaction. Was this an appropriate movie to show for Armistice Day, which was meant to honor our soldiers who had sacrificed so much? Didn't *A Time for Greatness* insult our boys by questioning the cause for which they had fought? Or the *way* they had fought it, or the act of fighting itself—or something? The exact complaint about this movie was never completely clear. There were earnest, endless, patriotic, *ridiculous* discussions about all this for a couple of weeks. I know—crazy, right? Mostly it was our parents who were upset. I got so fed up with the stupidity, I sat down and wrote a letter to the school newspaper, *The Sagamore*. I wrote that it was a sad day when we could not all agree that war was bad, and that Brookline High School was no less patriotic for having shown this innocent movie and debated this important topic. With all that, I was still careful to say that my uncle Charlie had served in the Pacific during the war. (Uncle Charlie used to tell us kids that he had fought "the battle of San Diego" and he had not killed anyone but the defenseless potatoes he'd peeled to death. I left that part out of my letter.)

My sister, Katie, had been the editor in chief of *The Sagamore* the year before. (Katie was a star at *everything* she ever did. *Nobody* was better than my big sister. I mean, *of course* she was editor in chief. What else would she be? Katie was *perfect*.) I think that is why the paper decided to print my letter—because Katie's sister wrote it. I was told that the letter would have to be edited for length, and that the copy editor assigned to the job was Danny Larkin. Later, Dan told me that he volunteered to edit my stupid letter to the editor just so he could meet me. I believe it; for someone who ended up talking for a living in court, Dan never liked to just come out and say what he wanted.

We met at the *Sagamore* office after school one day. Empty room. Just the two of us. A few typewriters and wire baskets on desks, piles of paper everywhere. A calendar on the wall with the next pub date circled in red (the newspaper came out every three weeks).

Danny presented my letter to me, marked up in ink. The crinkly onionskin typing paper was curled and wavy from the pressure of Dan's pen. He had not made many real changes. Mostly he just sprinkled my sentences with a lot of commas, like a chef grinding pepper onto a plate. The commas were mostly unnecessary, but Danny seemed very sure of his editing, and I understood that all those commas were his way of showing off for me.

"It's really good, Jane," he said.

"Thank you."

"I'll just—most of what I wrote there—why don't you just go ahead and read it. I'll just wait. I'll, uh, okay."

I started to read but he could not keep quiet.

"Why didn't you come out for *The Sagamore*?"

"Danny, I can't read it if you keep talking."

"Right, sorry. I'll let you read."

"Okay."

"It's just, your sister could have got you in."

"Katie's the writer in our family."

"I'm not so sure."

I squirmed. My impression of Danny was that he was very confident, a little contentious—always talking in class, always raising his hand, knowing the answer, never changing his mind even when teachers corrected him. It was cute to see him bumble trying to talk to a girl.

"Could I make one little suggestion? Maybe you could add a sentence about how sometimes war is necessary. Because, you know, if we'd left it up to the Quakers, then maybe we'd all be speaking German now, y'know? I mean, nobody *likes* war, but sometimes you have to do it. It's like going to the dentist."

"Do I really need to say that? Seems pretty obvious."

"Not to some people."

"It is to me."

"They'll want to argue with you. Especially 'cause you're a girl."

"Let 'em. I don't care. I hate arguing."

"Then you shouldn't have written this letter. It's gonna make people argue."

"Maybe. I don't know why I even wrote the stupid thing."

"It's not stupid. Someone had to say it. Someone smart like you."

This may have been flirting, too, but a different kind than I was used to.

"I'm glad you wrote it."

"Why didn't *you* write it, then?"

"You beat me to it, I guess."

"Write it now. It'll be better coming from you."

"No. Nobody would listen if it came from me."

"Why not?"

"I argue too much already."

"You think they'll listen to *me*?"

"Of course they will. Everybody knows you, Jane. They'll read it just because you wrote it."

"Yeah? And then what? It's a letter in a high school newspaper. Nobody cares."

"I do. Don't back down, Jane. That's the important thing."

He seemed to relish saying my name, the feeling of it in his mouth.

"Why is that important?"

"Because if you back down, they win."

"Who wins? Who's they?"

He thought it over. "I don't know."

And we both laughed. And that was the beginning.

My little letter did run in *The Sagamore,* peppered with Danny's commas but otherwise essentially as I wrote it. My girlfriends and my parents and even Katie were impressed with it, but no one else seemed to notice, and the Quaker movie was soon forgotten.

But now Danny Larkin had his hooks in me, and one afternoon he stopped by my locker as I was gathering up my things to go home. He said, "Can I ask you something? Are you going to that *Carousel* dance?"

This was a dance in the school gym that had a *Carousel* theme, after the Broadway show.

"I think so. I'm sorry, Danny."

"You *think* you're going? Or you *are* going?"

"I think so."

"With who?"

"I don't know."

"You don't know? How can you not know?"

"I mean, I'm not sure. Why are you giving me the third degree?"

"It's _____, isn't it?"

I will leave out this boy's name. I suspect that, like most of us, he would not like to be judged by what he was in high school.

I made a face: *What?*

"What's the big secret?"

"Danny, you really— Look, not that it's any of your business, but he hasn't asked me yet."

"*Yet.* So you think he's going to?"

I shrugged.

"You *hope* he's going to."

"Why are you grilling me about this?"

"I'm not grilling you, we're just talking."

"This is just talking? It feels like arguing to me."

"Don't be so sensitive."

"Okay, well, thank you for the invitation. I really appreciate it, Danny, it was very nice of you. But I guess I'll just see you there."

He shrugged and shook his head.

"I won't see you there?"

"I doubt it. I don't really want to go."

"You don't want to go? But you just asked me to go with you."

Shrug.

"Danny, why don't you just ask someone else? You don't even need a date—just go. Lots of kids go without dates."

"*Eh*, it's not for me."

"But you want to go!"

"Not really."

"You just said you want to go!"

"No, I said I want to go *with you*."

At that moment, for just a moment, I thought I had made the wrong choice. I didn't want to go either; I wanted to go *with him*. Or at least I wanted to go with a boy who wanted to go *with me*.

I didn't, of course. This wasn't a Doris Day movie, it was high school. I went to the *Carousel* dance with _____. He was the sort of boy I used to attract and be attracted to. Danny Larkin was *not*. You would have chosen _____ too. He played on the football and baseball teams. He was popular and handsome. My friends all thought he was to die for. But he never read *The Saga-more*, not even my letter about the Quaker movie. He never even asked me about it. He was much more concerned with what was in my sweater than what was in my mind. I don't mean he was a bad guy; he wasn't. It's just that he and Danny Larkin were different types. And in high school, well, Danny was the wrong type.

But when the next big dance came around, the junior prom in the spring, I was not with _____ anymore, and Danny did ask me properly, and though my friends thought I could do better ("Why would you go with *him*? You're so pretty"), I said yes. The theme this time was Moon over Miami. The walls of the gym were decorated with cardboard palm trees and a big gold moon. The boys wore rented white dinner jackets with shawl collars, the girls wore puffy skirts and silky tops with spaghetti straps. Danny was an atrocious dancer, but he did not seem to realize it or care, he was so happy to be there with me. Afterward, we drove in his father's car to Jack and Marion's, a deli where we had sandwiches and gabbed until it was very late. When we finally got home to my house, near the top of the hill on Summit Avenue, we parked out front and I sat in the front seat for a long time waiting for him to get up the courage to kiss me. *Come on, already!* Later, he said he already knew he was going to marry me.

Now, tell me: does that sound like a monster to you?

A year after I went missing, almost to the day—he waited for the anniversary, a decent interval, until he thought no one would notice—Dan took his new girlfriend to Bermuda on vacation. It was a vacation we were supposed to take together. I had already arranged it all through the travel agent. They took the same flights I had picked, they stayed at the same hotel, the Southampton Princess. They walked on the beach and dressed up for dinner at expensive restaurants. They tried scuba diving, exploring the sunken wrecks in the shallow reefs near the shore, something I never would have been brave enough to do. She looked so lovely and glamorous, so much taller and thinner than me. I looked like a plow horse next to Dan's girlfriend. At the pool she wore this diaphanous cover-up over her bathing suit, and elegant dresses at night. She had good skinny legs and arms, and beautiful bony shoulders. Beside her, Dan marched around with his little bantam strut, the way he used to after sex or after he won a big case, like a little boy swaggering around in a Superman costume, so proud and happy. They belonged together, anybody could see that. They just fit. They were a couple, more so than Dan and I ever were, though we got along fine for a while, even loved each other. This was different. Dan never used to touch *me,* but when he lay beside her at the pool, he always had a hand on her somewhere, clamped around her ankle or laid upon her slim derriere, a presumption that she accepted comfortably, though she did not look like the type.

I read once, in some magazine, that "love thrives on impediment"—on wanting, not having. On yearning. Killing me had kept them apart for a while, which actually made them want each other more. Now, finally, the wait was over. The impediment was removed. I was the impediment.

IT was around this time, too, that Miranda saw a vision.

In the year since I'd gone, Miranda's appearance had changed. She was eleven, almost twelve. She was thinning out, beginning to look like the woman she would become. Her manner was different, too, I think, though it might be just a mother's imagination. She looked weary. I know it is strange to describe such a young girl as *weary,* but that is how she seemed to me. A light had gone out of her.

Oh, my poor motherless little girl. I know that my death is not the only cause of everything that happened to Miranda. Some people are just born with a melancholy nature, and adolescence is when it often shows up. Another child might have survived this whole thing. Another child might have grieved then recovered. Miranda could not. Her sadness arrived with all its furniture, intending to stay. When I see that little girl a year after my going, I feel such guilt. What if I had not disappeared? How would she be different today? It was not my fault, but the fact remains: I was not there for my daughter when she needed me.

So, picture Miranda. She is hanging out on the sidewalk outside the little market in Newton Highlands, on Lincoln Street. October 1976. Mid afternoon. She did not like to go home after school anymore, so in the afternoons she would hang around at a favorite park or at the public library, reading. She had a friend named Marybeth, a little brunette with a swinging ponytail, and the two of them sometimes spent the afternoon together. But generally Miranda preferred to be alone in the quiet time after school, and on this day she was standing by herself on the sidewalk when she saw me.

She first caught sight of me as I walked nearly a block away, coming straight toward her. She gaped as the vision shimmered into focus. Miranda's body went rigid.

She *did* look like me, this woman. Especially at a distance, at a glance, when all Miranda could see was her shape, the way she carried herself, her posture.

And as the ghost came closer, more details: the right coloring, the right height. Some things were wrong, of course, but Miranda seemed to ignore the bits that were off—the nose was wrong, the face was too thin—and she saw instead something deeper, something in the woman's expression that could only be Miranda's mother.

You see, don't you? To Miranda this was not a woman who *looked like* her mother; this *was* her mother. For a moment.

Then it dissolved. She knew it could not be. It was impossible. And the vision was gone.

Yet the illusion was so intoxicating, so warm, that she chose to robe herself in it and stay there, feeling her mother's presence.

The woman finally reached the store. She noticed Miranda, gave her a nod and a smile, and went inside. If she thought there was anything strange about the little girl's stoned expression, she gave no sign of it.

After a moment, Miranda trailed her into the little market. It was just a tiny storefront in a century-old building. Inside was a small room with refrigerator cases in the back and shelves along the right-hand wall. To the left was a counter where a man stood on a raised platform at a cash register, tiers of candy and cigarettes behind him. This man saw the little girl come in and said hello.

Miranda did not answer him. She stayed near the entrance, watching the woman who was and was not her mother, studying her, until she worried that the woman would notice and she retreated to the sidewalk.

She did not know what to call the excitement she was feeling, her beating heart, the happy thrill that followed a year of deadness, but I know what it was: it was love. Love of a strange kind, it is true, but then they are all strange, no two loves are exactly alike. Of course she knew by this point, only a couple of minutes into the encounter, that this woman was not me. The dream could not last, reality smashed it up. If the woman had really been me, then the only possible explanation for my appearing here would be that I had willingly run out on my family but chosen to stay in the area, in plain sight, shopping only a few blocks from my old home, then looked my own daughter in the eye and did not react at all. No. And yet, *something* had happened, some switch inside Miranda had been thrown, and she felt it would be a blow, a second abandonment, if this woman simply vanished as I had.

So when the woman came out of the store hugging a brown paper bag, Miranda said to her, trying to mask the urgency she was feeling, "Excuse me?"

"Yes. Oh, hello."

"I'm trying—I was wondering if you ever need someone to babysit. I do babysitting."

"Do you? You're so sweet. What makes you think I have babies to sit for?"

Miranda shrugged.

"Do I look that old?"

The little girl's Adam's apple seemed to expand in her throat. "No."

"It's okay, sweetheart. I'm just kidding." She winked.

"Oh."

"How old are you?"

"Thirteen." A fib.

"*Thir*-teen. Have you babysat before?"

"No."

"Hm. Do you have any references?"

"No. Except my father maybe? I live two blocks that way." She pointed.

"Do you have little brothers or sisters you've babysat for?"

"I have two brothers but they're older."

"Ah. Well, that's too bad. What's your name?"

"Miranda."

"Miranda. Miranda what?"

"Miranda Larkin."

"What a pretty name. Where did you get such a pretty name?"

"My mother, I guess."

"Well, I love it. It's a name for a movie star."

"Her name was Jane. She did not want me to have a boring name like hers."

"Is that so?"

"That's what she said."

"Well, she picked a beautiful name for you, Miranda. Not boring at all. I tell you what: you give me your phone number and maybe we can try it for an hour or two sometime. I have two little girls. They're seven and nine. You could come meet them. How does that sound?"

"Good." Miranda smiled. Her face almost cracked, it had been so long since she'd looked *forward* to something, not back.

The woman hoisted the grocery bag up against her shoulder and cradled it there while she fished around for a pen in her purse. This was a big leather shoulder bag that drooped against her waist and seemed stuffed with all sorts of happy cluttery mothery things. Miranda loved even the sound of those things clacking around in the woman's purse, so like my heavy, overstuffed purse, which Miranda used to rummage around in.

"Okay, shoot," the woman said when she had found a pen.

Miranda recited her phone number and the woman scribbled it on the crumpling side of the shopping bag.

"You're gonna call?" Miranda said.

"I promise." The woman let her pen drop down into the open mouth of her purse, then extended her hand and Miranda shook it. "It's very nice to meet you, Miranda. My name is Mrs. Bowers."

Miranda watched the woman leave, then she quick-marched away, too, escaping before the magic of the encounter could dissipate. She wanted to carry it home with her, this hopeful new secret.

AND Jeff? Well, there is something you have to understand: if ever a boy was perfectly made to frustrate his father, it was my Jeff. He was forever tossing wet towels on his bedroom floor. He left his dresser drawers open every time he got dressed. (Once the entire dresser tipped over when Jeff opened all six drawers at once.) He would dump his things wherever he happened to be, leaving a trail behind him as he went—book bag, jacket, sneakers, socks. He had elaborate justifications for his sloppiness. Why ever wash a bath towel, he would say, when the towel cannot be dirtier than you, since it only touches you at your cleanest, after you've just bathed? Why close a drawer or make a bed when you are just going to reopen the drawer and unmake the bed in a few hours? Why clean a soap dish when the dirt *is* soap? Why fold under-pants? He was Dan's perfect opposite. Dan liked his underpants *ironed*. He insisted his socks be folded, not balled. He washed his hands in scalding-hot water, even to the point of having to wave them under the water a few seconds at a time. Dishes required even hotter water, the hottest that Dan could get out of the kitchen faucet. He scrubbed each dish without mercy, then, holding it gin-gerly by the edges, he rinsed it under the boiling water, then filed each steaming dish neatly in the dishwasher. And books! Even I used to get in trouble with Dan over the books in the den. He would flip out if I put a paperback in with the hardcovers, or a trashy novel among his serious-looking histories and biographies. He didn't like it if I added a book that was too beat-up. (Dan had a magical ability to read an entire book yet leave it looking un-touched. I never could. My books always had cracked spines or torn dust jackets, no matter how I tried to baby them.) Sometimes I did these things anyway, just to needle my husband, but with Jeff it was unintentional. He was oblivious, like a dog that frustrates its owner by shedding. When I was there, I kept the peace by discreetly cleaning up after Jeff or nudging Dan to laugh about it. I called them Oscar and Felix. It was cute, it was a running joke.

But in the first year or so without me, the differences between them took on a sharper edge.

One sunny Saturday morning, Dan watched from the kitchen window as Jeff mowed the backyard. The whole house vibrated with the buzz of the lawnmower engine.

Jeff pushed the mower in goofy, wandering lines up and down the long yard. He was wearing cutoff denim shorts and a T-shirt and his favorite sneakers, green suede Puma Clydes, which he always fought us for, even though they cost thirty dollars and wore out in half the time. He trucked along behind the lawnmower, bent at the waist, often looking down at his feet rather than in the direction of the lawnmower. Sometimes on his wavering path he would miss a spot, and he would have to circle back to trim the patch he'd missed, then try to figure out where he had left off.

Standing at the kitchen sink, Dan watched all this with growing annoyance. From his position, elevated above the yard, he could see the crazy, drunken tracks the lawnmower was leaving in the grass. He tried to ignore it—the carelessness, the lack of discipline—but eventually it was just too much. It *offended* him. He marched out to the yard, gesturing with his hand in the air, turning an invisible key, telling Jeff to turn off the lawnmower.

The lawnmower shut down, and there was a sudden, luxurious quiet.

"What on earth are you doing?"

"You told me to mow the grass."

"Look at this! Who taught you to mow like that?"

"Honestly, I have no idea what you're talking about."

"You don't? You don't even *see* it?"

"See what?"

"The mess you're making."

"Are you joking? What mess? I'm mowing the lawn like you said."

"Look again."

"I'm looking!"

"Look at the grass!"

"*What* grass? It's *all* grass!"

"Look at the pattern you're making."

"The pattern? Who cares about the pattern?"

"I do!"

"Why?"

"That's not the point! Why don't you just do it the right way?"

"There is no right way."

"There is. Why don't you just make the lines straight, like a normal person?"

"You're mad because the lines in the grass aren't straight? Are you fucking serious?"

"Watch your language. I'm mad because you're doing the job wrong."

"You *can't* mow the grass wrong. That's not even possible. Either it's mowed or it's not."

"This is our house, it's our property, I want you to take care of it."

"It's the backyard! No one even sees it! *We* don't even see it. No one comes out here."

"I see it!"

"Oh my *God,* Dad, it doesn't matter. It's grass."

"It does matter! Everything matters."

"How can *everything* matter?"

"Jeff, everything you do matters, *especially* when no one's looking."

"Why?"

"Because this is who you are. If you cut corners on this, you'll cut corners on the next thing, and the next. How do you think that's going to go in the real world? Are you just going to tell your boss, 'It doesn't matter, it's good enough'? No! The way you mow the grass is the way you do everything."

"*That's* why you're so angry?"

"Yes. Just do it right."

"Honestly you just sound mental right now."

"Jeff, this is our home, okay? We live here. And every time we look out and we see the yard looking all crazy like this, it sends a message. You know what that message is? The message is: 'This place doesn't matter anymore, we're just letting it go. We're just letting everything go.' And you don't care."

"The grass says all that?"

"Yes. The grass says all that. Lookit, just do me a favor and do it right, okay? Go up and down in a straight line, like a typewriter, nice and neat, not like some drunken lunatic did it. Back and forth, back and forth. It's not so much to ask."

"This is . . ."

Dan took a deep breath and exhaled through his nostrils. Patient, intransigent.

"Fine. Whatever. Straight lines."

"I don't even know what you're fighting about. The whole thing'll take you five minutes. Just go back over it."

"Wait, go back over it? You mean mow the grass I already mowed?"

"Of course!"

"You want me to mow the same grass twice?"

"That's the right way. You can't leave it like this."

"Oh my God, I wish Mom was here."

"All right, enough, we're not starting that." Dan waggled his hands: *none of that.* "This discussion is over. Just do it."

"Fine."

"Fine. Okay. Thank you."

Dan stood there a moment, unsure how to resolve the thing that still seemed unresolved between them, and when he could not think of a way to address it, he turned and walked away as Jeff raised his middle finger to his father's back.

THAT fall, Alex went away to college, yet another loss, leaving only the three of them. Life went on. The daily routine reasserted itself: up and into the shower in the morning, school, activities in the afternoon (sports for Jeff, ballet twice a week for Miranda), homework in the evening. The children were left to sort out their feelings mostly on their own; their father did not believe in "psychobabble" or the professionals who practiced it. The unresolved mystery of my disappearance made it impossible for the kids to grieve and get it all out and move on as best they could, the way they might have if I had just died in my bed.

To the public, within a year my case faded from memory. The strangeness of the story was not enough to hold people's interest forever, and the plot had stopped dead. In the end, most of the public believed I had been killed, I think. From that camp, about half thought Dan had done it. There were a few who figured I had just up and left, which was not as farfetched in 1976 as it might be now. It was easier to disappear then, to create a new identity, a new life. Missing-spouse stories used to show up in the news, especially the dishy supermarket tabloids, which I loved—the husband who went to take out the garbage and never came back, that sort of thing. I used to be fascinated by these stories, ironically enough. Sometimes the papers would print the epilogue too: the husband or wife who turned up years later, living under an assumed name. Those stories were even more delicious to me. The most popular destination for these runaways seemed to be Florida. I don't know why. I guess that, like water running downhill, they headed south until they ran out of road. In any case, my story was over. The revelations were at an end, and people moved on.

For the children, obviously, things were much, much harder.

One night in November, the reduced family sat down to supper, still at their old places around the Formica table in the "breakfast room," which was what the realtor who sold us the house called the little nook off the kitchen. We never actually ate breakfast there. Breakfast we wolfed down at the kitchen counter, standing or on stools, reading the newspapers that were always scattered there, listening to *The Today Show* on the little black-and-white.

We used the breakfast room only for supper, but we went right on calling it the breakfast room anyway, probably because, when we first bought the house, Dan and I were tickled that we could afford a place with a room dedicated just to breakfast. Now, with Alex and me both gone, Jeff and Miranda still went to their accustomed places at the table, which left my old spot unoccupied.

To his credit, Dan made an effort to maintain supper as a nightly family ritual, as it always had been. He learned to cook a few things—very, very badly—especially a tarragon chicken dish that Jeff liked. (He liked it so much we called it "Chicken Jeff.")

Dan was not as successful at drawing the children into conversation, although, to be fair, Jeff and Miranda never talked as much as they used to. Dinners were generally quiet and sullen, unless Miranda was in one of her loopy, effusive moods (rare now) or Dan was cross-examining the kids about their day. Most nights, you could hear the silverware clink on the plates or the *yom-yom* sound Jeff sometimes made when he chewed.

On this night, Dan put down his fork and knife and said that he had an announcement to make.

"I have good news and bad news," he said. "Which one do you want first?"

Jeff: "Bad."

"Okay. There's something I need to do that I think maybe could be a little difficult for you kids. For all of us. I need to go to court about your mother. I need to get a judgment—a judge has to say your mother is officially dead. It's just for legal reasons. It's just a technical thing."

Miranda: "But you said she's not dead, you said we don't know."

"It's true. But she's not here, and we are, and we need to go on. The sun comes up and we need to go on with our lives as best we can."

"But you *said*."

"It's true, Mimi, I said that. It's just, we need to do certain things so we can go on living. There's a lot of stuff you kids don't see, stuff that moms and dads have to think about."

Jeff: "Like what?"

"Well, like insurance. Or like I need to be able to sign papers as your sole parent, for school or hospitals or whatever. Or like making plans for my estate. What if *I* died? What would happen to you kids?" Dan had thought this last item was a dull, lawyerly point, but he saw the horrified look on Miranda's face and immediately backtracked. "It's not going to happen, Miranda. It's just an example."

Jeff rolled his eyes. His lips tightened. He gave Miranda a look, and she relaxed. It was a look only Jeff could have given her. It said, *It's okay, I'll be here even if Dad dies.* Miranda adored Jeff. She looked up to Alex, but she adored Jeff. (I remember when the kids were young—eight and ten or so—we used to go on walks in the neighborhood, and Miranda would ride piggyback on Jeff's back. That is an image I will always keep of those two: Jeff carrying his little sister on his back as she jumps up and down with excitement or lays her head on his shoulder, him bent nearly double under the weight of her.)

Jeff: "How can a judge know if she's dead or not?"

"He can't. No one can. But it's been a year, there's a presumption. The law allows a surviving spouse to petition for a judgment like this so we can . . . you know, kind of close the books and move on."

"You keep saying that, *move on.* What if I don't want to move on?"

"What else can we do?"

"Show a little faith. Wait for her."

"Jesus, Jeff, look around you! Do you see her? You think she's just going to walk in the door? She's not here. It's just me. What do you want me to do?"

"I don't want you to do anything. Why do we *have to* do anything?" Jeff looked down at his plate. He could not tolerate his father's expression now, his cool logic, the smug, lecturing tone. He thought that if he could, if he were bigger, he would smash his plate right in his father's face.

"There comes a time."

Jeff shook his head but kept his eyes down, avoiding his father's face.

Miranda looked stricken. Bad as Dan's message was, she was even more uncomfortable seeing her father and brother spar like this. It made the whole family feel fractured, fragile. It could all fall apart so easily, the family could spin into pieces and she would be left alone.

Jeff: "What was the other news, the good news?"

"The good news." Dan made an encouraging, phony little grin. "The good news is Sarah is going to move in with us."

Long silence.

"That's the good news?"

"Yes."

"Oh God."

"Won't it be good to have a . . . a mother in the house?"

"She's not our mother."

"That's not what I meant."

"You can't just pick a new mother—"

"That's not what I meant—"

"—some random woman and call her our mother."

"—and you know it. Come on, Jeff, you're not listening. Jesus, give me a break, would you? All right, I shouldn't have put it that way, all right? I'm sorry if I offended you." He turned to Miranda, seeking a more sympathetic audience. "How about you? Don't you think it'll be nice to have another girl in the family?"

"No."

"No? Don't you like Sarah?"

Miranda shrugged.

"Well, Sarah likes *you*. She loves you both."

Jeff: "*Loves* me? She doesn't even know me."

"Of course she does. And she'll get to know you more. She *wants* to know you more, if you'll let her. That's your decision."

"Apparently it's not."

"Well, you know, Jeff, you could give her a chance, let her in a little."

"Let her in. It's our house. Don't we get a vote on who can live here?"

"It's not our house, Jeff, it's my house."

"So it doesn't matter what I think."

"Of course it matters. But it's not your decision. I'm a grown man. I don't leave my life decisions up to a thirteen-year-old. *I* decide who I live with, who I spend my life with. That's how the world works."

"Who you spend your *life* with? Are you going to marry her?"

"I don't know. Someday, maybe."

"You do know, don't you? That's what you really want, that's what this court thing is all about, isn't it? You don't care about your will or the insurance or whatever. You just can't marry your girlfriend while you're still married to Mom."

"That's part of it, yes."

The boy looked around the room at an invisible crowd with a shocked expression that said *Can you believe this?* He was equally scornful of his father and proud of himself for uncovering the secret.

"Is that so wrong, Jeff? Do I have to spend the rest of my life alone, like a monk? Is that what you want? Just tell me, what's the right thing to do? And I'll do it."

"Nothing. The right thing is for you to do nothing."

"For how long?"

"I don't know. Longer than this."

Dan sighed.

Miranda: "What if the judge says Mom is dead but he's wrong and she's really alive?"

"I don't know, Mimi. I don't think it's going to happen."

"Why?"

"I just don't."

"But why?"

"Because it's been a long time now. I don't think your mother would just leave us like this. If she's alive, great. But . . ."

Miranda slumped. "Are you going to give her Mom's ring?"

"What ring, Mimi?"

"The one with the hearts."

This was my engagement ring. It had a beautiful pattern of interlocking gold hearts, each containing a tiny diamond. Before it was mine, the ring had belonged to Dan's grandmother, a woman who was once so poor—according to family lore—that she had worked in the window of the Jordan Marsh department store sewing ladies' gloves.

Once, not long before I disappeared, Mimi asked me to take this ring off so she could see it.

I can't take it off, sweetie. It doesn't come off. My finger's too fat.

You mean you never take it off?

That's right, I never take it off.

Even when you go swimming?

Even when I go swimming.

Even when you take a shower?

Even when I take a shower.

Even when you go in the garden?

Even then.

Even when you poop?

Yes, you little stinker, even when I poop. I never, ever take it off. It's pretty, isn't it? Isn't it beautiful, Mimi?

Dan said, "You mean Mom's engagement ring? I don't even have it."

"Where is it, then?"

"I don't know. I guess it's on her finger, wherever she is."

"No one can have it."

"Okay." Dan looked at his daughter with a mystified expression. Why couldn't he have had simpler children?

Miranda left the table and ran upstairs to her room. She did not come out again that night.

Nor could Dan get her out of bed for school the next morning. He tried coaxing and threatening, but she lay under her covers insisting she could not do it, she did not feel well, could she please, please, please stay home today, just this once? Dan finally relented, not out of kindness but exasperation; he had to get out of the house and go to work. My sister spent the day at the house with her. Kate took Mimi at her word that she was sick even though there were no symptoms. Later, Miranda's bouts of depression would become more obvious—longer-lasting, vertiginous, paralyzing—but that day Kate saw no cause for alarm. Mimi lay around the house most of the day looking exhausted, lethargic, dazed, until her mood started to lift in the afternoon and gradually she came back to herself, and Aunt Katie taught her how to play gin rummy.

As for Dan's announcement, Sarah did move in a few weeks later, into my house, into my bed. She bought new white sheets. She boxed up my clothes and put them in the attic. All this though I was not dead yet, officially. I was only missing, until a probate judge declared otherwise.

There was another surprise: Sarah did not come alone.

SOMETIMES I feel a sadness so heavy it won't let me up. If I think about certain things—my kids, my sister—it is like filling my coat pockets with heavy stones. It happens when I think about my marriage too.

For a long time, Dan and I were happy. We made a good couple. Everyone said so. Not alike, but compatible. All around us—in our town, among our friends—we saw marriages worse than ours, marriages like cyclones. We knew couples who cheated and gambled and drank (though we all drank too much back then).

We knew couples who argued endlessly; for naturally argumentative people, contradiction is just a reflex, and a marriage between two of them is like watching rams crash headlong into each other over and over. We had none of these problems. Dan and I were the steady ones. It was not a perfect marriage, but there are no perfect marriages.

I can't imagine what I did wrong, how I displeased him. For seventeen years, I cooked and cleaned for him. I dieted and dressed for him. I bathed the kids, fed the kids, drove the kids—he did not even know their schedules or their friends' names. I watched him get drunk at parties. I listened to his stories over and over, about defendants and lawyers who meant nothing to me, and I reacted on cue—nodded, laughed, agreed, always agreed. I smiled and smiled for him. I fucked *his* way, when *he* wanted to. I never, ever made fun of him, even as a joke, because he could not stand to be teased. I did everything I could—everything—and it wasn't enough.

And here's the thing: I never knew how unhappy he was. He hid things from me. My husband had secrets.

When I think about it, honestly, I am a loaded gun.

Well. Not anymore. I can't be upset. I can't *be*—I don't exist. I am not.

Back to the story. My marriage.

You want to understand my marriage? You need to know one thing: Danny's family was rich. I don't mean a *little* rich. I don't mean country-club rich or fancy-car rich. I mean name-on-a-hospital rich. I did not marry him *because* he was rich, of course. I married him because he was sweet and good, and I loved him. But I can't say I was unaware of it, either. And I liked it. Who wouldn't? My girlfriends gave me dreamy, envious looks when they thought of me swanning around in some mansion like Princess Grace. My parents teased me by calling him "Roosevelt." I liked all that too. Only Katie was unimpressed. She never thought he was worth it. Anyway, when Danny proposed, I wasn't going to turn him down because he was rich, now was I?

Maybe that was the problem. I could never be rich, no matter how much money I got. I could never be like Dan. Even at the end, right before I vanished, when one of the kids would do some low-rent, uncouth thing—when Jeff would clean the drips off the ketchup bottle by licking it, or take a drink of water by lowering his head into the kitchen sink and slurping from the faucet—I always thought, *That's my side of the family.*

For his part, Danny could be vain about his family's money, as if the fortune was somehow his accomplishment, but he could also be touchingly insecure about it. When I asked him on one of our first dates, "Is it true you're rich?" he said, "No, my parents are." I thought he was being cute. I didn't understand the distinction. I should have listened harder.

DAN and I got engaged right before our senior year in college, but he did not want to tell anyone. He said it would be our little secret—for how long, he did not know. I worried he was keeping his options open in case he got cold feet; really, he just wanted to put off telling his parents. I forced his hand, not accidentally, by spilling the secret to Katie and a few close friends, and word began to filter out until finally I had to insist he tell his parents before they heard it from someone else. By then it was December.

He arranged for us to have dinner at his parents' house, with hints that some momentous news was to be revealed. I got dressed up in my best clothes. Danny wore a coat and tie.

The Larkins' house was not especially grand. Inside, it was lovely and stuffed with beautiful art and antiques, but from the outside you would not have known it was a rich family's house at all. The dining room was sumptuous, though. White tablecloth, silver candlesticks, cut-crystal stemware, gold-rimmed china. Above the table was a crystal chandelier. At dinner, Mrs. Larkin kept a little sterling-silver bell by her plate; when she rang it, out through a swinging door came the family's maid, a stout, cheerful black woman, in uniform, to serve and clear the dishes. As a twenty-one-year-old girl, I was awed.

When Danny sprung the news of our engagement, Mrs. Larkin smiled as if she already knew. She was thin, with prematurely white hair, a hawk nose, and dark skin. Not a beauty, but she had an attractive, candid self-confidence. A presence. I had already begun to study her behavior, to mimic her—the way she moved, her tart opinions—so that she would not be disappointed in me.

"Well," she said, "that's wonderful news. And when will I become a grandmother?"

"Millie!" her husband said.

Me: "Not anytime soon, I hope."

"Well, it was just a question."

We all laughed, and my future mother-in-law went right on eating and chatting as if oblivious to my embarrassment. She was not oblivious, of course. I don't think she ever had an oblivious moment in her life. She just did not care what we thought of her.

Mildred Larkin was a one-third heir in the Coachman Shoe Company, which her father had started. At its peak in the 1940s and '50s, Coachman was a massive enterprise, the second-largest employer in Boston, after Gillette. As a girl, Mildred went to private school then to Simmons College, which was a luxury for women at the time. But of course there was no place for a woman in the business. Those jobs went to her two brothers and later to Mildred's husband. So all of her smarts and her wit were confined to the dinner table and her overmatched family, and occasionally the ladies at her do-gooder luncheons. What a waste of a terrific mind.

After dinner but before dessert, as the maid was bustling in and out, fussing and clearing the dishes, Mrs. Larkin said to me, "Come, we have a minute. There's something I want to show you."

She led me up the stairs. I remember looking up at her nubbly wool skirt and her spindly, bowed legs and thinking she was very old. She had arthritis, which swelled her knuckles and her knees and made her move stiffly. In fact, she was only fifty-three.

In her bedroom, she went to a large jewelry box and began to rummage through it. "I want you to have something, something of mine."

"Oh, Mrs. Larkin, you don't have to."

"I want to. It's not just a present, though; it's mine. A present would be *from* me but it wouldn't be mine. You understand the difference?"

"Yes."

She and her husband slept in separate beds, and I sat down primly on the bed that seemed to be hers. She returned with a chunky gold necklace, not at all my style (or my budget, I'm sure), but she seemed so pleased when she clasped it around my neck that I said nothing.

"Come look."

She stood behind me at the bedroom mirror. "There. That's lovely, isn't it?"

"Yes. But it's too much. Really, you don't have to."

She put her hands on my shoulders. "I can certainly see why he chose you."

"Thank you."

"Do you like it?"

"Of course I do. It's lovely."

"Good. Then keep it. I like it too. I like it better on you than on myself. It's a sturdy piece; it needs a sturdy girl." She squeezed my shoulders—in a friendly way but also with a kind of professionalism, as if she were sizing up a horse she might buy. "Maybe when you wear it, you'll think of me."

"Of course I will. Always."

"Come, let's sit down. I want to have a chat with you."

"Shouldn't we get back downstairs? They're waiting."

"Let 'em wait. We've never really talked. I want you all to myself."

Here was the real reason for my new necklace: it was the price of a private audience with me. We sat down on opposite beds, facing each other.

"Jane, have you ever met my father?"

"No, but I've heard a lot about him. Danny worships him."

"What has Danny told you?"

"That your father came to this country because he was poor. And he started the company."

"Poor. Poor doesn't begin to describe it. He came here when he was fourteen years old, with nothing but the clothes on his back, speaking not a word of English. When he first got here, he lived on the street. Twenty years later, he started the company."

"He must have been very smart."

"Oh, he was smart and he worked hard, but a lot of people are smart and work hard. You know what he was?" She whispered: "He was *lucky*. The shoe industry was still wide open. There weren't big national brands like now. Most shoe companies were still regional. But everything was changing. New ways to make shoes, ship them, sell them. To do it faster, cheaper, better. There was *opportunity*, you see? That's why he was lucky. Tell me, did you ever have Coachman shoes, sweetheart?"

"Yes."

"They were very expensive, weren't they?"

"Yes."

"And your parents did not have much money, did they?"

She was shameless! "No," I admitted.

"So why did your mother buy them for you? Why did she spend all that money?"

"Because she said they were the best."

"Yes, exactly. They were the best. Do you know why I'm telling you all this, Jane?"

"Not really, no."

"Parents do for their children. Just like your mother did for you."

"Oh. Yes. They do."

Mrs. Larkin looked at me, took my measure. She frowned, as if I had not understood something, so she tried again, with a different approach. "Do you know how my father met my mother? Has Danny ever told you?"

"Yes. He saw her in the window at Jordan Marsh, in town."

"That's right. When she was your age, my mother was making gloves. They used to have sewing girls in the window, to show the customers the quality. Now, what kind of a girl takes a job sewing gloves in a department store window?"

"I don't know."

"I'll tell you: a poor one. A poor one, Jane. You see, that's what my parents come from. It's not what Danny comes from, but it's where I come from. It's what I was taught. I was not born rich. My family got rich in my lifetime. That makes a difference, and I'll tell you why. Because we haven't had money long enough to be careless with it. We can still remember being poor. Ask my father about it sometime. Ask him how it feels to be hungry. And cold."

The subject made me uneasy. My family never talked about money, except to assure ourselves that it can't buy happiness and you can't take it with you and so on.

"My Howard grew up poor too. When I met him, he didn't have a pot to piss in. He came up here from Washington, Pennsylvania. He was a dentist with no patients. It was the Depression; nobody went to the dentist, nobody could afford it. So he decided he'd open a practice in pediatric dentistry because he figured parents would spend money on their kids' teeth even if they wouldn't spend it on their own."

"That was clever."

"It didn't matter. He wasn't lucky. Turned out, nobody had money for dentists, period. So when we got married, my father gave him a job at Coachman and that was the end of Howard's career as a dentist."

"Did he like it at Coachman?"

"Hated every day of it. Retired as soon as he could."

"That's very sad."

"Not at all. Howard is very happy now. He's retired, he plays golf, we go to Palm Beach in the winter. He has a good life."

"But all those years he was miserable."

"Yes, well. Happiness is a privilege. First you need a roof over your head and food in your belly, then you worry about being happy. Does Danny make you happy, Jane?"

"Very."

"Good. I'm glad. Howard's made me happy too. I married a handsome boy, and he married a rich girl; we made a good deal, the both of us. We've had a good life."

"There must have been more than that. Didn't you love each other?"

"Of course! And we love each other even more now. The only problem was my father. He thought Howard was a gold digger."

Mildred's eyes sparkled with meaning.

I could not think of one thing to say.

"Oh, it's all right, Jane. Don't be shocked. It was natural for him to be suspicious. Howard *was* a gold digger. But it didn't matter, you see? Because I wanted him."

"Oh."

"And by the time Howard gets any gold, he'll be too old to enjoy it anyway. That's the way my father arranged it. All the money is his, his and my mother's, until they die. Until then, technically I'm not worth a nickel. I stand to inherit quite a bit, of course, but that may not come for many, many years. And when it does, there is no provision for the grandchildren—Danny will get nothing, not until Howard and I both die. That's the way this family works. Each generation takes care of its own. Each generation works for what they get."

"I see."

"I want you to know that, sweetheart, right up front. There isn't going to be any money for Danny. Or for you. Not for a long time, maybe not ever. I intend to live a very long time."

"I don't want any money. I never—"

"I know, Jane. There's nothing to be upset about. I'm just being honest with you. We're both adults, aren't we? We're grown women, and we both know that some girls would look at Danny as a golden goose. So we need to be frank with each other. Is that all right? Can I be frank with you?"

I nodded. I did not tell her what I really thought of her insulting little speech.

"Do you know what my father likes to say about why he got into the shoe business? Because when you step in shit, it's not your hat that gets dirty." She leaned forward to confide: "That's us." She winked. "Come. It's not so bad." She stood me up and scrubbed her palms up and down the outsides of my arms to jostle me out of my tears. She arranged the necklace so it sat just so. "Such a beautiful girl. We're going to be good friends, you and me."

On a Saturday morning in March 1977, Jeff woke up—rousing slowly from the deep, drugged sleep of a teenage boy—to hear Sarah's voice downstairs. Not her words, just the unfamiliar timbre of a woman's voice, for the first time in over a year, transmitted through the timbers of the old house up to his room.

Outside, a car idled.

He stood up stiffly and, fingering apart the slats of a Venetian blind, he looked out to see Sarah's teal-green Olds Toronado in the driveway with smoke wisping out of the tailpipe. He grunted and shuffled off to the bathroom.

When he came back into his room to dress, he peered out again. Sarah's car was still in the driveway, engine still running.

Downstairs, in the front hall, he found a pile of cardboard boxes, which his father and Sarah were ferrying down to the basement. Apparently Sarah's belongings.

The happy couple came up from the basement.

"Hey, kiddo," Dan said, resolutely cheery, using a nickname he never, ever used.

"Good morning," Sarah said, more cautious.

All at once, Jeff felt sour, toxic—unreasonably, he knew, but he couldn't control his own venomous mood. Resentment swelled up in him like sewage. Sarah's presence here, so early in the morning, moving in, a constant intruder. His father's expectant face and obnoxious, chipper tone of voice, intended to manipulate him. It was all too much to bear.

He said, "You left your car running."

"I know. Jamie is out there."

Jamie was Sarah's daughter, a girl whose existence—here was another galling detail for Jeff to swallow—whose very *existence* they had hidden from Jeff until only a few weeks earlier, when Dan had revealed that slipping Sarah into the family might be more complicated than he had let on. The two families had all gone out to dinner to "celebrate" and give my kids a chance to meet this girl, their new stepsister. Even Alex came, arriving by cab from Cambridge like a movie star to a premiere. They went to Pier 4, the kids' favorite (expensive) restaurant, which was reserved for birthday dinners and special occasions—another clumsy attempt to manipulate him, Jeff thought, to buy him off.

"You left her out in the car?"

"I didn't leave her. She wouldn't come in."

"Why?"

"I don't know. Why don't you go ask her?"

"*Hn.* Okay, I will."

Now, Jeff was being gallant here, I think (I hope), but it was obvious that he was happy for an excuse to leave Dan and Sarah. He ambled to the kitchen cabinet, got himself a packet of Pop-Tarts, and left the open box on the counter, all in an unhurried way, to show his father that he would not be hustled out of his own house. A teenage boy has a thousand ways to say "fuck you."

Outside, as he shivered in the winter cold, Jeff saw Jamie sitting in the front passenger seat so he got into the driver's seat beside her. Bench seat, nothing between them.

Poor Jeff, this was the closest he'd been to a girl in months. The only females at his school were a few middle-aged secretaries and one spindly math teacher. He was not especially shy but he had no patter, no idea what girls might be interested in talking about. The only thing he wanted from them—sex—he did not have the nerve to ask for. Jamie Bennett was a little older than Jeff, a grade ahead in school. She was pretty, and so curvy and full, swaddled in her puffy down jacket, that she must have seemed to Jeff like some ripe, juicy peach dangling from a branch. It was simply impossible for this boy to sit next to her and not think of her body. Yet, for all that sexual electricity, he felt oddly calm in that car, too, closed in with her, quiet, warm, safe. Their problems were all locked outside with the cold. In fact, their situation was just so weird—strangers soon to be stepsiblings, in the shadow of my mysterious absence, and Dan and Sarah's unseemly happiness, and the quasi celebrity the case brought to the family—that he thought Jamie might be the only girl on earth who could understand what he was feeling. He actually thought she had it worse, in a way: Jamie's mother was *choosing* to enter this fucked-up family and dragging her along. It was not *Jamie's* mom who had disappeared, after all. Jeff was comfortable with her for another reason too: the word *stepsister,* with its whiff of incest, made her off-limits and thus easier to talk to.

"Did they send you out to check on me?"

"No."

"You just came out here for no reason?"

"No. Didn't want to be with *them*."

"Me too."

He opened the crinkly white Pop-Tarts envelope. "You want one?"

"What kind is it?"

He checked the package. "Strawberry."

"No frosting."

"My mother never let us have the kind with the frosting. Too much sugar."

He slid one of the Pop-Tarts out of its envelope and offered it to her. She shook her head.

"You don't want to live here?"

"No."

"Me neither." He took a bite then said, while still chewing (an old, terrible habit of his, by the way), "Your mother just said she doesn't know why you're out here."

"She knows."

"She knows you don't want to live here?"

"Yeah. She said she's sorry I feel that way but it's happening anyway."

"I bet you my father told her to say that. It sounds just like him."

"Maybe. I am *not* living here."

"You're freaked out because of the whole . . . what happened? Or you just don't want to live here?"

"No, it's because of . . . what happened. Your father—well, never mind."

"No, you can say it."

"I can't live in the same house as him, that's all."

"You're scared of him."

"I'm terrified of him. Aren't you?"

"No."

"Never? Not even a little?"

"No. He's just my father."

"So then you think he didn't do it?"

Long silence.

"I don't know."

"Then how can you not be afraid?"

"I don't know. I'm just not. Doesn't make any sense, does it?"

"No. Unless you're suicidal."

"Maybe I am. The other night I had this dream—"

"Ugh, only boring people tell you their dreams. You're not going to tell me some stupid dream, are you?"

"Well, not anymore."

"No, go ahead."

"Nah. It's stupid. Never mind."

"No, tell me your dream. I want to hear it. Is it the one where you show up for a test and you haven't studied and you don't have any clothes on?"

"No. Though I have that one too. How did you know?"

"*Everyone* has that dream, Jeff."

"Do you?"

"No. I do my homework. So go ahead. What's the dream?"

"Okay. So in the dream, I'm at the doctor's office, and the doctor tells me I have this fatal disease and I only have like a week to live."

"That's it?"

"No. The weird part is, I am totally happy. Because it means I don't have to go through with it, y'know?"

"Go through with what?"

"Growing up. The whole next thirty years. You ever had that one?"

"No."

"Oh."

She gave my Jeff a consoling little smile—oh, sweet, kind girl, thank you!—and he said, sheepish, "Me neither. I was just making it up. Anyway, that's why I'm not afraid of him, if you see what I mean."

"I do."

"You know, we have a room all made up for you. Mimi did the whole thing. She made a sign with your name on it and put it on the door. She thinks she's getting a new sister."

"I can still be Mimi's sister. She's sweet."

"She's not sweet. People only think she's sweet."

"She is! Maybe you're the one who's not sweet."

"What about your father? You could go live with him."

"He's not interested."

"Why not? Did you ask him?"

"I don't really know him. He's not around. You know . . ." Her voice ebbed away.

"So where will you go?"

"My friend says I can come live with her."

"That'd be a shame. I mean, for Mimi." Awkward smile. "You're wasting gas, you know. You should turn the engine off."

"I'm not sure I can turn it back on. I've never done it before. We'll freeze."

"I can turn it back on."

"Okay, go ahead, then."

He turned the key on the steering column, switching off the engine. The car got very quiet. They heard voices of pedestrians. Immediately the cold began to seep in. The intimacy of their little sealed chamber was not the same without the warmth and the grumble of the engine, and they felt less comfortable together, less willing to confide.

Jamie rubbed her hands.

"Back on?" he said.

"Back on."

He restarted the car.

"How do you know how to do that? You're too young to drive."

"I don't know. Just monkey see, monkey do."

"Do you think I'm crazy to be afraid of your dad?"

"I think you'd be a little crazy *not* to be afraid of him."

"But you're not."

"I just try not to think about it, y'know? I try not to think, ever. About that."

"Does that work?"

"Not really. But what else can I do? Where am I gonna go?"

"So what if he hurts you?"

"He won't hurt me."

"Or Miranda."

"If he hurt Miranda, I'd kill him."

"Okay. Sorry, I didn't mean to upset you."

"No, no, I'm fine. I'm just sayin'."

"It's none of my business. I'm not like this usually. Sorry."

"It's all right. It's not like I never thought about it."

She slumped in her seat, still feeling she had gone too far. And also not far enough—she hadn't gotten any real answers to her own dilemma.

Jeff: "Do you get along with your mother?"

"I used to. Do you get along with your father?"

"I don't know. I don't think he likes me very much."

"Why not?"

"I just kind of rub him the wrong way. Something about me. But he's not so bad."

"He's not so bad except for this one little thing." She held her fingers a quarter inch apart.

Jeff snorted.

Jamie laughed, clapped her hand over her mouth. "I'm so sorry. I shouldn't have said that."

"So he killed his wife, so what? He only did it one time."

"Oh my God, stop! It's your mother! That's terrible."

They stopped laughing and awkwardness filled the car.

"What was your mother like?"

Jeff considered the question. His vision began to blur, and he wiped his eyes with his thumb and forefinger. "She was nice" was all he could come up with. (Oh, Jeff. Break my heart.) "She was really nice."

Jamie sat back and stared through the windshield, unsure where the conversation could go from there.

"I wish we could just get out of here," Jeff said.

"Me too."

A beat.

"We do have a car."

"But we don't have a driver."

They shared a sly look.

Jeff put both hands on the wheel, at nine and three.

Jamie: "Oh no. We can't."

"Well, technically we *can*. I think you mean we shouldn't."

"No, I mean we *can't*."

"If we can't, then I guess I can't do . . . this."

He moved the gearshift into reverse, and the car immediately rolled backward until he was able to stomp on the brake pedal. The car stopped with a lurch.

"Stop! You're not allowed to do this!"

"I know! It's great, isn't it?"

Tentatively he raised his foot off the brake and backed the car out onto the street.

"You can't drive!"

"Stop saying I can't. I can. I am!"

He put the car in drive and they rolled down the street slowly, slowly. At the stop sign, he braked too hard and they were jostled. They shared another look, the same dopey grin.

"Where should we go?"

"Home!"

"Sorry. No such place."

"Go back!"

"No. Let's go someplace far away. How about California?"

"I don't want to go to California."

"Sure you do."

They rolled down the block toward the lake, Jeff focused, Jamie's mouth hanging open.

"Do *not* crack up my mother's car!"

"Jesus, this is the biggest car I've ever seen. Who drives a car like this? It's like driving the Hindenburg."

"Not what I want to hear right now."

"Right, sorry."

"Just keep your eyes on the road. If you mess up this car, she'll kill me."

"You? What about me?"

"She can't kill you. You're not hers."

"No, I am definitely not hers."

They rolled down the street, letting the engine move them at idling speed, like a boat drifting with the breeze. Gaining confidence, Jeff began to experiment with the gas pedal.

"Turn on the radio."

"No! You need to concentrate!"

"Radio!"

"Okay! What station?"

"BCN."

"What number is that?"

"Wait, you don't listen to BCN?"

"Oh my God, look at the road! You're going to get us killed!"

"Yes, I am," he said as he negotiated a twisting stretch of road along the lakeside. "Yes, I am."

The next week, when Sarah moved in, her daughter moved in, too, without argument. Miranda had her new sister after all.

IN March 1977, Detective Glover set out for Cleveland, ten hours by car due west from the Newton Police station, on I-90 all the way, no turns. He left on a Friday morning and made the drive with as few stops as possible. Once out of Boston's orbit, he lost the radio signal, so he drove most of the way in silence, with only the sound of the road passing beneath his car. There is always an illusion on long highway trips like this, especially after you have been driving awhile, that the car is not moving; only the outside, the trees and road signs whizzing past, are in motion. That is how I think of Tom Glover that Friday morning, moving west against the eastward spinning of the earth: he was suspended at a fixed point in space while everything else rushed by. Because that is what happened to this poor, sweet man, I think. He got stuck in time, looking for me, while the rest of the world moved on.

The trouble, you see, was that my case never quite went away. People saw me, or thought they did, in all sorts of places. I was in Santa Monica, California, and soon after that in Petaluma. I was in Mobile and Montreal, and Portland, Oregon, and Spokane and Vancouver. (The Northwest must have been a good place for ghosties like me to reappear.) I was in some out-of-the-way places, too, places I'd never heard of: Benson, Minnesota; Plano, Texas; Las Cruces, New Mexico. These sightings usually followed a news report that showed my picture. Often the witness was a New Englander far from home, more familiar with the case than the locals. The reports came in to local and state police, sometimes to the FBI (which did not investigate ordinary missing-person cases), and all of them were passed along from agency to agency until they finally reached Tom Glover's desk. Every one of these leads he ran down, in one way or another.

That was even more difficult than it sounds, for two reasons. First, in 1977 there was no way to prove a person's identity definitively except fingerprints. Glover did have samples of my fingerprints. (There was no proper, ink-rolled example of my fingerprints, of course. I'd never been arrested. But the cops were able to collect "latents" from objects that only I would have touched: my hairbrush, the drawer pulls on my dresser, a plastic Bic lighter on my night table.) The only other "scientific" way to conclusively prove that one of these doppelgangers was actually Jane Larkin was a scar on my right shoulder, which my mother told them about, a detail that the cops withheld from the public. (The scar was from when I was nine or ten years old. I was riding my bike and decided—God knows why—to find out what would happen if I rode full-speed into a deep pothole on our street. Well, here is what happens: the bike stops, the little girl goes sailing over the handlebars, and she lands on her shoulder.) So, for Glover, the work of ruling out suspects was slow and meticulous.

The second thing you must understand is that people go missing a lot more than you might think. There are thousands of unsolved missing-person cases every year, and even if you exclude the dreary, tragic cases involving runaways, people who *want* to disappear—people in unhappy or violent relationships, people who lose hope because they are in debt or in trouble with the law, people who are mentally disturbed or addicted to drugs or alcohol—that still leaves a lot of people who vanish for no apparent reason at all. A lot of these are murder victims, but the fact that their bodies have gone missing makes it impossible to know precisely how many. (And the poor communication between jurisdictions means that a nameless dead body found far from home would likely never come to the attention of the detectives searching for her.) All we know about the disappeared is that they were here and then they were not. One by one they vanish, here and there, year after year, until whole crowds of people are simply gone, missing, absent. So for Glover, the needle-in-a-haystack aspect of this investigation was particularly difficult, because the haystack was very large.

Glover was not alone, thankfully. My daddy had a saying: *Be bold, and mighty armies will rally to your side.* Something like that happened for Glover. He had only to ask a local police department to run down a lead for him, and it would be done. Anywhere, anytime. Once he explained the situation, no local cop ever refused Glover's request for help. Always a detective was willing to track down a "Jane Larkin," ask her a battery of questions, even submit a written report and a fingerprint card. This included cops in far-flung, undermanned departments whom Glover could never repay, and even foreign police departments in Mexico City and Paris whom he could not speak to directly, but only through a translator. The vast majority of leads were eliminated this way.

The woman in Cleveland was one of the few would-be Janes that Glover wanted to question personally. She did look like me, though the resemblance was not as close as these men seemed to believe (which is probably a good argument for more female detectives). She acted suspiciously: paid for everything with cash including rent and utilities, refused to provide (or could not provide) any ID to her landlord. A Cleveland PD detective—a lumpy, acne-scarred, take-no-shit old guy named David Poirier—knocked on her door pretending to be a building inspector, to avoid spooking her. She refused to allow him in, but Poirier was able to glance around the apartment from the doorway. To him, it looked as if she had not unpacked. She told him her name was Jane Setera; there was no record of a Jane Setera registered to vote or drive at that address. She seemed skittish. He suggested Glover get his ass out there before she took off. If she bolted, Poirier would have no way to detain her; she had not committed any crime.

When she opened the door to Glover and Poirier, she froze.

Glover held his badge wallet up for her. He announced they were police and wanted to speak with her. He was already searching her face.

She blinked at him a moment, too, his marred handsome face, then past his shoulder at Poirier, whom she seemed to recognize. She winced, apparently chiding herself for not seeing through Poirier's ruse earlier. When she came back to Glover, he was still gazing at her as if he recognized her, like an old friend or lover.

She had a thinner face than mine and good bones. She wore her hair short, like Mia Farrow, a style I would never have been able to pull off (I would have looked like a chipmunk with that hair). She did not look quite like me, but she did look—at least to their eyes—like a woman I might have become if I'd set my mind to it.

"May we come in?"

"No, you may not."

"We just want to talk.'

"I said no."

"You haven't done anything wrong. We're just trying to find someone."

"Who?"

"Someone who's lost."

"I don't know about anything like that."

"Good. Then this won't take long, and we'll leave and you'll never see us again. But if you won't help us, then we can't just leave you alone, you understand?"

She hesitated.

Glover stepped forward, into the doorway, gently forcing her to let go of the door and step back into the room. There was nothing aggressive in his action; it was more like a dance step than a forcible entry.

The room was grimy and small.

"You're Jane."

"Yes."

Glover had never seen me in person, only my photograph. In this woman's presence, he felt so close to me, so close.

"Is that your real name?"

"I don't really want to answer any questions. I think I have a right—"

"Look, I'm not going to tell you— We're not going to do this, okay? I came a long way to see you. You're not in trouble, you're not under investigation for any crimes, not by me. I don't care what you've done or what was done to you, whatever the reason is you're holed up here, I don't care. You understand? I don't care. I just need your help. I just need you to be straight with me for five minutes, and then I'm gone. I'm looking for someone. Okay?"

"Okay."

"I'm looking for a woman named Jane. She disappeared. She lived near Boston. That's where I'm from. This detective here thinks you might be her. He thinks you're my Jane."

"I'm not."

"Then who are you? What's your real name?"

"Jane Setera."

"Your *real* name."

"Jane Setera."

"Why are you here?"

"I can't tell you that."

"Why? Did you do something? Did you hurt someone?"

"No! Of course not. Someone hurt *me*."

"Who?"

"My husband."

"And where is he?"

"It doesn't matter."

"It does. Prove to me that you're being honest."

"Make him go." She nodded toward Poirier. "He lied. I don't trust him."

"Okay. Dave?"

Poirier left, tactfully clicking the door shut behind him.

"Who's the woman you're looking for?"

"Why does it matter?"

"I want to know."

"Her name is Jane Larkin."

"What did she do?"

"Nothing."

"Then why are you looking for her?"

"Because she's missing."

"Someone hurt her?"

"I don't know."

"But you think I'm her."

"I think she's dead, actually. But you might be her, yes."

"Why do you think she's dead?"

"It's just a feeling."

"Who killed her?"

"Her husband."

"If you think she's dead, why are you here?"

"Because I have . . . doubt. I need to know."

"Does she have kids?"

"Yes, three. Do you?"

"If I had kids, they'd be here with me."

"Can you show me an ID?"

"No, I trashed it."

"How old are you?"

"Thirty-eight."

"What's your real name?"

"Margaret."

"Margaret what?"

"Margaret Ann Furman."

"Is that your maiden name?"

"No. Daugherty."

"Husband's name?"

"Michael."

"What's his middle name?"

"He doesn't have one."

Glover's eyes narrowed.

"Really. It's true."

"Where were you born?"

"Long Branch, New Jersey."

"What hospital?"

"Monmouth Medical Center."

"Date of birth?"

"Five, eighteen, thirty-eight."

"What's your sign?"

"Taurus."

Her answers were swift, pointed, specific.

"What's the name of your grade school?"

"Garfield."

"First grade teacher?"

"Miss Phillips."

"Who was your best friend in first grade?"

"Sandra."

"Sandra what?"

"She was Levine then."

"Where does she live now?"

"Asbury Park."

"What's her name now?"

"Stancill. S-T-A-N-C-I-L-L."

"What's your birth date?"

"I already told you."

"Tell me again."

"Five, eighteen, thirty-eight."

"What high school did you graduate from?"

"Long Branch High School."

"Year?"

"Fifty-five."

"Are you in the yearbook?"

"Yes."

"What's the date of your marriage?"

"June 12, 1960."

"Where did the wedding take place?"

"Newark."

"Where?"

"At the Essex Hotel."

"Did you get a marriage license?"

"Yes."

He nodded. It was the wrong Jane. He would check out her answers later—have someone look up her yearbook page, pull her birth certificate and marriage license—but it didn't matter. He already knew. By then, she would have disappeared anyway.

"There's one other thing. Jane Larkin has a scar, on her right shoulder, here." He reached his left hand across his chest to point at the back side of his shoulder.

The woman stepped close to him, looked at him in a frank, unembarrassed way, and she unbuttoned her blouse enough to slip it off her shoulder and turn her shoulder so Glover could see her unmarked skin.

MIRANDA went on a Friday afternoon to Mrs. Bowers's house where, with the two little Bowers daughters, they baked chocolate chip cookies, an activity Mrs. Bowers contrived as a test for Miranda, to see how she might work out as a babysitter. It was all so intoxicating for Miranda. The afternoon *flew* by. Miranda loved *everything* about the Bowerses, she decided. She loved the bright, clear light of their house, particularly the gleaming, modern kitchen with its brushed-steel appliances. She loved baking cookies, which was an activity I used to do with her. She felt an instant kinship with the two little girls, shining children of seven and nine who looked up to Miranda as an elder in a way she had never felt before. It was as if she had entered a mirror image of her own family, sunny and bright where hers felt secretive and clouded.

Most of all, she could not help loving Mrs. Bowers. To Miranda, she looked less and less like me physically as the afternoon wore on, but it did not matter. She reminded Miranda of her mother anyway, in some mysterious, inarticulable way. Miranda felt a daughterly devotion to this woman, which she knew was unreasonable, crazy, but which gave her such a delirious high that she had no wish to talk herself out of it. She watched Mrs. Bowers in a sly way, when she thought her spying would not be seen, and she noted every move: the way Mrs. Bowers tucked her hair behind her ear, the way her eyes squinted when she smiled. These were mannerisms Miranda would adopt herself.

When the cookies went into the oven and the bowls and dishes were all piled into the sink, the two girls pulled up kid-size chairs in front of the oven and sat down to watch them bake, as if the oven window were a TV.

Miranda bustled around the girls, a happy little hen, displaying the sort of motherly concern that she imagined babysitters ought to have, until Mrs. Bowers said, "Come, Miranda, I want to have a little talk with you."

They went to the front of the house, to a living room that managed to be formal but not forbidding. They sat, Mrs. Bowers in a chair, Miranda on an adjacent couch, so that their knees nearly touched.

"Well," Mrs. Bowers said, "the girls clearly adore you. You have two new friends."

"I like them too."

"If you'd like to sit for them sometime, of course we'd love to have you. I think you're wonderful."

Miranda beamed for her.

"There is one thing, though. I need to ask you, sweetheart— I know . . . what happened."

"Oh."

"So I need to ask you: Are you okay? I mean, are you able to do this?"

"Yes."

"Does your father know about this? About us?"

"Not yet. I thought . . ." Her voice trailed off.

Mrs. Bowers looked down at the floor. She knitted her fingers together and squeezed them until the knuckles whitened a little.

"We're going to have to make one rule. There's always rules, aren't there?" Phony grown-up smile. "Your father can never come here. Not to this house, not even to the driveway to pick you up. If you need a ride, we'll pick you up and we'll bring you back home."

"I understand."

"I don't mean to hurt your feelings."

"It's okay."

"Is it, Miranda?"

"Yes. I don't mind."

"I'm sorry. But it's a strange situation."

"I know."

"Of course you do. I'm sorry." She took Miranda's left hand in hers, raised it, and kissed it.

Miranda was quiet. She was aware of the stain on her and that she should be grateful when generous people like Mrs. Bowers accepted her anyway.

"It's okay," Miranda said. "My mother has a rule—had a rule—that my father's clients weren't allowed to come to our house. They were bad people sometimes."

"I'm not saying your father is a bad person, Miranda."

"Yes, you are."

"No, sweetie. It's just complicated, isn't it? Life is complicated sometimes."

"Yeah."

1958–1961

I was married! I was a *wife*! Of course, we were both so young—I was twenty-one on my wedding day, Dan was twenty-two—that it was a laugh to call ourselves these things, *husband, wife, Mister, Missus*. We were kids playing house, tourists in Marriageland. It was the happiest I've ever been. When I was a little girl, of course I imagined being married, but it was all so dreamy and vague. So much depends on the boy, doesn't it? Now I had a boy—the best boy, the *perfect* boy for me—and the dream was real. I had a husband!

Our first home was a one-bedroom apartment in Brighton, which was tiny and gloomy and made us deliriously happy. We ate our meals in the kitchen. We played cards with a few other young couples, boozy games of gin rummy and canasta, always for money, that ran late into the night and left us all hungover and cigarette-smoky the next day. There was sex, too, fumbling, tentative, electric sex. In theory we were trying to get pregnant; the reality was that we were exploring the whole messy, mysterious business—the squelch and stink of it, the ravenous, jointed squirming—and it made us both go a little crazy. Danny could not get enough of me, could not keep his hands off. "You're a greedy boy," I used to tell him. We were not as expert as kids today or as brutal, but we had each other, we had such *trust*. Our bodies fit together, we were so perfectly paired *mechanically,* that I could not imagine ever being with another man or him with another woman.

We had been married less than a year when I got pregnant with Alex, and the whole euphoric interlude came to an end.

Still just kids ourselves, we moved to the suburbs to play at being parents. We bought an adorable little three-bedroom brick house in Newton. The down payment came from Dan's parents. They called it a loan, but Dan assured me we would not have to pay it back, and he shooed away my objections. He was always able to finesse the money politics of his family, which I could never fathom. Anyway, the Larkins' money was the Larkins' problem. I had my own family to build. Once we moved in, I launched into getting my new house ready for my new baby—scrubbing, painting, decorating.

But things were different. The jump to the suburbs altered my marriage in some weird way. We had moved only a few miles, but we were never the same after settling in Newton. Maybe we were *too* settled, too content. Or maybe the fizzy first year of a marriage is meant to subside, like day-old champagne. Maybe that is the whole reason the newlywed period is so happy: it cannot last. In any case, we never got back the bliss of those first months when we were newlyweds. Danny did not like what pregnancy did to my body. Neither did I. The doctor told me the more weight I put on, the harder it would be to take off after I had the baby, so I starved myself to stay skinny. It did not work. I watched helplessly as my belly and butt expanded. Even my feet and ankles swelled up. I felt like a balloon. My new husband lost interest in sex pretty quickly, but he was attentive in every other way, maybe even more than before, doting on his pregnant wife in adorable, old-fashioned ways. He called me "little mother."

It was around this time that Dan decided to go into law. It was what he wanted—Dan was no businessman—and his way was blocked at Coachman Shoe anyway. Dan's father had walked away from the company, and now a crowd of uncles and cousins stood to inherit control.

As it turned out, Coachman was about to enter a long, steady decline. In the 1960s and '70s, shoe manufacturing mostly moved overseas. Fashions drifted away from the formal styles that Coachman was known for. The company—led by all those uncles and cousins—could not adapt.

Of course, Coachman's problems affected us too. The Larkins' fortune was tied to the company's stock. By 1975, when I vanished, my in-laws were well-off but no longer rich. There would be no pot of gold for Danny and me. That was fine, I thought. We could make our own way, and no one could accuse me of gold-digging now. Even Danny took morbid pleasure in watching the company struggle. He felt his father had been treated shabbily there, and Danny always liked a good grudge. He couldn't help himself.

But I'm getting ahead of myself.

Back in '58 when Danny and I were first married, all we knew was that Danny had no future in business. He was free to follow his heart. So he ran up the pirate's flag and went into criminal law.

He attended law school at BU at night. Days, he worked for a rascally lawyer named Ronnie Collins, which was Danny's real legal education. Every night he came home with a new story. The one where Ronnie had his client's hair dyed before trial to foil a cop who had described him as gray-haired. The one where Ronnie split the seam in the seat of his pants but gave a theatrical closing argument anyway, pacing back and forth to make sure the jury saw the flash of his underpants, like a bunny's tail. Or the one where Ronnie picked his nose during the prosecutor's closing argument to distract the jury. Danny always said that everything he knew about trying a case, he learned from Ronnie Collins. But there was a difference: Ronnie was vulgar and Danny was not. Danny had good manners and good breeding, and in his own practice he would snare the wealthy clients who would not have considered a low-rent hustler like Ronnie Collins. But that was only a question of style. Under the surface, they were both pirates. With Danny it was just a little harder to tell.

So there it was. Life was good. Dan had found his life's work. I had a husband and a baby on the way. My God, we were happy.

AFTER I disappeared, Dan was happy with his girlfriend too. She moved into our house, and Dan was utterly blissful. A newlywed again.

Picture this:

One night the new, merged family sat in the den watching TV. Dan and Sarah on the couch, she with her feet crossed in Dan's lap. Jeff and Jamie in separate chairs. Miranda on the floor, on her stomach, chin propped in her hands.

Sarah moaned, "Mmm."

The three kids looked over to see Dan idly massaging his girlfriend's feet. Sarah with eyes closed, back arched. She was practically purring.

"Oh my God, gross," Jamie said. "*Ew.* Just stop."

Jeff made a retching sound.

The two of them fell out of the room together and up the stairs, with groans and eye rolls like soldiers under a mustard gas attack.

"What?" Sarah said. "What did we do?"

Dan shrugged.

"What about you, Mimi?" he said to the last child in the room. "Do you think we're gross too?"

"Kinda."

Miranda scrunched up her nose. It *was* gross. Not just the hint of sex. It was gross because Dan had never rubbed *my* feet when I was alive or demonstrated his affection so freely in any other way, at least in my daughter's presence. Now, by choosing Sarah, Dan was necessarily rejecting me, which meant—to trace the steps of Miranda's thinking—he was abandoning Miranda, too, since the little girl could not imagine herself as anything but my daughter. I was part of her. I was in her skin and her hair and her bones.

The thought of it—of losing her father now as well as her mother, of being truly parentless—stirred a familiar sadness in her. It was just a little fall at first, a fatal shift in mood. She dreaded this feeling, the bump, the first arrival of sorrow, like the first sniffles and sore throat that signal the onset of an illness. Once her dark moods started, she could not control them. Her body seemed to thicken and slow down, as if the blood was sludging in her veins. There was no choice but to ride it out, however long the gloom lasted, two or three days, sometimes more. She was young, but she already knew all this.

Dan should have known it too. He should have seen it in my baby's eyes. It was not complicated.

Miranda *wanted* him to see it, certainly, to sense her need and come for her.

But of course he did not. Miranda got up and left the room, and Dan never took his hands off his girlfriend's slim, lovely feet.

IT was not all sadness for Miranda, though. She was in love too. Her visits to the Bowers house a few blocks away became more frequent. After babysitting on a few Saturday nights, she began to go just to visit, often in the afternoon after school, preferring to sit with Mrs. Bowers rather than be at home alone or with Sarah. This became a routine. Miranda would bring homework or books to read, and she was always happy to play with the two little girls. Around five, when the family began to anticipate Mr. Bowers's return from work, Miranda would slip out, invariably to find her own home duller and sadder than the one she'd just left.

Mrs. Bowers allowed Miranda to come and go, at first with a little wariness, then with real love. If I could return to life even for a few hours, I would thank this kind woman for welcoming my quirky little girl in her home, especially with the shadow over our family. (You see, Jeff and Miranda? There *are* good people even in this story.)

How kind was she? Listen:

One afternoon Miranda found herself alone in the kitchen with Mrs. Bowers. The girls were playing four square in the driveway, and Mrs. Bowers occasionally went to the window to glance at them or she smiled at the sound of their voices. Miranda had been reading *Tess of the D'Urbervilles* but she'd put the book down beside her.

"Can I ask you something?" Miranda said.

"Sure."

"It's kind of personal."

"Okay."

"Do you think I need a bra?"

"A bra. Oh my. Well, let's see. You *could* wear a bra, I guess. Do *you* think you need a bra?"

"Sorta, yeah."

"Are other girls in your grade wearing bras?"

"Some are."

"Do you *want* to wear one?"

"Yes. I kind of—" She sat up straight, shoulders back, straining to look down at her own chest. "I think I'm sticking out. Am I?"

"No!" (This was not exactly true but bless her for saying it.)

"You look beautiful, Miranda! But if you'd feel better, then you could wear one. Why not?"

"Where should I get it?"

"Oh, any department store."

"Will you take me?"

"Me? It's your first bra. Don't you think it should be someone you know better?"

"I *want* it to be you. Anyway, no, there isn't anybody else."

"That can't be true. There must be somebody."

Mrs. Bowers did not know about Sarah, the quasi stepmother. Miranda had never shared that mortifying detail of her family story.

"What about your grandmother?"

Miranda actually chuckled at the thought of discussing boobs and brassieres with either of her grandmothers. My mother would make too much of it; Dan's mother too little.

"What about that aunt that you told me about?"

"Katie."

"What about Aunt Katie? I'm sure she'd take you."

"It would be weird. I'd have to call her just for this. I don't want people to talk about it. I want to just . . . do it."

"Oh. Okay." Mrs. Bowers made a concerned face. "I don't know, sweetie. It feels a little strange."

"Please. Please take me."

Mrs. Bowers smiled, relenting, indulgent. "All right, then."

"Yes! Thank you!"

Beaming, Miranda jumped up and ran to hug her. She wrapped both arms around Mrs. B's back and laid her head on the woman's shoulder, eyes closed, and squeezed her tight. In that moment, Miranda felt so much love for this woman and so much comfort in the press of her body against Miranda's—how perfectly they fit!—that she could not let go.

Mrs. Bowers returned the girl's hug, then relaxed her arms to signal it was time for the embrace to end. But when she understood that Miranda did not intend to let go, she pulled the girl in, kissed the top of her head, and laid her cheek down on the spot she'd just kissed. She must have found it impossible not to love Miranda, but she must have known, too, that that kiss was a mistake.

In my time, the kids had always done homework in their rooms. Dan insisted they needed quiet and solitude so they could concentrate. Personally, I always liked to have people around even when I was trying to focus, and I suspect the solitude did more harm than good. But Dan won, and it became the kids' habit to scatter to their rooms after dinner. They would emerge one by one, an hour or two later, bleary-eyed and starved for TV, when they had finished their work. Even Alex, who outgrew his little room by junior year—we used to joke that soon Alex would be so big he would have to back into his room like a hermit crab into its shell— still secluded himself there every evening until he graduated.

That all changed when Jamie moved in. She and Jeff began to do their homework together in the den. It seemed like a small thing. Jeff was being kind, changing his routine so that his new stepsister would not feel lonely in her new home. Jamie was in an odd situation socially, too, because she had not transferred to a school in Newton but stayed on at her old school to finish the year, which meant she had no friends in her new hometown.

One evening in early spring, Jeff was at the little card table in the den, struggling with his Latin, as he always seemed to. He had a bored look on his face—he was a teenager now but could still look just like a little boy—and his eyes wandered to Jamie. She was sitting on the couch with her legs crossed, books scattered around.

She sensed his gaze, raised her head. "What?"

"Nothing."

"Stop it."

"Stop what?"

"Staring."

"I'm not staring."

"What do you call it, then?"

"It's just where my eyes were pointed."

"Well, point them somewhere else."

"Like where?"

"Anywhere but me. Get back to work."

But he didn't look away. He couldn't.

And any girl would have known.

DANNY made good money as a lawyer right from the start, but he spent it as fast as he made it. He liked good things, expensive whiskey and wine, cigars, Rolexes, cars. He liked visiting New York to have suits custom made or to shop at Paul Stuart. He insisted we join his parents' golf club, which was so outlandishly expensive I begged him not to. My husband seemed ethereally unaware that money could ever run out.

It drove me crazy, and Danny knew it. At restaurants, he used to shoo me ahead so he could overtip the valet or the maitre d'. One restaurant host in particular—at Charley's in town—used to make a fuss over Danny and sneak us to the front of the line. He would come fetch us from the crowd and escort us through the bar right to an open table. Then Danny would swipe the tip into his hand with a gesture the two of them seemed to have practiced. "Always nice to see you, Mr. Larkin." To Danny it was all so ordinary, "A little grease, Jane, it's just the way things work." If I objected to any of his lavish spending, he had a stock answer: "It's my money. I made it. No one can tell me what to do with it."

He was so at ease, so complacent, that I began to think the crazy one was me. So after a while I stopped arguing. He was right: it *was* his money. He was making plenty. And what was the point of having it if not to spend it? So I spent too. I collected

Courrèges sweaters and Dior dresses and a Corum gold-coin watch. All our friends seemed to be doing the same: we spent every penny we had, and then some. Why save it? At some point, it no longer seemed strange when, despite all the money Danny was earning, we sometimes could not make the mortgage payment at the end of the month. Yet I knew, at the same time, that it was wrong. I *knew* it. I was not like Danny—I was acting, he was not.

One year—it must have been 1965, Miranda was a baby—we made a big mistake. We were living month to month as usual. Come April, we realized we had not set aside money to pay taxes. (Danny hated taxes, would not talk about them, considered them legalized theft.)

We went to his parents and asked for help. His mother said no. "You got into trouble, now you get out of it."

I was shocked. I could not imagine my own parents denying me help, no matter how irresponsible I'd been.

But Danny was more than surprised; he was furious. It never dawned on him that his mother's cool logic was just like his own. Even her peremptory judgment—*you got into trouble . . .* —could have come right out of Danny's own mouth.

Danny and his mother had a huge fight, and when we got home, he called her to scream some more, all to no avail.

After the kids were settled in bed, we sat in the kitchen trying to figure a way out.

Danny was seething. He was drinking Chivas on ice, the glass nearly filled.

We began to run through all the possible sources of quick money we could think of. Did Danny have clients with unpaid bills? Clients who might be willing to pay in advance, maybe in exchange for a discount? Danny suggested he had some clients, connected guys, who would lend us money, but we agreed it was a bad idea.

I said, "Your mother's right, you know. It's our own fault."

Danny's eyes burned. "Our own fault how?"

"How? Danny, come on. It's not like we didn't know tax day was coming. It's not like we never paid taxes before."

"We made a mistake, all right? It's a mistake. People make mistakes. That's different from what *she* did."

"What *she* did? Your mother? What did she do?"

"She knifed us."

"Oh, Danny, come on."

"She did. She knifed us right in the back. Don't you see that?"

"That's a little dramatic."

"Is it? Is it *dramatic*, Jane? Let me tell you something: we're in this position for one reason—my mother refused to help us."

"It's her money."

"No. It's family money. We're family too. We have a right to *some* of it, surely."

"No. Not a right."

"Jane, you don't get it. She's just holding it for us. It's not really hers."

"Well, it's hers for now."

"She didn't earn it, though, did she? So how is it hers? Like a fuckin' queen: *You got into trouble, now you can get out of it.* Fuck you! I go out and I *earn* my money. I hustle and I fight and I scratch and claw every day. Every fuckin' day. And what does she do? Did she earn that money? Did she?"

"No."

"No. So how is it hers? It's not."

"I don't know, Dan."

"You don't know?"

"Well, how is it yours?"

"Simple: I'm her son. Jesus, you're a pea-brain sometimes."

"Don't call me that. I'm not a pea-brain."

"Then stop talking like one."

A moment. Dan settled down. These little storms overtook him sometimes.

I said, sullenly, "We could sell one of the cars."

"We're not selling the cars. It wouldn't be enough anyway. The minute you drive them off the lot, they lose half their value."

"Well, there must be some money somewhere, Dan. It can't all be gone."

He got up with his drink, retreated to a corner of the room, leaned against the counter. "I do have some money I could get to."

"You do?"

"Clients' money. I'm just holding it. I could borrow from that. Nobody'd ever know."

"What happens if you get caught?"

"I get disbarred."

"Forget it."

He frowned, reluctant. "I have some other money too. Some cash."

"Cash? Where?"

"Banks."

"No, you don't. I see all the statements, I balance the check-book."

"It's not a bank account. I mean actual cash. In safe-deposit boxes."

"You have—what? You have cash in safe-deposit boxes? Why?"

"For a rainy day."

"Why didn't you tell me? All this worry and fighting was for nothing?"

"It's *my* money."

"It's *money*, Dan. That's what we need now, is money. Why would you hide that?"

"It's not completely"—he searched for a word that was opaque, diplomatic, but even here he could not allow himself the imprecision—"legal."

"Oh no, Danny. What are you up to?"

"Nothing. I have some clients that like to pay me in cash."

"And you don't want to pay the taxes."

"That's part of it."

"What's the rest of it?"

"Some of my clients aren't the nicest people. I don't ask where they get their money."

"You don't ask because you already know."

"Are *you* asking?"

"No."

"Okay then."

"Is there anything else you haven't told me about your clients?"

"Jane, this is my work. I'm a lawyer. There's no need to tell you every last detail. This is what it is."

"Okay. So we can use it to pay the taxes?"

"It's not that easy. There's some risk."

"Why? It's just attorneys' fees. You earned it, like you said."

"These aren't fees. I can't just put it in the bank."

"Jesus, Danny, what's going on?"

"Sometimes these guys need to put their money somewhere. They want to invest in something—a bar, a restaurant, maybe they want to buy a building, a laundromat, a parking lot, whatever. They want to invest, same as everyone else. Only it's more complicated for them. So I help them. We set up a little corporation or a trust, and we buy the building without their name on it. Or we put *my* name on it. That kind of thing."

"You mean money laundering."

"Listen to you, J. Edgar Hoover. I don't mean money laundering. It's just paperwork. I'm not doing anything illegal, Jane, believe me. I wouldn't do anything to endanger us, you know that."

"And yet you're hiding money in safe-deposit boxes."

"Well, I can't exactly walk into a bank and hand the teller a suitcase full of cash, can I?"

"There's no law against it."

"It's not smart."

He was bullshitting. And I was prepared to accept a little bullshit, I guess. Anything to get out from under.

"So we're going to pay the IRS with a suitcase full of cash."

"No. I'll manage it, don't worry. I'll scatter it around. It'll be okay."

"You're sure?"

"Yeah. Don't worry, I'll take care of it."

I never asked Dan how he got the money into our checking account. I assumed he went around to different branches making small deposits. I never asked him how much money he had stashed away, either. I chose not to know. All I can tell you is when tax day came, we wrote checks to the feds and to the Commonwealth of Massachusetts, and those checks did not bounce. That was enough for me.

There was one other thing. Listening to Dan, I got to thinking: Maybe he had a point. Maybe it would be smart for a girl to put away a little cash somewhere for a rainy day. A wife should have options, too, just like her husband. So I started to sock it away just like Danny. I called it my fuck-you money.

DRAW a circle around our house outside Boston, with a radius of around two hundred miles. That was the range, Detective Glover figured, that Dan could have traveled by car in ten unaccounted-for hours on the day of my disappearance. That circle covers an enormous area: New York City and most of New York State, all of Vermont and New Hampshire, and Maine almost as far north as Bangor. Somewhere in that area, he thought, my body must be hidden, in some shallow grave or lake bed or newly cemented basement.

Now, from the center of that circle, move your finger to the perimeter at about eleven o'clock, and you will be pointing at Trout Lake, Vermont.

Outside this town, there is a vast, dense old-growth forest.

For Glover, the theory that my body might be buried in these woods was intriguing. There had been a hazy report of a white Thunderbird like mine in the town on my last day, though the car was a popular model and color. It was also the only wilderness that he could connect Dan to—as far as Glover could find, the only rural area Dan knew at all. Our family had visited Trout Lake the summer before I disappeared. It was our family vacation that year. Dan had been in this forest before, and the detective doubted that such a meticulous man would risk this mission in an unfamiliar place. It was probably a coincidence—a white car, a family vacation. But what if?

Glover discounted the possibility that Dan would have sunk the body in the lake or in one of the smaller ponds nearby. Dan had no access to a boat and no experience with them, and he would not have wanted to involve anyone else. Also, on a lake in broad daylight there was a greater risk of being seen, and some risk that the body would not stay submerged. No, the forest, he figured, not the lake.

It did not add up to much, honestly. Glover knew it. But there was so little to go on. The one mistake he would not make was to give up too soon.

So, ten months after my disappearance, he came to check it out. He snooped around this tiny Vermont town, asking if anyone had seen Dan or either of our cars on November 12, 1975, or a few days before. (I disappeared on November 12, but Glover guessed that Dan might have come earlier to dig the hole, so he could get in and out quickly.) Of course nobody remembered anything. Too much time had passed.

He pulled credit card slips from gas stations in the area, at least the ones that kept them around, hoping to get lucky. He did not find anything. That also meant nothing; Dan would have been smart enough to pay cash.

The detective did track down the cabin that we'd rented, by the big lake. He even walked in the nearby woods a bit, searching the ground for irregular features, fresh dirt, breaks in the ground. These were impossible to find; the forest floor was irregular everywhere he looked, and the thick undergrowth would have covered any scars long before.

Imagine Tom Glover in those woods, the only one still looking for me. He must have understood the futility of coming up here. Another shot in the dark. But he did it anyway.

Now pan out, think again of that circle on the map, four hundred miles in diameter. From New York City to the Canadian border. And one man to search it.

Here's the thing: he was very, very close.

ONE Saturday around noon, Miranda wandered into the kitchen to find Sarah at the sink, putting the finishing touches on a cleanup. To accommodate Dan, this required that the sink itself be washed, Windexed, and dried after all the dishes were done, because he believed that "the sink is the last dish that you wash." This seemed to be what Sarah was doing as she swabbed the sink with a dish towel to prevent water spots.

That morning, Miranda was already in an unsettled mood. None of her "real" family was around, just Sarah and, somewhere in the house, Jamie. Miranda had spent the morning in her bedroom with the door closed, reading, listening to music on cassette tapes, daydreaming.

Sarah gave her a kindhearted smile. "Hi. You hungry? Can I make you something?"

Miranda adjusted her new bra, tugging down the elastic under her armpit with a now-familiar, peevish gesture.

Sarah seemed to notice Miranda's tic and her new bra, but she said nothing. "We have some nice turkey I just got."

"No, thank you."

"'No, thank you,' you're not hungry? Or 'no, thank you,' you don't want turkey?"

"I'm not really hungry."

"Are you okay?"

"Yeah."

Sarah dried her fingers with the dish towel but never took her eyes off Miranda.

"You're sure there's nothing I can do for you?"

"No." Miranda's tone was a little puzzled but not hostile.

Sarah came over to Miranda and stood in front of her. "I'm not so bad, you know."

"I know."

"You could give me a chance."

"Okay."

Sarah leaned forward and hugged Miranda, laying her chin on the girl's shoulder.

Miranda stiffened. She became aware of Sarah's perfume and of her own breathing, in, out, in, out, and her spine rigid as a broomstick.

Sarah moved back but kept her hands on Miranda's arms, a gesture of warmth.

This was as close to Sarah as Miranda could remember being. Up close, the impact of Sarah's beauty was blunted. You could disassemble her appearance into its component parts: lean face, blond hair, fragile nose, sinewy neck, blue-gray eyes. There was something else, too, behind all that—a thrumming tension about her, like a wire pulled taut—and this Miranda did not think was so pretty at all.

Miranda felt nothing at all for her. No anger or hostility, no warmth or pity. She could not remember ever feeling this flat, wooden response to anyone. A bundle of unruly emotions, like a bag of angry cats—that had always been Miranda. She was disappointed in herself at feeling so little, since Sarah was reaching out to her with obvious kindness. But it was easier to feel too little than too much, it was a luxury to be indifferent.

"Okay," Sarah said. "I just wanted you to know."

"Know what?"

"Just that—I don't know. I'd just like us to be friends someday, that's all."

"'Kay."

"This must be hard for you. I know that. It's a difficult age anyway, isn't it? If you ever want to talk or you have a problem, I'm here, okay?"

Miranda squinted. She could not quite make out what problem Sarah was referring to. My disappearance? The bra? Something else?

"Because I'm a mother, too, right?"

"Yeah."

"Only I'm not the right mother, am I?"

"No."

"No. I suppose not. Okay, well. That's all I wanted to say."

Miranda turned and stepped softly back up the stairs to puzzle over all this, having completely forgotten why she'd gone down to the kitchen in the first place: for lunch.

For years, they would both wonder what they should have said, whether it would have made any difference. Miranda still does.

A few days after Miranda's odd conversation with her quasi stepmother—too soon for coincidence—Dan did a strange thing: he came to the Bowers house one Friday night to pick up Miranda from babysitting. He had never done that before. The timing of his arrival was odd too. Mr. and Mrs. Bowers had come back from a restaurant only a minute or two earlier when they heard Dan's car horn.

The nasal, European *meep* of Dan's Mercedes was not expected, so they did not immediately respond.

In the kitchen, Mrs. Bowers was asking Miranda how the evening had gone, as she fished in her purse for five dollars to pay Miranda.

In the front hall, Mr. Bowers was taking off his sport coat and rolling up his sleeves. He was always a little irritable and standoffish around Miranda, which made her feel—as it was intended to make her feel—like an interloper, an unwelcome guest. Understandably, she tried to avoid him. Here, though, he was keeping his distance for a simpler reason: he was tired, a little drunk, and did not want to be bothered with the oddball babysitter his wife had dug up somewhere. He just wanted Miranda out of the house so he could take off his shoes, flop down on the couch, and release an enormous fart that he'd been brooding like a hen.

When the horn sounded again—*meep-meep*—Miranda knew what it was, and she knew it was trouble. The one rule of babysitting here—that her father was forbidden—came straight from Mr. Bowers. Miranda understood as much without being told.

He said, "What the— Who is that?"

More sounds: Mr. Bowers going to the window, the car door opening and closing, footsteps on the stairs, the doorbell.

Miranda came out to the front hall as Mr. Bowers was opening the door.

In the doorway, Dan looked up at Mr. Bowers, who was burlier and much taller. Dan wore a bland, pleasant expression, as if unaware that his presence might be provocative. "Is Miranda here?"

Mr. Bowers opened the door wider so Dan could see his daughter. "Who are you?"

"Dan Larkin." Hand extended. "Glad to meetcha."

Ignoring the hand: "I don't appreciate you being here."

"Daddy, I *told* you."

"I know, I'm sorry. I just thought I'd save Miranda the walk. Anyway, I've wanted to meet you two. I feel like my daughter has a whole 'nother family!" Big smile, not returned. "I just wanted to say hello and thank you for being so nice. Come on, Mimi, let's get out of these people's way. It's getting late."

"Don't come here again. If I see you around here, I'm calling the cops."

"For coming to pick up my own daughter?"

"You heard what I said. Don't come back."

"Ah. Okay. Come on, Miranda, let's go."

Miranda hesitated, repelled by both men. She looked back at Mrs. Bowers, who stood a few feet behind her.

"It's all right, Miranda," she said. "Do as your father says."

Miranda gave her a brief hug goodbye and whispered, "I'm so, so sorry. I told him not to come, I promise. I *told* him."

Mrs. Bowers patted her on the back. "You better go."

Mr. Bowers stepped back to make a path for Miranda, who slipped past him. He said to Dan, "You stay away from my family."

With Miranda now safely in his possession, Dan put his hands into his pockets and said, with false innocence, "Well, I'd like to, but how can I stay away when you've got my daughter working here?"

Mr. Bowers felt a strong urge to throttle this little man—Dan had a way of inspiring this feeling—but his face betrayed nothing. He swung the heavy door shut, causing the pictures to rattle on the wall, then, for effect, he shot the dead bolt.

He said to his wife, "This ends now. This is over. I'm done talking. This is lunacy."

BACK in '75, there was a restaurant in the North End that Dan liked called the Scotch 'n Sirloin. We started going there before my exit, and afterward he kept right on going with his new pretend-wife. The restaurant was about what you would expect from a place called the Scotch 'n Sirloin: a steak house for guys, especially guys more interested in scotch than sirloin. We had fun there, Dan and I. It drew all kinds of people, hairy-handed goons with unbuttoned shirts all the way to manicured suburban professionals in suits, like Dan. It was a couple of blocks from Boston Garden, too, so it was always mobbed before and after Bruins and Celtics games.

One Friday night Dan took Sarah to a hockey game then to the Scotch 'n Sirloin. She hated hockey—hated all sports, really—but she was intent on pleasing him, so she went along. (I used to go along, too, for years. And I'll tell you what: I liked the games a lot more than Sarah did, especially the Bruins' wonderboy, Bobby Orr.)

The restaurant was crowded. Over the clatter, Dan was told there was a one-hour wait for a table. He slipped the maitre d' a little packet of folded bills, and he and Sarah went to the bar to wait, he anticipated, for a lot less than an hour.

Dan took Sarah's drink order (white wine, in a hockey crowd—oh, Sarah, you poor thing) and made his way through the crowd at the bar.

Waiting to catch the bartender's eye, he found himself next to a woman who appeared to recognize him. She did an obvious double take then stared right at him, without embarrassment. She wore a thin, strappy top despite the cold weather, revealing freckled shoulders. Her hair was feathered back like Farrah Fawcett's.

Dan sensed her eyes on him. He ignored her.

The woman said, "You're that guy, aren't you?" She had a thick Boston accent: *Yaw that guy, ahn-cha?*

"What guy is that?"

"Don't play dumb. You're the one that killed his wife."

"No. Sorry. You must be thinking of someone else."

"Yeah, okay, Mickey the Dunce, whatever you say."

He turned away. Smoothed his canary-yellow tie. Searched for the bartender.

"What's your name? Tell me."

"It's Dan."

"You here with someone, Dan?"

"Yeah."

"Who?"

"Never mind who. None of your business."

Dan finally caught the bartender's eye and ordered his drinks, a white wine and a vodka gimlet.

When he turned back to the woman, she was sliding a cocktail napkin across the bar toward him. "Here. Use it."

There was a phone number written on the napkin.

"That's for me?"

"No, it's for the guy next to you. Could you give it to him, please?" She shook her head. "Of course it's for you, knucklehead."

"You think I killed my wife, but you want to give me your number?"

She leaned in close and whispered, "You're a star."

"Not a very smart decision, is it?"

"You said you didn't do it."

"I didn't do it."

"So what's the problem?"

"What if I'm lying? How would you know?"

"Are you lying, Dan?"

"No."

The drinks arrived. He paid the bartender, stood waiting for the change.

"Does it bother your girlfriend that you might be lying?"

"Who says I have a girlfriend?"

"You said you're here with someone. She ever ask you if you're lying? You know she's thinkin' about it, climbin' into bed with you every night."

"She doesn't have to ask. She knows me."

"You don't know what she knows, *Dan*."

The bartender dropped the change on the bar next to the napkin. Dan picked up the bills, tossed a couple back down on the bar as a tip. Hesitated. Picked up the napkin, folded it once, enclosing the phone number, and slipped it into his pocket. Left without looking at her.

When Dan handed the glass of wine to Sarah, she said, "Friend of yours?"

"No. Some woman."

"What did she want?"

"My autograph."

"Did you give it to her?"

His eyes had been scanning the room but now he looked at her. "No."

"You want to go back and finish your conversation?"

"No." But his eyes quivered, as if drawn to other, more promising things: the crowd, the bar. He had to point his eyes at Sarah consciously and hold them there. "Of course not."

It was a look I had seen on Dan's face more than once. Sarah must have guessed as much.

ONE afternoon, Miranda steeled herself to ring the doorbell at the Bowers house, intending to apologize for bringing the wolf to their door. She was not allowed inside. Mrs. Bowers, in jeans and Tretorn tennis sneakers, slipped out to sit with my little girl on the front stairs. She explained, kindly but with no ambiguity, that Miranda could not come to their house anymore, not to visit, not to babysit, not to see the two girls, whom she loved like sisters and who loved her too. Miranda had the strange sense, which sometimes accompanies big moments, of doubleness, of stepping back to watch herself as she went through the conversation. She seemed to hear only snippets. A phrase would stick like a dart—"I have to put my family first," "nothing to do with you"—and she would not quite hear the next few sentences. "Please," Miranda begged, "just give me one more chance. It will never happen again. I swear. I'll talk to him. I'll make him promise."

There is no sense dwelling on this moment, or the days and weeks that followed. My daughter just broke. You will have to imagine the aftermath, the twelve-year-old girl in tears. As a mother, I just can't go there with you. This, not my disappearance, was the low point for Miranda. My going away had been an uncertain, unfinished thing, with no clear beginning or end. This was definitive. She was alone now. The full weight of her loss, her unmothering, became clear. Miranda remembers the moment to this very day, sitting on the moldering wood steps in front of that house as Mrs. Bowers explained, "Sweetie, I can't be that for you." Picture it all if you want to. I'm going to look away.

WE had dinner once with Katie and her husband. This was, oh, a year or so before I disappeared. I remember it for two reasons. The first was that Dan made an ass of himself at dinner. We went through two bottles of wine, most of which Dan drank, since Katie and her husband, Stephen, were not big drinkers. But it was not just the wine that made Dan so obnoxious that night. By then, he was different from the boy I had married. Not in any shocking or unpredictable way—far from it; the Dan Larkin of 1973 or '74 was a natural evolution of the boy I had met at Brookline High, who felt so free to spill his commas all over my letter to the editor of *The Sagamore*. He wore his hair and his sideburns longer, and his shirt open one or two more buttons, but the biggest difference was that, at thirty-eight, he had found the persona he would inhabit as an adult, the character he would play: arrogant, argumentative, pontificating, scrappy.

He and Katie were oil and water, always had been. Their tangling never seemed to bother either of them. Katie was serene in a conflict—she seemed to give Dan's opinions no more weight than she would a teenager's—and Dan was positively radiant when debating. But I always hated it. I wanted them to get along, if only because I needed to have my sister around and I was always afraid Dan's occasional boorishness would keep her away, that sooner or later he would go too far even for her.

It was after the meal when the trouble started. The four of us around my dining room table, lethargic from a meal I had labored over from *The Joy of Cooking*. At the head of the table, Dan slouched in his chair. He had brought a bottle of Chivas to the table and insisted that Stephen join him in drinking a glass. Dan had slipped off his fancy two-tone silver-and-gold watch and was turning it idly in his hand.

The talk had turned to marriage. There had been a rash of divorces in our circle at the time, and the natural life span of marriage was on our minds.

After gossiping about a couple we knew—a man who had left his wife abruptly—Dan said, "I think all married men are a little unhappy, secretly, at least the ones who marry young."

"Like you?" Kate said. "You married young."

"Not me in particular. Just generally. I think it's common. It makes perfect sense. We marry too young. All of us men. Before we've sown our oats. Don't you think so, Stephen?"

"No, I do not."

"How old are you?"

"Forty-one."

"And you don't feel any . . . ambivalence?"

"About my marriage? About my wife? Of course not. I mean, I feel like—you know, I wish I was *younger*, but I don't have any regrets about my marriage. It's the one thing I've done right."

Kate clasped her hands over her heart and pretended to swoon. I said, "Aw."

"You're not being honest. I get it. Kate's here; I understand."

"Actually I'm being perfectly honest."

"Well, let's put it this way: I know lots of guys—not me, just guys like me, not old but not young anymore either—and they're all feeling this way. Is this all there is? Is this all I get?"

Stephen: "'Is this all I get?' Around here? These people have everything—fancy cars, fancy watches, fancy houses, fancy schools. And they're bitching about 'Is this all I get?'"

"Maybe they shouldn't feel that way, but they do. They're unhappy."

"Unhappy? Because they're getting old? Tell them to grow up! This is life! Enjoy it, it'll be over soon enough."

"Okay, right, but isn't that the point? Life is short. They're starting to realize that. Time is starting to run out."

"Time is short for everyone, Dan."

"But not equally. We don't *feel* it the same way, men and women. I'm just being honest here. The men I know— Okay, think of it like this: A young man is like a rising stock, like IBM or Coke. And the stock gets sold too soon, while it's still going up. So what happens? The guy looks around, eight, ten, fifteen years later, and what does he say? He says, 'I sold too low. I should have held out. I'm worth more than I got.'"

Kate: "So the woman, in your little metaphor, she's a sinking stock. She's worth less, eight or ten years in."

"No, well—what she's *worth*—well, yes. But look, this isn't just me talking, this is society, this is what we're taught. And let's be honest, if we're looking at men and women as a marketplace, as assets, in purely economic terms, then yes, our society assigns a higher value to a young, sexy woman than to a middle-aged mother."

Me: "Middle-aged!"

"Not you, Jane! I'm not talking about you."

Stephen laughed out loud. He was lanky, wry, soft-spoken, detached. "Dan," he said, "I advise you to stop now."

"Stop? Are you crazy? I'm just getting started." A little grin. "No, the point is just—again, in purely economic terms—a woman is sold closer to her peak value than a man. Before she begins to depreciate. And her peak value comes earlier than a man's does. That's all I'm saying. I don't know what there is to argue about. These are just facts."

Me: "Oh, good Lord."

Kate: "So does it matter that the *reason* for the woman's depreciation is that she spent all those years giving birth and changing diapers and cleaning your house and washing your clothes, while you went off to work so you could . . . appreciate?"

"In economic terms, no, it doesn't matter, because the market doesn't care. It looks at a woman and sees what it sees."

"And of course by 'the market,' you mean 'men.' *Men* look at women and see what they see."

"I didn't invent the system, Kate, I'm just describing it."

"Janie, I'm so sorry to hear about your depreciation. You must feel terribly depreciated right now."

"Oh, believe me, I do."

"And here you are with a husband whose value has skyrocketed! You lucky thing."

"I'm a lucky gal."

Stephen sat up, with a professorial, inquisitive expression. "So, Dan, if your market theory is right, then isn't this an inefficiency that costs the woman more than the man? You seem to be assuming that, if this middle-aged couple were to divorce—"

Me: "Would you stop saying middle-aged!"

Stephen: "Yes, sorry, right. If this couple—of indeterminate age—were to divorce, you're assuming the man would then reenter the market at a higher value than the woman, whose stock has fallen. But that's not how markets work. In a real market, the woman bought low because there was some risk built into the price of her husband's stock. The young man she married might have turned into a bum, his stock might have tanked. She took the risk, now she's entitled to the upside. Why doesn't she get to keep the profit?"

"Well"—Danny smirked—"I never said it was a perfect metaphor."

There was laughter. This is as close as Dan could get to backing down.

Kate said, "The scary thing is I'm not completely sure you're kidding."

"I'm not kidding."

"Oh, Danny. Allow me to save my husband from himself—of course he's kidding."

Dan tried, finally, to gauge his audience's reaction. "Of course I'm kidding," he said, with a mischievous expression. He looked around the table at each of us. Three against one. "Of course I'm kidding."

I told you this dinner was memorable because Dan made an ass of himself. That is true but it's not the whole story. I did not care about Dan's stupid theory of men and women as shares in a human stock exchange; I had heard him say similar things before. What really made the evening stick in memory was Katie and her husband's reaction. Their forced smiles, the knowing glances they exchanged. I understood. I got a glimpse of Dan as they saw him. Not amusing; obnoxious. Not witty and bracingly honest, as Dan saw himself; just crude and unkind. It made me ashamed, as if I had let down my big sister. I could almost hear them talking in the car on the way home: "How does she stand it? How does she put up with him?" Earlier in my marriage, I might have been defensive, I might have tried to see my husband in a more generous light. But that night I knew—that is, I *felt,* deep in my bones—that they were right. My husband had turned into a man I did not like.

Worse—much worse—I understood, finally, that my husband did not love me.

We got to bed late that night, after Katie and I cleaned up the kitchen.

Sitting up, my back resting on the headboard, I watched as Dan got ready for bed. He strutted from the bathroom to his closet, folded his sweater-vest, and hung up his slacks carefully, all the while whistling under his breath, evidently unaware of how our guests had perceived his little performance that night.

"Do you really think I'm a sinking stock?"

"Hm? Oh, *pfft.*"

"Do you think I've lost value?"

"I think we're all getting older, we're all losing value. You and me both."

"But that's not what you said. You said men actually gain value as they get older. Their stock goes up."

"Well, it does, generally. Men are the breadwinners, and at our age everyone knows which ones win the bread and which ones don't. That's all."

"And my stock?"

"I like your stock, Jane. You're reading too much into it. We were just talking."

"I don't know if I believe you. Let me ask you something. If we weren't married, if we were both single and we met at a party or something, would you be interested in me? Am I a woman you'd go after?"

"Jane, of course I'd go after you. Every time I see you, I see the girl I met in high school. How could I not go for that?"

"No, but if we'd never met before, if you were just meeting me for the first time now, as we are. You wouldn't, would you? Because your stock is higher than mine. That's what you mean, isn't it?"

"It's not the same thing. Because I did meet you a long time ago. I couldn't meet you for the first time today."

"I know, but *if*."

"I don't know, Jane. It's a pointless discussion."

"I don't think so. I don't think it's a pointless discussion."

He smiled and shrugged. That was his answer.

It is hard to believe the night could actually get worse from here, but it did.

To my surprise, Danny reached for me in bed that night. I was hopeful enough, or dumb enough, to think he might be trying to make up for his comments or to make me feel better. When you have known a man as long as I'd known my husband, maybe you are slow to see changes, maybe you still see the boy rather than the man who has displaced him. Also, I was concerned about how little sex we were having. So I was glad he touched me, I did not want to say no, even if I was tired and not especially eager. I went along. I allowed him to maneuver me onto my knees so he could bash away at me from behind, a position I hated but Dan preferred. After a while, he began to poke himself into my rear end. We never did it that way, and I never wanted to. At first, I thought he had just lost his focus or was making a kind of invitation. I moved away, I said no. He whispered, "Let's try it." When he tried again, I pulled forward, away from him, lying flat. "Stop it! What's wrong with you?" He said, "What's wrong with *you*?" Then he got on top of me and he did it anyway. I did not scream because the kids were in the house, though when he first pushed his way in, I yelped—high-pitched, an animal sound—and he clamped his hand over my mouth but he did not stop.

When it was over, I was too shocked to be angry. I was not sure what it meant, how to think about it. I went downstairs to get away from him.

Danny came down, puzzled at first that I was so upset, then

annoyed that he would have to stay up to comfort me, then insulted that I did not want him near me—that I was being ungrateful for his gallantry in coming to console me. So he went back upstairs.

I tried to convince myself it was not a big deal. Just a bad night, he'd been drinking, things went too far, it happens between husbands and wives. But a few days later, when I could not stand the secret anymore, I told Katie what he had done. She said it was rape; I said it was not. Neither of us even considered reporting it to the police. She said I should leave him, that's what she would have done.

I did not leave him, of course. I stayed. As time went by, the incident sort of felt like a dream, you know? Like I might have imagined the whole thing, and I was glad I had told Katie just so I had someone to confirm my own memory of it, to tell me I wasn't crazy. Anyway, I decided it was best forgotten. I had three children, so I stayed. I never talked about it again, and I swore Katie to secrecy too.

But everything was broken after that. I thought I could put it back together again somehow. I was wrong.

A hundred years after she was shut out of the Bowers home—or maybe only a few weeks; Miranda lost track of time for a while—my little girl trudged to the lake, a block from the house. It was August now, end of summer, always a mournful season for her. The day was so thick with humid heat, you could hear the air ticking like a hot oven.

At the lake there were some older kids, teenagers lounging in the grass in their bathing suits. The braver girls wore bikinis. The boys eyed them like predators.

Miranda took a seat on a bench in the shade, as far from the sunbathers as possible. She wished she'd brought a book, not to read it but to wall these people out. Her sadness made the sight of happy people infuriating, isolating, as if the world were a big, rollicking party that she was not invited to. Yet she still wanted to be near them, to spy on the party.

A policeman came to stand by her bench. He wore a short-sleeve navy blue summer uniform and Ray-Ban aviators.

Miranda looked up. There was no mistaking him, the blot on his forehead. "It's you," she said.

"It's me. You mind if I sit here?"

"It's a free country."

Tom Glover sat down at the very end of the bench, leaving a wide space between them. He took off his glasses, folded them, put them in his shirt pocket.

Miranda: "What are you doing here?"

"Working."

"Here? Doing what?"

"Watching the lake."

"In case someone tries to steal it?"

He smiled. "In case someone tries to jump in."

"They're not supposed to jump in?"

"They're supposed to go over to the swimming area, where the lifeguards are. It's safer. They're not supposed to jump in here."

"Everybody jumps in here."

"I know."

"Why don't you stop them?"

"It's too hot. I'm not gonna hassle a bunch of kids for swimming."

"But you just said it's against the law."

"True." He folded his arms, stretched out his legs in the direction of the lake, and slid down on the bench a little. "You think I should arrest 'em all? Or just shoot 'em?"

"I just figured, if it's a rule . . ."

"Well, I don't think we'll descend into anarchy if a few kids jump in the lake."

She turned to look at him. His uniform with the Newton Police shoulder patch, polished black shoes. He looked handsome in it.

He said, "How come you're not swimming?"

"Don't feel like it."

"You don't like swimming?"

"No, I just don't feel like it right now."

A beat.

"You doing okay, Miranda?"

"No."

"You want to tell me what's going on?"

"No. I don't really feel like talking."

"Okay."

They sat awhile, watching the party. Laughter, chatter, splashing.

"You're not going to find her, are you?"

"I don't know."

"That's not what you said before."

He grunted. "I'm still looking."

"I know you won't find her. It's okay. You don't have to lie."

"Why do you think we won't find her?"

"I just don't believe him anymore."

"Your father, you mean."

No response.

"Why don't you believe him?"

"I just don't."

"Did something happen?"

Miranda thought of her dad standing in the doorway of the Bowers home and their reaction to him. But she did not want to tell Glover about this because she did not want to get anyone in trouble; and she did not want to admit to Glover that she had betrayed her own mother by falling in love with Mrs. Bowers; and, most important, she did not want to confess that when she saw how frankly terrified the Bowerses were of her father—how they *hated* him, how they were *sure* what he had *done* and what he *was*—she had seen him as they did and she knew they were right. All of it was literally unspeakable. So she said simply:

"Everybody thinks he did it."

"Do you?"

"Yes."

He turned his head toward her but said nothing.

"I didn't used to think it, but now I do. I changed my mind."

He stretched his arm across the back of the bench and contacted her shoulder briefly, cautiously, then pulled it back and refolded his arms.

"I just want my mom back. But I know I can't have that, so I just need to get used to it."

"You'll never get used to it."

"How do you know?"

"I lost my father when I was young."

"He died?"

"No, he just left. My parents split up, then we didn't see him anymore."

"Is that why you want to find my mom so bad?"

"I don't know. I don't think so."

"Why do you care so much, then?"

"Maybe 'cause of you."

"But you don't even know me."

"Of course I do. A little. Is there anything you want to tell me, Miranda?"

The girl said nothing.

"Well, we don't have to talk." He looked at her. "If you don't feel like it."

"Okay."

"I'll just sit here with you, make sure nobody bothers you."

"Can I ask you something? When your father left, how did you know he wasn't coming back?"

"I'm not really sure. I guess it's like you said: I just didn't believe in him anymore. I waited and waited, and then one day I just stopped."

"Oh."

Glover put his sunglasses back on and looked out at the lake, the swimmers, sunbathers. "Goodness, it's hot," he said.

Oh my, this is a sad story, isn't it? I must be *tormenting* you. And things are about to get much worse, I'm afraid. But there were happy moments.

Here is my Jeff, in love:

It was around midnight. Jeff and Jamie were on the living room couch, making out with such passion they seemed to be devouring each other. Is it weird for me, the boy's mother, to say these two young people were beautiful together? Well, I don't care. Because my son, who had been lost, was so happy with this girl in this moment. As they kissed, he kept smiling, and his smiles interrupted the kissing, and that made her smile, too, and he had to force himself to relax his lips enough to go on kissing this pretty girl, this girl who felt to him like a gift from heaven, a gift that he did not deserve. What Jeff was feeling was not just teenage horniness—though there was plenty of that, I'm sure. It was *wonder*.

They kissed silently because they didn't want to wake up the sleeping house. The relationship was a secret. It had to be, because of their parents, the weirdness of the arrangement, the possibility they might become brother and sister one day if Dan and Sarah were to marry. They couldn't bring themselves to talk about this, to use the words *brother* and *sister*, so they simply ignored the awkward fact, kept it secret from themselves, and all the secrecy made the affair even more electric because it was theirs alone. There was no audience for it, they were not performing love for anyone but each other. Only they knew, only they understood. They were two alone.

On this night, though, they were not alone.

Dan was watching from the doorway, in the shadow of the hallway, in stocking feet. Watching his son. More intently, he was watching Jamie, who twisted her body to meet Jeff's mouth, whose T-shirt Jeff had lifted just enough to grip her torso on either side. There was a slack, almost sorrowful expression on Dan's face. He must have been impressed that his son had fooled him. Jeff, who was so lazy and sloppy in so many things, had been so disciplined in this.

But it was Jamie, not Jeff, who commanded Dan's attention. You must think Dan was just horny for this girl—who, yes, might have reminded him of me at a younger age. But I think his feelings were a little like Jeff's: he was not horny. What he felt was wonder, and yearning, not for the girl but for the passion she embodied, the possibilities. After all, Dan had once been the boy on the couch with a pretty girl in his arms, many years before. But all that was over for him now.

Somehow Jamie sensed Dan's presence. There had not been a sound, but she pulled back from Jeff and looked toward the door.

"Did you hear something?" she whispered.

"No."

"I think somebody's watching us."

"No way. They're asleep. Come on."

He pulled her back to him. In that moment, he did not care about the risk. My lost boy had found love. His only concern was *right now*—this moment, this girl, this ecstasy. The world had taken Jeff's mother but now it had begun to repay the debt, and maybe, just maybe, he would find his way home again.

THE last time I talked to my big sister, Kate, was the day before I disappeared, Tuesday, November 11, 1975. We spoke on the phone in the morning, as we often did, after we got our kids off to school and husbands off to work, and had a quiet moment to ourselves in our empty houses. It was our sister time. Katie was not a big phone talker generally. She was always doing something else while we chatted—reading the paper, clearing the dishes, smoking a cig, with the phone clamped between her ear and her shoulder. She had one of those princess wall phones with an extra-long cord, and you could tell when she was moving around the kitchen as we spoke. Her attention would drift in and out. So I usually did most of the talking, which, she liked to say, was my greatest talent.

ALL THAT IS MINE I CARRY WITH ME   163

There was no one better to talk to. She was the smartest person I ever knew. She always knew what to do, she always knew the right answer. I was unlucky in my choice of a husband, but I had the best big sister.

That morning, I confessed to Kate that I thought Dan was getting ready to leave me.

"Did he say that to you?"

No, I told her, it was just kind of a queasy feeling. All Dan had said was that he was unhappy, but that everyone was unhappy at our age, every man anyway. Was that true?

"No, Janie, of course not. Why would every man be unhappy? It's ridiculous."

Well, that was what Dan had told me. I didn't know what to do. Dan was just drifting away, losing interest. He was acting a little mean. The truth was, I didn't trust him anymore.

"Be patient. All marriages have ups and downs, right?"

No, some have only downs.

"Jane, are you sure the problem isn't that *you* want to leave *him*?"

I told Kate that *she* probably wanted me to leave him.

"Maybe," she said. "But it doesn't matter what I want. The question is what do *you* want?"

I didn't know. Maybe we could both use a little break, a vacation from each other. A time-out. Couldn't every marriage benefit from that?

"You mean a separation."

What an awful word. I didn't even know what it meant, legally.

"It means what it says: you separate. What do you think it means?"

No, I certainly didn't want that. I didn't want to feel like I failed at being a wife or that I was responsible for breaking up my family.

"Who says it's you that failed? You don't have to be unhappy forever, that's all."

And that was true, wasn't it? You don't have to be unhappy forever.

WHAT did Dan want? In the end, he got rid of the woman he didn't want (me) and he got the one he did. He got everything he wanted, but the wanting didn't stop. Is that how all men are?

One night around nine o'clock, not quite two weeks after he had spied on Jeff and Jamie on the living room couch, Dan found himself alone with Jamie in the kitchen.

There was a palpable awkwardness between them. The girl, suspicious but not entirely sure whether Dan had watched her kissing Jeff, was eager to act as if nothing had happened. To wish away the whole uncomfortable possibility. By this point, it seemed to have worked: the old man never mentioned it, never even let on that he knew Jamie and Jeff were together. So she must have imagined the whole thing, right?

For his part, Dan could not get the image out of his mind. The girl on the couch. He could not think of her the same way, now that he knew her body was activated, weaponized.

When she first came into the kitchen, Jamie exchanged a glance with Dan, then went to the sink with her small plate and glass, which she hoped to rinse quickly, file away in the dishwasher, and slip out of there, away from him. But there was a clutter of dishes in the sink, and she felt an implicit duty to clean up the entire mess, to be a good guest in the Larkins' home—which was not and would never be her home.

So she stood at the sink for a few minutes, her back to Dan, saying nothing, quick-rinsing one dish after another, trapped. She did not hear Dan come up behind her, and when she felt his hand on her, weighing her right buttock, she froze for a moment, wordless, before she could gather herself enough to spin away from him and say, "Oh my God, what are you *doing*? What is *wrong* with you?"

"Sorry. I misunderstood." But he wore a satisfied little smirk that communicated his true feelings: not sorry, no misunderstanding, certainly no regret.

"You are *such* a creep," she said, rightly. "I have to get out of here."

She ran upstairs.

When she got to her room and slammed the door, Dan had not moved but was still smiling, not at her reaction, I think, but at the memory of touching her, the feel of her, the weight of her bottom lingering on his palm. Whatever would happen next, whatever price he would have to pay, he seemed to think the grope had been worth it.

I tell you: this was not the man I married.

THE cops brought Dan in one last time to question him, on the morning of Tuesday, January 17, 1978. They must have known the case was lost. They had been waiting for new evidence to turn up; none ever did. As a practical matter, the investigation had already ended.

Dan certainly understood the situation. The detectives had asked him politely to come to the Newton police station for an update, a bit of theater that would not have been necessary if they could have brought him in the usual way, in handcuffs. They had been reduced from bullying to begging. So Dan accepted, blithely.

He was shown into an interrogation room, one he had been in twice before for interviews on this case. He entered with his usual rooster strut, wearing a tailored suit and a blood-red tie.

Across the table, seated in a row: two state police detectives and Tom Glover. And in the corner of the room, a technician of some kind wearing a funereal dark suit, seated at a boxy machine that, from the back, might have been anything at all but that Dan immediately recognized.

"The gang's all here," he said

On Dan's left was a big mirror. He stepped up to the glass and tapped it with one knuckle, making a hollow sound, then he slipped off his eyeglasses and held his nose right up to the surface of the mirror and peered into it.

"Who else is watching? Am I allowed to ask?"

"Couple of detectives, a DA."

"Well, why don't we just invite them all in, since we all know who's here anyway? Wouldn't that be more honest?"

"It's better if you just have a seat here with us," the lead state police detective said. This man—his name was Freeman—had a buzz-cut, square-jawed look like an old Marine. Dan found him thoroughly uninteresting. Not a worthy foe.

"Have it your way," Dan said. "So much for honesty."

There was one chair on the side of the table opposite the detectives. Dan slid this chair back from the table so that he had room to cross his legs. After arranging his jacket to avoid creasing it, he crossed his arms, too, so that he presented himself to the cops as a complicated knot.

The second detective, brighter looking—and higher ranking, Dan presumed—said, "We'd like to end this today, one way or the other."

"Would you? So you have some news for me, then?"

"No."

"No updates, no breakthroughs?"

"No."

"Is this being recorded?" Dan glanced around the room. "I have a right to know that."

"Yes, it is."

"Good. And your friend here, Silent Sam"—he nodded toward the man in the corner—"who is he?"

"A polygraph expert."

"Oh, a polygraph expert. Is that like a phrenology expert? A voodoo expert?"

"It's a lie detector expert."

"Oh, good Lord, are you this desperate? You have no idea what happened to my wife, do you? All this time and you have nothing."

"We'd like you to take a lie detector test."

"Forget it."

"Why? What are you afraid of?"

"I'm afraid of charlatans like Silent Sam over there."

"Why would you refuse a lie detector unless you're lying?"

"Really? We're going to do this? All right, please make sure the following statement is recorded and included in your reports of this interview: I would refuse a lie detector because there's no such thing as a lie detector, and you know it. It's a bunch of hocus-pocus. You're going to hook me up to a machine to measure my blood pressure and my heart rate, and from that you're going to guess whether or not I'm lying? Please. What you have there—and I'm being kind—is an anxiety detector. That's all you can measure. The trouble is, some people can lie without getting anxious. And some people—most people—will get pretty damn nervous if you drag them into a police station, hook them up to that machine, and accuse them of murder."

"An innocent man would jump at this chance."

"An innocent fool, maybe. Why don't you try a Ouija board instead?"

"Are you refusing the test?"

"How about this, detective: *You* take the test. We'll hook *you* up to the machine, and I'll cross-examine you right here and now. I'll ask you questions, I'll accuse you of murdering my wife. What do you want to bet I can make your heart race a little?"

"Are you refusing the test, Mr. Larkin?"

"Oh yes, I am refusing the test. And for the record, and for the men behind the mirror and for the evening news, I am also refusing to let you perform a séance or read my palm or ask the Amazing Kreskin what happened to my wife."

"You realize I'll have to draw an inference from the fact you refused the test."

"And what inference is that?"

"Consciousness of guilt."

"Ah. I think you've already drawn that inference. Here's the inference *I'm* drawing: you all failed. Your assignment was to solve this case and you failed. I begged you—I *begged* you—to find my wife, and you failed. All of you. And I promise you—believe me, I do not bluff—if I read in the paper that I refused this test today, I will say in public what I just said here, and I assure you the story people remember will not be 'Man Kills Wife,' it'll be 'Clueless Cops Botch Case.' I do not just sit back and take punches; I punch back. You will not bully me. This is my business, this is what I do."

Dan stood up and buttoned his suit coat. He always enjoyed making speeches, especially when he got to dress down men taller than himself, which was most of them. But it must have bothered him that Tom Glover had remained silent.

He said, "What about you, Mr. Glover. The smartest man in the room is usually the quietest. What do you think about all this?"

"I think you killed your wife."

ON my last day—Wednesday, November 12, 1975—I stirred from sleep at the sounds of Dan showering and dressing. He was never very quiet. He seemed to think that the noise he made was a kind of service to the rest of the family, a gentle way of waking everyone up. So he would blow-dry his hair with the bathroom door open, or whistle or hum as he went about his morning routine. He was evidently in a good mood that morning. He was not going to the office or to court, he said; he had a brief to write and would spend the day at a law library downtown. That meant he could stay at home a little later than usual and even drive Miranda to school if she wanted (of course she did). He wore his usual dapper suit, however, because you never knew when you might be pulled into court.

So we had a rare family breakfast together, if you could call it a family breakfast with the kids drifting through the kitchen in various stages of getting dressed, gathering up their books and gym clothes, wolfing down their food, while I assembled three lunches for them.

Dan sat at the center of this chaos eating his muffin with a fork and knife, his red necktie flung over his shoulder. Since he never helped get the kids off to school in the morning, he was at a loss how to pitch in. But he was unusually kind to me—unusually kind, I mean, by the standards of our increasingly chilly marriage. He gave me a little smile as if to say, *Look at these beautiful kids and this crazy, happy home we've made together.* As if he was just now discovering his own family.

He made me see it, as well. My three kids. And my handsome man, too, in his trim suit and fancy glasses, and his childish, innocent self-importance. How precious it all was. That breakfast made me just a little hopeful. Stupid me.

Dan waited for the boys to leave in Alex's car. Alex was pissy because his little brother always made them late, Jeff was morose because he had to suffer Alex's lecturing.

Car key in hand, Dan attended upon Princess Miranda, who was intent on dawdling in the house as long as possible, to make the most of her ride to school.

He even dabbed a little kiss on my cheek before he left with Miranda.

Was it all an act? I had no suspicion, certainly. Why would I?

An hour and fifteen minutes later, he came back.

I heard his car pull down the driveway and the back door open.

I called downstairs, "Dan? Are you all right?"

"Yeah, just forgot something."

It didn't feel right. He never forgot anything, this meticulous man.

The thought flashed in my head that we might have sex now. The house was empty. We had not done it in weeks, but Dan had been a little warmer to me lately. It felt like the right moment. It would be good for us. I had just showered too. I had on a good bra. I was ready if he was.

"Did you get all the way into town?"

"Yes."

"So what happened?"

"I told you, I forgot something."

"What did you forget?"

"It's nothing. Don't worry about it."

He did not come upstairs right away, so I went back into the bedroom to finish dressing and picking up.

His shoes creaked on the stairs, then he came into the room without his suit coat. His red necktie was off; it dangled from his right hand. His cuffs were turned up. His watch and wedding ring were missing.

I said, "What's that look? What are you up to?"

"Nothing."

"What happened? Did you mess up your tie?"

He nodded.

"You came all the way home for that?"

He shrugged.

I picked up some folded clothes of Dan's and began to put them away in his bureau.

Dan crossed to a little side table where I keep my cigarettes, and he took off his glasses and put them down.

Then he came and stood directly behind me as I continued to work. He was a small man but still taller than me, and I was in bare feet as well, so I sensed him behind and slightly above me. He was playing a game. We were so close.

His arms reached over and around my head in an odd way, laying the necktie loosely around my neck—not the way a man typically lays a necklace on a woman, but with his forearms crossed so that his left hand was behind my right shoulder, his right hand over my left shoulder. He was very delicate about it, even wary, the way you might loop a collar over the snout of a skittish dog, ready to jerk it if the dog snapped.

I still did not understand what was happening.

Behind me, I felt him wrap each of the tie-ends one time around his fists, drawing up the slack.

I was about to say, *Dan, what are you up to?*

The tie zipped tight around my neck, across my Adam's apple. A shock of pain. My head snapped back then forward.

We crashed forward into the chest. Dan pressed me up against it to hold me still.

Somehow the strap slid up my neck to the soft fold under my chin, where it sunk in. I clawed at it but it was clamped tight all around and I couldn't get my fingers under, couldn't get ahold of it.

No air.

Another bolt of pain, in my right foot. I had kicked the heavy bureau in front of me.

Somehow we fell to the floor. Dan's weight was on my back, his lips by my ear, his clenched breathing, straining.

My mouth made no sound at all. I did not scream, I could not even speak. No air, no gasp, no breath, no voice.

I knew now that I was dying.

The more I struggled, the tighter he pulled the noose.

My lungs clutched and convulsed—a frustrated, instinctive *need* to inhale, to inflate—but this was more distant, under the other things: air, foot, agony.

How long? Minutes, seconds? It all happened so fast, kids, so fast.

Then nothing. I broke through. In an instant, there was no pain, no panic. I was not dead. I knew exactly what was happening. I knew Dan was on top of me, still squeezing and hauling up on the rope like he meant to pull it right through my neck. I felt my spine arch backward as he pulled. But I felt no pain. Dying brought a kind of anesthesia. And a wonderful warm feeling: relaxed, calm, peaceful.

BOOK 3

1

Hell is the red-eye from San Francisco. Not the takeoff, when everyone is fresh and hopeful, and not the landing, when everyone is relieved and hungover and morning-after sweaty. I mean the squalid, endless middle of the flight, when the plane is lit only by a dim reddish glow, and the passengers snuffle in their sleep with their drooly mouths hanging open and no shoes on their oniony feet. You think: We are packed inside this metal tube, and if that tube ever cracked apart—like in Lockerbie—we'd tumble out of the sky and splatter on the ground. We are delicate little animals with thin, elastic skins and twiggy bones. It's a wonder we live as long as we do.

I am coming home to bury my mother. My sister Mimi called yesterday morning—no, it must have been two days ago; it is now 1:30 A.M. California time, 4:30 Boston time—to tell me that Mom's remains were dug up by a construction crew in Trout Lake, Vermont, beside a lake where we vacationed once when we were kids. She said a three-man crew was clearing a building site out of the forest, using a big Michigan loader to level the ground, when they shoveled up Mom's skull. It was so faded and dirt-stained that it looked like a rock at first. Only when they turned over the next scoop of earth did the crew realize what they had found.

Maybe that is why, in this flying tennis ball can, surrounded by sleepers, my mind is revving with morbid thoughts: A human head is just a brain-case. The bottom half is complicated by holes, all the inputs in the human body: food hole, air holes, sight holes, sound holes. (Other holes, the waste outlets, are located, wisely, as far from the intakes as possible while still permitting the creature to run and jump.) But above all the head-holes is the essential, magical part, the bony dome that helmets the brain. We are like Russian dolls: inside my head is my skull, inside my skull is my brain, and inside my brain, somewhere, is me, Jeff Larkin.

At Logan we shuffle off the plane like refugees or prisoners of war, stiff and defeated, all swearing silently never to take the red-eye again.

Miranda is waiting at the gate, smiling, expectant. No one else on earth is ever so visibly excited to see me. She is dressed in full bohemian weirdo mode, in some kind of daffy scoop-neck peasant blouse, baggy jeans, black Doc Marten shoes. Her wrists are armored with bangles and string bracelets. Her hair is swirled up on top of her head, a few flyaways artlessly left to dangle around her face. My sister has always affected a careless indie style, as if she would never stoop to mere attractiveness. She is oblivious (I think) to how lethally attractive this makes her to men.

She bumps a kiss onto my cheek and hugs me around the shoulders, pinning my arms to my sides.

I didn't miss you at all, she says.

I didn't miss you either.

You ready to go bury your mommy?

I can't imagine a better way to spend the day.

All right, then. Can we go get breakfast? I'm *starving*.

Absolutely. Burying mommies is hard work. We'll need our strength.

So I know what you're thinking. We should be all solemn and tragic when we talk about our mother, and in public we are. But it's tiresome, trust me. Anyway, when your family is ridiculous—not just in the ordinary sense, but actually the object of ridicule—what else can you do but laugh along with the joke? Here's what I've learned as I approach my thirtieth birthday: Don't face up to your problems with honesty and courage. That's just crazy. You're better off burying them under an avalanche of sarcasm. It's not a foolproof method. Sometimes problems come unburied. They wiggle up out of the ground like earthworms after a rain. When that happens, my advice is: just fire up your Michigan loader and bury the little fuckers all over again. That's the tricky part—the part Miranda can't always manage. Anyway, this is how we talk, Miranda and me, and I'm not going to apologize for it. *You* try living our lives, then you can criticize.

So we wander around Central Parking awhile because Miranda has no idea where she left her car.

This place is crazy! How does anyone find their car in here?

I don't know, Meem. I think they just take the closest one.

We finally find the car, and Miranda navigates out to the road. She sits very erect in the driver's seat, as if this is her first day in driving school.

So what happens now, Mimi?

Nothing. We can't do anything till the DA decides what he's going to do.

What about the funeral?

Can't have one. The DA has to release the body. Or the bones, whatever. It's evidence, I guess.

Jesus. How long is that going to take?

Nobody knows.

Who tells you these things?

The DA's office. They assigned us a social worker.

Great. So what do we do in the meantime?

We have breakfast.

What about Dad? Have you talked to him?

Not since they found her.

And before that?

It's been a while.

Weeks?

Months.

Jesus, Mimi. Who calls who? Does he call you or you call him?

I call him. But I'm not going to anymore.

Yeah? Why not?

I just can't.

I should call him. Fuck.

Do what you have to do, Jeff.

I haven't talked to him in . . . a year? More? I should call him. What about Alex?

Team Dad all the way.

There's a shock. I guess I have to call him too. God, this is a root canal. Maybe you should just take me back to the airport. Nobody knows I'm here yet.

Aunt Katie knows.

Really? Where is she in this whole thing?

She wants Dad's head on a spike.

Like you?

Miranda considers before answering. She says, I'm not sure. Sometimes I want his head on a spike, then sometimes I just want to forget the whole thing and move on. I want to just be normal.

You mean this isn't normal?

Ha ha, Mr. Funnyboy.

She takes me to a place called the Blue Diner. (You've got to hand it to Miranda, she has a sense for the poetic.) We take a booth and both order pancakes. Together, we feel like kids with adult privileges: we can order pancakes whenever we want to.

So tell me about California. Do you surf?

I do not surf. I'm the only one.

How sad for you. And how's it going with the wife?

This is more sarcasm. I do not have a wife. Probably never will. Miranda is talking about my girlfriend. Ex-girlfriend as of forty-four days now. Her name is Rachel. The thought of Rachel occupies my brain like a baseball-size tumor.

Please tell me you're not still parking outside her apartment and spying on her?

I shrug.

Jeff, what are you doing? That's crazy.

I know, I know. But it's not spying. It's just, if I happen to be there and I happen to see her, what's the harm?

You're a stalker! Can you please find a new hobby?

Does drinking count?

Sure. Just promise you'll stop obsessing about her.

I'm trying.

She's not worth it. You'll be okay.

How do you know she's not worth it? You never met her.

I just know.

And how do you know I'll be okay?

Because you're always okay.

Mimi, I am *never* okay.

Well, you better be okay this time. This family can't have two fucked-up children, so get your shit together, big brother.

Weirdly, that actually works for a moment. I feel a little brighter, a little less fucked-up, just because Miranda needs me to be.

I read your story, Mimi. It's really good. I liked it.

Thank you.

Have you showed it to anyone?

Just you.

You should show it to Phil.

Phil Solomon?

Yeah. He's writing a book, a novel.

He is not. Phil? Can he even write?

I don't know. Nobody knows. Including him.

Well, don't show it to him. It's personal. I don't know what to do with it yet.

You can't publish it, you know. You used everyone's real names. And you showed Dad murdering Mom. And Aunt Kate's story about him raping Mom? Are you crazy? You can't publish that.

Well, I don't think anyone's rushing to publish it. I didn't write it to publish it, anyway. I just wrote it to get it out.

Like taking a shit.

No, not like taking a shit, you pig. Now I want to show it to Phil just so I can have another adult to discuss it with.

So can I ask about it? Okay, I liked that it was in Mom's voice. That was kind of cool. I liked hearing her voice. I don't even know if that's what she really sounded like, but it felt good. Only I was thinking, if the story is told by a dead person, doesn't she have to explain where she is? Like, what's it like to be dead? Is she here? Is she in heaven?

Why does it matter where she is? Why does everything have to be so explicit and obvious?

It's just kind of a natural thing you'd want to know from a dead person, isn't it? What happens when you die?

Jeff, you are such a . . . *man*. It's a story, it's imagination. You just go with it.

It's a story but, I mean, come on, it's only *kind of* a story, right? So is she, like, a ghost? Or just a literary device? What *is* she?

I don't know. She's whatever you want her to be.

You don't know?

Of course I don't know. I've never been dead. How would I know?

I'm just sayin'. If I was writing it, I'd talk a little about how this dead person is able to tell the story, so readers don't wonder.

So go write your own story.

Hey, I'm just giving you feedback.

All right, well, thank you for your insightful feedback. Now can we talk about something else?

Sure. How's your love life?

Okay, maybe something *else*?

Ooh, listen. You know what you could do? If Mom is a ghost, she could come back and haunt Dad.

Oh my God, are you drunk right now?

Only a little.

Okay, forget the story. Jesus, Jeff. Let's talk about my love life.

Great. How is it?

That was a trick. I don't have a love life.

Really? No boyfriend? No . . . *other* friend? Like, really none?

None. I live in a nunnery.

Good.

Why good?

Because you'll bring home some crunchy hipster jackass, and I'll have to pretend to like him.

What would you rather I bring home?

I'd rather you just buy a dog. What about your old rich guy? What happened to him?

Oh my God, that was ages ago. He's long gone.

Good. What a cliché. A sugar daddy.

I know. Just don't tell Alex. I don't need the lecture.

Well, looking on the bright side, you actually did something boring. That's kind of comforting.

He had a Porsche, y'know.

Of course he did. That's what rich guys with small penises do. They buy Porsches.

Why don't they just buy small underpants?

They buy both. Didn't anyone tell you?

No! Nobody told me. My big brother moved to California so I have to find this stuff out on my own. You could have warned me about rich guys with small penises.

I wanted you to find out the hard way.

Oh, you're super funny, Jeff. Excellent penis joke.

The waitress arrives with the pancakes. She overhears the last comment and raises her eyebrows.

I give her the crazy sign, nodding toward Miranda and drawing circles with my finger beside my temple.

The waitress grants me a noncommittal smile and leaves.

So are you going to call Jamie while you're here?

Mimi, why would I do that?

Because it's the nice thing to do? Because she's a friend?

Your friend, maybe.

Of course she's your friend! She was your sister.

She was not my sister. For someone who talks about penises so much, you're a little confused about biology.

Well, she's still *my* sister.

How does she look?

After all these years, that's what you want to know?

Yes.

So shallow.

Penis owners are all shallow, trust me.

Believe me, I know.

So tell me.

She's gorgeous.

She is *not* gorgeous. Stop it.

I think she's gorgeous.

All right, whatever. Just tell her I said hi.

I'm not your secretary. You want to say hi, call her and say hi.

I *don't* want to. *You* want me to.

I don't care what you do. I just thought—since you two used to—I just thought you might want to talk to another human being sometime.

Well, you were wrong. I don't want to talk to any human beings, ever. I'm like a tree.

Trees say a lot, actually. You just have to know how to listen.

Oh, please. Weirdo. Are they coming to the funeral, Sarah and Jamie?

I doubt it.

Who's going to show up for this thing? We could have this funeral in a phone booth.

Dad said it's going to be private. Immediate family only.

Dad said?

Yeah. Only Aunt Katie says it's not up to him. She says Mom's family is having the funeral and Dad's not invited.

Well, that's awkward, isn't it?

If he shows up, Aunt Katie says she'll have him arrested.

Well, sure. What else would you do? When the guy who murdered your sister shows up at her funeral, you don't just offer him a Kleenex.

Stop it. Not funny.

Maybe we'll have two funerals. Split up the bones like french fries.

Stop it, Jeff. That's not funny.

I am not happy when I make these jokes. I don't know why I do it. Yes, I know it's my own mother, and yes, I know it's not funny. I hate myself for it. Believe me, my self-loathing dwarfs whatever little loathing you might already have conceived for me.

I'm going to see him.

Good.

Come with me, Miranda.

No way.

Please. Don't make me go alone. He's your father too.

I'm not the one who ran away.

This is a little stiletto, and it leaves us both silent a moment.

I'm going to ask him, Mimi, straight out.

You never learn. Go ahead, ask him whatever you want. You know what he's going to say.

Please come. I don't want to go by myself.

I can't, Jeff. I can't handle that right now. You can do it. You're strong enough.

I'm not. You overrate me.

Uh-uh. You go, you can handle it. I can't look at him right now. I can't listen to his bullshit.

I know what you think happened, Mimi. It's right there in your story. But we really don't know.

Before they found the bones, maybe we didn't know. Now we do. We need to stop fooling ourselves.

Miranda is right, of course. I know she's right, but I can't quite accept it yet. Not yet.

So how are you doing, Meem? Your mood. All this, it's terrible timing for you.

No, it's okay. I'm good. I feel like they gave me the tools I need.

She is referring to the shrinks at the Wharton Center, a wonderful, miraculous psych hospital in western Massachusetts where Miranda spent two snowbound weeks last March to deal with a paralyzing depression. I came out from San Francisco to see her. Our father did not come from Boston to see her.

Yeah? Like what tools?

Just tricks, kind of.

Tell me one.

It'll sound stupid.

Not to me.

Well, there's one I use called the Rocky technique.

Rocky, like Balboa?

Mm-hm.

Show me.

So you just, when you feel it coming on? It kind of feels like this . . . heaviness, sort of. Like your body is . . . slowing . . . down. And you just *know* that feeling. Your mood starts dropping and there's nothing you can do and you're starting to go over the edge. So what you do is, you close your eyes and make two fists, and you imagine this cloud coming at you, this huge cloud. And you picture yourself sticking out your chest and raising your fists like Rocky and shouting, *Bring it on! Give me the pain!* And you imagine this cloud enveloping you, and while you're in this fog you keep shouting, *I love it, I love pain! I'm stronger than you! You can't break me!* And you keep doing that until the cloud passes, and then you imagine yourself standing in the sun, with a clear blue sky. And you open your eyes and you feel better.

That works? Really?

Yeah. Makes me feel like a warrior.

Across the table, above her plate of pancakes, my sister holds up her fists in a pretty good boxing position, right fist at her chin to block a punch, left fist extended to jab her opponent. In slow motion, she throws a big, looping right hook toward my cheekbone. Her arm barely reaches halfway across the table. Pow, she says.

So I drop Miranda at her apartment, and in her car I go "home." Along the way, I pass my old grammar school and playground, the houses of old friends, a meandering tour of my childhood. It is all subtly changed, unfamiliar, dissociating, unsettling—weird. But then, my whole life lately has this trippy, mournful vibe.

By the time I force-march myself to the front door of my old house, my head is a riot of ideas and grievances and regrets. I am not ready to see Him.

Then he is standing in front of me, the object of my obsession but so much reduced in person, so small and mediocre that he seems unworthy of all the attention. The whole thing—a lifetime of shaping myself around the anvil of my father and what he may or may not have done—it all feels futile and foolish, something I ought to have outgrown years ago.

He is wearing a shabby terry bathrobe and apparently nothing else. No Rolex, no collar pin, no cat's-eye ring, no pocket square. Just a pair of tortoiseshell-and-wire-framed eyeglasses. The lenses have thickened since he was younger, when he used to slip off his glasses and gesture with them constantly. His curly hair is messy and, at fifty-seven, he is starting to go gray. His morning beard also shows a little gray, which gives his complexion an ashy tone. Between the lapels of his robe, a bristle of silver curlicues is grayer still. His bare shins and feet are thin and hairless and smooth as bone.

I feel a little guilty catching him like this, stripped, undignified. He was always so proud of his appearance.

He doesn't seem to care. With a little of his old cocksure manner, he says, *Hell*-o, stranger.

Hi.

This is a surprise. Why didn't you call ahead?

Didn't know I was coming.

I step into the old house, which seems smaller and darker than I remember it but mostly unchanged. More than anything, it feels empty, abandoned.

Come here, he says.

He pads over to kiss my cheek. I bend down to accept a kiss, and he puts a hand on the back of my neck.

Why am I doing all this? Why am I pretending? Why is he? We both know what the situation is.

Come, sit down.

He leads me into the kitchen, which is worn and dingy. The walls and cabinets need painting. But everything is in place. There are no dishes or food in sight, and, true to form, he has Windexed the sink to a shine.

Coffee?

No, I just had breakfast with Miranda.

Did you? Wonderful!

Yeah. I guess.

How is she?

She's good.

You came back for the funeral?

Yeah.

Good. I'm glad. Where are you staying?

With Mimi.

You can stay here, you know. There's plenty of room. Your old room is still there.

It's okay, Mimi's got room.

He nods. He seems determined to keep things light, superficial.

So you have a big birthday coming up. The big three-oh.

Yeah.

My thirty-year-old son. I can hardly believe it.

I wince, but not for the reason he imagines. I don't give a shit about turning thirty. It is June 1993, I was born in July '63. It's just math. Who cares? I am wincing because I know now what this guy is. I *know,* don't I? We both know. What the fuck are we talking about? How long are we going to keep this up?

How are you doing out there? Are you still . . . ?

Bartending, yes.

I hear the little voice in his head: *Why would a grown man waste his time bartending?* But he keeps it bright:

Great. You enjoy it?

Not really.

Oh. So what's next, then?

Dad, I need to ask you something. Those bones.

The bones, yes. We can finally have a funeral. But the DA is dragging it out, isn't he? He wants to torment me. Eighteen years. Eighteen *years* of this, and *still!*

He waits for some affirmation from me, but I say nothing.

Ah, he's got a job to do, he's got a job to do. I get that. I shouldn't say this stuff to you, Jeff. I don't mean to put you in a position. I know how you must feel.

Do you?

Well, I know how I feel. I'll leave it at that.

And how do you feel?

Destroyed.

Destroyed. That's an interesting choice of words.

Is it? Why?

It's passive. You make it sound like something happened *to you.*

It did.

It did, huh. Dad, I need to ask you something. 'Cause I am trying to get my head around this, I mean I am *really* trying. How on earth did Mom's body get buried there? Of all places.

He gives me a long look. I don't know, he says.

You knew that place. You'd been there. How does this happen?

I don't know. That's the honest truth. What else can I say?

That's just not good enough. Nobody's going to believe it.

It's the truth. I promise you.

I keep hoping there's some innocent explanation. Is there? What is it?

I've been racking my brain, Jeff. Maybe she drove up there for some reason. She did that once before, you know. She went up there looking at places for the next summer, for our next vacation. So I figure she must have gone up there again and she ran into the wrong guy at the wrong time. That's all I can figure.

Then how does her car end up at the train station right here?

Whoever did this to her must've dumped the car there. Covering his tracks.

I shake my head.

You don't believe me?

I don't know. I want to, I really do. But I'm having a hard time, y'know? It doesn't make any sense. What would be the motive?

Motive? Who knows. People do crazy things. I've seen it. Crimes like murder, rape—there isn't always a motive. It doesn't work that way. Sometimes people just do things. Maybe it's just a crime of opportunity. This woman shows up in a little town. She's an easy target. She isn't from around there, nobody knows her. And your mother wasn't the most streetwise person.

No. That's not what happened.

Why do you say that?

I just don't believe it. Those bones, Dad. Those bones change everything. Don't you see that?

Jeff, I'm telling you the truth. It's all I can do. What else can I tell you?

That's what you always say.

Tell me what I can do to convince you. I'll do anything. Test me. Give me a way to prove myself.

You can't.

Exactly. There's nothing I can do, there's no way I can defend myself against . . . suspicion. Against doubt. Don't you see that? Don't you see the position I'm in? It's impossible. There's no *proof*. It's just rumors.

There *is* proof now. You know there is.

What proof? A few bones? What do those bones have to do with me?

Look, why don't we just— What do you care what I think? It doesn't matter what I think.

Of course it does. It matters very much to me. More than anything else. Much more than what *they* think.

He is looking at me in an imploring way, but I have nothing to say to him.

Look, Jeff, I know we haven't always—I know I'm not the father you might have wanted. You haven't spoken to me in, what? Five years?

You haven't spoken to me either.

I know. I'm not accusing. I don't want to argue. I only mean that, whatever flaws I might have had as a father, I never lied to you. Now, you know that's true. Even when it was something you didn't want to hear, even when I knew you were going to get your back up, I always said it straight out, to your face, didn't I? I was always honest with you. Well, I'm telling you now: I'm not lying. I promise you. I promise you.

Even in his ridiculous bathrobe, even worn down with anxiety, he was a good lawyer. I'll give him that. He identified my weakest point—doubt—and he planted his flag there.

I'm sorry. I'm just having a hard time believing you.

Well, let's talk about it, then. Tell me why. Let's keep talking.

No. You know what? Let's not. I can't talk about this anymore.

Okay, we'll pick it up later, then. You must need some sleep.

No. I mean, I don't think we should talk anymore, ever.

Jeff, what? Come on. You don't mean that.

He gawps, and I understand that the hurt he feels is real. I find some lame, pathetic comfort in that. That he cares about my approval. That simply leaving him, withholding myself from him, my mediocre self, is painful to him. Good.

Jeff?

I'm gonna go now, I tell him.

And that's it. That's all there is. Saying goodbye to my father ought to be a grand gesture, the climax of something, but it happens quietly. No tears, no violins. It feels perfunctory, a formality. Like signing the paperwork on a deal that we agreed to a long time ago. It is almost a relief. I bet he feels the same way, deep down, happy to be rid of me. All we have ever done is fight. Where is it written that fathers and sons have to get along?

On the way out I notice a photo of my mother on a table in the living room, in a silver frame. Not much older than the big three-oh herself. It is a picture I remember.

Can I keep this?

Of course. Go ahead.

I don't expect I will ever set foot in this house again. So, okay. Good. I'm fine.

HERE is one thing that has changed since my mother's skull rolled out of the dirt in Vermont: no longer do Miranda and I imagine that she might be out there somewhere, living under some other name. As nutty as that sounds, Mimi and I have always preserved that possibility, whispered about it. Well, we would say, it's possible, there's no way to disprove it. We worked out all kinds of crazy theories explaining why Mom would hide herself from us: mental illness, amnesia, kidnapping, brainwashing, a threat of harm, a cult (okay, that was mine). Miranda adored this game. She made up elaborate stories about Mom sustaining a head injury that magically erased her memory or convinced her that she was some other woman. She liked to imagine Mom in picturesque places like Key West or the south of France. Wherever she was, in

Miranda's dreams Mom was always happy. Well, those fantasies are all over now.

The district attorney is not the fantasizing type, either. After waiting eighteen years for a break in the case, it takes him only twenty-four hours to come to a decision, once the lab confirms the identity of the bones using the new science of DNA.

He does have the decency to invite the family to his office in Cambridge to explain the decision in person. We assemble there on a perversely fine morning in June. Sunny, temps in the eighties. The entire city, usually so gruff, is uncharacteristically cheerful, as summer-starved, sun-drunk New Englanders tend to be when the warm weather finally arrives.

The DA's office occupies half of one floor in a molded-concrete 1970s courthouse in Cambridge. It does not even feel like a courthouse to me. There's no patinaed old woodwork, no marble statues. Just generic county-government office space. Thin carpet squares laid over a concrete floor, flimsy walls painted Government Beige, fluorescent lights, water-stained acoustic-tile ceilings. The office could as easily be the Registry of Motor Vehicles or the Office of Weights and Measures.

Around quarter to ten, we begin assembling in the waiting area.

Aunt Kate is already there with Uncle Stephen. She smiles when Mimi and I arrive and rises to hug us. She fusses over me in particular because I have been away. But her face looks hardened, gaunt. There are bags under her eyes.

Next to arrive is the detective from Newton, whose name at first I can't remember. Mimi air-kisses him in the same way she did Uncle Stephen, laying her cheek on the stained side of his face. Then she reintroduces him to us. His name is Tom Glover, which of course I should have remembered but I'm terrible with names.

Alex processes in like an emperor, wearing a suit that must have cost more than my car. He shakes everyone's hand firmly, in turn, as if we have all come here to meet with *him*. Good Lord, my brother can be a jackass.

His wife is with him. A yuppie like Alex, a Harvard MBA with frosted hair who works in business consulting doing God-knows-what. Her name is Laurel Marcus. She uses her maiden name because, she says, *Laurel Larkin* is too hard to say and *Laurel Marcus-Larkin* sounds worse, but I think it is really because she is so alarmingly complete, so perfectly *finished* that she could no more remove her name than she could remove her nose. Still, she has a softer manner than Alex, and the self-possessed awkwardness of an only child, and no long history with us Larkins. Also, she seems to genuinely love Miranda, which goes a long way with me. (Alex and Laurel have three young kids, too, aged seven, nine, and eleven. I find these spoiled children more insufferable every time I see them. At this rate, I expect that very soon my nieces and nephews will be suitable only to be sewn up in a burlap bag with a wolverine and tossed into the nearest river.)

And that is it. Our whole oddball, de-parented family gathered in one room at last. Aunt Kate is now the eldest among us. My mom's parents died a few years ago, never knowing whether the case would be solved. Mom's mother—my grandmother—was convinced that my dad killed her beloved Jane, and she despised him until her last breath.

We are met by a young woman with the baffling title of *victim-witness advocate*. She escorts us through a heavy locked door, past a maze of cloth-walled cubicles, to a windowless conference room.

There we are joined by the district attorney himself, an unsmiling, square-jawed man named Martin Leary, and his top assistant, a doughy guy in a baggy suit whose name I do not quite catch. Chris Something-or-other.

District Attorney Leary greets us one by one. He is not a natural politician. I am sure no one has ever met him and thought, *There goes the next governor of Massachusetts.* He speaks in a terse, cautious way. His movements are stiff.

We sit down around an oval table. We Larkins have no appointed leader, but Alex and Aunt Kate both radiate a natural, effortless authority. The rest of us fill in between them like the dimmer stars in a constellation.

District Attorney Leary says: I want you all to know how difficult this case has been for me. Not just professionally, but personally. I am haunted by this case. I think of your mother—your sister, Kate—I think of her every day. And I have for years. I mean that sincerely. Every day, for years. I want you all to know how very much we want this case closed. We owe that to Jane and we owe it to you. Nobody, and I mean nobody, wants this case prosecuted more than me. Obviously there's two sides to it. I don't know how each of you feels about Dan Larkin's role in all this, and honestly I don't want to know. For you three children especially, he's your father and I would never ask you to choose. The decision has to be mine. I have to do what's best for the case, not what's best for you. So, end of speech.

The district attorney leans back and crosses his arms, then seems to realize his body language is wrong, and he promptly unfolds his arms again, leans forward, and lays his arms on the table. I find all this ungracefulness weirdly reassuring. A man this socially clumsy cannot afford to lie. He could never get away with it.

So I have some difficult news for you, which is that we are not going to indict the case at this time.

Aunt Kate's hand flies to her mouth, a rare loss of composure.

No one else reacts.

I've studied this question and discussed it with colleagues, and the evidence just isn't there. I am truly sorry, but that's the fact of the matter. Obviously the discovery of your mother's remains is a big, big break. One of the enormous holes in the evidence until now has been the lack of proof that your mother was actually killed. That's no longer an issue. But it's not enough. It's a circumstantial case, which is okay; we win circumstantial cases all the time. But there just isn't enough to charge anyone right now. Now, having said that, I want you to understand that this case is not closed. It will not be ignored or inactive or anything else. We will pursue the case aggressively, as we always have. When I charge your mother's murderer someday, I'm going to nail him, I promise you that. But I'm not going to endanger the case by rushing ahead with incomplete evidence.

Silence.

Kate says at last, Rushing? It's been eighteen years.

He nods. I know.

What if someday never comes? What if this is as much proof as you're ever going to get?

Then there's still no sense in charging anyone, not if we already know we're going to get a not-guilty. If the case isn't there, it isn't there.

But what possible other evidence could there be at this point? What are you waiting for?

I don't know, honestly. I can imagine all sorts of evidence coming up: physical evidence, a new witness, a confession of some kind. We'll have to wait and see.

We've been waiting eighteen years.

Things can change. Believe me, I've seen it happen. Cold cases do get solved. New evidence does turn up.

Aunt Kate shakes her head. She looks both disappointed and a little scornful of this man who is so fastidious in his preparation, and perhaps so risk averse, that he cannot actually act.

Alex says, as if to soothe but actually to silence her: Aunt Kate, Mr. Leary has a duty to do what he thinks is right.

Jesus, I mutter.

Alex, my parents are dead, my sister is dead, I'm fifty-nine years old. I don't have forever. I think we should be honest: if it doesn't happen now, it's probably never going to. That's what this means, that's what he's telling us. Your father gets away with it. Is that what anyone here thinks is right? Does anyone think this is right?

Aunt Kate, you're assuming he did it. If there's no evidence pointing to him, then maybe he didn't do it.

Kate's face tightens, holding back the words from escaping her mouth.

Miranda says, No one's said his name.

A beat.

I have been determined not to speak at this meeting. Though I am as intimately involved as anyone here, I feel like an interloper. I live far away. I *feel* far away, from all of this, from Her, from Him. But I find myself saying to the district attorney, Can I just ask you: do you think my father did this? I'm not asking whether you can prove it in court. Just, do you think he did it?

Yes.

Do you have any other suspects?

No.

Any evidence that points to someone else?

No.

How sure are you that he did it? Like, percentage-wise?

That's hard to say.

I'm just asking what you *think*. Your *opinion*. Are you *sure* he did it?

I'm sure, yes.

A hundred percent sure?

I can't put a number on it.

Isn't it possible that some stranger did this? Maybe my mom went to that little town on her own that day and someone attacked her, some crazy man? Maybe she was robbed or . . . or raped or just murdered for no reason, out of the blue? That happens, doesn't it?

It's possible, yes.

So you have doubt?

No. I'm just acknowledging the possibility. We're human beings, we're working with incomplete information—I might be wrong. It's possible. That's not the same as doubt.

That makes no sense. You just said you're sure. Now you're saying there's a chance you're wrong.

There's always a chance I'm wrong. My job requires that I make decisions anyway. I'm not an appeals lawyer or a journalist who comes along after the fact; I don't have the benefit of hindsight or new evidence. I have to make decisions based on the imperfect information that's in front of me right now. So even if I make the right decision, the *reasonable* decision, someday I could be proven wrong. My job is to accept that possibility and make decisions anyway. There's no other way. Someone has to decide. Right now, that someone is me.

And you've decided on my dad.

I have.

Dan Larkin killed my mother.

In my opinion, yes. I'm sorry.

I lean back in my chair, feeling a little stoned.

Alex says, I think we need to remember that Dad has rights too. I don't *accept* this assumption that he did this. He *is* our father, Jeff, he's *your* father. You owe him something.

I *owe* him? What do I owe him?

Loyalty. Gratitude.

Gratitude! For killing my mother?

For your existence. He brought you into this world.

Ai, Alex, let's not do this.

Kate says: Alex, doesn't Jeff owe all those things to his mother too?

Yes. Of course, Aunt Kate. You know what I mean.

I don't. What do you mean, Alex?

Look, we all know—I'm sorry, but we all know Jeff and Dad don't get along. You moved three thousand miles away from him.

I moved three thousand miles away from you too.

Aunt Kate says, That's enough.

Jeff, I don't mean to fight with you. I'm just saying, you have to be fair to him too. That's all.

I *am* being fair. You just heard the DA say Dan Larkin killed his wife. Then you decided to ignore that and blame me instead.

I heard the DA express an *opinion*. Well, I have an opinion too. I disagree with him. *Dan Larkin killed his wife?* Do you even hear yourself? Who talks like that? Those are your parents you're talking about.

Well, Kate intervenes, it doesn't matter. None of our opinions matter, do they, Mr. Leary? It doesn't matter what we want. The decision is yours and yours alone.

It does matter. Your family's input is something I listen to and I consider and I give great weight to. But yes, in the end it's my decision.

And your decision is already made. You won't charge Dan with killing my sister.

I can't. I'm sorry.

You keep saying that, *I'm sorry*. What does it even mean, you're sorry? You're not sorry enough to charge the man who you're absolutely sure killed my sister.

Tight-lipped, the DA nods.

And if I tell you, as Jane's sister, that I would rather take the chance of a not-guilty, that I would rather see him tried for what he did to my sister, even if it's a longshot, than see him get off scot-free?

I'm sorry, I can't do it. If we indict him and he gets off, then it's all over. We get one bite at the apple. I can't waste it if I don't think we have a realistic shot of a conviction. I also have a professional duty not to charge anyone if I think the evidence isn't there.

Alex says: Aunt Kate, he has no choice.

Aunt Kate eyeballs Alex, registering his betrayal but determined not to be distracted by it.

So what are we supposed to do? My sister is dead. What am I supposed to do?

The district attorney shakes his head, patient, nonjudgmental, but intransigent.

Nothing, he says. There's nothing any of us can do but wait and hope for another break.

OUR audience with the district attorney ends with a few announcements. Mom's bones will now be released for burial, we are told.

Later today, the DA will issue a press release announcing his decision. We are admonished not to speak too much to the press, if we are contacted, lest we complicate a prosecution at some hazy time in the future.

We accept all this information in defeated, submissive silence.

Awkward handshakes all around.

To Aunt Kate the district attorney says one last time: I know you're disappointed. But I hope in time you'll understand my position. We are on the same side, you know.

She gives him a forbearing smile, like an adult might give to a child.

Kate says, May we borrow the room for a few minutes before we leave? I'd like to have a moment together as a family. It's a lot to process.

Of course.

The DA and his assistants file out.

On his way after them, Glover tells Miranda, I'll catch up with you later.

Mimi takes his hand in hers and thanks him for coming.

Waiting for Miranda to release his hand and with all our eyes on him, Glover looks stricken.

Aunt Kate watches this interaction with a curious expression. Miranda, *you* asked him to come?

Yes.

Why?

Because he's my friend.

He's a police detective?

Yes. But I wanted him here. He knows everything about the case.

Miranda has a way of sounding more naive than she actually is.

Kate says to Glover, You stay.

She closes the door, sits back down.

Detective . . . what was it?

Glover. Tom. Tom Glover.

What do we do now, Detective Glover?

Um, basically it's like the DA said: there's nothing you *can* do.

I don't accept that.

That's the way it is. It's his decision. That's how the system works.

Then we have to change the system. We have to change his mind, don't we?

Alex groans. Aunt Kate, respectfully, what are you talking about? You just heard the DA say there's not enough proof. That's it. Let it go.

No. I will not let it go. We're talking about my sister.

And my mother. And not for nothing, my father too. I shouldn't have to keep saying this: he has rights, he deserves some consideration.

Alex, I love you, I've loved you since the day you were born, and I'll love you till the day you die. But I can't just look the other way. Don't ask me to do that.

I'm not asking you to look the other way. I'm asking you to accept reality. At some point we have to move on. For all of our sake. How long is this going to go on?

Is that what you kids think? Jeff? Miranda? Is it time to move on? Is that what you want to do?

Mimi's head is down.

Kate: Do we think he did it? Isn't that the real question?

I say, I don't know. I don't know anything.

And it is true: my thoughts are swirling. I genuinely don't know what I believe. More than that, what bothers me now is that I am being *forced* to think about it, forced to visit this uncomfortable subject, forced to think at all. What I want, really, is to be in San Francisco, far away, with a beer and a spliff and a head as empty and light as a float in Macy's parade.

Miranda lifts her head and declares: I think he did it.

She looks around the table at each of us, gauging our reaction, but nobody has any extra emotion to give.

Aunt Kate says, Well, that's two guilties, one not-guilty, one not sure.

There are others in the room, of course, the spouses and Glover. But they don't get a vote.

Alex sulks: Just to be clear, I didn't say not-guilty. I said he's entitled to the benefit of the doubt, just like anyone else. Process matters. We need to respect the process.

Aunt Kate: All right, so two guilties, *zero* not-guilties. Detective, what can we do? We need to get this case into court. How do we do that?

I don't know.

There must be something.

Glover: Find more evidence.

We've waited eighteen years. More evidence probably isn't coming. So what else? Think. Who can we talk to?

There's no one else to talk to. Like I said, it's the DA's call.

Well, there must be someone above him. Who do we appeal to? Who could order him to proceed?

The AG and the governor. Technically. Good luck with that.

Who could persuade him, then? Who would the DA listen to?

I don't know. Maybe George Bailis.

Okay, a name finally. Great. Who's George Bailis?

He's a lawyer. Back when all this started, he was the DA's right-hand man. The DA was old and sick. Bailis was the whiz kid. Nothing happened without a nod from George Bailis. He's the one who decided not to charge the case in the first place, twenty years ago.

How do you know that?

I was in the room. I was looking right at him.

Why would the DA listen to this George Bailis?

Because he ran this place for years. He's like the pope.

Where do we find him? The Vatican?

I have no idea.

Well, he's a lawyer, right? He can't be too hard to find. These people don't hide.

Kate stands and snaps up a yellow pages from a bookshelf in the corner.

Alex says: Aunt Kate, this is wrong. I don't agree with this.

Alex, if you don't want to be a part of it, I understand, honey. But this was my sister. As long as there's something I can do, I'm gonna do it.

BAILIS's office is downtown, on a narrow, shadowy block off Franklin Street, in a tomb-like, granite-front, prewar office building. In the lobby, the directory announces, in faded gold lettering, that this is the Stratford Building, a pretension that makes me want to escort this exhausted old building off somewhere private and shoot it.

We squeeze into a small elevator for a rattly ride to the third floor. Luckily, only four of us have come: Aunt Kate, Miranda, Glover, and me. Still, we have to stand uncomfortably close to one another.

Mimi grins at the awkwardness. This is cozy, she says.

She is right to smirk. This whole errand feels unserious. We all know we are humoring Aunt Kate. My aunt can be bullish but she will accept it soon, she will have to. It is time to bury Jane once and for all.

For my part, I am already thinking ahead to the funeral. Will the coffin be sized for an adult, in which case it will be mostly empty? Or will it be shoebox sized, for the few bones that remain? Will the bones be tied down or wrapped to keep them from rolling and clattering? Will one of us have to make a speech? Not me, I hope. God, just get me to the plane, get me a Stoli on ice, get me home to S.F. and a chilly, foggy oblivion. That's all I want.

By the time we arrive at the LAW OFFICES OF GEORGE M. BAILIS LLC, I have this weird feeling that we have come to a charmed place. The obscure building, the antique elevator, a dark hall-way—it is like a fairy tale, like we have passed through a series of secret doors and passageways to reach the Hidden Cave. The office itself is nothing so grand. Antique tables with crackled surfaces, a wavy oriental rug, a reproduction of a second-rate painting of a three-masted sailing ship. It is all so small and shabby, a cheap imitation of my father's bigger, slicker office.

Bailis comes out to greet us promptly. His whiz-kid days are long behind him. He is thin and grave. His hair is more salt than pepper. He wears mouse-brown shoes with a gray suit and a cheap tie that my father wouldn't be buried in.

When the cop Tom Glover explains who we are, Bailis says, Yes, of course.

When Aunt Kate thanks him for seeing us, he says, I remember your name.

He seems to have been expecting us, all these years. I am tempted to apologize for not coming sooner.

Bailis leads us to a conference room that looks out, through a venetian blind, onto an air shaft. There he listens with an impassive expression to Kate's recap of our frustrating meeting with the district attorney.

Already Mimi and I are exchanging glances: now it is Bailis who is humoring Aunt Kate.

When Kate is done, the lawyer—the pope—asks, What is it you want me to do?

Glover asks if Bailis will intervene with the DA, get him to reconsider his decision.

Bailis: It won't do any good. He won't listen. He's too timid, always has been.

Kate: So Dan just gets away with it? There's nothing we can do?

Bailis reprises the same tired, rote legal advice we just heard an hour ago: If the prosecutor will not charge him with the crime, there is nothing we can do. Only the government can initiate a prosecution for murder. Blah, blah, blah.

Aunt Kate shakes her head. She looks like she might cry, which is something I have never seen and never thought was possible.

Bailis says, There is another way. If you're absolutely determined, you could sue him.

Sue him? For *murder*?

Yes. Well, for wrongful death, technically. Infliction of pain, infliction of emotional distress, loss of companionship.

Sue him for money, you mean.

That's right. But the money isn't the real point. The point is to have your day in court. It's a way—it's the *only* way—to establish the truth in a public forum. To hold him accountable.

But we don't have enough proof.

For a criminal case, maybe not. In a criminal case, the DA has to prove guilt beyond a reasonable doubt. In a civil suit, all you need is a preponderance of the evidence. Fifty percent plus a feather.

You think we could do that?

I'd have to look at the evidence, but my guess is that if it was a close call for the DA at the higher standard, it will be an easier decision for us. The other benefit of course is that we get to conduct our own investigation, collect our own evidence. We get discovery, we get to depose witnesses. We can swear Mr. Larkin in and ask him questions under oath. If that's what you all want.

Aunt Kate: I've never heard of it.

Bailis shrugs.

She looks across the table at Miranda and me. It would have to be up to you kids, she says. You've been through enough already. I won't force you to do anything.

Of course, just an hour ago Aunt Kate was perfectly willing to override Alex's wishes. Apparently she considers Miranda and me more fragile. She is not wrong. I just wish it wasn't so obvious.

Bailis: I would add one other point. This will sound awful but you have a right to know. In a civil suit like this, for damages, the best plaintiff is the one who is most damaged, who's sustained the greatest losses and is the most sympathetic to a jury. In this case, the children are the obvious choice as the lead plaintiffs.

Aunt Kate: No. I'm the one who should be out front on this.

Well, again this will sound awful but it's true: a dead mother is worth more than a dead sister.

Kate blinks at him.

Miranda: This is crazy. You want us to sue our own father? Me and Jeff? Really?

I tell him, It's a bad idea. I can't even keep a houseplant alive. I don't think you want me for this job.

Bailis: I don't want you to do anything that you don't want to do. I'm just telling you, as a practical matter the case is worth a lot less without you two.

Miranda shakes her head.

Aunt Kate: I don't think it's a good idea. I'm not comfortable putting the kids out front like that.

Miranda: Hey, I don't want to be the one to say no if this is what you guys want—Aunt Kate, if this is what you want.

What do *you* want, Miranda?

I could do it.

I don't know, sweetie. I'm not sure you could. I'm not sure I should let you.

Bailis: What about you . . .

Jeff.

Jeff. What do you think?

I don't think I could sue anyone, honestly, let alone my own father.

Okay.

I just don't believe in it.

Okay.

What would be the point? Money? Money isn't going to bring her back, money isn't going to make me any happier.

That may be true. But, again, it's not about the money.

You keep saying that: it's not about the money. Of course it's about the money. That's the whole point of a lawsuit.

Not to me. Look, we use money as a punishment because we have to. We have no choice. It's the only thing we can take from him. It's the only form of justice available to us. The government keeps a monopoly on physical punishment—on the power to drag people away in handcuffs and lock them up. So we use the tools that are left to us. It's not perfect, I grant you, but it's what we have.

It just doesn't feel right.

Okay then. Look, I'm not trying to talk you into anything. But can I ask you one question, just to satisfy my own curiosity? What do *you* think happened here, Jeff? What do you really think?

The DA said he was sure.

What about you? Are *you* sure?

I don't know.

I get the feeling you *do* know. Am I right? It's okay to say it, if it's how you feel.

A moment passes.

Yes. I think he probably did it.

Are you sure?

Fifty percent and a feather.

Fifty percent and a feather won't do. You have to be sure, otherwise it doesn't make sense to go ahead with this. It's just too hard. You have to be sure.

Another pause.

Yes. I'm sure.

Well then, that's an awful burden for a young man. That's a lot of weight to carry around.

You can't manipulate me.

I would never try. It's just, I've been carrying this case around too.

Not like I have.

No, not like you have. Of course.

And what do *you* think? Did my dad do it?

Yes, he did.

How sure are you? Fifty percent and a feather?

Let me put it this way: I made a terrible mistake not indicting this case twenty years ago.

And if you had?

He'd be in Walpole, I promise you.

So now you want to fix it. *Your* mistake.

It's too late to fix it. You can't go back. That's one thing old men know. It was my mistake; I have to live with it. But maybe we can make things just a little better. For everyone.

With money?

With the truth.

But you'll keep the money just the same.

You don't have to keep it, Jeff, if you're uncomfortable with it. Give it away to charity if you like. Make something good come of all this.

I have no idea, at this moment, if the great George Bailis is just another greedhead shyster or if he actually means what he's saying.

I tell him: Well, honestly, everything I touch turns to shit lately. I'm not sure I can handle this right now.

Mimi is looking at me with an expression that is so crestfallen I have to look away. It's like she has seen me the way the world sees me, not as her big brother but as the loser I really am, and she is disappointed. I am disappointed too. I have always been content to disappoint myself and delighted to disappoint others, but I can't stand disappointing her.

Aunt Kate, what do you want?

I want you kids to be at peace.

But for you. What do *you* want?

I want my sister back, that's what I want.

Kate breathes out a long, resigned sigh.

But since I can't have that, I want the man who did this to her to pay. Somehow. If not in prison, then maybe this is the only way. There has to be a price for doing this. Otherwise it's just—the world is—the whole thing is just . . . wrong.

What started as an unserious errand to a lawyer's office to humor my aunt has left us all feeling devastated.

Bailis says, Well, I suggest you all go think about what you want to do. Obviously it's a big decision. In the meantime, let me leave you all with this thought: *somebody* always pays. Your mother paid, obviously, with her life. But for a long time now, you've paid too. All of you. You, Jeff. Your sister, your whole family. The question isn't whether someone should pay; the question is who. You? Or him?

IN the days after meeting with the attorneys, Miranda slips into a funk. It is nothing dramatic at first, just a modulation to a lower key. She is quiet, somber, dull, fatigued. I am boiling with the idea of suing Dad, awed by it, terrified, exhilarated by it, but Miranda won't talk about it, even leaves the room if I bring it up.

I have been staying on Miranda's couch, in her little one-bedroom apartment in Somerville. Beside the couch, piled up on my open suitcase, is a bird's nest of all the belongings I brought with me, plus a whorl of bedsheets and blanket, which I ball up every morning and toss onto the pile. On the day after our meetings, when the district attorney's decision not to prosecute is on page one of the *Globe,* Miranda comes to sit beside me on this couch, among my tossed-off things.

Mimi, is there anything I can do for you?

No.

Do you have any meds or whatever that you can take?

She gives me a stern look. I am being ridiculous.

You want to do your Rocky thing?

No.

Bring on the pain! I love pain! Yo, Adrian!

It's okay, Jeff. You don't have to worry, you don't have to fix everything. I'm just a little upset, that's all.

I do worry.

Well, stop.

Don't you *want* to feel better, Mimi?

No. I want to feel just what I'm feeling.

Okay. Sorry.

How can you *not* be upset, Jeff? I don't know where we go from here.

By the second day, Miranda has retreated to her bed. Until now, I haven't really understood what Mimi's depression looks like as it sets in; I have only seen the bottoming-out and, more often, the aftermath, the slow recovery. So I can't be sure if this is the real thing or, as Miranda insists, just garden-variety sorrow, a normal reaction to a very bad day. But as the hours pass, her grief becomes *physical:* how ill she looks, how vacant her expression, how bone-tired she feels. It is like she is fighting an infection, which in a way she is.

I hover around her as much as she will tolerate, but eventually she always demands to be left alone.

The second night, I have a skittish anxiety that she will hurt herself, so I sneak into her room to sleep in the chair beside her bed.

Next morning, I wake up in the chair. My neck aches, the vertebrae crunch as I move my head.

It is early.

Miranda is sleeping on her side, facing me, oddly peaceful.

I whisper to her, Mimi, you've got to snap out of this. I'm all alone here.

She does not stir.

That day she does not come out of her room except briefly to eat and use the bathroom. She takes a long nap in the afternoon and nods off again, in her bed, after dinner. At what point do I call a doctor? At what point do I overrule Mimi's wishes and call for help?

Around ten, I check on her. The bedroom has the clammy stink of illness. This is not the romantic tristesse you might imagine from movies. It is more like a fever.

Miranda, you want anything to eat? I could get you something.

No.

You might feel better if you ate. You must be hungry.

No response.

Miranda, please try.

No response.

Mimi, listen to me. Give me something to do or I will go crazy.

She gazes at me, as if it has never crossed her mind that her suffering might affect someone else. She says, making up an errand for me perhaps: I'd like to see Jamie.

JAMIE answers her phone after four rings. Her voice is instantly recognizable, same cadence, same distinctive tone, though a little deeper now, thicker. A grown woman's voice. My voice must be different too. The last time Jamie Bennett heard me speak, I was sixteen years old. But I am afraid what she will hear in my voice is not maturity but defeat, failure, compromise, dissipation.

On the phone, we barely speak, and we certainly don't acknowledge our awkward history. Jamie and I are both beside the point; Miranda is asking for her, that is all that matters, so Jamie will come.

When she arrives, about a half hour later, there is a little thrill in seeing her, of course. At thirty or thirty-one, she is exactly what I imagined. Transformed yet familiar. Not "gorgeous," as Miranda promised, but *correct* in some mysterious way. She is the standard, the template. I measure other women, consciously or not, by a simple test: How does she compare? Is she more or less pretty, smart, clever, kind, etc. than Jamie Bennett? This is the enduring power of first love: it is definitive, it imprints on you.

Jamie betrays no such emotions upon seeing me. She smiles, but in a way that is polite and measured. I am tangled up in a bad teenage memory. I can't blame her.

She tells me it is good to see me and, with a pat-pat on my shoulder like a benevolent aunt, she moves quickly past me to Miranda's room.

There she sits down on the edge of the bed beside my sister, strokes her hair, and says, Sweetie, what happened?

I close the door and leave them alone. Already I feel a sense of relief about my sister. Help is here. Whatever it is that Miranda needs right now, Jamie has it and I do not.

WHEN she emerges a half hour or so later, alone, from Miranda's room, Jamie slips into the chair opposite me. She sits straight as a ruler and fixes her eyes on me.

So, she says.

So.

I lie tossed across the couch, where I have been doping myself with Oreos and stupid TV, waiting. But I sit up now and click off the TV in a guilty way. I want to be present, serious. As steady and grown-up as Jamie seems to be. I want to match her.

How is she?

She'll be okay. It takes time. This happens. You look tired, Jeff. How are you?

You mean in the last couple days or the last fifteen years?

Both.

Terrible, in both.

Miranda says you're going to sue him.

We're thinking about it, yes.

She's not sure she can do it.

It's pretty obvious she can't, isn't it?

Can you?

I don't think so.

That's understandable.

They want me to be the lead plaintiff. The front man. Mick Jagger.

And what do *you* want?

You know me: I'm not Mick Jagger. I'm the bass player, I'm the guy whose name no one remembers.

I remember your name.

Do you?

Of course.

That's good.

The lawyer must think you can do it or he wouldn't have asked.

He says I have the best case because I'm the victim's child. I'm the most damaged. I have the winning lottery ticket: a dead mother.

And what do you say?

I say I have a sister who's been catatonic for forty-eight hours just thinking about this, and I have a brother who's playing for the other team. So I guess I'm the only candidate.

No one's forcing you to do anything.

No.

So part of you must want to do it.

Part of me thinks I *have* to do it.

Why? Why would you have to?

For my mother.

Is that what she would want?

No. Actually, I think it's the last thing she would want. What she would want is for all of us to just get along. One big, happy family.

Jamie makes a face: *Too late for that*.

Can we talk about something else, Jamie?

Why? What else could be as important today?

Because I'd like to think there could be a time, someday, when you could look at me and not think of the murder.

Okay. So what should we talk about?

Tell me about you. What do you do?

I'm an executive assistant.

I don't even know what that means.

It means I run errands.

Yeah? For who?

A man who owns art galleries.

How many art galleries?

Three. Boston, Wellesley, P-town.

Is he gay?

Why would you ask that?

Just the P-town thing.

Oh.

Also, I'd really like him to be gay.

You would?

Kind of, yeah.

Aw. Thank you. Yes, he's gay.

Good. Is he a good boss?

Oh God, no, he's a tyrant. I think he hired me just so he can have someone to yell at.

That sounds pleasant. Where do you live?

Brookline.

With your husband.

Don't have a husband.

Do you want one?

No. One tyrant in my life is enough.

Fiancé? Boyfriend? Dog?

No. Maybe. Yes.

Maybe a boyfriend?

Well, define *boyfriend*.

Do you *think of* this person as your boyfriend?

Hm. I don't know. Sometimes.

Is he taller than me?

Honest answer?

God, no.

He's very short then.

You're a terrible liar. I hate him already. He's not worthy of you.

You might be right about that.

You said yes to the dog?

Yeah.

Tell me about your dog. He's not some little runty fuckin' thing, is he? I hate dogs that are the size of gerbils.

He's maybe seventy or eighty pounds.

Good. What's his name?

Stanley.

You named a dog Stanley?

He was already named when I got him. Whoever named him Stanley also left him at the pound.

What is he?

He's a mutt. Mostly shepherd, I think.

Does Stanley like the boyfriend?

Stanley likes everyone. He's not very bright.

Okay, how about this: If the boyfriend were allergic to dogs, would you get rid of the boyfriend or Stanley?

If he were allergic to dogs, he probably wouldn't have become my boyfriend.

You said before he wasn't your boyfriend.

I'm just using your word.

Okay, whatever. It's a sudden thing, he develops a dog allergy overnight.

That's not realistic.

It is. A man in Fresno was hit by a dump truck, and when he woke up he was allergic to dogs.

Wow. Is that so? I must have missed that story.

It's absolutely true.

Okay then. If my boyfriend, who is not actually a boyfriend, were hit by a dump truck in Fresno and he woke up with a mysterious dog allergy, I would definitely get rid of him.

Of course you would. You'd have to. Because what was he doing in Fresno?

Exactly.

Can I ask you something? Do you remember the day we went driving in your mother's car?

Of course I do. Except as I recall, *you* went driving.

You made me do it.

I did not!

You egged me on.

That is so not true. I was a helpless victim.

That memory? That's one of my favorite things.

Mine too. You were so . . . unafraid, Jeff.

I was pretending.

What's the difference?

I don't know.

Miranda says some girl out there broke your heart.

A little bit.

I'm sorry.

She didn't love me. It's not her fault.

That's very mature of you. But you're still left with a broken heart.

Not broken. Just cracked a little.

That's not what Miranda says.

No? What does Miranda say?

She says you're not yourself. You're drinking too much, sleeping till noon.

That's not myself?

It didn't used to be.

No, you're right, it didn't.

It's not something to joke about, Jeff.

Oh, I disagree. I'm the best joke I know.

Not to me.

This is too much, too close to home. I am anxious to point the spotlight away from me:

How's your mother? Does she still hate me?

She never hated you, you know that. It was never about you.

How is she?

She's good. Remarried.

She did the right thing, getting out, taking you away.

She didn't have a choice.

I know. I understand. She did what any mother would do.

It had nothing to do with you, Jeff.

I know. Sorry. Shouldn't have brought it up.

What are you going to do about the lawsuit?

I really don't know. What should I do?

It's not for me to say. He certainly deserves whatever he gets.

A beat.

Well. It's getting late. I better get going.

Okay.

We both stand. For a long, awful moment we stare at each other.

I ask, Are we a hug or a handshake?

Hug. Definitely.

She steps forward to bestow a chaste hug.

I cinch her up close, my hands on the flat of her lower back, and I lay my head on her shoulder. Her body is comfortable, strong, thick. And I can't help it: what I want, in that first moment, is to fuck Jamie Bennett as soon and as heroically as I possibly can. To lose myself in it, spend myself, forget myself. But a sense of tragedy suffuses the whole thing (*Remember when we drove in your mother's car?*) and deadens my idiotic libido. Hasn't yearning steered me wrong too? (*Miranda says some girl out there broke your heart.*) And by stages my desire declines, reduces to a mere idea, a thought, de-eroticized, manageable, minuscule, and I am happy to send it eeling away. What remains, what I want then, is just to stand here, with my head on her shoulder and her body crumped tight against me, for as long as I can, for as long as she'll let me. That's all I want. Just to rest here awhile.

She bends to me, as a tree bends with the wind. What she is feeling, I have no idea.

Then the moment is over.

Okay, Jeff. I think I better go.

AROUND four the next day, I am back in the waiting area of George Bailis's office.

Scattered on a coffee table in front of me are the copies of *Massachusetts Lawyers Weekly* I have been flipping through, oddly fascinated, for nearly two hours.

In the hallway, the elevator door rattles.

With no more evidence than this sound, the secretary, Donna, nods at me: *This is him.* Donna and I have formed a little alliance.

She seems impressed that I have stuck it out this long to see her boss.

When Bailis enters, she announces, Mr. Larkin has been waiting to see you.

Has he?

I stand up.

Why didn't you call ahead, make an appointment? I wouldn't have kept you waiting.

I didn't really think it through. If I had, I probably wouldn't be here.

Bailis frowns. With his ruined face, his beat-down slouch, the battered boxy lawyer's briefcase dangling from his hand, he seems very old for a fifty-something man, which is what he must be if Glover's math is to be trusted. There is only a little glint in his eyes, a hint of quickness, to suggest the whiz kid that Glover remembers.

Well, he says, I'm glad you didn't think, then. Come in, come in.

The receptionist extends to him a bouquet of phone messages on pink slips of paper while, with her other hand, she offers to take Bailis's briefcase.

He refuses both, leads me directly to his office.

In the office he plops down in his desk chair and opens a bottom drawer to prop his foot on.

Sit down, Jeff. You're alone today. Where's the rest of your crew?

They don't know I'm here.

Ah. Okay.

I'm not sure what to tell them. I'm not sure I can go through with it.

That's understandable. It's a big step.

I keep thinking, you know: What if we're wrong? What if we're destroying my father's life and we're wrong? Because this case is going to destroy him either way, isn't it?

Probably.

And I'll be responsible, won't I?

Partially.

You really think my father did it.

I do. I've told you that.

See, this is what I don't understand. You seem so sure. How can you be so sure?

I look at the evidence and decide. What else can I do?

That's what the DA said. I just don't think I'm wired that way. To *judge* people. If we're wrong, I don't know if I could live with it. The responsibility.

I don't envy you. You're too young to have to make a decision like this.

It's just that I don't want to hurt anyone.

Well, it's actually pretty easy to go through life without ever hurting anyone or getting anything wrong or making a mistake. Just never *act*. Never do anything. Leave the world exactly as you found it.

At this I close my eyes, rub my brow. There is a knot in my brain.

Bailis comes out from behind his desk and tactfully closes the office door, then takes the chair opposite mine, in front of his desk. The office is not very big; our knees nearly touch.

Can I ask you a question, Jeff? What is your relationship like with your father?

Right now?

Right now.

I don't have one.

What does that mean? You don't speak at all?

No, we don't.

When was the last time you spoke to him?

It had been years, then I just saw him a few days ago. I accused him.

And what did he say?

He said I was wrong, he didn't do it. He *insisted*. I haven't spoken to him since. I don't know that I ever will.

I'm sorry.

It's no big deal.

It's a very big deal. What would you *like* your relationship with him to be?

It doesn't matter what I'd like. It's not up to me.

Why not?

Because I can't change him.

Why would you want to change him? Why not just accept him as he is?

You know why.

No, tell me.

Because of what he did.

A minute ago you said you didn't *know* what he did, you still had doubt.

I don't have doubt. I have . . . resistance. I don't *want* this. I don't want it to be true.

I don't blame you, kiddo.

Do you have kids, Mr. Bailis?

I have a daughter.

How old?

Thirty-two.

Are you a good father?

I'm an imperfect father.

Are you a good-enough father?

I don't know. I try to be.

I'm an imperfect son.

There's no other kind, Jeff.

Yeah, but we don't all sue our fathers. We disappoint them, not sue them. What if I decide not to go ahead with it? What happens to the case?

I think it probably ends there. If the children are opposed, if they still believe in their father, it's unlikely a jury would go against that.

But we wouldn't be opposed. We just wouldn't be participating.

How is a jury supposed to tell the difference?

What about my aunt Kate? She has a right to a lawyer, doesn't she?

I suppose. She has a right to a lawyer; she doesn't have a right to me. And I wouldn't bring the case if I thought you and your sister didn't want it.

Are you trying to pressure me to do it?

Just the opposite: I'm trying to ease the pressure on you. Here—

He goes to his desk, rummages around in the papers on the desktop, and brings a manila folder to me.

Here. Look this over. See what you think. It's my file on your mother's . . . disappearance. I kept a few reports from the DA's file.

Is that legal?

I don't know. You'll have to ask a lawyer.

He winks.

Okay. I'll check it out. Maybe I'll find something everyone else missed, right?

No. You won't find any answers in there, just facts. Old police reports, photos, grand jury transcripts. A bunch of puzzle pieces that don't fit together. But go on, read it, maybe it'll help you decide.

I'll bring it back.

Keep it. If you decide not to go ahead with the suit, I'll have no more use for it.

But you hung on to it all these years.

Exactly. Maybe it's time for all of us to move on.

Can I ask you a question? Did you know my father back then?

Of course.

Did you ever try a case against him?

Many times.

He was a good lawyer, wasn't he?

He was an excellent lawyer.

What did you think of him personally?

He was an excellent lawyer.

Ah. That's what I thought. Why didn't you like him?

He was difficult. But lots of lawyers are difficult, I suppose.

You mean he was an asshole.

Lots of lawyers are that too.

What was it, then?

I didn't trust him.

He lied to you?

In this job everybody lies.

Do you lie?

Of course.

No, you don't. I don't believe that.

Sure, I do. If I have a client who I know is guilty, and I stand up in court and say he is not guilty, haven't I lied?

No. It's like a poker player saying he has a full house. It's not lying; it's how the game is played.

It's how the game is played. Exactly. That's why I shouldn't bad-mouth him.

Okay, so maybe he lied a little back then. Doesn't mean he did this.

No, it doesn't.

You think he was capable of it.

I think in the right circumstances anyone is capable of anything.

I'm not.

You underestimate yourself.

Overestimate, you mean.

Bailis makes a face: eyebrows raised, head tilted. *Whatever.* He says, Maybe you overestimate your father. You wouldn't be the first son to do that.

In the waiting room, he tells me, Just let me know what you want to do. Any decision you make will be the right one. You'll know.

The *Lawyers Weekly* is still on the coffee table where I left it.

Can I have this?

Sure.

———

ALEX invites me to play golf at his country club in Brookline. This has never happened before. I have no interest in golf or country clubs or, for that matter, in Alex. But it is hard to say no to my brother, whose invitations feel like commands. He says *You wanna play golf?* with the same presumption that a rich man says to his driver *Will you bring the car around?*

I am supremely uncomfortable here. The club is snooty, the members are an army of farcical old-money clichés. And here am I, in rumpled khakis and old sneakers.

Alex is wearing a trim, fitted golf outfit. He looks like a very tall acrobat.

It is a muggy morning, and I am sweating more than anyone else on the course, I'm sure.

Of course I have no chance against Alex. His golf game is picturesque. With his long body and long clubs, he is like a windmill. He generates power effortlessly with great lazy, looping swings. He has a trick of backspinning the ball so that, on landing, it snags the surface with talons and sticks there. Me, I don't play golf, and this course is not for beginners. It is short but difficult, full of sand traps, water hazards, hillocks, tall grass, and narrow fairways. It is infuriating. It is designed to be infuriating. Even the fairways are pimpled and rolling like the surface of the ocean.

I scuffle through seven holes, hitting five balls into the woods, losing two of them. There is a foursome creeping up behind us, and I am anxious about holding them up. Alex and I barely speak. I am miserable.

But on the eighth hole something miraculous happens. The hole is a short par 3 with a fairway that bends to the right. The only way to play it, Alex instructs me, is to drive the ball to the elbow of the fairway, where the path to the green turns, then pitch to the green from there. By dumb luck and for the first time today, my drive is on target. I know nothing about golf, but in the magical *snick* of the three wood off the tee, I can feel what draws golfers in: the little elation of a ball well struck, the rapture of watching it arc toward its goal. The momentary taste of rightness, of perfection—*yes!*

High on this little success, as Alex and I walk to our cart then ride down the side of the fairway, I let my guard down a little, I begin to imagine that Alex and I can be real brothers. So I disgorge a pet theory:

This has to be the stupidest sport. I mean, isn't it? How many hours have you spent playing this game, and for what? To learn the skill of hitting a little ball with a stick? What on earth is the point? What are you going to do with that skill? Think what you could have accomplished.

You could say that about any sport. What's the point of throwing a ball through a hoop? What's the point of hitting a ball over a net?

Yeah, but golf is especially ridiculous. It takes so much *time*.

Right, Jeff, because you use your time so wisely. You're so busy.

It's not even good exercise. I mean, look at us. We're riding in a *cart*, for Christ's sake. We're like invalids! This is a sport?

You're just saying that 'cause you suck at it.

Yeah, I suck at it, but I suck at a lot of things. I suck at open-heart surgery, I suck at playing the trombone; I would never say those things are stupid.

We arrive at my ball. It may have been my first decent drive all day, but I am still a good ten yards short of Alex's ball.

You're away, Alex says, because he is a dick.

I have no idea which club to use for any given shot, so I have to ask Alex, What am I hitting?

Seven iron.

I take this club from my bag, which Alex has borrowed from a friend of his because Alex's own clubs are much too long for me.

There's golf *courses* too. What a complete fucking waste of real estate. Look at all this. We can't find a better use for this land?

No, Jeff, we can't.

This game probably made sense at the start, in Scotland, because that whole country looks like a fucking golf course. You didn't have to build anything. You dug a few little holes and, boom, that's a golf course.

You've never been to Scotland, Jeff. Hit the ball.

Golf courses and cemeteries: biggest waste of real estate in America.

Just hit the ball.

So I make a few golfish gestures. I stand back to look at the flag and visualize the ball arcing toward it. This is a technique Alex has shared with me: imagine yourself succeeding, and you will. I take a relaxed practice swing. I stand over the ball and waggle the clubhead. I am ready. But then—what happened?—I am not ready. I have waited too long, the ready moment has passed, and now I am thinking too much: *I can par this hole. The drive is the toughest part. If I can just hit this green. Don't think. Just relax . . .*

I shank the ball off the heel of the club. It dribbles away to the left, not more than twenty feet.

I fucking hate golf.

It takes practice.

I'm taking a mulligan.

You can't take a mulligan. We're playing here.

Exactly, we're *playing*. Do you even know what that word means?

It means somebody wins and somebody loses.

No! That's not what it means at all. Anyway, you must be up by twenty strokes.

Eleven.

Who cares, Alex? Look, what if I just concede? You win. Now we can play just for fun.

Then what's the point of playing?

Exactly! There is none! It's a *game*.

It's not a game; it's competition. That's not pointless—it's *life*.

Life is golf?

No, life is competition. It's *like* golf. It's a metaphor.

It's not a fucking metaphor! Alex, we're hitting a ball into a fuckin' hole in the ground. What's metaphorical about that?

Ai, this is your whole problem: You want everything to be easy. You don't want to work for anything. That's the metaphor.

What? Do you know what a metaphor is?

Jeff, do you know why people play golf?

No, but you're about to tell me, aren't you?

They play golf because it's *not* easy. They want to challenge themselves. That's not you. God forbid you ever challenge yourself.

Wait, all that because I suck at golf?

No, it's not just golf. You have problems here, so you run away to San Fran.

Nobody calls it San Fran.

And when that doesn't fix it, you drink yourself stupid. You're thirty years old, Jeff—thirty!—and what *are* you? Your whole life is a mulligan. It's one long excuse. A mulligan is a kind of lie. It's avoiding responsibility.

I have no idea what that means. I just want to hit the golf ball again.

Let me ask you something: What do you think you're up to with that lawyer? Suing Dad?

What does that have to do with anything?

I'm just wondering. What kind of guy could sue his own father?

Let me guess: the kind of guy who would take a mulligan.

I'm being serious, Jeff.

Okay, let's be *serious.* How about: the kind of guy whose father killed his mother.

Oh, that is such bullshit. Naive, sanctimonious, melodramatic, self-righteous bullshit. You don't even believe it yourself.

I do, actually. Not the naive, sanctimonious part.

You can't believe it. It makes no sense. It's completely ridiculous.

Why?

Because this is your own father. You get that, right?

Yeah, I get it. It's not a complicated point.

Then how could you do it? How could you even consider it? You're going to blow up your own family? What the fuck is wrong with you?

Is that a trick question? What's wrong with me is I have a conscience.

A conscience?

Don't worry, I'm trying to get rid of it.

Is that what you tell yourself? It's your conscience? Well, aren't you precious.

You know what, Alex? I just *got* it. I thought you wanted to play golf. What an idiot I am! This is why you brought me out here, isn't it? So I'd be trapped on a golf course and you could grill me about this.

No, I thought we could talk about it like adults.

Why would you ever think that?

Jeff, if you do this . . . I don't know what. If you do this, there'll be nothing left. You'll destroy the whole thing, what little we have left. You won't have a family to go back to.

Do I have one now?

Yes! I'm right here! What am I? I'm your family.

Not your best argument.

What about Miranda? What about Dad?

What about Mom? Oh, right.

He groaned. Jeff, I get it. Something bad happened to you. You lost your mother.

I didn't lose her. She wasn't a set of keys.

She *died*, okay? It was a tragedy. A complete fucking tragedy. It was cruel, it was awful. And you're not the only one who got hurt, by the way. But it was a long time ago, and nothing we do will ever change it. The world just keeps on turning. What else are we going to do?

So just forget it?

No, don't forget it. Just stop feeling sorry for yourself. Stop thinking of yourself as a victim your whole life and start *building* something instead. Stop blaming other people. *Help* yourself. Man up. Jesus.

Man up? Really? Like for the big game against Yale?

No, like: be a man. Your family needs you. You're not a kid anymore.

I'm starting to think you're not going to give me that mulligan.

Jeff, stop, all right? If you won't do it for yourself, do it for Miranda. She needs you. Help her, don't pull her under the waves with you. Help your family. Help your family.

You mean help Dad.

Yes, help your father. Is that so ridiculous?

It is, actually.

Jeff, here's how I think about it. It's real simple. I want to make things better, not worse. That's it.

That's it? That's your big idea?

Yes. I want to put this family back together again, at least a little.

Alex, that's not realistic.

Of course it is.

The whole family's broken. Everyone except you.

Then heal! Change! At least try.

I'm trying, Alex. Believe me, I'm trying.

Are you? Are you making things better? If not, *why* not?

He obviously believes it too. To Alex anything is possible. Why not, indeed? What has he ever failed to achieve? Imagine yourself succeeding, and you will. Who am I to say he's wrong?

Alex, it's a lie. You're all worked up about a mulligan—

Oh, I don't give a fuck about the mulligan.

—but you're willing to look the other way on *this*? I don't get you.

I'm not looking the other way on anything, Jeff. I'm just trying to prevent you from making a huge mistake. That's all.

AFTER the district attorney's decision not to prosecute, it takes nearly a week to release my mother's remains. Aunt Kate and my father argue for days over who will arrange the funeral—who will control the bones—until my father relents, allowing Kate to plan a short, unpublicized family-only graveside ceremony, to keep away the gawkers. Her hatred of my father is total. When he makes a public statement to a *Globe* reporter that the DA has cleared him of the crime—including the cliché about *Where do I go to get my good name back?*—Aunt Kate calls the same reporter to clarify that the DA has said no such thing and that the family still considers him Jane Larkin's murderer. She seems to be daring him to sue for slander. Dad is right, however, that he has not been charged, so presumably he has some right to be heard on the question of his wife's burial (or reburial). In the end, he allows Kate to make the arrangements, but there is no way to prevent him from attending.

So, on a warm morning in July, our little family stands together in a graveyard in West Roxbury. Mimi and me. Alex, his wife and kids. Aunt Kate and Uncle Stephen. Nine people, that's all that's left.

A full-size casket is suspended on thick canvas straps above an open grave, with bunting draped around it to hide the view down into the hole.

A dozen folding chairs.

A man from the funeral home stands nearby. Balding, florid complexion, black suit. A drinker, I imagine, though who would begrudge him? He has agreed to recite some rote funereal comments, relieving us all of the obligation to speak.

Dad arrives last. I suspect he wants to minimize his time here, around Aunt Kate especially. He marches toward us with theatrical dignity, a man with a grievous duty to perform but also with nothing to hide. His suit is tailored, charcoal gray. I have to hand it to him: the man knows how to dress. His coat is buttoned despite the heat. I am struck again by how gray his hair is, though I saw him only a couple of weeks ago. How handsome he is, the sort of guy you would pass on the sidewalk and think, *That must be someone important*. I am struck, too, by how little I feel for him today. Not love or hate or anger or anything at all. He is just a guy I used to know.

Alone among our group, Alex steps forward to greet him. A handshake, then a shoulders-only man-hug. Neither of them is a hugger. The disparity in their heights only makes it worse.

The easy bit done, Dad comes to stand awkwardly in front of Mimi and me.

He sticks out his hand toward me. He knows it is safe to do this, that I will not embarrass him. There is a phrase in the newspapers a lot lately: President Clinton is said to be "conflict averse." It describes me, too, and I accept the handshake dutifully. God, at moments like this I loathe myself.

After me, however, comes the more volatile business of greeting Miranda. Dad stands before her a moment regarding her, as if she is a safe to crack or a bomb to defuse. He says, Hello, Mimi.

Hello.

Not *Hello, Daddy*. Just *Hello*.

He puts a hand on each of her upper arms, a gesture meant as a modest hug, I guess, but it comes off as a sort of wrestler's hold. Grasping her this way, he kisses her cheek.

She recoils from his kiss, but only a little, and half-heartedly. When it is over, Mimi's eyes are brimming.

Sweetheart, he says.

Aunt Kate tells him: Dan, just get away from her.

Dad, leave her alone, please.

Dad bristles but goes to stand with Alex.

The man from the funeral home makes a short speech, welcoming us, explaining that he understands the family wants as brief a ceremony as possible. He knows we are not a religious family, but at Aunt Kate's request he will read a single Bible passage. It is from Proverbs, he tells us, as he opens a worn softcover Bible:

A wife of noble character who can find? She is worth far more than rubies. Her husband has full confidence in her and lacks nothing of value. She brings him good, not harm, all the days of her life.

The passage goes on at length, a litany of the noble wife's deeds:

She selects wool and flax. . . . She gets up while it is still night. . . . She watches over the affairs of her household. . . . Her children arise and call her blessed.

Through it all, Kate glares at Dad.

When the funeral director finishes the peroration—*Honor her for all that her hands have done, and let her works bring her praise at the city gate*—he looks up to find us all slack-jawed. Mistaking our shock for grief, he mutters on our behalf, Amen.

He asks, Is there anyone who would like to say a few words?

Aunt Kate comes forward to stand by him. She is wearing a black skirt suit with a band collar notched at the hollow of her throat, like a priest's collar, and beside this professional funeralist she looks the much more solemn, more righteous. Kate has gotten so lean over the years; there is something hard and puritanical in her look now.

She says in an even, controlled tone: I was going to talk about my sister. I wrote down all these . . . remarks. I lay awake last night hoping I'd get it just right. I wanted to remember her. And *be with* her, in a way, just for a minute. She was beautiful and she was mischievous and she was fun and she was loving and she was *good*. I wanted to enjoy the memory of my sister here, all together. As a family.

A beat.

But Dan, Dan. You profane this moment by being here, *Dan*. Your presence here is an obscenity. It's monstrous.

Miranda murmurs, Oh my God.

Did you come here to bury her, Dan? Why don't you grab a shovel? It wouldn't be the first time.

Uncle Stephen says, Kate, stop. This isn't the time. You have to stop.

But Kate will not stop.

What is that look on your face, Dan? What does it mean?

Aunt Kate, please don't.

Would you please tell me *why*, Dan. Tell me why you did this.

Dad turns his head to his right, as if he would spare Kate the indignity of being seen this way.

Because I can live without my sister, I guess. I've done it long enough. But for the life of me, Dan, I cannot live without knowing why.

There is a long moment of silence. City noise, like distant applause.

She was so good to you, Dan. She gave you everything. And you took it all. Even her bones. Didn't you?

I didn't.

Yes, you did. Yes, you did.

No.

Why are you here, Dan? What is the point of you being here?

Same as you: I loved her. She was my wife. I lost her, too, Kate.

You don't belong here. You should leave.

No.

Kate's mouth is slightly open, tensed, so that the tips of her teeth are just visible in her skeletal face.

I have to go, then. I can't do this. Kids, I'm sorry. I'm very sorry.

Miranda pleads, Aunt Kate—

But Kate is already walking away. Head down, as if the footing is uneven and she might trip if she looks up.

For a moment Uncle Stephen hesitates, then he bustles off after her without a word.

I am watching them leave when I hear my father say: I'd like to say something.

Miranda says, Oh my God, please don't.

Dad says, with little practiced gestures of his arms honed over years in courtrooms: I'm sorry you kids had to hear that. Your aunt Kate is very upset, obviously. I don't bear her any ill will. People can say what they like. I loved your mother very much. Very much. And I miss her terribly. Don't let anyone or anything make you think otherwise.

And that's it. That's all Dan Larkin has to say about his wife of seventeen years, now dead for eighteen. That's all the sorrow and memory he can muster. *I loved her very much*.

Alex says, We know, Dad.

Mimi and I say nothing. There is simply nothing to say anymore.

The funeral man, with an exquisite sense of the macabre, says in a soothing, priestly voice—as if nothing odd has happened here—This is the end of the service. If any family members would like to stay as the casket is lowered into the grave, you are welcome. If not, the service is concluded.

I say, I'll stay.

Miranda grumbles into my coat sleeve, Please make him go, Jeff.

Dad, you have to go.

My father then takes a step toward Miranda, presumably to comfort her. She is his daughter, after all. He says, Miranda.

Get! Out! she orders.

Dad, go.

Get *out*! What is *wrong* with you?

Something in Mimi's rising voice seems to break him a little. His iron posture slips, his shoulders round forward perceptibly.

Okay. I'm sorry. I didn't mean—

He turns and walks off. I can only hope that Aunt Kate has already left the parking lot or we may have another funeral before the day is over. Maybe there is a discount if we buy in bulk.

Alex's wife, Laurel Marcus-but-not-Larkin, says, We should get the kids home. They don't need to see this.

She glances at the coffin meaningfully, and Alex nods.

I don't want to see it either, Miranda says.

I do.

Why, Jeff? It's ghoulish.

I don't know, Meem. It just feels like something I want to do. It's okay. Go wait by the car. I'll meet you.

When we are alone with the coffin, me and the funeral man, a quartet of shadowy men with shovels appears in the shade of a tree nearby, uncertain if their cue has come. He waves the shovel crew over. They avoid eye contact, avoid conversation. They move quickly, efficiently. The bunting around the coffin is pulled away and laid on the grass, near a neat conical pile of dirt covered by a tarp. Hand cranks are attached to the straps that support the coffin. The cranks are turned, the coffin descends. Afterward, the straps are tugged out from under it.

The men flip the tarp off the dirt pile and, avoiding my eyes, they begin the work of refilling the hole they dug a few hours ago. The dirt and stones clatter on the wood coffin. Then a softer chatter, then a sifting sound, dirt falling on dirt, as the coffin begins to disappear.

I step forward and hold my hand out for the shovel held by one of the gravediggers. Can I do this?

He hesitates, unsure.

It's okay, I assure him.

He hands me the shovel. His fingers are stained with dirt.

The others stand aside to let me work. They seem unsure whether I want them to help, so I give them a little wave and say, It's okay, I'll do it.

The shoveling is easy. There has not been much rain lately; the ground is dry. The soil is loose and light. It is good to be moving, to be doing. Oddly, the chore is not sad at all. It feels productive, useful, practical. It is satisfying to fill this hole. I do the work carefully, spread the dirt evenly; I do not want to screw it up as I usually do. This is the closest I have been to my mother in nearly eighteen years, which is longer than I'd been alive when she vanished. It is the first thing I have done for her in all that time, and I feel helpful, a good son, as if I am standing at her elbow in the kitchen all those years ago.

I had a mother once. How odd. I wish I could have a moment with her, as Aunt Kate said. Just a few minutes to visit. I would like to hear her voice. I would like to do right by her. Not for *her* (she is past caring) but for me. I would like to go back to the place where I lost my way and choose a different road.

IN the afternoon, still wearing the suit and tie I wore to the funeral, I go into town to return Mr. Bailis's case file and tell him I'm in.

He comes to the lobby of his office. His shirt collar is crooked. His belt is cinched tight, causing his pants to bunch. Does he live alone? Is there no wife to fix his collar, to ask why he is losing weight?

When I give him the news, he only nods and says, Okay.

You have your lead plaintiff. Larkin versus Larkin. Isn't that what you wanted?

It's not what we want. It's what we have to do.

I thought you'd be happier.

I am happy for the opportunity. It's just, it can't end well, can it? But here we are: damned if you do, damned if you don't.

THE next morning, Miranda drives me back to Logan to catch a flight to SFO.

At the gate she says with fake offhandedness, Jamie asked me to tell you goodbye.

Did she?

Yeah.

She's totally in love with me, isn't she?

I don't think so. She called you Steve.

See, now that's funny.

She bear-hugs me in her guileless way and tells me, I won't miss you.

Why don't you come with me, Miranda? You'd love San Francisco. It's all a bunch of hippies burning their bras. You'll fit right in.

Do you have any idea what a decent bra costs?

I mean it, Mimi. Come. Why not?

Because it isn't home.

She gazes at me earnestly, hoping I will agree.

Jeff, just make me one promise, okay? Stop drinking. For a while, at least. And forget that girl.

That's two promises.

No. The drinking and the girl are the same thing.

The girl, fine. Can I at least keep the drinking?

No.

You sound like Alex.

Maybe Alex is right. You're better than this. This isn't you.

I'm *not* better than this. This *is* me. I am exactly *this*.

That's not true, Jeff. I love you but please, please get your shit together. For me.

Miranda is right, of course. It is time to grow up, put childish things aside. Lord knows, this isn't the first time I've heard it. She is wrong about the drinking, though. Drinking is the symptom, not the disease. The disease is unhappiness. And it seems to me that I am done with it, it seems to me that it is time to stop. All the romantic obsession, the rumination, the melancholy, the indiscipline—the whole Sad Young Man routine. It is beginning to feel like a coat I have outgrown, a coat I am ready to take off.

But first, a drink. Maybe two. As soon as the plane has steadied and we are comfortably missiling west, I order two nips of Stoli and a glass of ice. The stewardess brings me two packages of peanuts, too, in fiendish, unopenable packets. Breakfast of champions. I empty both mini bottles into my plastic United Airlines cup, and I settle back among the travelers with their neck pillows and their *People* magazines, who have never heard of Jane Larkin.

2

Fourteen months later. September 21, 1994. Five days before the trial is scheduled to open.

I am back in the conference room in Mr. Bailis's little office. I am resolved that the only way to deal with this situation is to immerse myself in it—in the details of trial strategy and evidence. The only way out is through. So I am poring over transcripts of depositions—sworn testimony, under oath, conducted by the lawyers—which have been the greatest part of Bailis's "discovery" (wonderful term) over this long pretrial period. Before me now is Jamie's deposition. The deposition took place in this very room, last April. She may have sat in the same chair I am occupying now.

MR. BAILIS: Were you ever afraid of Dan Larkin?

WITNESS: Yes.

MR. BAILIS: Why? Did he ever behave in a way that frightened or concerned you? Or made you afraid for your safety?

WITNESS: Yes.

MR. BAILIS: Or your mother's safety?

WITNESS: Yes.

MR. BAILIS: What did he do?

WITNESS: He touched me in a way that was inappropriate.

MR. BAILIS: Sexually inappropriate?

WITNESS: Yes.

MR. BAILIS: Did he ever hit you or injure you physically?

WITNESS: No.

MR. BAILIS: But he touched you in a way that you considered unwelcome?

WITNESS: Yes.

MR. BAILIS: How many times?

WITNESS: Ten or twelve. Approximately.

MR. BAILIS: Over how long a period?

WITNESS: Almost a year.

MR. BAILIS: Did you report it to anyone at the time?

WITNESS: Eventually.

MR. BAILIS: Who did you report it to?

WITNESS: My mother.

MR. BAILIS: And what was her response?

WITNESS: We moved out of the house.

MR. BAILIS: All right, let's talk about this.

I have read this deposition several times already.

Mr. Bailis has told me that as the client, I have a perfect right to see the evidence. He holds back only his own handwritten notes. He is humoring me, I think, but I am helping him too. There is something lonely and monastic about Mr. Bailis's life. He seems to enjoy my presence in the office. This is the second straight day I have spent in the conference room studying his papers, and he stops by every few hours to check on me.

Coming into the room at the end of an afternoon, he asks, So what do you think, counselor? You don't look happy.

Some of these are hard to read.

Yes. But this is the business we're in.

Anyway, I think we're gonna lose. We don't have anything solid.

It always seems that way. Look.

He takes my yellow legal pad and flips to a blank sheet. He draws a vertical line down the middle of the page, creating two columns. Above the left column he draws a minus sign, above the right column a plus sign.

All you do, he tells me, is put down every piece of evidence, every argument, every fact, in one of these columns. Either it's good for us or it's bad for us. Then you try to move everything in the minus column to the plus column. From this side to that side. And that is the entire practice of law.

What if you can't move it?

You can always move it.

That's it? It takes three years of law school to learn that?

Well, you don't learn how to be a lawyer in law school.

Where do you learn, then?

Here. Doing what you're doing right now. There were lawyers long before there were law schools. How do you think they learned?

He winks. He seems to brighten the closer the trial gets.

Time to go home, Jeff. We don't have to find all the answers tonight.

THAT evening, I am at a restaurant in Brookline Village. Waiting for Miranda and Jamie. The place is casual, crowded with tables, open kitchen, noisy, clattery, cozy.

When Jamie arrives, she makes her way over. It is a pleasure to watch her. Something about her square-shouldered walk and her heart-shaped face framed by curls.

I stand and we hug cordially.

You're here early.

If you're five minutes early, you're ten minutes late.

She gives me the side-eye. Who are you and what have you done with Jeff Larkin?

It's something my dad used to say.

Where's Miranda? I feel like I'm crashing. You don't mind that she invited me?

Of course not. She's not here yet.

I think she wants to lock us in the linen closet together.

She thinks it's what *I* want.

Jamie wrinkles her nose: *Let's not go there.* You look different. Did you change something?

No, I don't think so.

A waitress comes by to take our drink order.

Jamie, to me: What are you drinking?

Just water.

Really?

Really.

Okay then. To the waitress: I'll have the sangria.

The waitress leaves.

Jamie, can I ask you something before my sister gets here? I read your deposition.

Well, that's embarrassing.

How come you never said anything?

I did.

To me, I mean.

She looks down.

And why did you wait so long even to tell your mom? If you were scared, if he was putting his hands on you—I don't get it. Why would you wait?

She does not answer. She is not prepared for this conversation.

We don't have to talk about it if you don't want. It's just, why so long?

You mean you don't know?

No.

Because of you.

A beat.

Because if I told, I knew I'd never see you again.

Oh. Oh.

It's okay, Jeff. It was a long time ago.

It's not okay. I wish I'd known. I would have killed him.

Thank you.

I mean it. It makes me so angry, even now.

Well, it's over. And the lawyer said I won't have to testify, so no one ever has to know. He said it's not relevant.

I think it's relevant.

Eh. It happened long after your mother disappeared. What would it prove?

If my dad had a thing for young women, and his wife wasn't young anymore? If he saw something he couldn't have, and he tried to take it anyway? I think that's relevant. But all that—that isn't what I meant. I don't know if it's relevant to the case; I'm not a lawyer. I meant it's relevant to me.

Well, look, there's a kind of man that every woman knows to stay away from. He was one. There's no reason for you to be upset, though. Not now.

Not sure I agree with that.

I'm a little happy that you're upset, honestly. Thank you.

I'm glad your mother got you out of there. Even though.

Me too. Even though.

Miranda arrives with a flutter, like a bird flapping down into a nest, all smiles and apologies and cheek-kisses. My two favorite people, she says.

Miranda has a manic, false quality tonight. She is working to be happy, laboring against the outgoing tide.

She says to Jamie, Are you okay, sweetie? You look upset.

I'm fine.

What horrible thing did he say to you? You two look so serious.

We were just talking, that's all.

About what?

Jeff was just telling me about the trial.

The trial. I wish we could think about *anything* else. At least it'll be over, right? We'll ride the roller coaster to the bottom and then we'll finally be able to get off.

I tell her: Mimi, I've told you, don't think that way. You're going to be disappointed. The roller coaster isn't going to stop.

So what am I supposed to do?

Just protect yourself a little, that's all.

How? How do I do that? Can *you* do that? You didn't use to. I don't know what happened to you.

Maybe I'm getting old.

Well, stop it.

Jamie lays her hand over Miranda's and squeezes it, which is probably what I should have done.

AFTER dinner, Miranda makes a point of vanishing so I will be alone with Jamie.

We walk to her apartment, a fifteen- or twenty-minute stroll on a pleasant September night.

She says, Did you mean what you said to Miranda, that you don't think the trial is going to make any difference?

I said it wouldn't be the end for her. For me, it will be. I need to start my life.

Thirty's late to be starting your life.

Thirty-one. And I know.

Well, you still have a few good years left.

Thank you for that.

When we reach her apartment building, she says, Do you want to come up?

I think if I come up, things are going to go a certain way.

That's kind of the idea.

I don't—I'm not in the habit of turning down offers like that.

Jeff, I'm not exactly in the habit of making them.

It's just, I kind of have this feeling like, if things ever . . . went a certain way with you, I kind of want everything to be perfect, you know?

You might be waiting a long time. Perfect is a big word.

I know. I just don't want it to be part of this whole thing, something we just did because we were under stress, because the trial was coming up. I want it to come *after*.

After. Okay.

Is it?

It's fine, Jeff.

It doesn't feel fine. It feels like I'm blowing it right now, like this is the moment.

Who knows. Life.

Yeah. Life.

Just don't wait too long, okay? Don't think so much.

I'm working on it.

She goes inside, and I do not. I stand on the sidewalk already knowing our moment will never come. I can go in now, still. I can change my mind. But I don't. I walk away.

FOUR days before the trial is set to begin, my father calls with an offer to settle. Settlement offers are not unusual, Mr. Bailis tells us. It would be surprising if he did *not* offer to settle, at least half-heartedly. (What's to lose?) But it is obvious that, even in this run-of-the-mill interaction, my dad can't help pissing off Mr. Bailis. Rather than convey the offer to our attorney, as lawyers ordinarily do, my dad cuts Bailis out of the loop by calling us directly with an invitation to meet. With a bully's eye for weakness, he invites Miranda first, the most pliable and sentimental of us plaintiffs. Once she has accepted his invitation, the rest of us are trapped. Rather than meet at an attorney's office, he asks to meet at his own home, at the dinner table where we grew up eating as a family. It is all so transparently manipulative—an appeal to emotion, to family loyalty—that I half admire him for sheer ballsy shamelessness.

But it is also emotionally obtuse. Whenever I am in that house, I can't help but think of my mother. Time has not scrubbed her from this place. She is in the floorboards, she is in the walls. She is in the creaky dining room chairs where, on a Friday morning, we now gather to hear the great Dan Larkin plead with his children for mercy. How could he not know that, sitting around the table where we ate dinner every night at six, his children would be reminded of her? That we would feel angry, not nostalgic, and certainly not loyal to dear old Dad.

He sits at the head of the table with some papers in front of him. He is wearing a suit. The buttonhole in the lapel of his coat winks open, a real handmade buttonhole, not the usual fake stitched-on kind. He has taken off his necktie to suggest he is weary, beleaguered, at the end of his rope. But it is all so stiff and stagy—so careful. (I know it sounds ridiculous to say that my father can't even take off his tie without seeming phony, but I'm telling you: nothing this guy does is spontaneous, nothing. This is a man who makes a point of sitting in a different spot on the couch every day so the cushions wear evenly. I promise you: he thought long and hard about leaving off that necktie.)

Opposite him, in my mother's chair, is Kate. He had to include her; she is a named plaintiff, he needs her agreement on any settlement. But she seems so far from settling with her sister's killer that it's surprising she even showed up. Probably she came in order to prevent a settlement, not agree to one. It is also striking, as she sits in Jane's chair, how alike and how different she looks from her sister—a skeletal, stony, sculptural version of my mom. And of course Aunt Kate is much older today than Mom ever got to be.

Miranda, in "her" chair from childhood, wearing her hair pulled back and a six-inch cuff of bracelets on her left wrist.

Mr. Bailis with his old briefcase.

And me. Amid all this emotion, I am preoccupied, absurdly, not with the murder or the settlement, but with the fact that I had a chance to sleep with Jamie Bennett last night and I passed it up. It is shallow, I know, to be thinking about getting laid right now, but I am *alive* and my mother, God bless her, is not.

The only one missing is Alex, whom Mimi has lately been calling Benedict Larkin. Alex is not a plaintiff but he is still a member of the family, and his absence is noticeable. I presume it was carefully calculated too: my dad knows I will say no whenever, wherever, and whyever Alex says yes.

Dad explains his offer: It is everything he has. Two-point-eight million dollars in cash (that's tax-free, he tells us, waggling his finger), his entire life savings. He will include the house we are sitting in, too, after a life tenancy that would permit him to live there until his death.

As he spells out his proposal, eyes dart around the table. The number is actually low and dishonest. His inheritance alone will be much larger than what he is offering, unless the Coachman Shoe fortune has completely vanished. No doubt he has some cash hidden away too.

He finishes with this closing argument:

I've thought about this carefully, about what's best for all of us. None of us wants this lawsuit. It's foolish. None of us can win, surely you know that. I've spent my whole career in courtrooms and I can tell you: nobody wins. I don't want to face my own children in court, and I want you kids to have whatever peace you're looking for. Your complaint asks for twenty-five million in damages. That's insane. I don't know where that figure came from. I don't have anything like that kind of money. There's no chance you'll actually recover that number. It's just not realistic. The real purpose of asking for an outrageous verdict like that is to destroy me; I don't know how else to interpret it. It's to wipe me out for good. I'm asking you to be reasonable, and in exchange we can all be spared what's about to happen. It's not too late. All I'm asking is to keep the clothes on my back and a roof over my head. I'm not a young man; it would not be easy for me to be wiped out like this, believe me. If you don't trust me, I have a letter here—let me find it; here—from a forensic accountant documenting that this is all the assets I have. This is literally everything you could possibly win in court. It would be a complete victory for you. You can't get blood from a stone.

Kate says, It's not everything. You're not admitting what you did.

Kate, you know I can't do that.

A confession is the only thing that matters. I don't need money, I don't need a house. I need the truth. Finally.

You can't ask me to confess to murder. There's no statute of limitations for murder.

Is that the only reason?

No, Kate, of course not. I didn't do this.

Then why settle?

Because the truth doesn't matter. I can't win this case, and you know it. The moment I walk into court, I lose. It doesn't matter what the jury says. I'll *look* like a killer just sitting there. That's what this is really all about, isn't it? You'll convict me in public whether you prove your case or not. I'll be smeared. That's why you're doing it.

Kate shakes her head. No. Not without a confession.

Kate, be reasonable. We're talking about a settlement, not a surrender. Both sides have to give something. That's what settling means.

How can I settle over something as important as my sister's life?

And how can I confess to a murder I didn't commit?

Well then, Dan, it seems we're at an impasse.

Miranda says: If there's a way to avoid a trial, I would like that.

Silence.

Dad says, It's a lot of money. It would really help you kids, which I would love to do. And you can't win a penny more by going to trial because there isn't a penny more to collect.

Miranda: What do you think, Jeff?

Mimi, I think we should be honest. Since we're all putting our cards on the table, I think Dad is right about what he's saying, about how a trial is going to suck for everyone. And it is a lot of money. But I also think Aunt Kate is right: we owe Mom something. Somebody has to stand up for her. And there's also me and you, Miranda. We need to be able to walk away with some finality about this. Dad's not offering that. I don't blame him, really. If he confesses to murder—

Jeff, that's not why—

I know, Dad, I heard you, I get it, you didn't do it. But the fact is, if this jury comes back with a guilty verdict—

Mr. Bailis corrects me: Liable, not guilty. This is a civil action.

Okay, liable then. If the jury says he did it—even if the standard is just fifty percent and a feather, more likely he did it than not—then maybe things change in the criminal case too. Maybe the public gets interested again, maybe the DA looks at the case again. I think Dad knows all that too. He's priced that into his offer.

I don't know if I want Daddy in prison. I don't want to be the cause of all that.

Thank you, sweetie.

Miranda winces at the endearment.

What do you recommend, Mr. Bailis?

Jeff, I can't tell you what to do. It's your decision. I can say that this discussion should not be happening here, with your father present. We should go somewhere where we can hash it out in private.

There's nothing to hash out, Kate says evenly. I'll take this out of everyone's hands. I'm not settling. I know I said I wouldn't go ahead without you kids, but I don't feel that way anymore. I've come too far. If you kids want to settle, if you feel that's right for you, then you should. I'll love you no matter what you do. But I'm going to see this through.

Kate, that makes no sense!

She folds her arms.

I'm giving you *everything*. Everything I have. But you need your pound of flesh.

Yes, I do. I need my pound of flesh.

How much is that? What's a pound of flesh actually worth? Give me a number.

I don't know, Dan. Let me ask you: How much do you think my

sister's life was worth? Two-point-eight million plus a house? Seems a little low to me.

I've never gotten anywhere with you, Kate. Why did you even come today?

To watch you suffer.

Oh, stop it. There's no talking to you, there's no reasoning with you. You've always hated me, even when Jane was here. You've always been a bitch.

He spits the last word. It was not a mistake that he said it, the word did not slip out. He is relieved to have said it finally.

Kate brushes it off—she literally makes a brushing movement with her hand on the surface of the table, flicking away invisible crumbs with royal contempt.

Kids, she says, I can't tell you what to do. Just don't sell yourselves cheap.

Mr. Bailis says, I think we should all take a little time to think about it.

I say: No. I don't need time. I'm in. Mimi, if you want to bail, that's okay. It won't affect anything either way now. But I'm with Aunt Kate. Let's see this through.

I take a deep breath and exhale slowly. An odd, unexpected sense of relief comes over me. My shoulders and back relax. I had not even known I was carrying so much tension.

Miranda says, Then I'm in too.

You kids are making a big mistake. You have no idea what you're starting. None!

Mimi and I exchange a nervous glance, because he is right. We have no idea where any of this is leading.

Just remember, I tried to avoid this, for all of us. There's nothing more I can give. I have nothing left to lose.

But there is, and he knows it.

8:30 Monday morning. Courtroom 12B.

Waiting for the trial to begin, two court officers in uniform loaf near the judge's bench. The clerk—a round-bellied guy with a comb-over—comes in and out of a door at the back of the courtroom. At one point, the clerk summons over a court officer, and the officer fetches a pitcher of water, which he places on the judge's bench. They all look competent and bored.

The courtroom is modern, a little grungy, with a high ceiling. There are two jury boxes (I don't know why—are there trials with two juries?); in the second jury box a small TV camera has been set up on a tripod. The camera has no markings to identify what station it represents.

In the gallery, there is still plenty of room on the benches. Three reporters have grabbed spots in the front row center, a TV reporter in a stylish pantsuit and two frumpy print reporters beside her, clutching little spiral notebooks in their laps.

Our group of plaintiffs—Miranda and me, Aunt Kate and Uncle Stephen, and George Bailis—sits in the corner nearest the door. In the washed-out, shot-on-video light of the courtroom, Miranda looks ashen. She hasn't been sleeping.

In the other corner is my father with just two supporters: Alex and my grandmother, Mildred. Grandma Mildred is ninety years old. Alex and Dad sit on either side of her like Praetorian Guards.

I am shocked by her appearance. She is shrunken, rheumy-eyed, her back bent—no longer her old commanding self. But she still wears an elegant wool skirt suit and low heels with an unmissable chunky gold necklace, similar in style to a necklace she once gave my mother. Her brittle snow-white hair is still coifed. I have not spoken to Grandma Mildred in many years, since Grandpa's funeral. My mother's murder and our grinding suspicion of Dad created a rift that will never heal. Still, it seems unforgivable that she might die without my ever speaking to her again. She is a link to my earliest childhood. Her simple presence here opens up memories, nostalgia, longing.

We *have* to go say hello, Mimi.

No, we don't.

She's our *grandmother*!

Then let her come say hello to *us*!

She's ninety years old! Are you mental?

We trudge like children, feeling Mom's invisible hand on our shoulders (*Kids, go say hello to your grandmother*), the twenty feet or so across the courtroom gallery.

Dad and Alex glower up at us. It's hard to take them seriously, though, not just because I don't care what they think, but because, sitting together like this, they look absurd, six-foot-five Alex and my dad who claims to be five-eight. (On FBI surveillance tapes in the early eighties, Boston mobsters were heard talking about my father. They referred to him as "Little Hands" and "the midget." So there you go.)

Bent as she is, my grandmother seems unable to tilt her head up to face me, so I kneel in front of her.

Grandma, it's me, Jeff.

Oh, Jeff. Isn't this horrible?

It is. How are you feeling?

She shakes her head and emits a little groan.

I'm happy to see you, Grandma.

Her hands are in her lap, spotted, and knobby and gnarled with arthritis. I sandwich her rough hand between mine. It feels papery. She lays her other hand on top of the stack and says, Oh, we loved your mother. I don't know what could have happened. I don't know what happened.

I can't be sure if she is rambling like an old woman or if she is playing me. She doesn't know what happened? Really? Her eyes are unfocused, heavily lidded, and moist with emotion.

I tell her, I'd better go, Grandma. They're going to start soon. Do you want to say hello to Miranda? She's right here.

Miranda!

Mimi kneels and delicately embraces her grandmother, careful not to muss Grandma's hair.

Miranda, the old woman repeats. She raises a clawed hand to touch the back of Miranda's head. Then: Miranda, what is wrong with you? How could you *do* this? To your own family?

Miranda's head draws slowly back against the weight of Grandma's hand until she is free. She stands and says, How could *I*? She turns and marches directly out of the courtroom.

Aunt Kate jumps up and hurries through the swinging door after her.

AT ten past nine, a court officer announces, All rise!

The judge sweeps into the courtroom, a woman around fifty years old, straw-colored hair, unsmiling. She is the Honorable Justice Christine Maginnis, the clerk tells us.

The whole entrance is so perfunctory and quick—and I am so taken by this judge, who has a scrappy, tomboyish, don't-fuck-with-me vibe, but also a triple string of pearls and elegant makeup—that the whole ritual of the judge's entrance is over before I can sort out my thoughts. I am still getting to my feet when everyone else is already sitting back down.

The clerk announces in an absent drone: Calling civil number 93-dash-0410, Jeffrey D. Larkin, Miranda S. Larkin, and Katherine A. Witner, all individually and on behalf of Jane A. Larkin, deceased, plaintiffs, versus Daniel M. Larkin, defendant. The complaint alleges that the defendant did cause the wrongful death of Jane A. Larkin by malicious, willful, wanton, or reckless actions; that the defendant did cause Jane A. Larkin to experience conscious pain and suffering prior to her death; and that the defendant did cause the plaintiffs to suffer the loss of companionship of Jane A. Larkin. The complaint also seeks punitive damages.

He looks up with a bland expression.

The clerk's blasé, been-there-done-that manner is strangely comforting. Here, my family's strange history—the whole amorphous, incomprehensible load of sorrow that I've been lugging around—fits neatly into three ancient definitions: wrongful death, pain and suffering, loss of companionship. Simply giving these things a name reduces them, uncomplicates them. This is what you have lost, no more, no less. This is the precise nature of your grief. Wrongful death, pain and suffering, loss of companionship. I never had the terms to describe it before. My injury. Or as the lawyers say, my complaint.

Counsel, please identify yourselves for the record.

Good morning, Your Honor, George Bailis on behalf of the plaintiffs.

And, Your Honor, Daniel Larkin appearing pro se, on my own behalf.

The judge regards my father for a moment without comment. Is she reacting to the fact that he is representing himself? Or something more?

Are there any preliminary matters?

Bailis says, Yes, Your Honor, there are a few preliminary motions, which you have before you. I would like to raise an additional matter, as well: I would point out for the court that the defendant acting as his own attorney in this case raises several issues. There is the possibility of his blurring the line between attorney and witness. In his capacity as a lawyer, the defendant will be tempted to speak to the jury directly, to *sneak* in what amounts to testimony, rather than testifying properly as a witness from the stand, under oath and subject to cross-examination. I would simply ask that the defendant be warned not to break this rule.

My father responds: Your Honor, the trial hasn't even begun yet. Mr. Bailis is free to object at any time, to anything I do, as he sees fit.

Yes, Mr. Bailis, I will rule on any objections as we go. Is there anything else?

Yes, Your Honor, I have a motion for a ruling on the admissibility of statements of the victim in this case, Jane Larkin. Under General Laws chapter 233, section 65, statements of a deceased person are admissible and should not be excluded as hearsay so long as—

I'm aware of the statute, Mr. Bailis. Mr. Larkin, any objection?

To the statute? No. Without a proffer as to the nature of the statements, it's impossible for me to say anything now. I would reserve the right to object at the time if I find any of the statements improper.

Good. Done. The motion is denied. I'll rule on particular statements as necessary. Next?

Your Honor, I have a motion to bar the defendant from introducing evidence that he was not arrested, indicted, prosecuted, or convicted in a criminal case. There is a long-standing rule in Massachusetts that such evidence is not admissible in a civil action because the standards of proof and the nature of the acts to be proven are quite different in a civil setting. The fact that a prosecutor may have concluded there is not evidence beyond a reasonable doubt says nothing about whether the simple preponderance-of-evidence standard here is met.

Mr. Larkin?

Your Honor, the adequacy of the evidence against me is the entire issue in this case. It will be impossible to defend myself if I am barred from discussing it.

The motion is allowed, as far as it goes. However, the defendant may discuss the sufficiency of the evidence against him provided he does not suggest that the lack of a criminal prosecution argues for his innocence here. Agreed? Good. Next?

The remaining motions are Mr. Larkin's, I believe.

Yes, Your Honor, I have several motions. The first is to exclude evidence that I refused to take a lie detector test. Such evidence is incompetent in Massachusetts—

The motion is allowed.

There is also a motion before you to exclude statements taken that relate to a lie detector test, which might open the door to such evidence.

Denied for now. I'll rule on objections at the time.

I have filed a motion to exclude all references to the term "murder" in the plaintiff's opening statement.

Denied.

I have a motion to exclude evidence concerning my own financial situation or the possibility of an inheritance.

Denied.

I have a motion to exclude evidence of a Caribbean trip.

Denied.

Motion to exclude evidence of other bad acts.

Denied.

Motion to exclude evidence that I invoked my Fifth Amendment privilege against self-incrimination.

Denied.

I renew my objection to the use of television cameras in the courtroom.

Denied.

A beat.

Is that all?

Mr. Bailis organizes his little pile of papers, tapping the edges on the table to neaten the pile. He has not even had to argue against any of the defense motions. Just stood there. *Snick, snick, snick,* go the papers on the tabletop.

Sitting behind my father, I watch him glance across at Mr. Bailis. He flips open his suit coat and props his right fist on his hip. His posture is straight, shoulders square, head high, like a Prussian general. Just by looking at his back, I can tell: he is pissed.

Good. Fuck him.

The judge asks, Is there a request to sequester the witnesses?

No, Your Honor.

No, Your Honor. I want the witnesses here. I want my children to see how absurd this is. I want that second jury.

Mr. Bailis, just for reference, is it your intention to call Mr. Larkin to the stand?

It is, Your Honor.

Mr. Larkin, I presume you're aware of that? And of your Fifth Amendment rights?

I have every intention of testifying, Your Honor. I have nothing to hide and nothing to fear.

All right, then. If there's nothing else, Mr. Clerk, you can bring in the jury venire. Let's get moving.

NEXT morning.

I have already learned, after sitting in the back of the court-room all day yesterday through interminable hours of jury selection, that trials are like baseball: most of the time, nothing much happens; the action is all concentrated in a few moments. My father with his balled-up fist on his hip, glancing across at Mr. Bailis—that was a moment, a tell.

The next moment comes during opening statements.

Today, the courtroom is full, like the premiere of a Broadway show. The spectators are a professional, wised-up crowd; they knew not to waste time yesterday watching the dull work of jury selection.

The district attorney himself is here with his first assistant, the same two men we met a little over a year ago who refused to prosecute this same case. If they feel any embarrassment over the decision, they are not showing it.

Mr. Bailis has finished what seems to me an unexceptional speech. He is not a natural performer. He is a technician, doubly burdened by his duty, as plaintiff, to lay out the facts of the case methodically.

He began, One afternoon in November 1975, a little girl named Miranda Larkin came home from school to find her mother missing. . . .

For the next twenty minutes or so—it felt much longer—the jury watched him, poker-faced, attentive but unmoved.

Now my father is before the jury, and he is everything Mr. Bailis was not: theatrical, bombastic, passionate. A "hot" personality after Mr. Bailis's cool one.

He overacts in ways that seem very familiar to me:

There is not one *iota* of evidence, not one *scintilla* of real, direct proof. *Where* are the *witnesses*? Where is the *witness* who *saw* or *heard* any of the things you would expect to find in a case involving bloody murder? Where is the *witness* who heard the victim scream? Where is the *witness* who saw a body? Where is the *witness* who saw the murderer running from the scene? Where is the witness who heard a confession? Where is the policeman who found blood on the defendant's hand? Where is . . .

It is all predictable TV-lawyer stuff. Only my dad's strutting, preening style makes it interesting.

Unfortunately for Dad, his evident ego seems to put off as many jurors as it impresses. One man in particular—back row, far left—smirks and looks away, as if Dad's bombast has set off his bullshit detector.

Still, I admit I feel a perverse pride in my father's performance. In all these years, I have never actually seen him in court, and it is instantly obvious why he is so good at his job. He is a murderer, a liar, and a virtuoso lawyer, and these things seem not unrelated. Am I crazy to be a little proud of him? (Answer: yes. I know this.)

Then comes the moment. Dad has exhausted the subject of the insufficiency of the evidence against him—the *not one iota, not one scintilla* business. It is time to close the deal. With a little less bravado, in a softer tone, he makes eye contact with each juror in turn and tells them:

At every moment of this trial, ask yourself: Who among you would stand up, step out of that jury box, and trade places with me? Who would be accused of a violent murder based on . . . nothing? How would you prove your innocence when there was never any proof against you in the first place?

At that, Mr. Bailis starts getting up to object, but the damage is already done. He crouches over his chair a moment then drops back down without saying anything.

The juror in the back row, far left, blinks awake, sits up a little straighter. His bullshit detector has gone quiet.

LATER the same morning. It is around eleven-thirty. The energy in the courtroom is flagging. Everyone is drained—judge, jury, lawyers. Lunchtime is coming into view.

Mr. Bailis has called Detective Glover as his first witness. Glover is our Virgil; in over ninety minutes of testimony, he has walked the jury through the entire investigation. He is the one detective who has worked the case from the start, who knows every piece of evidence—the missing red necktie; the car scrubbed clean; Jane's unhappiness in the marriage; the family vacation in Trout Lake, Vermont, where the body was ultimately found. His memory is strong. He is a seasoned, professional witness. He is also a diffident, involuted guy, and his laconic manner works here. He comes off as steady, reliable, not an attention seeker. By the time his direct testimony ends, I feel confident he has done his job of establishing our case in the jurors' minds. More important, it is quite clear that he believes Dan Larkin murdered his wife.

All he has to do is survive the cross-examination.

When Mr. Bailis sits down, the judge says: Mr. Larkin, it's eleven-thirty, we've been going quite a while. Would you like to take a break before you cross?

No, Your Honor.

All right then, you may proceed.

Dad goes to a little podium, places his yellow legal pad on it, then comes around to stand in front of the jury box. He rests his hand on the rail before the jurors, almost one of them, asking his questions from their position, without notes.

Lieutenant Detective Glover, what shall I call you, Lieutenant or Detective?

Either.

Let's go with Detective. Detective, how old are you today?

I'm fifty.

Fifty. So if my math is right, when you were assigned this case, nineteen years ago, you were thirty-one years old.

Yes.

That's awfully young to be the lead detective on a homicide, isn't it?

It wasn't a homicide when it was assigned. It was a missing-person case.

And is that how the case remained, officially, a missing-person case?

Yes.

Had you ever worked a missing-person case at that time?

No.

Had you ever worked a homicide?

Not on my own, no. Only as part of a team.

And yet you found yourself working this very difficult, unusual case. At age thirty-one. Alone.

Not exactly. Lots of other detectives came on. The whole department was available. There were state police, too, and the DA's office. It was never just me.

But it was you I kept meeting, wasn't it?

We spoke several times, yes.

Just you.

Yes.

Never had a partner. I never met with you and anyone else?

Not usually, no.

And it's you here today still, isn't it?

It is.

No other cops have stuck with the case all this time, have they? Just you.

Just me.

And no other cops are going to testify in this case, will they?

Bailis: Objection

Judge: Sustained.

You told the jury a moment ago that *This is a circumstantial case but, taken together, the evidence is strong.* But that's not what you've always believed, is it?

At what time do you mean?

Well, even years after my wife disappeared, you continued to investigate whether she might be living somewhere else, didn't you? Under an assumed name, an assumed identity?

I did.

So obviously even you weren't convinced she'd been murdered.

It was my job to run down every lead.

Detective, don't be cute. If you didn't think there was any chance Jane might be in Cleveland or Petaluma or any of the other places you went, you wouldn't have bothered going, would you?

No.

No, of course not. So you obviously thought there was a chance, however remote, that she might be alive.

Yes.

You had doubt.

Bailis: Objection.

Judge: Overruled.

You can answer the question, detective. Did you have doubt that Jane had been killed?

I considered it very, very unlikely she was still alive.

But not impossible.

Correct.

So it's fair to say that this circumstantial evidence, which taken together is so strong, still leaves room for doubt.

Objection.

Sustained. Move on, counselor.

Detective, let's look at that circumstantial case piece by piece.

All right.

You testified earlier that on the day Jane disappeared, you thought my car had been recently washed. Tell me, if a man takes his car to a car wash, do you generally take that as an indication he has committed murder?

Generally, no. In combination with other evidence, I might. That's how circumstantial cases work.

That's how circumstantial cases work? By piling up innocent actions to create a false impression of guilt?

Bailis: Objection.

Judge: Sustained.

Detective, shall we ask the jurors if any of them have washed their car recently?

Bailis: Objection.

Judge: Sustained.

In your direct testimony, you said that there was dirt under my fingernails.

Yes, that's what I observed.

But that otherwise my hands seemed to have been scrubbed clean.

Yes.

And I changed my necktie?

Yes.

And my shirt?

Yes.

And therefore I killed my wife?

Bailis: Objection.

Judge: Sustained.

Shall we ask the jurors if any of them have washed their hands today? Or changed their clothes?

Bailis: Objection.

Judge: Sustained.

Bailis: Your Honor, may I be heard at sidebar?

Judge: Yes.

The lawyers stand together at the far side of the judge's bench, out of the jury's hearing, and mine. Looking up at the judge, Mr. Bailis makes an argument in a low mumble. My father answers with a shrug that says: *Who, me?* The judge seems to warn him, but as he returns to his spot near the jury box—with his back to the judge and Mr. Bailis—he gives the jurors a look: *Do you see what's going on here?*

Detective, you testified that on the date of Jane's disappearance, you found my manner to be nervous and evasive.

I don't believe I said nervous. I said you seemed wary and evasive.

Is that because of anything in particular that I said?

No.

Just my manner?

That's right.

It was just a feeling you got, then? A sense?

Something like that.

You simply divined that, on the inside, I must be hiding something.

That was my impression, yes.

Based on your vast experience with murder investigations, at age thirty-one, in Newton, Massachusetts?

A person knows when he is being lied to.

How many murders a year, on average, happen in Newton?

On average? Zero.

Fair to say you were very inexperienced at the time you drew this conclusion?

It's fair to say I hadn't investigated many murders.

Yet you found my emotions unconvincing.

Yes.

Had you ever met me before that day?

No.

Did you know anything about me?

No.

We'd never met, yet somehow you knew how I behave when I am—what was it?—wary and evasive?

It was the sense I had, yes.

Is it ever wrong, this sixth sense of yours?

Bailis: Objection.

Judge: Overruled.

I don't know.

Well, this is quite a skill for a detective to have, isn't it? The ability to know what other people are thinking even when they've said or done nothing suspicious.

Bailis: Objection.

Judge: Sustained.

Bailis: Your Honor, I would ask for a curative instruction. This can't go on.

Judge: Ladies and gentlemen of the jury, I am going to instruct you to disregard the last question. Put it out of your mind as if you never heard it. The lawyers will have a chance to make their arguments to you later in the trial. Mr. Larkin, pose a proper question, please. Don't make speeches.

Detective, you still believe that taken together the evidence is strong?

Yes.

When the search warrant was executed at my house, you took all my suits and shoes. Were those clothes analyzed for evidence of the crime?

Yes.

And what was found?

Nothing.

The shovel that was taken from my garage—what evidence was found on it?

None.

And my car, which you tore apart for evidence. What did you find in it?

Nothing.

And in Jane's car, which was discovered at the train station? What did you find?

Nothing. It was wiped clean.

By *wiped clean,* you mean no evidence was found?

I mean we found evidence to suggest that the car had been wiped down to remove any fingerprints or other evidence.

So there was no evidence in that car pointing to me or anyone else?

Correct.

None at all?

Correct.

And yet taken together the evidence is strong?

Yes.

You testified that no witnesses could confirm that I was at the Social Law Library, where I claimed to be on the day of the disappearance.

That's correct.

But there are also no witnesses who say I *wasn't* there, isn't that so?

It's very difficult to prove a negative.

Well, it may be difficult but it's also your job. You've suggested to this jury that I wasn't where I claimed to be. Do you have any witnesses or evidence to confirm that?

No.

No? Not a single witness?

No.

Not a shred of real evidence?

Only the lack of witnesses to corroborate your story.

So, for all you know, it's possible I was exactly where I said I was that day?

A beat.

It's possible, yes.

In the back of the courtroom, my eyes drift from the Q&A to the spectators, the judge, the jurors, the details of the courtroom itself. I stop listening. I have never watched a cross-examination before. It is at least possible that they all go this badly. But I doubt it. It will go on a long time, it seems. There is a lot to cover, and Dad is in no hurry. He is like a cat tormenting a mouse before killing it; it isn't cruelty, just instinct, the pleasure of acting according to one's nature. Dad is nowhere near satisfied yet, but I think we can look away.

———

NEXT morning, around 9:30.

Miranda is on the stand, called by Mr. Bailis to recount her experiences in the first hours of my mother's vanishing.

My sister's testimony has been reported in the media and has drawn a predictable crowd of lawyers and ghouls. The district attorney is there, as well, as he has been since the opening statements.

Miranda is a wreck. She hardly slept last night. I have told her that when she is up on the stand, if she starts to lose it, she should look at the tattoo on her arm: *Omnia mea mecum porto,* all that is mine I carry with me.

Whatever butterflies she may be feeling, Miranda relates her story in a steady, unemotional voice. Coming home from school to an empty house. Waiting for hours alone. The long night. The appearance of Detective Glover the next morning.

It is all very sad, but none of it incriminates my father, so he is not contesting any of it. He raises no objections or distractions. Just listens, downcast.

It has not been going on very long—we are only twenty minutes or so into Miranda's testimony—when the courtroom door opens and a woman enters. She stops in the doorway, uncertain where to go, where to sit. There are no empty seats in the gallery.

The courtroom goes silent.

On the witness stand, Miranda—who has been telling the jury about how Detective Glover questioned Dad on the morning after my mother vanished—stops speaking.

The woman looks across the room at Miranda, twenty feet away, and she smiles gently.

She is my mother.

Beside me, from Aunt Kate, a sudden intake of breath through the nostrils. Jane!

She cannot be my mother. She is too old. Or is she? Is this what my mother would look like at fifty-eight?

The ghostly moment goes on, a fermata, until Dad turns in his chair to see what is going on.

Mimi beams for this woman, puts her right hand over her heart, and mouths the words *Thank you*. She is the only one who seems to know who the woman is.

Then I understand. It is Mrs. Bowers, who so reminded Miranda of our mother years ago.

I stand and gesture to Mrs. Bowers, offering my seat, as if she were an old woman on a subway car.

She declines the offer with a shake of her head. Crossing her arms, she settles herself against the doorjamb. She will stand where she is to watch Miranda testify. Something about her posture suggests she will stand there until Miranda is done, all day if she has to.

Aunt Kate continues to stare at this woman.

On the witness stand, Miranda seems to sit a little straighter, stiffened, as if the real Jane has actually showed up. She says into the microphone, I'm sorry, I forgot the question. Could you repeat it?

WHEN Miranda's direct testimony is concluded and Mr. Bailis has sat down, I am deeply uneasy. Miranda has gone over a lot of the same material that Detective Glover talked about: the business about the missing necktie; my mother's belongings undisturbed in the bedroom—the hairbrush, cigarettes, jewelry—nothing stolen, no sign of struggle; my dad's oddly flat demeanor in the first twenty-four hours of my mother's absence, punctuated by scripted, unconvincing displays of anger or fear. In this big courtroom, under the unforgiving eyes of the judge and jury, it all seems inadequate. There is nothing here, no smoking gun, and there will not be. Increasingly I comfort myself with the mantra *fifty percent plus a feather*. We do not have to eliminate all doubt, we just have to cross the fifty-yard line.

Miranda looks drained by her testimony. The prospect of taking the stand has terrorized her. She feels guilty about betraying her father by testifying, but she would feel equally guilty betraying her mother by not testifying. Her face shows exhaustion and relief at being nearly finished.

Dad stands up for his cross. He is in a tricky position. He cannot be seen by the jury to be beating up on his own daughter; at the same time, he *has* to attack her testimony. She is trying to ruin him; he has to answer.

This time he takes a position right next to the witness stand, as close to Mimi as he can get, no doubt so the jury sees him alongside his daughter, father and child, co-victims.

Miranda.

Yes.

I know this is hard for you. I am so sorry you've been put through this.

Mr. Bailis: Objection.

Judge: Sustained. Pose a question.

My father nods, mournful, reluctant.

Miranda, do you remember the last morning we all spent together with your mother?

Yes.

You remember we had breakfast, before school?

Yes.

It was a nice breakfast, wasn't it?

I suppose.

There was no fighting, no arguing?

No.

Everybody was happy?

Yes.

Mom was happy?

I think so.

Do you remember your mom teasing me that morning about how I ate my breakfast?

Yes.

What did she say?

That you shouldn't eat your muffin with a fork.

And we all laughed about that, didn't we?

Yes.

Including Mom?

Yes.

You remember that because it was our last meal together, don't you?

Yes.

You've gone over it in your head a thousand times.

Yes.

I have too. Where were we sitting, me and you? Do you remember?

At the table.

And where was Mom?

In the kitchen.

Dad's tone is gentle, nostalgic. He is practically taking Mimi's hand and walking her through it.

And where was Jeff?

Late.

Why was Jeff late?

Because he was always late.

(This is not true, by the way. I was occasionally not late.)

And where was Alex? Do you remember that?

He was there too.

When you went off to school that day, you weren't worried about any trouble between your mom and dad, were you?

No.

You weren't worried that Mom was unhappy?

No.

She did not seem upset or angry or sad, did she?

No.

And I did not seem upset or angry, either, did I?

No.

Just an ordinary morning.

Yes.

That night and the next day, do you remember sitting with me, waiting for Mom to call or to come home?

Yes.

Where did we sit?

On the couch in the den.

We sat right next to each other, didn't we?

Yes.

You weren't afraid of me, were you?

No.

You were *never* afraid of me, were you? I never did anything to make you afraid, did I?

No.

And your mom never said anything to suggest that she was afraid of me, did she?

I was a child. If she was afraid, I don't think she would have said anything to me.

True, you were a child, but you were *her* child. If your mother thought I was dangerous in any way, don't you think she would have given you some warning?

Yes.

She would have done everything in her power to protect you?

She would have.

But she never said anything like that, did she?

No.

She never gave you any reason to think she was afraid, did she?

No.

In fact, for many years after her disappearance, you believed I had nothing to do with it, isn't that true?

Mr. Bailis: Objection.

Judge: Overruled.

I believed you, it's true.

Miranda, do you think it's possible that kids sometimes imagine things about their parents? They get wrong ideas about them?

Objection.

Overruled.

I guess so.

Because of course parents don't tell their kids everything, do they?

No.

Miranda, are you aware that, just a couple of weeks before she disappeared, your mom made a trip to Trout Lake, Vermont, to find a cabin for our family vacation the next summer?

Objection.

Overruled. Mr. Larkin, I presume you will be offering evidence to support that?

Yes, Your Honor, my own testimony.

The witness may answer.

I did not know that. I've never heard that before.

No, she never told you. She only told me afterward. It was going to be a surprise.

Objection.

Sustained. Pose a question, Mr. Larkin.

So it's possible your mom drove herself to that little town again and you would have no idea of it?

I guess it's possible.

That makes things less suspicious, doesn't it? That there was an obvious reason for her to have been in the very town where her body was ultimately found? That there is a simple, reasonable explanation for her body being found there? And it has nothing to do with me.

I don't know.

You don't know or you'd rather not say?

I don't know.

Miranda, I'm so sorry you've been put in this position.

Objection.

Sustained. The jury will disregard the last statement.

I haven't been *put* in this position, Daddy. I chose to be here.

My father pauses, repeats the word back to her: Daddy.

Miranda does not answer.

The point is, there may be facts about your mom and dad that you weren't aware of, isn't that so?

There may be.

There may be. You're not sure, are you?

Miranda's hands are clasped in front of her, resting on a little shelf in the witness box, like a confession booth in church. Without hurrying but also without warning, Dad puts his hand on top of Miranda's prayerful hands, and he squeezes them with a reassuring jostle, then he quickly withdraws his hand before Miranda—or Mr. Bailis—can react.

Dad repeats the question: You're not sure, are you?

About what?

About what happened to Mom. Nobody is sure.

I *am* sure.

Dad nods. He will leave it there, he will not push his daughter any further. Another glance at the jury is all he needs to communicate his message: *doubt, doubt, doubt.*

DAY three.

Tom Glover and Miranda had essentially the same weakness as witnesses: they were vulnerable people. Because they were unconfident, they seemed to be hedging and tentative, and because neither had the sort of kill-shot evidence that might clinch the case, their testimony felt weak, insubstantial.

Aunt Kate has never been vulnerable, and she has a kill shot.

Kate was always Jane's confidante. Every day the two sisters chatted, sometimes just to check in, other times sharing intimate details of their marriages. They usually spoke in the morning, after their kids had left for school. My mother would sit in the kitchen, drinking coffee, gabbing on the phone that sat on the counter. Like an old baseball glove, the phone itself showed signs of my mother's constant talk: it was discolored by her coppery makeup, which rubbed off on the dialer and the mouthpiece.

Now, on the stand, Kate reports what Jane told her.

(An out-of-court statement from a dead person generally is not admissible in court, but a Massachusetts law allows such hearsay in civil suits, provided only that the judge finds the statement was "made in good faith and upon the personal knowledge" of the deceased person who said it. So a pattern develops: my dad objects to Kate repeating something Jane told her—*Objection, hearsay.* To which the judge responds, *I find the statement was made in good faith and upon the personal knowledge of the declarant.*)

Jane believed her husband was unhappy in their marriage. She suspected he was fooling around and that he wanted to leave her. But she also thought he would not risk a divorce. In those days, divorce settlements tended to be generous to women, especially those who had been spurned rather than copped to "irreconcilable differences," and especially those ex-wives—the vast majority, then—whose earning power paled beside their ex-husbands'. Money was Dan's weakness, Jane said. He was obsessed with it, always scheming for quick cash. His parents were wealthy, it was true, but Dan never seemed to have enough. He spent like a rich kid—watches, clothes, cars, travel, all of which dazzled Jane—but the couple never had the cash to keep up. Dan's parents hoarded their money. They told Dan that he would inherit nothing until both his parents died, which would probably come too late to help Dan. (The presence of Dan's mother in court certainly confirmed that.) Jane did not have her husband's rich-kid nonchalance about money, his assurance that money would always appear when needed. She fretted about it, and told him so. They argued.

Dan's unhappiness was not primarily about money, though. Kate describes dinners with Dan and Jane when he would insult or berate her over some small thing. He had always been a nasty guy, Kate says, but by 1975 he seemed very obviously to have fallen out of love with Jane. Neither Kate nor Jane had any idea about Sarah Bennett, Dan's girlfriend, but Kate was not surprised when Sarah showed up, either.

Led along by Mr. Bailis's questioning, Aunt Kate describes a dinner, about a year before Jane's disappearance, when Dan said: I think all married men are a little unhappy, secretly, at least the ones who marry young. He had a theory about marriage: Young men are like rising stocks whose value peaks around age forty or fifty. Therefore a man who marries young is bound to feel he sold too low on his own stock and is now stuck with a depreciating asset—his wife.

To this point, Aunt Kate's testimony is unflattering but not fatal. The man she is describing is a jerk but not necessarily a murderer.

But the kill shot I mentioned is not my dad's unhappiness. It is his capacity for violence. This was always going to be a difficult hurdle for us to clear. Is it believable that a man who had never been violent before would suddenly murder his wife? Could we convince the jury to accept that possibility?

In her unwavering, reportorial tone, Aunt Kate repeats Jane's description of the night Dan raped her.

Dad does not object. He filed a motion before trial to exclude this evidence, which the judge denied. Now he does not want to underscore the incident by trying, and failing, to keep it from the jurors' ears.

It takes Aunt Kate only a few minutes to describe the facts of the rape, but the impact in the courtroom is immediate. Even our skeptical juror—back row, far left—sits up, his face screwed tight with concern.

When Dad stands up to cross-examine Kate, he positions himself dead center in the middle of the courtroom floor, equidistant from the witness, jury, and Mr. Bailis. I am fascinated by the little tactical decisions he makes, the stagecraft. Now he is like a boxer dominating the center of the ring: his position forces Aunt Kate into the ropes.

She looks unfazed. Even in a corner, she could knock him out.

Kate, he says, pointedly using her first name, do you remember when we first met?

Not offhand, no.

Would it refresh your memory to hear that it was in high school? We worked together on the school newspaper. Do you remember now?

Not really. That was a long time ago.

You would agree, though, that you've known me even longer than Jane did.

Since you murdered her, yes.

He smiles, forbearing. What I mean is, you met me before she did, isn't that right?

Yes.

And you never liked me, did you?

Until Janie started dating you, I never thought about you at all.

And since then?

I never liked the way you treated people, my sister included. That's true.

And your sister knew this about you, that you did not get along with her husband?

I certainly didn't make any secret of it.

And yet we continued to socialize, we continued to see each other as couples, didn't we?

Yes.

You never refused my company?

That would have meant not seeing my sister.

You never saw me act violently?

No.

Toward your sister or anyone else.

Personally, no, I never saw it myself.

In your testimony, you described how, as a young man fifteen years or so into my marriage, I seemed unhappy to you.

Yes.

Do you think that's uncommon, for a man to feel less . . . *enthusiasm* for his marriage as time goes on?

Uncommon? I would have no way of knowing.

Really? No way of knowing? Are you familiar with the common statistic that more than half of marriages in this country end in divorce?

Yes.

Then you would agree, at least, that it is not uncommon for married couples to become unhappy, disenchanted, bored?

Apparently.

Men and women both? Husbands and wives?

Apparently.

So if, as a younger man, I did not find my marriage as . . . *compelling* as I once had, that would not be so unusual either, would it?

If you say so.

It's a yes-or-no question, Kate.

No.

Unhappy marriages are common, divorces are common, wouldn't you agree?

Yes.

But wife-murder is very, very uncommon. You would agree with that, too, wouldn't you?

Yes.

Therefore a lot of couples lose their passion for each other without it leading to murder?

I suppose.

And yet in my case, and only in my case, you suggest to this jury that feeling disillusioned with your marriage is sufficient cause to murder your wife?

I didn't say it was sufficient cause.

So it's *not* sufficient cause?

Dan, nothing could ever be sufficient cause to murder your wife.

But you're suggesting it was enough for me, aren't you?

It's impossible for me to say what *you* would find sufficient, Dan. Janie would have been better able to answer that question.

Objection.

The judge: Sustained. The jury is instructed to disregard the witness's last answer.

About this so-called rape—that's the word you used to describe this incident, isn't it?

That's the word I used because that's what it was.

Did you tell your sister the same thing, that she'd been raped?

Yes.

So you must have encouraged her to report it to the police?

Yes.

But she didn't, did she?

No.

So she disagreed with you?

About reporting it? Yes, she did.

Did you tell her to report it once or more than once?

More than once.

And yet you never convinced her, you never changed her mind. Doesn't that suggest that she thought you were exaggerating what happened? That she didn't believe she'd been raped at all?

No. It suggests she didn't want to destroy her family by turning in her own husband for a violent crime.

Violent? Was she injured in some way?

You don't have to be injured to prove you've been raped.

Was she injured?

Not as far as I know.

Well, did she ever tell you she was injured?

No.

So she was not injured, she did not think she'd been raped, and she did not want to file charges. Isn't that all true?

Yes, but lots of women—

Lots of women but not Jane, isn't that right? Not your sister, not my wife.

She did not want to do anything about it, it's true. That doesn't prove anything.

So the only one who did want to do something about it was you.

Yes, I did.

Did you ever tell Jane to leave me, to divorce me?

Yes, I did.

But she did not do that either, did she?

No.

She did not hate me as much as you did.

No.

No further questions.

Dad has turned his back and is making his way to the defense table when Aunt Kate says, If she'd left you like I told her to, she'd be here today.

Dad turns to look at her, weighing his response.

Mr. Bailis has explained to me the basics of cross: If it's done right, only the questions matter, because the questions contain the answers. And don't be greedy. Make your points and sit down. This isn't a TV show, witnesses do not crumble, even if they are flat wrong, even if they are lying through their teeth.

I am guessing that Dad will sit down. His cross has been effective enough to blunt Aunt Kate's testimony, or at least to complicate it. He landed a few jabs. It's enough.

But Aunt Kate has always known how to bait this man. Something about this stiff-necked woman he cannot abide.

He says, If she'd left me, like you told her to, you would still hate me.

Objection!

Sustained.

And you would still say anything—

Mr. Larkin!

—to hurt me.

Mr. Larkin. The objection is sustained. The jury is instructed to disregard the last statements by defense counsel and by the witness. You are not to consider them. You are to give them no weight. You are to erase them from your minds. Mr. Larkin, are you done?

Yes, Your Honor.

AFTER a break, a chance for tempers to cool, Sarah Bennett takes the stand. Her serene manner is a welcome relief from Aunt Kate's intensity. She wears very light makeup, a dove-gray dress, no jewelry but a watch on a brown leather band.

Jamie is in court, too, to support her mother. She says nothing either to me or Miranda; I guess none of us know what to say.

Technically Sarah is a plaintiff's witness, but her testimony is so neutral—in content and tone—that one suspects if Mr. Bailis had not subpoenaed her, Dad would have. Her story is all aftermath, denouement, cleaning up details. Yes, her affair with Dan began when Jane was still alive, and yes, she knew from the start that Dan was married. She knew the affair was wrong but did not feel like she had a choice in the matter; the heart wants what it wants. No, Dan never said anything especially negative about Jane. He never told Sarah that he would divorce his wife, let alone harm her. Nor, she says, did the fact that she ultimately left Dan have anything to do with this case or with any fear of Dan.

Why did you leave him, then? Mr. Bailis asks.

The relationship had just run its course. He just wasn't the man I wanted to spend my life with.

That's it?

That's it.

I can't help looking across at Jamie. What must she be thinking? What would the jury think if they knew about my dad pawing a teenage girl, less than an hour after hearing that he also raped his own wife? But Sarah is right to protect her daughter. I would, too, for the simple reason that Jamie is alive and my mom is not, and enough damage has been done already. (Jamie will not testify at the trial. Mr. Bailis has chosen not to call her.)

The highlight of Sarah's testimony—the Moment, as I have been calling it—comes during her description of the blissful vacation in Bermuda that she took with my dad only a year after Mom disappeared.

Mr. Bailis patiently reviews the details of the trip, all of which my mother had planned for herself and Dad—the flights, the hotel, the restaurants and activities. The fact that they waited for the one-year anniversary of Mom's vanishing before they took their trip to Bermuda. Sarah readily agreed to all of it.

You were the stand-in, weren't you? You were the woman who took Jane's place on that vacation?

That's not how I thought of it.

Did Dan seem upset at all, to be on this vacation that he'd intended to take with his wife?

No.

Did he express any grief or anger, any feelings at all, over his wife not being there for this trip that they'd planned together?

No.

No. He was happy.

He was.

He was in love.

I think so, yes.

One year later, he'd gotten exactly what he wanted, didn't he?

Sarah pauses. This is the Moment.

Objection.

Sustained.

Sarah is not allowed to answer, but her answer doesn't matter. As Mr. Bailis likes to say, the question contains the answer.

THE medical examiner's testimony is inconclusive. After eighteen years underground, the body is too decomposed to reveal much about the crime. What he adds are details.

The hole in my mother's skull was likely caused postmortem.

It is likely (but not certain) that she was buried without

clothes on, presumably to encourage decomposition or to hinder identification if the body was found. Otherwise one would expect to find more durable clothing materials—buttons, zippers, belt buckles, the small eyelets and nails in shoes, synthetic fabrics—even after the soft natural fabrics themselves have decomposed.

And one detail that I wish I never heard: a human body buried at a depth of six feet, uncoffined and unembalmed, in ordinary soil, will decompose to a skeleton in eight to twelve years. My mother's corpse probably skeletonized more quickly than that, he believes, due to the shallower depth of the grave and the moist, highly acidic soil of the lakefront site. The witness was reluctant to assign a precise number of years to this process, but he guessed the corpse skeletonized within seven to ten years.

Which means that for more than half the time I have been dreaming of my mother, she has been only bones. The total weight of those bones today, his report notes, is just fourteen pounds.

AFTER two hours of testimony, Mr. Bailis puts a final question to my father (too dramatic, too easily parried):

Did you kill Jane Larkin?

No, I absolutely did not.

WHEN the jury returns its verdict, and the courtroom is instructed to rise, my father does an odd thing. He stands and buttons his coat. He looks briefly at the jurors filing into the box. Then he turns fully around to face the crowd in the back of the courtroom. His own mother and loyal Alex on his right. The mob in the middle, including reporters and the district attorney. And finally his mutinous relatives on the left, Miranda, Aunt Kate, and me. He makes a formal little bow, tipping from the waist, no more than ten degrees or so, like the conductor of an orchestra. Is he thanking us? Is he telling us what is about to happen?

The clerk hands the verdict papers to the judge, who reads them impassively and returns them to the clerk.

The clerk: Do you have a verdict, Mr. Foreperson?

We do.

The clerk reads from the papers: Special Verdict questions. Question one: Did the defendant, Daniel Larkin, cause the death of Jane Larkin? Answer: No.

Miranda immediately bolts from the courtroom, hands cupped over her face.

I cannot move. I am frozen.

BOOK 4

On Sunday, October 15, 2017, the following article ran on page one of *The Boston Globe*.

A Cold Case, Decades Old, Nears Closure

In July 2016, a man named Norris White, age 78, serving life without parole in a Lancaster, California, prison, began to experience the classic symptoms of a heart attack: tightness in the chest, numbness in the left arm, difficulty breathing. Fearing that his time among the living was almost up, White decided to unburden himself of a secret. Over the next several weeks, first to his jailers and then to various law enforcement agencies, he gave an extended account of his career as a serial rapist and murderer of women.

White had already been convicted of murdering three women in Los Angeles and two more in Texas. He had also been tried and found not guilty of murdering another in Florida, and been arrested on suspicion of killing two women in Ohio but released without charge.

Now he confessed to killing at least sixty women. There might have been more, he said; he couldn't be sure. The killings occurred from the early 1970s until 1994, in 24 cities in 16 states. He claimed multiple murders in several states, and at least five each in New York, Ohio, Kentucky, Florida, Texas, and California. Norris White led a nomadic life. The longest he ever lived in one place was three years, in Jacksonville, Florida. He preyed on women whose death would not attract attention, usually sex workers or drug addicts. But he was also an opportunist, and he would deviate from his pattern when the opportunity presented itself.

An FBI expert on serial murderers came to California to interview Norris White. The expert found him genial and eager to help. White had a remarkable memory for his crimes. He was able to recount many details. He even drew colorful head-and-shoulder portraits of the victims, in crayon, to help identify them. The expert had no doubt White was telling the truth. He was given a polygraph test anyway, which he passed.

White felt no compunction about any of the things he was describing. He told the FBI man that he simply did not consider what he was doing to be wrong, any more than a normal man would consider it wrong to have ordinary consensual sex with a woman. The expert wrote a report on the case in which he noted that there was nothing odd or off-putting about Norris White's demeanor or appearance. He was a burly man but his manner was quite gentle.

In the year or so since Norris White's initial confession, detectives have corroborated 34 killings with certainty, using DNA evidence. Other cold cases also have been officially closed, even without DNA confirmation, based on the accuracy of White's descriptions, especially of non-public information. In almost all of these cases, the victim was sexually assaulted and strangled to death. It is likely that Norris White is one of the most prolific serial murderers this country has ever seen.

It is also virtually certain that Norris White murdered Jane Larkin, a Newton woman whose disappearance on November 12, 1975, has vexed investigators for more than four decades.

In the years since she went missing, suspicion has centered on her husband, Daniel Larkin, a criminal defense lawyer, now retired. He has never been criminally charged, however, and has steadfastly maintained his innocence.

In 1994, Mr. Larkin was the subject of a civil suit brought by his wife's surviving relatives, including two of Mr. Larkin's own children. The suit alleged that he murdered his wife. The jury in that civil suit found Mr. Larkin not liable for damages.

Now the mystery seems to have been resolved.

In his confessions, Norris White described the killing of Jane Larkin in detail. He remembered her clearly, he said, since she was so unlike his usual prey.

In the fall of 1975, White was living near Trout Lake, Vermont, in a ramshackle apartment he shared with three other men. Then 37 years old, he had come to Vermont only a few weeks earlier, when a friend offered a place to stay. A native of Akron, Ohio, White had been living in Cincinnati before coming to Vermont.

Ms. Larkin, then 39 years old, apparently came to the town seeking a rental cabin for a family vacation planned for the following summer, reprising a vacation the Larkins had enjoyed a few months earlier, in August 1975. It seems to have been only her second or third visit to Trout Lake.

White had been hired by the town to do maintenance work. That day he was assigned to work on an unpaved road in the woods, "clearin' brush, fillin' holes," he said. When Ms. Larkin drove up, White was holding a shovel provided to him by the town. According to White, she asked for directions to one of the lakeside homes.

Eighteen years later, in June 1993, her bones were discovered buried in the forest nearby.

White was able to describe many details about the murder. Jane had a distinctive scar on her shoulder, he recalled, and drove a white Ford Thunderbird with a brown landau roof. He remembered that she had a flyer from a local realtor with a listing for the rental cabin.

Norris White left Trout Lake immediately after the murder. He was not fleeing, he claimed, he simply found Vermont too rural and dull for his taste. In total, his stay in Vermont lasted only a few weeks.

There is no DNA evidence available in Jane Larkin's case, but investigators have concluded she was indeed murdered by Norris White. In May, law enforcement agencies in Massachusetts and Vermont officially closed the case. No charges were filed; it would have been an empty gesture. Several states had already begun proceedings to extradite him; prosecutors in Vermont would have to wait in line, probably for years.

Norris White did not have years. He died on September 4. To the end, he never expressed remorse for what he did to Jane Larkin or any of his other victims. He seemed not even to understand why he should feel such an emotion.

The families of Daniel and Jane Larkin declined to comment for this story. Mr. Larkin's daughter, Miranda Larkin, stated that her father, now 81, is unable to respond to interview requests. He has battled Alzheimer's disease for many years, according to Ms. Larkin, and suffers from the dementia typical of that disease, including confusion and extreme memory loss.

1

I am in a foul mood. Alex and Miranda—with Jeff's connivance, I suspect—have bullied me into touring a retirement community called The Willows. I'll be safe here, they tell me. Meet wonderful people. Wonderful activities, wonderful dining. If it's such a fucking country club, why don't *they* move in?

My daughter warns me several times to be nice.

In the lobby, we are met by the director, a woman with flyaway hair and a bossy presence. Built like a brick shithouse. (My libido still notices, long after my decrepit prick, curled up like a dog beside a fire, has lost interest in the whole business.) There is some insufferable chat in her office, then we are trooped past a dining room with white tablecloths, a deserted gym, a dark-wood library, even a hair salon. In an "activity room," a group of women is tying yarn in knots. Finally a few boxy apartments. It is all very posh. I'm sure it is outrageously expensive.

When it is done, I point out that we have not seen the memory unit.

The director's eyes flicker toward Miranda and Alex, but she says brightly, Of course.

Miranda says, Daddy, you're a long way from needing the memory unit. You're in the middle stage.

Nonsense. The middle stage. Don't bullshit a bullshitter.

The memory care unit is on the sixth floor of the building, behind a locked door.

Entering, we come into a large, open common area. On our left, in a kind of living room, a dozen or so residents are seated in a semicircle around a younger (fortyish) woman who is leading them in a dance, a seated version of the hokey-pokey. A version of this song is playing on a little portable speaker, quite loudly: *You put your right foot in, you take your right foot out. You put your right foot in and you shake it all about. You do the hokey-pokey and you turn yourself around . . .* The woman is relentlessly cheerful. She shouts directions to the dancers and sings bits of the song. All right, left foot! Here we go! But the dancers are lethargic. They extend a foot, dangle a foot, retract a foot, all in a listless, dreamy way. A few do not move at all. One is in a wheelchair. There are only two men in the group. Neither dances.

Only one woman, vivid and smiling, has gotten up out of her chair. She dances a graceful, salsa-like hokey-pokey that makes me wonder what is in her head, what is in her past. Eyeing us, the salsa dancer seems to grasp why we have come. She directs her gaze at me, performs a bit of the hokey-pokey dance—left hand in, left hand out—as if inviting me to join her.

The staff are all women wearing scrubs with colorful tops, except for one older gentleman who wears slacks and a wine-colored polo with THE WILLOWS stitched on the chest.

The director informs us that there are activities throughout the day, all aimed at improving cognition and encouraging physical movement. All activities take place inside this locked unit.

We are led down a long hallway, past residents' bedrooms. On the walls are vintage black-and-white photos: Monroe, Sinatra, the Beatles in their mop tops, JFK, Ted Williams and Joe DiMaggio.

A few very old residents are seated in the hallway, almost motionless. As we pass, one or two face us with wooden expressions. Most of the rooms are empty, though in one doorway I glimpse a withered foot, pink with blue marbling, tangled in the bed-sheets. Bulletin boards by every door are decorated with family photos, including pictures of the occupant as a younger, more vibrant person.

There are no rooms available to rent at the moment, our guide tells us. *At the moment.*

At the end of the long hall, we come to a final space, a small sitting area. A few armchairs arranged by a window. A table with nothing on it—no books or magazines.

A woman waits here, in a chair, hands laid in her lap. She is quite old. In her nineties, I imagine. Her hair is ashy gray. It hangs loose over her shoulders. White housecoat. Eyes a little yellow and cloudy.

This is Janice, we are told. Hello, Janice.

The woman does not respond.

How are you today, Janice?

No response.

You're looking well, the director tells Janice.

I'm ready to go home now, the old woman murmurs.

You are home, Janice.

I'm ready to go home now, ready to go home now. . . .

IN the car on the way home, I am silent. Has so much time passed already? How has the end come so close so quickly? I thought I had *years.* The shock of it weighs on me, almost literally: I feel heavy with it, I feel pinned to my seat.

My daughter says, You're awfully quiet.

Mm.

You want to talk about it?

I'm never going into that place.

All right.

Never. Promise me.

All right. No one can make you.

Promise me.

I promise. You never have to do anything you don't want to do. We just thought it might be good to explore the options.

We both know, if I go in, I'm never coming out.

You make it sound like a prison.

It is a prison. Those people are locked in.

For their own protection. Daddy, I told you, that's a long way off. The memory unit is for down the road. It's for later. We just wanted you to see this place because they *have* a memory unit, for when you need it. You can transition from one stage to the next without moving to a whole different community. That's a good thing, it's a luxury. We're lucky we can afford it.

Some luxury.

We have to face facts. You have a disease, you're going to need care. I know it's difficult, but we can't just pretend it isn't happening.

Did you see those people? They were zombies.

They were not zombies. They were people. With an illness. They're doing the best they can. And they did not seem unhappy.

I'm not going to be a zombie.

Daddy, you can't think of it from the point of view of today. You have to think of it in terms of what you'll need *then,* when you get to that stage. That could be many years away. Who knows how you'll feel then?

We need to find another way.

What other way? What other way? Tell me. I'm doing all I can, and it's not enough. Even now, it's not enough. Daddy, someday you'll need more help than I can give you.

I don't want help. I'm nobody's burden.

You're never a burden. Don't use that word.

It's exactly what I am.

Not today. Look, we're having a nice conversation.

Today. *Pfft.*

We shouldn't have even gone into the memory unit. I told you. You were the one who *insisted* we see it.

I have a right to know the truth.

I'm just saying. You may see the situation differently in five or ten years.

I don't have five or ten years. We both know it.

This disease is unpredictable. Nobody knows for sure how fast it will move, how much time you have.

Just promise you'll never put me in there.

I already promised, Dad. But what are we going to do? We need some kind of plan for what's next.

We need a different plan, then.

THE girl is arguing on the phone:

I do *not* think you're crazy. I never said that. . . . No, no, I did not say that. I said you're not being fair and objective. This is a heavy thing. It's hard to wrap your brain around. . . . No! Obviously I don't trust this con man. It's not just him. The cops believe it, the DAs believe it. Why would they do that if there was no basis?

She is being patient but I can tell she is mad. She says, Oh my God, Jeff, would you stop? Why would they want to close the case so badly after all this time? No one even *cares* anymore, no one's even *heard* of it. They want to *solve* it, not just close it. . . . So what? We've been through this a thousand times! He didn't remember details like that because he was a vagrant and this was forty years ago! . . . I know, you're a lawyer. . . . Who cares if he couldn't name his roommates? What difference does it make? Look what he got *right*. . . . It was in the newspapers, yes. But that was years ago, *years* ago. . . . They were *not* feeding him details. They were asking questions. How could they ask about a crime without describing it? Why would they want to feed him details? . . . Oh my God, now you *do* sound crazy, Jeff. These people are all on our side and they're professionals with lots and lots of experience—why would they do that?

Listening, she puts her hand on top of her head then extends her arm like *What are you talking about?* Then, into the phone:

I know, cops get things wrong. Yes, confessions can be false. I've heard you, I believe you. . . . I understand, Jeff. I get it. . . .

She raises her free hand again, frustrated.

Would you stop with the ring! Who cares about the ring? It doesn't *matter*. I can think of lots of reasons why the ring wasn't there. How about: It was buried with the bones for forty years! Or maybe White *did* take the ring off her finger and he just forgot he did that. This all happened forty years ago, Jeff! The surprise would be if he got every little detail exactly right!

She listens for a long time. Then:

Jeff, is it possible you're so convinced Dad's guilty, and you've felt this way for so long, that you just can't accept the idea he's not. Isn't that possible? . . . Do you have any idea how crazy you sound? . . . They did *not* write the confession for him. Stop. That's ridiculous. . . . They did not feed him details. Why would they— . . . Jeff, I'm tired, I'm not going to fight with you. . . . All right, *you're* discussing, *I'm* fighting. . . . Because you're wrong, Jeff, that's why. I love you but you're wrong. . . . I can't. We're going in circles now. Can we just—

When she hangs up the phone, she lets out a groan.

She turns and sees that I have been listening. I am sure she is mad at me.

Oh my God, I'm sorry. Did you hear all that, Daddy?

I nod.

Do you know what we were talking about?

No. Are you in trouble?

Am *I*? The girl looks like she is going to cry. She says, Yeah, I think I am.

EMPTY kitchen. Midday. Hot weather. Warm sunlight.

I am standing at the counter. Light-headed. The room swims

around me. Objects waver, the edges of things tremble—counters, cabinets, appliances.

From the doorway, the girl says: Hey, Daddy, what are you doing?

I'm a little . . .

Do you want something? You hungry?

No. I just, I just . . .

Are you all right? What's wrong?

She steps into the room cautiously, with a curious expression, comes around the counter.

Did something happen?

Her gaze travels from my eyes down to my hands, which dangle at my sides. She takes up my wrists in her hands and lifts them. They are glistening red with warm blood. Particularly the left hand.

Oh my God! Daddy, what happened? Oh my God, what happened?

Searching for the source of the blood, she raises my arms by the wrists to inspect my hands. Blood has been puddling in my left hand, caught in my cupped fingers; this pool now spills back down my wrist and over her thumb.

My pants are smeared red at my left hip. There is blood on the floor; it has already begun to soak into the old maple planks, turning it dark brown. A sharp knife is on the floor.

My wrist is slick. It slides in her fingers. The pain is very slight. Only a little burning or itching. Not as much pain as I expected.

What did you do? Are you all right? What did you do!

She lets go of me to snatch a dish towel.

On my wrist, blood oozes from a neat incision. I press the wound against my chest to stanch the blood, reddening the front of my shirt.

She tugs the arm away from my chest. Her eyes widen. She swaddles the wrist tight in the towel.

What happened? What were you doing?

I don't know.

What were you trying to do? Come here, we have to rinse it. What were you *doing*?

Over the kitchen sink she unwinds the towel and tosses it aside, holds all four of our hands under the cold water as the blood dilutes and runs clear. She works her fingertips over my palms and between my fingers to rub away the rest.

We should go to the emergency room.

We're not going to the emergency room, Daddy. If you walk in with this, they'll give you a psych evaluation.

What does that mean?

It means maybe you don't get to come home tonight.

How do you know?

Because I know.

But *how* do you know?

Here, hold this. Press on it. I'm going to go get some bandages. We need to get you cleaned up. Daddy, what were you *thinking*?

Sorry.

Don't ever do this to me again.

She hugs me. I don't remember her ever doing that before.

Not this way, Daddy. Not this way.

A man sits opposite me.

Do you mind if I record this? he says.

I don't mind.

I'd like to talk to you about your life and your illness if that's all right with you.

Okay.

We've actually met, many years ago. I don't know if Miranda told you. I'm an old friend.

I don't remember you. You'll have to forgive me, there's a lot I don't remember now. This disease.

It's okay. Can I ask how you're feeling today, in terms of your illness?

Good.

Can you describe it to me, what it feels like? I have to say, you seem very present, very alert, articulate. Much better than I expected, to be honest.

Well, I'm working very hard to be, um, equal to this conversation. I'm concentrating and thinking very hard. Also, I have good days and bad days. I never quite know what I'll be capable of from one day to the next.

This is a good day?

This is a good day.

Are your days mostly good or mostly bad?

Bad.

Miranda tells me you're in the middle stage of the disease. Does that sound right to you?

No.

Why not?

Because I've lost so much.

In terms of memories?

Yes. And the ability to think.

What is that like? Can you describe it?

The past just falls away. It's a constant deterioration. I lose more every day. Every day I wake up and take an inventory of what's been taken away and what I still have. It's just a constant taking-away.

Has it accelerated, the memory loss?

Yes.

Do you remember anything about the old days?

Yes. But you lose a lot. The details. There's a kind of fog in your brain. You have a sense that those memories must be out there in the fog but you can't see them. You can't see anything clearly, you can't *think* clearly.

That must be frightening, to be lost in the fog.

I have to accept it. I decided long ago that I would not resist this disease.

That's remarkable.

I've had many years to get used to the idea.

What *do* you feel, then, if not afraid?

I don't feel anything.

You must feel something.

I feel ashamed sometimes, embarrassed. People want to feel capable and normal, and I am not capable or normal anymore.

Angry?

No. I'm not an emotional person. Things happen; why shouldn't they happen to me?

Miranda says the disease has changed you, made you more mellow, kinder, gentler.

I don't know. It may have.

It's not how you used to be, if you don't mind my saying. You used to be very proud, very argumentative, assertive.

Well, one thing the disease takes from you is confidence. When you feel incapable, when you feel dependent, then you behave differently. You live a different way.

And you've done that?

It's not a conscious choice, but yes.

I wonder if it might even be a blessing. To set aside some of those negative emotions—vanity, aggression. To be changed in such a fundamental way.

It's not a blessing. I wouldn't say that. I wouldn't romanticize this disease. It is eating me. And it will keep eating till I'm gone.

And then what?

Then you have a decision to make.

And you've made that decision, Miranda tells me.

Yes. I've made that decision.

Why now? You don't seem unhappy. You've lost your memories, or some of them, but you seem very sharp to me. To an outsider, it seems like you still have a lot of time left.

Well, the nature of this decision is that you have to do it when there is still a lot of time left.

When you are still competent to make the decision, you mean.

Yes.

And you do feel entirely competent? You understand the decision, what it means?

I do.

Miranda gave me this document you wrote. "This is to memorialize the decision I have made to end my life before my disease compromises my quality of life in ways that are unacceptable to me. No one has played any role in this decision but me. No one has offered advice or assistance of any kind or participated in any way. The decision is solely my own and the act itself, when the time comes, will be solely my own." Is that how you still feel?

Yes.

It seems very lawyerly, if you don't mind my saying. You created a paper trail.

Yes.

So no one else will be blamed.

That's right. We live in a country where—where we can't control our own lives, we can't choose how we die. So I have to do this alone.

Miranda says you cut yourself with a knife a few months ago.

Yes.

Because of the memory loss, the confusion?

Yes. Because of the disease.

It seems to me that the memory loss has already happened, to some extent, and yet you seem quite content, you're not upset at all. I might even say—and this might just be the writer in me, it might just be me romanticizing, as you say—but the memory loss might even be the reason you feel so peaceful now. You've lost your past, but your past wasn't all good. Maybe some memories are better lost. You've been through some difficult times, I can tell you. Maybe it would be easier for us all to forget our past—all the mistakes and regrets, the grudges—and just live in the moment. No past, no future. It sounds kind of Zen.

That's not how I feel.

So why? Why now? Because the disease is accelerating?

Because it's accelerating, yes. It's changing. It's not just the forgetting. It's something else.

The fog.

Something in the fog.

Dementia.

Yes.

You feel this?

I am aware it's happening.

How? What does it feel like? I want to know.

Why do you want to know?

I'm a writer. I'm writing about you.

Why would you write about me?

You've led an interesting life, Mr. Larkin. I'm writing about what's happened to you. Is that all right with you?

I suppose.

I want to understand you, what it feels like to be you. So people can understand your position, what you've been through. I want to pry your head open.

You want to pry my head open.

Yes. What would I find if I did?

Nothing. Fog.

So tell me. I feel like I'm meeting one of my characters. I've never had the chance to do that before. What are you thinking right now, about your life, about the case, about Jane?

I'm not thinking anything.

I find that hard to believe, honestly. I find you very elusive.

I'm not. I'm sorry. I'm not trying to be.

(After a long pause:) I have to ask—I'm sorry, but I have to ask you once, straight out. There's no way to avoid it. Do you know anything about Jane's disappearance?

What?

I'm sorry, but I have to ask. Do you know anything about what happened to Jane?

I don't know what you're talking about.

Jane.

I don't know any Jane.

You don't remember her?

No. Who is she?

She was your wife. People thought you did something.

What did I do?

I don't know.

What did I do? Tell me.

I don't know. I don't think you did anything, honestly. But I have to ask. It's my job.

I don't know what you're talking about.

Okay. I'm sorry. I didn't mean to upset you. *Shh*. It's my mistake. I'm sorry.

(I am trying to whip my sluggish mind for information. But I have nothing, I have nothing. My brain is empty. Who *is* this man?)

Do you mind if we keep talking, Mr. Larkin?

Who are you again? Why are you here?

I'm writing a book. About your family. There was a crime.

I don't know anything about a book.

It's all right. I'm an old friend of Miranda and Jeff, an old family friend. That's all. I'm your friend.

You're not my friend.

I am, I promise you.

I don't understand.

The man stares at me, searching. He has bland features and a benign expression, but he *wants* something. He drops his head, disappointed.

No, he says, I'm sure you don't understand. I believe you.

I'm sorry.

It's okay, Mr. Larkin. I'm the one who should be apologizing. I'm sorry for upsetting you. Your daughter asked me to come. She wanted me to talk to you.

So you can write your book?

So I can write my book her way, I think.

You won't make me look like a fool? The way I sound. I have trouble finding words sometimes. I'm not myself anymore. This isn't me.

It's okay. I can sharpen things up a little. I can find the words for you.

My daughter says, finally, Do you have enough, Phil? I think he's getting tired.

Yeah. Of course.

We still have a long time ahead of us, don't we, Daddy? We're just making plans, that's all. I just wanted my friend to meet you before it's too late. But we still have years together. Years.

2

Night.

Sound of a car in the driveway.

I go to the window to peek out. It is a funny old beat-up car.

A man gets out. Middle-aged. Sloppy like the car. Beard, base-ball cap, potbelly.

He walks around to the passenger side, opens the door, talks to someone inside:

Would you get out already? . . . No . . . I'm not carrying you. . . . No . . . It's not that I don't want to; I *can't*. . . . Because you weigh too much. . . . I didn't say fat. I said you weigh too much. . . . Just stand up. . . . Of course you can. . . . No, I told you, I'm not going in. . . . Because I'm not, that's why.

Offering his hand, he draws Miranda up out of the car. She stands with her head bowed, eyes closed, heel of her palm on her forehead.

Okay, you ready?

Just a second. How's the car?

The car is fine.

How's the fire hydrant?

Better than the car.

Oh God. I'm in such trouble.

You're not in trouble. I'm the only one who knows. Can you walk?

No.

All right, come on, get on.

The man turns his back to Miranda and bends over.

What are you doing?

I'm asking for a prostate exam. What do you *think* I'm doing?

Ew.

Knucklehead, I'm giving you a piggyback.

Oh.

Get on.

You're too high. I can't get up that high. Bend your knees.

They're bent.

Bend them farther.

If I bend them any farther, I won't be able to get back up.

But the guy does bend his knees a little more, and Miranda drapes herself over his rounded back and shimmies up onto him.

Okay, go.

The man grunts and sways, but he is able to straighten up.

Oh my God.

You used to be stronger.

No shit. You used to be skinnier.

Can you do this?

I'm only taking you as far as the door.

The man clumps to the stairs with Miranda on his back. I lose sight of him from the window, though I can hear his burdened footsteps as he climbs the wooden stairs and heaves his way to the front door.

I open the door before he can ring.

Oh. Hi, Daddy.

What happened?

Nothing. Everything is fine.

Who's this?

This is your son Jeff.

It is?

He nods at me with a wince.

Is she okay? What happened?

She's fine. She's drunk. She's just being dramatic.

I am not being dramatic. Bring me to my room.

Mimi, for God's sake, I just told you!

Can you just— Can we not do this now? Just bring me to my room. It's just a house. What do you think is gonna happen? It's just a house, for Chrissake.

He bears her up the stairs, stooped, hand clamped on the railing.

When he comes back down, he says, She's out. In the morning she won't remember any of this. Neither will you, I guess.

No. Probably not.

She takes good care of you?

Yes. She's very nice.

Too nice. Lucky for you.

I say nothing.

You must be the luckiest asshole on earth.

I let this insult pass too. I ask him only, You wanna come sit down?

No. I'm going home.

You sure?

Yeah.

Did you two go out tonight?

No. Miranda called me to come get her.

What about her husband?

He narrow-eyes me like he is mad, then he grunts at me like I'm just a dummy—which I am—and I know I have made a mistake.

She doesn't have a husband.

Oh.

Mimi shouldn't be drinking. I've told her that. She can't do it. Fucking amateur hour.

Drinking's bad for you.

Drinking's bad for *her*. She doesn't drink. This is all your fault.

Me?

Yes, you. Driving her crazy. Making her run around after you, taking care of you.

I have no idea what he means.

Tell Miranda I'm taking her car. Tell her—never mind, I'll text her tomorrow. You won't remember. I'll take it with me. I know a body shop, I'll take care of it.

Thank you.

Why are *you* thanking me?

For helping.

Yeah, well. I'm bringing her car to the shop, I'm not donating a liver.

Of course.

He humphs and studies my face. He makes me a little afraid. His anger, his size.

Do you even know who I am?

No. Who?

I'm your son.

No. I know who my son is.

Do you? What else do you know?

Come sit down.

No. What's my name? Tell me.

I don't know.

That's what I figured. Miranda told me to stay here tonight. She says you need watching or you'll wander off or set the house on fire or something. But you seem fine.

I'm okay.

You're not going to burn the house down, are you?

No.

Good. Because I'm not staying here. Don't you go making trouble, okay? Give her the night off, for once.

Okay.

Enough is enough with you.

Okay.

He puts his hand on the front doorknob and takes a moment to look at it. The doorknob is old, tarnished brass. Its surface is textured with a design of tiny flowers. The knob is loose, and he rattles it.

You should sell this house. It's nothing but trouble.

What on earth is this man talking about?

You don't fool me, he says.

I'm not trying to fool anyone.

You might fool Mimi, but you don't fool me.

He leaves, using Miranda's keys to lock the door from the outside.

OUTSIDE. Cool night air. The houses are all dark. The night sounds are nice.

A woman's voice behind me says, in a whisper-talk, Daddy, what are you doing?

What a silly question. I'm not doing anything, just standing.

Do you know what time it is?

No. What time is it?

It's almost one in the morning! I thought you were in bed.

I'm not tired.

Come in. It's late. It's time for bed.

I'm not tired.

So what are you gonna do?

Go for a walk.

A walk? Now? Where?

I don't know.

She scrunches up her face. She has a nice face.

Okay, wait, let me get my shoes on. Don't move. I'll be right back. Don't move.

Later, I am walking when she runs up beside me.

I told you not to go anywhere! I can't take my eyes off you for one minute! Here, put this on, it's freezing. Aren't you cold?

No.

She puts a coat on me and zips it up. When it is closed, she tugs on the zipper pull to test it. There, she says. Better?

Good.

Where are we walking to?

I don't know.

Well, the lake is this way. We could just keep going. How's that?

Okay.

There is not enough room to walk side by side on the sidewalk, so we stroll right down the middle of the street.

I like this, I tell her.

Me too.

My illness has taken so much from me but not this, not the dumb joy of walking on a chilly night, between sleeping houses, with dried leaves banked up in the gutters and on the sidewalks. Maybe I appreciate it more now, knowing it will go, too, in the end.

She clasps her hands behind her back. She is about my height but seems much bigger than me. Strong. I have a feeling she could pick me up like a baby and carry me home if she had to.

She calls me Daddy to remind me who she is, which I appreciate. I cannot recall her name right now. I realize how crazy this is, how ridiculous I am, but I do not want to ruin the moment by asking. The walking is so pleasant, the night is so perfect. I will feel sad later, maybe. Not now. I may remember her name in the morning anyway.

We come to a lake. She slips her arm around mine to lead me down a slope, past the trees, to the lakeside where the surface of the water riffles in the moonlight and city light.

It's beautiful, she says. Isn't it?

Yes.

Thank you for showing it to me.

I smile at her. Okay.

You happy, Daddy?

Yes. You?

No. I'm very sad, actually.

Why?

Because I hurt you.

No, you didn't. Don't say that. Don't ever say that.

Why not? It's true.

It doesn't matter.

Of course it matters.

No! Don't say that!

Okay. Sorry, Dad. You ready to go home? It's getting late.

Not yet.

ONE day—months later, it is spring now, the world is rainy and green—the woman comes to me with a sneaky grin, quivery with excitement: Daddy, come, I have something I want to show you. Don't worry, it's going to be fun.

She takes my hand and leads me to the living room. The coffee table has been cleared except for a small cardboard box.

What is it?

It's a memory machine.

She tells me to sit down on the couch in front of the box, and when I have, she says, Now close your eyes first and listen, okay? They closed? Keep 'em closed. Just listen. You used to love this record.

She turns on music, adjusts the volume.

It had to be you, it had to be you. I wandered around and finally found the somebody who—the beat is slow, strolling, sad—*could make me be true, could make me be blue, and even be glad just to be sad thinking of you.*

There. Just keep your eyes closed. Relax.

Some others I've seen might never be mean.

Just keep your eyes closed. Try and relax. Let's just listen for a couple minutes. Enjoy the music.

Might never be cross or try to be boss, but they wouldn't do.

When I was little, you used to listen to this one all the time.

For nobody else gave me a thrill, with all your faults, I love you still. It had to be you, wonderful you, it had to be you.

I don't remember it.

That's okay. Don't worry about it. Don't try to remember any-thing. It's not a test. Just relax and enjoy the music.

The song plays. A muted trumpet. Bass. The sad singer.

They say sometimes music can reach into a deeper part of the brain and unlock old memories. You may not experience it as a specific memory; it may just be a feeling, a stirring. Maybe it just *feels* familiar. Familiar and old and fun and *good*. But you don't have to feel *any* pressure. We're just listening to music, that's all. Just enjoying.

The song ends—*wonderful you, it had to be you*—and imme-diately it restarts in a loop. *It had to be you, it had to be you, I wandered around and finally found*—

She sings softly with the stereo: *Somebody who-o-o could make me be true, could make me be blue, and even be glad just to be sad thinking of you.*

I begin to bob my head to the music.

Are you enjoying it, Dad?

Yes.

Do you know this song?

I don't know.

Okay. That's okay. Just keep listening. You had this record. Do you know who it is?

No.

It's Billie Holiday. Do you remember Billie Holiday?

No. Did I know him?

No, silly. Okay, you can open your eyes now. You ready? You're doing great.

My daughter turns down the volume of the music but leaves it playing. She sits down next to me, gives my back a few scrubs with her palm to reassure me.

Now we're going to look at a few pictures, okay? We'll look together. You and me. How's that?

Okay. If you want.

Some others I've seen might never be mean. . . .

She takes the lid off the cardboard box, takes out an old photo.

The color is washed-out and yellowed. It shows a man wearing a fancy suit with a vest. Wide yellow necktie. His shirt is pale blue with a contrasting white collar. He has thick curly hair, aviator glasses. He stands up very straight, a drink in his hand.

Do you know who that is?

He's at a party.

He's at a party, I think you're right. But do you know who it is?

No, who is it?

Do you know *where* it is? Look closely. Look at the room. See if you can figure it out.

I don't know. Tell me.

It's this room! He's in this room!

He is?

He is! Look. You see the bookcase there? He's standing right there. Okay, that was kind of a trick question. Let's try another.

For nobody else gave me a thrill, with all your faults, I love you still.

She pulls out another photo. They seem to be arranged in order; she pulls out the top photo on the pile without hesitating or rummaging through the box. This picture shows a lanky, long-faced teenage boy. He is wearing a white oxford button-down. Looking into the camera with a serious expression.

Who's that?

Don't know.

Take your time. Who's that boy? He was your favorite. Your *favorite* favorite. Do you remember him?

No.

Okay, here's a clue: look what he's holding. What's that in his hand?

A ball.

A ball, good. What kind of ball?

A ball. What do you mean, what kind of ball?

Okay, never mind. It's a basketball. A basketball. Does that help? Who liked basketball?

You?

No, not me! Silly. Are you making jokes? Come on, who likes basketball?

Him.

Yes, him. Oh, you are so funny today. That's Alex. You remember Alex, your son.

Okay.

Okay, let's try another one.

Another boy. Longer hair, slouchier, wise-guy grin.

Who's that?

My son.

Your son! Right! Do you remember his name?

Alex.

No, this one is Jeff. Do you remember Jeff?

Of course.

Really? Or are you just saying it? Tell the truth.

I remember everyone.

Are you telling the truth?

Sure.

Okay, let's try another one. You ready? This one's super tricky.

Okay.

The song restarts. *It had to be you, it had to be you. I wandered around and finally found the somebody who . . .*

This photo shows a little girl. Blond. Beautiful.

It's you.

It's me. How did you get that? Were you just guessing?

No. I know you. I know my beautiful daughter.

You do?

Of course!

Oh my. That is so sweet.

She clasps her hands over her heart and makes a ready-to-cry face. She kisses me on the cheek.

Okay, should we keep going? This one is hard. I don't think you'll get it.

Some others I've seen might never be mean, might never be cross or try to be boss.

Photo of a couple, on vacation maybe, somewhere sunny. He with curls and aviator sunglasses, a fancy watch on his wrist, she with blond hair swirled up in an elegant bun, wearing a bright flower-print dress.

Who is this woman, do you know?

No. Should I?

There's no *should*. If you don't remember, it's okay.

I don't remember.

Her name is Sarah. Does that help?

I don't think so.

And how about him?

Hmm.

It's you again, silly! Now I know you're kidding! Okay, just two more.

The next photo shows a woman with white hair. I do not even wait for the question: That's my mother.

That's your mother! Excellent! She was my grandma too! Okay, last one.

The last photo shows a pretty young woman with a full face and warm half-smile. She is wearing hoop earrings. Her brown hair frames her face.

Take a good look. Who is this?

Do I know her?

You did once.

Are you sure?

Yes, I'm sure, Daddy.

You knew her too?

Very well. We both knew her. Take your time. Take a good, long look.

I pick up the photo and take a good, long look. I want to know the answer for my daughter. I am *supposed* to know. She thinks I once knew. She *wants* me to come up with it; that much I can tell from her expression, from the eager way she leans forward.

But my mind has gone blank. As it increasingly does. I don't know, and I don't know if I ever knew, and I don't know if I will ever know again or if that part of my self has crumbled away. Staring at the picture won't bring the memory back, because there is no memory to recover; I have never seen this woman.

But I *did* know her. My daughter tells me I did.

Increasingly, I don't know if I am sane and merely forgetful or if this is what insanity feels like, the mind going dark in chunks, disintegrating, vanishing. What will be in my thoughts when I reach the other side of this, when the erasure is complete? Will my head contain only silence? Or will something else swarm in to fill the emptiness—delusions, dreams, chaos? If this is how it feels to know I am slipping away—if this is the middle stage, as the woman says—then what comes next? What comes *after*?

I don't know.

It's okay. Try. Look at her face. You knew her once.

Who is it?

She was very special to you.

I don't know her.

My daughter covers her mouth with her hand and closes her eyes.

I tell her, I'm sorry. You're sad. What did I do? Why are you upset?

It's okay, Daddy, I'm not upset.

You are. Who is it?

It's okay, Daddy. It's no one.

SOMETIME later. I don't know how long; the days, weeks, months pass uncounted, unclocked.

I am in bed.

My daughter comes into the room, tells me "Good morning, Daddy," and with practiced movements she glides around the room opening the shades. How many mornings have begun this way?

Summer light softens the edges of things. The familiar details of the room—the woodwork aged to the color of honey, the pastel yellow walls—all seem freshly beautiful.

How do you feel this morning?

Good.

You remember what today is?

No.

She sits down on the edge of the bed, takes up my hand and kisses the back of it. She says, It's the last day. July twenty-fifth.

Oh. Yes. I know.

How do you feel about it? Are you ready?

I'm ready.

You're sure?

I'm sure.

And I *am* sure. It is time. Before I lose control, before the monster in the fog—dementia—can take what is left of me. I am not afraid; we are not meant to live forever. I am not bitter about my illness; all bodies fail. I am ready.

Okay. Come, let's get you washed up and presentable. Come.

She walks into the bathroom with me.

Do you need to use the toilet?

Yes.

Okay, I'll wait outside.

When I am done with a reluctant, sputtering pee, she knocks on the door. Are you ready?

Yes.

She comes back in, flushes the toilet. Are you showering today?

I shake my head.

Okay then. She puts toothpaste on a brush and hands it to me. Get brushing, she says. I'll get a washcloth.

When I am done, she hands me a pill. Do you remember what this is?

No.

This is the anti-nausea pill. You have to take it a few hours ahead of time.

Okay.

Okay, so put it in. Good. No, don't chew. Just put it on the back of your tongue and drink the water and it'll go right down. Good, like that. That's good. Did you swallow it?

Yes.

Pills are hard, aren't they? I hate pills.

Yeah.

She shows me the washcloth. You want to do this or do you want help?

Help.

Okay, arms up.

My arms go up on their own, with no urging from me.

She slides my T-shirt off, wets the washcloth in warm water and scrubs some soap onto it, then she wipes down my shoulders, arms, armpits, back, and belly, rinsing the cloth under the faucet now and then. That done, she gives the cloth a good rinse and wrings it.

Eyes closed, she says.

My eyes close for her, and she dabs my face with the warm cloth.

Sit.

She gestures toward the edge of the tub for me to sit. She kneels and wipes my feet, first the left then the right.

Up.

I stand, my pajama bottoms are lowered, she wipes my butt with the warm cloth, and she raises the pajamas again.

Okay, that's it. Feel good?

Yes.

We're getting pretty good at this, aren't we? Now, what are we going to do about that hair?

Does it matter?

Does it matter? Oh my goodness, do you know how you used to fuss over your hair when you were younger? *Of course* it matters. You want to brush it yourself?

No, you can.

Okay, hold still.

She fetches a brush from the drawer and fiddles with my hair awhile, chattering about how I used to be very particular about it.

I think that's the best we can do. You want to have a look? Come stand in front of the mirror. Good?

Good.

Excellent. Let's get you dressed.

She leads me from the bathroom back to the bedroom closet. She saunters slowly for me. I move slowly now. I speak slowly too. But I can tell she is bristling to move at her normal pace.

She opens my closet. Slacks and suits hanging on the right, the rest on shelves.

Do you want to pick? Have you thought about what you might want to wear?

No.

Well, let's pick something comfortable. I think you'll want to be comfortable today.

She hands me a clean pair of underpants.

Put those on. I won't look. Pajamas go in the hamper, Daddy, not on the floor.

Okay.

When I get my underpants on, I stand before her like a child.

She turns to show me a shirt, chattering—How about this? I like this color on you—but at the sight of me in my underpants, her offhand manner cracks for a moment. A little gasp escapes her. She closes her eyes and draws a deep breath, like an actress preparing to step onstage, and when she reopens them, she is back in character. We are treating my last day as if it was any other.

She says, I think this one is good.

Thank you, I tell her. Then: It's going to be okay.

She nods. Jeans? I think jeans. Jeans and sneakers. You'll be most comfortable that way.

When I am dressed, she looks me over and smiles. She hugs me. You look very handsome, she says.

Thank you.

What else? Are you hungry? You're not supposed to eat, but I think if you had something very light, it would be okay.

I'm not hungry.

Have you thought about what you might say to Alex and Jeff? You could write something, maybe. I could help you.

I don't have anything to say.

Anything you want to give them?

They'll take what they want, after.

What about for you? You have a lot of stuff, you know. Here, let me show you.

She goes into my closet, where a small safe is on the floor, purchased at Home Depot and deposited here when I became ill.

She says, We put all this stuff away so nothing would happen to it. You even knew the combination to the safe back then. Can you imagine?

She punches in a code on a keypad, which beeps with each button-push. She takes out a jewelry box and hands it to me.

Nothing to save it for now, right? You always liked fancy things. Watches and collar pins and cuff links. You were very dapper.

Was I?

Yes. Go on. Pick something out. Show 'em a little style.

I sit down with this jewelry box in my lap. It is a big leather-wrapped box. Inside are watches and rings, men's bracelets, even a necklace with some sort of tornado-shaped horn pendant that I must have worn at some point. Some things hidden in small jewelry bags.

My daughter plucks out a ring. You used to wear this one a lot. A cat's-eye ring. Here. Try it.

I try the ring on.

Too tight.

Try it on your pinkie. There, that's better. Do you like it? How about a watch? I never knew a man with so many watches. Pick one, I'll set it for you.

There's so much!

I know! It's like a treasure chest! Pick one.

What are these?

They're studs. You wear them with a tuxedo.

You want them?

Daddy, I don't wear tuxedos.

Neither do I. Take a watch.

No, the watch is for you. Pick one. Go ahead, they're all yours.

She sits beside me. The tattoo on her arm catches my eye, but she covers it with her other hand, intentionally or not.

How about this one?

Okay. Very pretty. Ooh, Rolex—very fancy. I remember you wearing that too. Let me see if I can set it. What time is it?

She gets up to check the time and set the watch, and I go back to rummaging in the box.

When she comes back, she is holding the watch loosely in her fingers. She says, I think I did it. It's a little fussy.

But I have something for her too. A gift. I hold it out for her in the palm of my hand.

I want you to have this.

What have you got there, Daddy? You don't have to give me anything.

I want to. I found it. Here, put out your hand.

She offers her hand, and I slide the ring onto her ring finger. It goes on so smoothly, it seems to settle in place at the base of her finger as if it had always belonged there. As if it might have jumped onto her finger on its own, like a dog onto its owner's lap.

She looks down at this ring. Her face falls, her mouth is open. She lowers her head to examine it more closely.

Oh no no no no no no no no. Daddy, what did you do?

The question makes no sense to me, but my mind is so untrustworthy I don't want to speak and embarrass myself.

Daddy, what did you do?

What's wrong?

Daddy, what did you do?

She backs away from me until she is against the wall, staring at the ring on her finger.

It's pretty. It has hearts on it. It's for you.

What did you do?

It's okay, you can have it. What's wrong?

She screams: *What did you do!*

What? I hear my own voice rising with confusion and fear. What did I do to upset her?

What did you do!

She rushes at me, grabs my shirt in her fists, and we topple onto the floor. She is above me, shaking me, screaming, What did you do? What did you do? What did you do?

I don't know. You're hurting me, you're hurting me.

When she has exhausted herself, her head falls onto my chest and she says one last time—now with resignation—What did you do?

(Bewildered:) What did I do?

Don't you understand? She never took it off. She never took it off.

Who?

She was wearing it that day. They never found it. You had it. Oh, Daddy. Oh my God. What did you do?

LATER, a man arrives. It has all been arranged. My sons and their families will not be here. No one can help me or they will go to jail. Only my daughter will be nearby—but not in the room—and this man to serve as witness so no one gets in trouble. This is what I requested, apparently. No ceremony, no hysterics.

My daughter is quiet. She is upset for some reason.

I ask what's wrong, is there anything I can do for her, to make this easier.

She says there's no use explaining. I wouldn't understand.

Is she angry? Why is she angry?

It's too late, is all she will tell me.

My head hurts. It is because I fell, she explains. I fell? When did I fall?

Together, the three of us go into my bedroom.

My daughter asks if I am comfortable.

I am.

Do you want to take your shoes off so you can lie down?

No, I'm okay.

Do you need to use the bathroom?

No.

Do you need anything?

I'm a little hungry.

I think you'd better not eat, you know, before. You could—it might come back up.

After, then.

At this, she shoots a glance at her friend, who seems uncomfortable.

Yeah, after. Daddy, I'm going to leave the room now. I can't be here for this, it's not allowed. You remember?

No.

My friend Phil is going to be with you. All he can do is watch, though. He can't actually help you. But if you have any questions, you can just ask him, okay?

Okay.

Do you remember what you're going to do?

No.

There are two glasses on your night table. One is the medicine. You're going to open the little bottle and pour it into the first glass and drink it. The second glass is just wine. It's a nice Barolo like you used to like. The medicine might taste a little bitter, so if you don't like the taste, you can drink a little wine and that will help. Then all you have to do is lie down on the bed and close your eyes and relax.

Why can't you stay?

Because what you're doing—what you've chosen to do—it isn't legal for me to help you. No one can. You have to do this yourself.

Her friend breaks in: Mr. Larkin, do you understand what's happening here?

Yes.

You're ending your life. You understand that, right?

Yes.

And that's what you want?

Yes.

And you know you can stop at any time. You don't have to do this.

I know.

The man nods, not quite convinced.

Okay, Daddy. I'm going to say goodbye. Can I give you a hug?

Yes.

She hugs me and I am happy. She kisses me on the cheek.

I tell her, I love you.

She nods. She says, Okay, I'm going to go.

Okay.

When she has gone and the door is closed, I go to the night table. Bottle, empty drinking glass, full wineglass. I take up the wineglass and sip. The wine is dark and earthy.

The man says, Do you remember what to do?

No.

First you're going to open the little bottle and pour it into the glass.

Which glass?

The empty one.

I put the wineglass down, pick up the small vial. There is a plastic wrapper over the top. I try to take it off by twisting it and picking at it with my fingernail.

I can't open it. It has a thing on it.

Keep trying. I really can't, you know, touch anything.

After more struggling, the man relents and comes over to help.

Okay, here you go.

He puts the plastic scrap on the night table then thinks better of it and slips it into his pocket.

Thank you. So what do I . . . ?

Pour it in the glass.

I pour the clear liquid into the drinking glass.

The man says, Do you know what that is?

No, what?

It's pentobarbital.

Pentobarbital.

It's poison. If you drink it, you'll die.

I understand.

You're sure?

Yeah.

Okay. Do you want to sit down first? I don't know how fast it'll work. Maybe you should sit down.

I sit on the side of the bed.

How much should I drink?

All of it, I guess. I'm not really sure.

I hold the glass under my nose. I do not smell anything. I take a small sip. The liquid is tangy but not awful. Still, I spit it back into the glass.

Does it taste bad?

Yes.

Try it with the wine maybe. You could take a little of one then the other.

It tastes bad.

Yes, that's what the wine is for. You want to try again?

I don't know. I'm not sure.

It's okay, you don't have to.

I'm not sure. I don't know.

Okay. Let's just stop right here, then. Do you want to stop?

Yes. I want to stop.

All right, I'll get Miranda. Just wait here.

I'll drink this one, though.

Just remember, the wine is the red one. Don't—well, never mind, I'll just take that with me.

He takes the glass of clear liquid, opens the bedroom door, calls Miranda's name.

Footsteps, bustling.

She meets him at the threshold.

The man tells her, He doesn't want to go through with it.

He hands the glass to the woman.

Why don't you wait outside, Phil.

Miranda—

It's okay. Go wait outside.

Miranda.

I'm just going to talk to him.

She steps aside so he can exit the room.

For a moment, he does not move. Then a sigh—a little heave of his back—and he steps out.

The woman comes in, holding the glass, and begins to shut the door.

The man puts his hand on the door to stop its closing. His face visible in the doorway, peering in, he says, *Miranda!*

She closes the door.

All That Is Mine
I Carry With Me

William Landay

A BOOK CLUB GUIDE

An Interview with William Landay

The following is an edited transcript of selected portions of an interview between William Landay and writer Christine Daigle, originally aired on the *Writers, Ink* podcast.

Christine Daigle: Your novel *All That Is Mine I Carry With Me* has four different points of view from four different characters, but they're in blocks, not interspersed or alternating the way that you sometimes see. It reminded me of the structure of the movie *Rashomon*. Can you tell me a little bit about why you chose this structure?

William Landay: I was very much influenced by Ian McEwan's novel *Atonement*, which is told with a similar structure and to me is a masterpiece of this kind of storytelling. The interlocking stories [in *All That Is Mine*] are an attempt to capture the differing experiences of the people involved—their perceptions and temperaments, their reactions, especially as they age. . . .

I've always thought of crime novels as a prism to look at wider, more universal issues. I don't find crime itself all that interesting, actually. In fact, I don't think of my books as crime novels at all; I think of them as novels that happen to involve crime. This missing-woman story seemed like an interesting way to deal with the topic of losing people as we grow up—how we adjust to growing up and saying goodbye to people—and learning to live with the void that they leave behind. The characters' differing experiences are a way to dramatize that.

So that was part of it. The other part was structural complexity, which, as a reader, I adore. Telling this story in chunks, from different points of view and different periods of time, involves the reader in a more active, engaging way, I think, as a sort of participant in the storytelling. The book presents readers with a series of puzzle pieces and invites them to put things together on their own.

One of the joys of reading *Atonement* is that the pieces don't fall into place until you reach the end of the novel, when new information recasts the entire story. Those last few pages of *Atonement* were one of the great reading experiences of my life. I remember the hair on my arms standing on end! And the idea of re-creating that experience for readers—that electric moment that books rarely achieve but all readers remember—just seemed like a magical thing.

We live in a digital age when we're deluged with information and text, yet those magical reading experiences are scarce. We've kind of learned to be skeptical about what we read, to keep it at arm's length. We've learned to keep our bullshit detectors dialed up to eleven at all times, because there's so much dishonest information coming at us. It's very hard, I think, for a modern reader to "suspend disbelief," as novel-reading requires. So I wanted to present a text that meets the reader where they are, at the center of these multiple media firehoses, with their filters up, and allows them to grapple with the text in a more active way, thinking and participating rather than just following along from page one to page last. This book really does require you to sit up straight and put some pieces together yourself. When the reader is engaged actively that way, it is an immersive experience. I hope that it will become one of those unforgettable books where you feel a part of the story, not just a spectator.

Daigle: It is definitely a book that when you're done with it, you don't just put it down and forget about it. You're really left thinking about what it all means. I know that a lot of times readers get something very different thematically out of a book than what authors intended. Did you think about the nature of truth, about investigating the philosophy of justice?

Landay: I think those things are all implicated; they're all there to some extent. I'm very wary about interpreting my books for readers, though. I want them to experience the story for themselves, especially a book like this, where the shifting perspectives and voices invite readers to withhold judgment, to consider the different attitudes of people who disagree about how these crimes and criminals should be treated. This case polarizes the family and drives them apart. The three children who are left behind by this woman's disappearance—an older brother named Alex, and two younger siblings, Jeff and Miranda, who are very tight but not alike—these three different personalities respond to the incident in different ways. I don't want to step on readers' opinions or emotions about what they see.

But I will say, from a legal perspective—I'm a former prosecutor, so I always think about how a case would present in court—this story does raise interesting questions about sufficiency of proof and, more broadly, about what we mean by guilt. As suspects age, is it possible for them to become less guilty? Can the passage of time—decades, in this case—or the staleness of an investigation or changes in their personality moderate their criminality in some way, make them less guilty in our eyes? Or are some crimes simply unforgivable, a stain that can never be removed?

I don't know. To some extent, these are moral judgments, not legal ones. That's a wonderful thing about a book like this: It transcends the easy labels that we tend to assign to criminals. We tend to monster-ize our criminals because it makes it easier for us to lock them away in a different category, to differentiate them from ourselves. In this case, everyone—the children, the missing woman, the primary suspect—is given depth and complexity as humans. So it's very difficult, I hope, to write them off as one-dimensional monsters.

Daigle: Absolutely. I'm curious if you have a character that you're excited for readers to read about and why that would be.

Landay: I don't pick and choose that way. Not in this book, anyway. One of the characters is a novelist whose resemblance to me is more than passing, so I suppose I ought to feel closest to him. But one of the nice things about being a novelist is that you get to try on lots of masks. I don't feel closer to that novelist character than I do to any of the others who populate this book. I will say that, until the very end—until the last edit, in fact—the name of that novelist-narrator was Bill Landay. So for me to tell you that he's no closer to my heart than any other may say something about where fictional characters come from. They all originate inside the writer, for better or worse—mostly worse, in my experience.

Daigle: That's interesting, because Phil Solomon starts off with writer's block. Do you want to tell me about that and where it came from? Is that a personal experience?

Landay: It's definitely a personal experience. I don't know if all writers would assign that term to it necessarily, but all writers know the struggle of trying to get a book going, pushing through various obstacles, slowdowns, resistance, whatever you want to call it. In this case, my last book, *Defending Jacob*, came out more than ten years ago and I didn't want to ignore that. I wanted to address it head-on and use the delay in some way, incorporate it into the story.

One of the things I was trying to do with *Defending Jacob*—which I took even further in this book—was to make it as authentic to my own experience as I could. *Defending*

Jacob was my third book, and the two previous books had been more traditional crime novels—"traditional" in the sense that they had a more hard-boiled tone and they involved street crime. When I proposed a third similar book to my editor, she told me to come down [to New York City] to talk about it. I knew right away I was in trouble—if it's good news, you don't need to take a train to New York just to be told how great you are. So we met and she told me, "You could go ahead and write another crime novel, but a lot of mainstream readers simply won't consider it. So if you want to reach a broader readership, you have to tell a different sort of story." And so the focus heading into *Defending Jacob* was to go the opposite way, to do the opposite of what I had done before. (Like George Costanza in "The Opposite" episode [of *Seinfeld*]!) That meant making things as close to my own life as possible, as close as possible to what felt authentic to me, rather than dreaming up some gritty noir crime story that was actually quite far from my personal experience. And so in *Defending Jacob* I set the book in the town where I actually live and posited a family that resembles my own in a lot of ways.

So [with *All That Is Mine I Carry With Me*] I wanted to continue in that direction, because I do feel that when you write from a place that is personally relevant to you, there is a kind of honesty in the writing that is hard to replicate if you feel like you're faking it—trying to write to a genre or copy someone else's template.

In that context, addressing the long silence after *Defending Jacob* seemed essential to me. When there's ten years between books, that's obviously a transformative, difficult experience. I thought it would be dishonest for me not to address that in some way. I also felt—especially in this day and age, when readers know so much about authors—it would've been the elephant in the room for readers who open up this book after having read *Defending Jacob* five, eight, ten years ago. Naturally they would be asking, "Where's this guy been?" I thought I could use that to my advantage. It plays into the opening act of this book, where the premise is that the novelist character has been blocked and is presented with the idea of telling this story about an old friend whose family experienced this crime, this mysterious disappearance of the boy's mother.

That lead-in has such an honest, confessional feeling to it. I don't claim to have originated this technique; some of my favorite books start with similar devices. Nick Carraway is obviously the most famous example, but I also think of *The Razor's Edge,* which was one of my favorite books as a teen. It's just such an enchanting, seductive way to open a book, for the writer to break that fourth wall and turn to address the reader directly. It's disarming because it calls out the pretense—the conscious pretense, the *pretending*—that novels rely on. As I've said, I feel that readers are on guard now in a way that they haven't always been. This is a sort of jiu-jitsu approach to their cynicism, their guardedness. It subverts the reader's wariness by addressing them directly: "Look, I know you're going to find this hard to believe, but here I am unmasked. Let me tell you a story that really happened." That voice leads you into the story, wins your trust—which is also why it becomes so interesting, and jarring, as the book progresses and the voices and perspectives begin to multiply and complicate.

Daigle: I think it's true, with the way things are, that people can be very cynical, and I think a human connection is so important to get people's interest now. In your bio you say that you have a philosophy that the author's place is offstage—hide your life, disappear. So how do you kind of reconcile those two things?

Landay: First of all, I'm a writer—I can change my mind anytime. I don't have to be perfectly consistent. The other thing is, even if I had put a character in this book called Bill Landay, he wouldn't be me, any more than Philip Roth putting a character into his book called Philip Roth would be the real thing. Once you [place your book] in the fiction aisle, you're free to do and say anything. So I don't feel bound by honesty or consistency—in my books, at least.

Daigle: You said no writer of any quality can base his novels on fact. Do you want to tell me what you mean by that?

Landay: The world is just so messy, and experience is so shapeless and undramatic, it has to be refined. People are always asking me, "Are you writing about cases that you were involved in when you were a DA?" I want to take them into any local courthouse, have them sit behind the DA, and watch what his day is actually like. It's mostly mundane—paperwork and waiting for judges to arrive, that kind of thing. All art is filtered in one way or another. It's all dishonest; it has to be to elevate and concentrate the experience of real life. So, no, I don't try to capture reality too closely.

Daigle: I want to ask you a couple more questions about author life in general. What do you think authors worry too much about that they shouldn't?

Landay: How they'll be received—by reviewers, by readers, by Amazon reviews, or anyone else. I always feel that the only audience that I'm ever trying to please is myself, and that is a much harder thing to do than please a reviewer, in my case. I'm always dissatisfied with my books, and the fact that I am dissatisfied with my books, that I am my own worst critic, immunizes me against the pain of reading negative reviews. I don't read reviews at all, really. I mean, I do sometimes give in to curiosity and peek at what people are saying, but I never take it to heart.

It's very rare that you hear a criticism of some aspect of your book that you weren't aware of previously. Generally, the flaws in your book—the bits that are held together with duct tape and chicken wire—are things that you are painfully aware of and you either couldn't fix or needed to leave as is because you were trying to serve some other purpose. You're building a very complex machine and sometimes you need to compromise on one aspect of the book in order to serve another. So the one thing I would say to writers is: Don't allow other people to be the judges of your success. The whole public aspect of a book's life is not where my focus is. Generally when I think of readers at all, I'm thinking of an individual reader somewhere, off reading in a quiet corner. I'm not thinking of "the public."

That's the beauty of a book. It's a unique art form in the sense that it's consumed in complete privacy. Even if you're reading a novel in a crowded subway car, your experience of the novel is completely internal to you. A novel comes to you as a script, as words on a page, and you bring to it your skill as a reader to lift those words off the page and perform the novel for yourself, in your head. So your experience of it is necessarily an interior one. That's a very intimate way to experience a story—and to meet a novelist. It's why, when I meet readers, they often feel as if they are meeting someone that they know, because in a sense they do. They have heard my voice more intimately than they will hear anyone else's, because my voice has been in their head. That is the one-to-one communion between writer and reader. That is the real power of the art form and the real goal of novel-writing and novel-reading.

Daigle: I agree. So I'm curious, what are you excited to explore in your fiction that maybe you haven't done yet but would like to?

Landay: I don't tend to think in terms of long-term plans that way. I tend to put everything into the project that's in front of me. Right now, I'm just grappling with the next project and trying to figure out what that next book is. And that's all I'm thinking about: the next book. I think that's the way most artists progress. You go project to project, and try to work at the extreme outer limit of your talent, and do the best you can with the tools you have at that moment—the tools being your own skill, inspiration, and the internal, substantive merits of the project you're working on—all of which hopefully will come together to make something special. But the arc of your career and the long-term themes that connect book to book or project to project should only be apparent at the end, and only to others, really.

One thing that marks writers whom I particularly enjoy is that their books are unpredictable. There is a throughline, of course—there's always the same hand behind it—but you don't know exactly what the next book is going to be. When you find a writer whose style and voice you like, you come to trust them and you're willing to follow them in a new direction. What I would like my readers to bring to my books is that same sort of faith and confidence—that when they open a book by Bill Landay, they don't know what the book is going to be exactly, but they have accumulated enough trust over time that they're willing to go along and see where this guy takes them. We all have favorite writers like that, where we open a book with a level of trust that accrues from each novel and that increments book after book. It's such a wonderful presence in your life when you have a writer like that.

I'm not one of those programmatic writers who is producing variations on the same story over and over. Sometimes I wish I were. I wish I did have a single note that I could just keep hitting. I think of Patrick O'Brian and his series about the British Navy. Wouldn't it be wonderful to not have to reinvent yourself with every book? Trollope famously would finish one of his monstrous Victorian novels, put down the last page, and immediately take a new piece of paper and start writing the next one. For every writer who's dealt with hesitation at some point, that's the fantasy: moving from one book to the next seamlessly. I have never experienced it, in part because I do try to do something different each time. Which means I am reinventing myself each time, or trying to. It takes time and it takes struggle.

Daigle: Absolutely. I have one final question as we wrap up. If you could offer one piece of advice to new and aspiring authors, what would it be?

Landay: It's very difficult because I do feel that the experience of each writer is idiosyncratic and is driven in large part by that person's individual temperament, skill, and interests. What works for me may not work for the next writer. The one thing I might say, as I look back, is that it's a long road, there's a lot of struggle, and there will be dark moments. Don't give up. Because if you have the talent and the drive, then you will improve from book to book. I have published four novels, but I've written more than that. The goal is simply to grow, to improve with each book. And for that, you have to keep going. When I started out, I was a lawyer, and writing was a nights-and-weekends sort of thing. Then, when I left to start writing full-time, my intent was just to write one book, just to see how far I could go. Now this lark that I thought would be a year or two is into its third decade. I hope that holds some inspiration for young writers, that this is a long road and there is something to be said for sticking with it. Just keep going. That's not always easy. And you have to be a little lucky as well. But just keep going.

Discussion Questions

1. *All That Is Mine I Carry With Me* explores a number of thought-provoking themes, including family, loyalty, grief, secrets, and the fragility of relationships. Which theme resonated the most deeply with you and why?

2. In addition to being a crime novel, *All That Is Mine I Carry With Me* is a family drama and a character study, following the Larkin family and the impact of Jane's disappearance over decades. How do these events shape the lives of Alex, Jeff, and Miranda as adults? And why do you think this case stuck so deeply with Detective Glover and the lawyer George Bailis?

3. The author takes care to emphasize how defining a case this was in public memory, writing: "In the fall of '75, believe me, if you lived in Boston, you knew who Jane Larkin was. The local media feasted on the story, particularly in the first few weeks after her disappearance." True crime is often sensationalized and prominently featured in news headlines and the public eye. Why do you think people become so invested in cases from afar?

4. What do you think the title of the novel means, aside from being the English translation of the Latin text in Miranda's tattoo?

5. Each part of the novel is told from a different character's point of view. How did that deepen the story? Did any section particularly stand out for you? If so, why?

6. Book 2, which initially seems to be written from Jane's perspective, turns out to have been written by Miranda as a creative outlet. What did you think of that section? What does it tell us about how Miranda has been impacted by her mother's disappearance and the long-unanswered uncertainty surrounding that event?

7. How does each of the characters change over the course of the novel?

8. There are many intense family scenes in *All That Is Mine I Carry With Me*. Which ones stayed with you most and why?

9. A little more than halfway through the novel, after Jane's bones are found and the DA decides not to pursue a case against Dan, there's a tense discussion among the family. Did you side with Kate or Alex, and why? What would you have done in that situation?

10. There are a number of secrets revealed over the course of the narrative, including Dan's assault of Jane and Jane's suicide attempt, neither of which was discussed for a long time. Why do you think Kate and Jeff keep these secrets? Have you ever kept such an impactful secret from your loved ones?

11. What message is Kate trying to convey with the Bible verse she has the priest read at Jane's burial ceremony?

12. While reading *All That Is Mine I Carry With Me,* did you believe Dan murdered Jane? Why or why not? When and how did you come to that conclusion? Were you thrown off by the red herrings?

13. How did you feel at the end of the novel? What message(s) did you take away from reading it?

About the Author

WILLIAM LANDAY is the author of three previous novels: *Defending Jacob,* which won the Strand Critics Award for best novel; *The Strangler,* listed as a best crime novel of the year by the *Los Angeles Times, Daily Telegraph,* and others; and *Mission Flats,* winner of the Dagger Award for best first crime novel. He lives in Boston.

williamlanday.com

About the Type

This book was set in Sabon, a typeface designed by the well-known German typographer Jan Tschichold (1902–74). Sabon's design is based upon the original letter forms of sixteenth-century French type designer Claude Garamond and was created specifically to be used for three sources: foundry type for hand composition, Linotype, and Monotype. Tschichold named his typeface for the famous Frankfurt typefounder Jacques Sabon (c. 1520–80).